HE WATCHED HER EYES
TRAVEL ABOUT THE BEDCHAMBER

"Do you like it?"

"Good heavens, Douglas, I wouldn't go that far," she said lightly. "It suits you, of course. For my taste it's too dark, too large, too harsh." She could have been describing him. "Its saving grace is the parapet walk."

His male vanity was piqued. He grasped her wrists with his hard hands, imprisoning her. "Do *I* have a saving grace?" he demanded, lust and anger suddenly blazing in his gut like banefire.

She searched his dark face and whispered, "I hope so, my lord. I pray for both our sakes that you have a sense of humor."

He released her wrists. "We go to Castle Douglas day after tomorrow. Perhaps my bedchamber there will be more to yer taste."

"Perhaps," she murmured, allowing her lashes to sweep to her cheeks. God, they were like two scorpions circling each other, looking for the most vulnerable spot to leave their sting.

"Perhaps I'll stay here."

"You, madam, will do as ye are told." His words had a hard, challenging ring.

She laughed up into his face. "You do have a sense of humor!"

THE FALCON AND THE FLOWER

winner of the 1989 *Romantic Times*
Award for Most Sensual Medieval Romance

"VIRGINIA HENLEY'S LUSTIEST, BAWDIEST, MOST DARING, AND HOTTEST historical romance to date . . . this is most definitely a must for fans of powerful, erotic, and passionate medieval romances."

—*Romantic Times*

THE HAWK AND THE DOVE

winner of the 1988 *Romantic Times*
Award for Best Elizabethan Historical Romance

"BOLD, LUSTY—and very SEXY . . . exciting adventures and hot love scenes." —*Romantic Times*

THE RAVEN AND THE ROSE

"Henley brilliantly interweaves a passionate love story with the turbulent events of the War of the Roses, an era unmatched for intrigue and drama." —*Romantic Times*

Books by Virginia Henley:

THE MARRIAGE PRIZE
THE BORDER HOSTAGE
A WOMAN OF PASSION
A YEAR AND A DAY
DREAM LOVER
ENSLAVED
SEDUCED
DESIRED
ENTICED
TEMPTED
THE DRAGON AND THE JEWEL
THE FALCON AND THE FLOWER
THE HAWK AND THE DOVE
THE PIRATE AND THE PAGAN
THE RAVEN AND THE ROSE

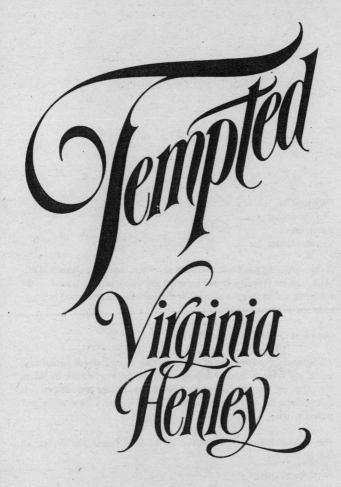

Tempted

Virginia Henley

Dell

Published by
Dell Publishing
a division of
Random House, Inc.

The trademark Dell® is registered in the U.S. Patent and Trademark
Office.

ISBN: 0-440-20625-1

Printed in the United States of America

Published simultaneously in Canada

February 1993

20 19 18 17 16 15 14 13 12

OPM

In memory of my father, Thomas Syddall

and

Dedicated to the real Tina (Moskow) and Damaris (Rowland). Two blithe spirits!

Chapter 1

'Twixt Wigtown and the town of Ayr,
Portpatrick and the Cruives o' Cree,
No man needs think for tae bide there
Unless he court wi' Kennedy!

 Valentina Kennedy, so named because she had been born on Saint Valentine's day, was more often called Firebrand or Flaming Tina because of her glorious red-gold hair, all molten flames and fire.

She brushed it back with a nervous gesture as she approached the tower room of Castle Doon. Her expressive golden eyes, usually so dreamy or sparkling with challenge, were now liquid with apprehension.

She straightened her shoulders and pushed open the door with a bravado she did not feel. Simply stepping over the threshold was an act of courage, for ever since she was a child this room had been dubbed the torture chamber. She had always played roughhouse with her older brothers, sometimes showing more daring and recklessness than they did and she felt quite cocky when she heard the servants call her a plucky little lass. But her mettle had deserted her the day they dragged her up to the torture chamber and showed her the crude instruments one by one, describing in grisly detail how Butcher Bothwick cut out a tongue or plucked out an eyeball. They had gleefully pointed out the red-stained flagstones and reached for a jar of black leeches they said would suck out her blood. Valentina flushed remembering what she had done when she saw Butcher Bothwick, the hairy giant who wielded these instruments of torture. She had fainted.

It was years later before she understood that Bothwick was the castle surgeon who staunched Kennedy wounds, lanced boils or pulled rotten teeth. A toothache was the reason for her being here today. She had never had a tooth pulled before, never even seen a tooth extracted from anyone else, but common sense told her there would be pain and there would be blood.

"Come in, lass. I've been expectin' ye," said the big man in a thick Scots brogue, flexing his muscles with pride, eager to show his finesse.

Tina was quite literally terrified, yet she had so much stiff Scots pride, she would rather die than allow this man to know her total fear of him.

"I ha' all in readiness," he said, taking up a pair of torturous-looking pincers in hands whose size made her tremble, for she knew with a certainty that they were too large to be capable of gentleness. Tina seemed rooted to the spot, unable to move, until Bothwick encouraged her, "I'm no' a monster, I'll no' hurt ye!"

She took a deep breath to steady herself, and his promise made her fear recede a little. She shrugged one pretty shoulder and walked boldly forward. He towered above her, so close she could smell the whisky on his breath. His bare biceps bulged above hairy forearms, clearly displaying his strength, and she knew he could easily overpower her if she resisted.

His fingers brushed her lips and he coaxed roughly, "Open for me, there's a good lass."

An inborn instinct for self-preservation made her shrink from him, backing away slowly and imperceptibly, but with dismay she saw him advance upon her with determination. She broke away from him and retreated hastily, no longer able to bear his touch. The couch was now between them. "Lie doon here fer a minute, an' it'll be over an' done wi'," he urged, but every instinct told her she would then be completely at his mercy.

Tina's mind seethed with uncharitable thoughts of her family. Her young sister had cast her a look that told her plainly Beth was most thankful she was not the one to suffer such a dreadful fate. Her loutish brothers slapped their thighs, hilarious that for once *fate* was being unkind to the willful beauty of the family.

"I've hardly complained at all! 'Tis not fair!" she'd cried, and they'd laughed all the harder at her predicament, winking at each other and demanding, "Who the hell ever said life was fair?" But it was her father she blamed the most at this moment. He'd issued his orders and none dared disobey him. Even her timid mother had blanched when Rob Kennedy, Lord of Galloway, had said, "She goes to Bothwick!"

"B-Butcher Bothwick? Oh Rob, must she?"

"Aye, ye heard me, woman—yer no' deaf, and I'll have no weepin' and wailin'." His fierce glance swept over all with a challenge. "Is there any in this room dares tae hint I dinna ken what's best fer ma ain family?"

Valentina's throat constricted, and her lovely full breasts rose and fell with her growing apprehension as the powerful man vaulted across the couch to trap her. When he slipped a thickly muscled arm about her shoulders to prevent a second escape, fear swept over her in a great wave. She squeezed her eyes closed as she felt the rough stone wall against her bottom, and she knew she could retreat no further.

He took her chin in his hand, forcing back her head. Her pleading eyes sought his. "Please, no. Can't we wait until tomorrow?"

"Dinna be a coward, lass—the longer ye wait, the more affeared ye'll be. We'll do it now!" he said decisively. "I'll be quick as I can aboot it."

To be called a coward was anathema to Tina. She gathered every ounce of courage and swayed toward him. His fingers touched her lips gently as he whispered, "Open fer me."

She did as she was bidden, and he slipped his fingers into her mouth. Her dark lashes swept to her cheeks, a low moan built in her throat, and as she felt him probing, she could not speak—she could not even breathe. Suddenly something inside her snapped.

She gathered all her strength and pushed the huge man away from her with a suddenness that sent him sprawling across the flagstones.

"Judas Iscariot!" he cursed.

Valentina was immediately contrite. "Oh Bothwick, I'm sorry." She reached down to help the burly man to his feet. "It's just that I changed my mind. Suddenly the pain disappeared and my tooth doesn't hurt anymore. There's no point pulling a perfectly good tooth."

"Liar!" he accused gruffly, rubbing a skinned elbow.

Suddenly she grinned and the older man thought he'd never seen such a radiant lass in his life. "I don't care if you call me liar, so long as you don't call me coward. Don't tell them I was afraid, for I certainly wasn't. When you put your fingers in my mouth, the pain vanished. You have the healing touch, Bothwick."

He grinned back at her reluctantly and put away the primitive-looking instrument he'd been holding. "Yer a liar, but yer a bonnie liar!"

"I'll go and see Mr. Burque. He'll give me something to help."

"Wheesht, lass, 'tis his muck give ye the toothache tae start with. Yon prancin' fop will rot every tooth in yer haid afore he's done."

Mr. Burque was the elegant French chef who had accompanied her mother to Scotland when she had married Lord Kennedy. When Bothwick saw the forlorn look on her face, he relented. "Away with ye tae the kitchens then. Nae doot his chocolate will cosset ye a wee."

* * *

Down in the castle kitchen Tina couldn't help comparing Mr. Burque's attractive hands with the thick, hairy ones of Bothwick. He was fluting the edges of a gigantic mutton pie, his long, slim fingers transforming the hearty fare into an artistic masterpiece. Tina sat upon his worktable, her foot propped upon a kitchen stool.

"Chérie, I'll be putting flour on your pretty gown," he warned.

"You'll be putting flowers on my grave if you don't give me something for this toothache," she said dramatically.

Mr. Burque was all sympathetic concern at her *cri de coeur*. He rolled his eyes and wrung his hands at her plight. Valentina laughed up into his attractive expressive face, thoroughly enjoying his company. He was better looking than most women, and the two had shared a rapport since she was a child. Mr. Burque lifted the lid of his precious spice box, selected a tiny treasure from it, and, holding it between elegant thumb and first finger, uttered a fanfare: "Ta-da!"

Tina sniffed the minuscule object and decided it was a clove. She opened her mouth for this man as trustingly as a baby bird, and he popped it against the offending tooth.

They were both startled by the loud, grating voice of Rob Kennedy as his imposing bulk filled the entranceway to the kitchen. He saw the two heads close together but had no fears for his daughter's chastity with yon prinking, prancing ninny of a Frenchman. "Did ye attend Bothwick as ye were bidden?"

Lady Valentina jumped down from the table and faced her father squarely. "I did, my lord. I took your advice and faced right up to it."

His florid face softened a mite. "Was there pain?"

"Hardly any," she assured him.

"Blood?" he commiserated.

"Not a drop," she said truthfully.

He shook his head in admiration. "There's a brave lass. God's passion, but ye get more like me every day."

She fervently hoped not.

Mr. Burque made a choking noise behind her, and Rob Kennedy's baleful eye fell upon him. "How much more time afore we sup?" he demanded.

"A mere *soupçon,* my lord," came the reply.

"Soups on? Aye, a good thick broth'll stick tae the ribs. None of yer French muck, mind ye!" he admonished.

"Peste!" swore Mr. Burque as the Lord of Galloway took himself off.

Unexpectedly, Kennedy's bulk again shadowed the doorway. "Tell yon pest we ha' guests fer dinner," he told his daughter.

"Take heart, Mr. Burque," she murmured. "He sails tomorrow, praise Heaven."

Her father's words made no impact upon Tina. They always had guests. Doon Castle was a warm, welcoming place atop the headlands above the busy seaport of Ayr. Kennedy hospitality was legendary but only for the invited. The Lord of Galloway was affluent and set the best table in Scotland. Kennedy captains dined alongside the young lairds and masters of the ruling clans.

The bachelor quarters of Doon Castle overflowed at the moment with red-haired young men from no fewer than four different branches of the clan. They had brought the wool from the first shearing to be exported via Kennedy vessels.

The racket that assaulted Tina's ears as she entered the dining hall was loud enough to raise the rafters. She liked nothing better than mingling with her brothers and first, second, and third cousins. She loved men's company, their laughter, their boisterous camaraderie, their coarse language. She secretly longed to be one of the lads. At her approach the young lairds abandoned their shoving match. She parted them like the Red Sea, then they closed about her, making her the center of attention.

"May I get ye some wine, Tina?" asked Callum Kennedy of Newark.

She rewarded him with a smile and announced, "I'll have ale like the rest of you." A leather tankard was pressed into her hand, and her eldest brother, Donal, censured her.

"Ale is a man's drink."

She flashed him a look of challenge. "Aye, I know—like everything else in life, it's devised to pleasure a man."

They hooted, and the air was thick with ribald rejoinders as they seized upon the age-old male-female bone of contention. "Well, I ask you, what pleasures are reserved for women?" she asked, warming to her subject. "You do the hunting and we tend the hearth!"

"Hark at her," said her brother Duncan, laughing. "Tend the hearth—she canna boil water."

"Jesu, an' a good thing or we'd all be poisoned," Donal said, teasing.

"You have armor and weapons, claymores, swords, and dirks. The knife I'm allowed is a pitiful thing compared to the weapon Duncan polishes day and night."

"There's no call tae bring my sex life into this," Duncan murmured to his cousin, who howled at his wit.

"I heard that aside, Duncan Kennedy, which only helps prove my point. That's another indulgence allowed men. The king holds the record for bastards, and the rest of you are in the running, except mayhap my wee brother Davie."

David, at fourteen, bristled at her remark. His was the only fair head in that sea of flames. "Are ye tryin' tae make me a laughingstock? I'm no' without experience. Yer a right bitch of a sister!"

"See what I mean?" Tina asked, laughing. "Men brag about their conquests, which only bring sorrow and shame to women."

An argument had broken out between Kennedy of Newark and Kennedy of Dunure. "Yer witless! The king no' holds the record fer bastards. 'Tis ma brother Keith," he announced with pride.

"Yer daft, man! There isna a Kennedy breathin' can compete wi' the Stewarts when it comes tae bastards."

His cousin gave him a shove that almost knocked him into the huge fireplace, and he came back in a rush with clenched fists flying. "I'll flay ye!"

Donal and Duncan each grabbed a combatant with a strong arm beneath the throat, effectively ending the skirmish, but not before blood had been drawn. Duncan said, "Robert Stewart of Orkney has seventeen sons, none born in wedlock, an' none tae the same mother."

Donal said, "This is no fit subject tae be discussin' wi' the little firebrand."

Now it was Tina's turn to be angered. "Because I'm female, I can't talk about bastards. I can't drink, curse, fight, or go off on a raid with the rest of you." A sudden unnatural silence fell on the gathering. Donal exchanged a furtive glance with Callum Kennedy, and immediately Tina scented something in the wind. She was wise enough to keep her mouth shut, however.

To fill the silence Andrew Kennedy, Lord of Carrick, took Tina's hand and said, "If ye'd accept one o' the proposals ye receive, yer husband would bring ye all the pleasure a lass could yearn fer."

A harsh voice, loud enough to raise the dead, cut through the conversation. "What's this o' proposals?" demanded Rob Kennedy, and once more the group of males parted, exposing Valentina to her father's wrath.

"I—I said no when Andrew asked me to marry. I have no wish to marry," she said faintly.

"No wish tae marry?" Rob Kennedy thundered, his face becoming a congested purple. His accusing eyes burned into her as if she had uttered an unspeakable blasphemy. "How many others have ye sent packing wi' a flea in their ear?"

"N-none," she whispered, and the brawny young men

behind her with heads like torches coughed at the bare-
faced lie she gave her father.

"Every last one of 'em in this room," revealed Davie, "as
well as Sandy Gordon last week."

Duncan's boot jabbed into Davie's shin before he was
effectively silenced, and Rob Kennedy looked as if he were
about to have a seizure. "Ye turned down the Earl o'
Huntly's heir?"

Lady Elizabeth and her younger daughter, Beth, chose
this moment to arrive in the dining hall. Tina's mother cast
an apprehensive glance over the gathering and faltered.
She wondered if she could stomach the Kennedys en
masse. Rob outwardly ignored their arrival, but it made
him put a curb on his outburst. "Attend me after dinner.
God's passion, but daughters can be a curse tae a man."

Andrew Kennedy, feeling protective toward Valentina,
asked her to sit with him. On her other side Donal warned,
"Father's right hot wi' ye. It'll pay tae use him softly."

She gave them both a grateful smile. "I'll handle Father," she whispered with bravado, but it ruined her pleasure in the chocolate truffles that Mr. Burque had made
especially for her, and the cursed tooth began its nagging
ache again.

At the far end of the hall two women in their thirties
dined at a table for the more important servants of Doon.
The castle steward eyed the two nursemaids with relish. It
was well known that the two women barely tolerated each
other, and he could see that at any minute entertaining
hostilities were about to break out between the foes.

Kirsty, a Scotswoman whose charge was Beth Kennedy,
the younger, sweeter daughter, could not wipe the satisfied
smirk from her face as she helped herself to the mutton
pie. She adjusted the severe neckline of her gown trimmed
with vair and whispered almost gleefully, "Trouble! Trouble is Valentina Kennedy's middle name."

Ada, the Englishwoman Lady Kennedy had brought with

her when she was but a girl, held on to her temper. Tina was her charge, but they were also friends and close confidantes. Ada was still an attractive woman who wore her hair in an upsweep to show off her long neck and dangling earbobs. "I warrant the poor animal which owned that mangy fur you're wearing didn't complain at losing it."

"Och!" Kirsty cried, compressing her lips until they disappeared. "Ye've an insolent tongue. 'Tis plain tae see where Flaming Tina gets it."

"I freely admit I've taught her to stand up for herself. If you make a doormat of yourself, people will wipe their muddy boots on you in this world," Ada said dryly.

Some of the smugness crept back into Kirsty's face. "My lord is incensed this time. I have my doubts she'll stand up tae him long."

"Rob Kennedy will ride roughshod over any who will let him, but he admires guts, even in a woman. That's something you'd know nothing about."

"If she were my charge, I'd soon whip some obedience intae her," declared the Scotswoman. The steward laughed in her face. God's passion, it would take a strong man in jackboots to whip obedience into Flaming Tina Kennedy.

Ada said, "She's sixteen, almost seventeen—a woman grown. She's too old to take orders from a nursemaid."

"Beth takes orders from me," Kirsty stated firmly. Ada wasn't about to start pulling young Beth to pieces but said, "They are different as chalk and cheese. Valentina is all comely, shapely fascination and beauty."

"And well she knows it," Kirsty accused, her eyes traveling down the tables to the men surrounding the tempting redhead. "She has a reputation for bein' a honeypot, an' no wonder, when ye've been in charge of her morals."

Ada was a widow who could not deny she enjoyed the company of men. "Jealousy ill becomes you, woman."

"In my experience men prefer a bit more innocence. They dinna like it when some o' the bloom has been rubbed off," Kirsty said maliciously.

"In your experience? There's a figment of the imagination." Ada had had enough and decided to silence her adversary. "Do you know what happens to spinsters on their fortieth birthday? Their holes make up!"

Kirsty gasped, turned beet red, and fled from the table. The steward was still choking on a mouthful of ale. Ada's satisfaction diminished somewhat when the page tugged at her sleeve. "Laird Kennedy wants tae see ye."

A pale Lady Kennedy followed her husband into the first-floor room he used for conducting his business. Valentina followed her in, and Ada brought up the rear, whispering, "One more day and he would have been gone."

Tina had a habit of shrugging one shapely shoulder, and Ada sighed with resignation. Sparks were bound to fly when two such volatile personalities came together.

Mother and daughter seated themselves while Ada stood guard behind Tina's chair. At one time Rob Kennedy had been a handsome man with a flaming torch of hair. Now it was sparse and gray. His florid face showed sagging jowls, and his paunch thrust forward as a testimonial to Mr. Burque's talent. He was still an imposing man, however, with his broad back and shrewd eyes. He stood with his backside to the fire and asked in a deceptively quiet voice, "Do I detect a conspiracy here?" His eye fell upon his hapless wife. "Just how many proposals have ye been keepin' from me?"

Elizabeth grew even paler. "Rob, I know nothing of this," she said softly.

"Know nothing . . . know nothing? God ha' mercy woman, do ye go through life wi' blinkers on? Ye know nothing—ye never do!" His voice had risen, and it had a grating quality that pierced the eardrum painfully.

"Please don't browbeat Mother," Tina said reasonably.

"I've no intention of browbeatin' yer mother—'tis ye I'll browbeat!" He locked eyes with her and demanded, "What earthly use are daughters tae a mon?" Silence. "I'll elucidate. Lasses, in especial ravishin' beauties like yersel, are valuable tae forge marriages between powerful clans tae preserve peace, tae extend power, and tae increase wealth." He turned on his wife again. "I shouldna listened tae ye. I shouldha sent her tae court—she woulda had a husband an' a bairn in her belly by now."

With great daring Elizabeth said, "The last Kennedy who went to court didn't manage to catch a husband."

"She did even better—mistress tae the two most powerful men in Scotland, Archibald Douglas, Earl of Angus, an' now the king hissel, if yer talkin' about ma wee cousin, Janet Kennedy."

"Don't you dare say that name in this house," Elizabeth whispered.

"Janet Kennedy? She's a bit o' a whore, but let me remind ye, woman, the Kennedys were Kings o' Carrick. We ha' the finest blood in Scotland!" he shouted.

"I was speaking of Douglas," Elizabeth said quietly.

Rob Kennedy cleared his throat. "Aye, well, I didna mean tae stir painful memories, Lizzy. Foul fall all the bloody Black Douglases."

Elizabeth had her handkerchief to her eyes. "May I leave? I'm feeling unwell," she pleaded.

He nodded, not trusting himself to speak until she had departed, then his invective burst forth like a dam upon the remaining pair. "Now see what ye've done! I should flay ye fer upsettin' yer mother!"

Tina was on her feet. "*You* did that when you brought up the profligate black-hearted Douglases."

He waved his hand dismissively. "Och, the woman's too sensitive. It all happened over fifteen year past an' best forgot. She acts as if Damaris was her sister rather than mine."

"Damaris was her best friend, her only friend in Scotland. The Douglas Clan poisoned her—mother will never forget!"

"That's no' the issue here." As he caught sight of his daughter's vivid beauty, he wondered how on earth he'd produced such an exquisite child. The fireshine played across her heart-shaped face and turned her hair to molten copper. She drew men like bees to a honeypot and it had been a puzzle to him why none had offered for her. His heart softened. "Lassie, I want a Campbell or a Gordon for ye."

"Father, I don't want to marry. Why can't you teach me to sail one of the ships so I could take the wool to Flanders?"

His face hardened again, and his accusing eyes came to rest on Ada. "Wheesht, woman, 'tis ye who's put these daft ideas in her haid! Why could ye no' make her gentle an' biddable?"

"My Lord Kennedy, Scotland is a harsh land filled with harsher men. I swore I wouldn't make the mistake of making Tina soft like her mother and Beth. Besides, she's too much like you to be gentle. As for biddable, it will take a very strong mate to make her that."

"Aye—even then I ha' ma doots. Tina, lass, listen tae yer old dad. Choose while the choice is still yers. Yer nigh seventeen. If ye dinna wed soon, Archibald Kennedy, Earl of Cassillis, will choose fer ye. 'Tis his duty as laird o' the clan. Or the king might force ye tae wed tae his advantage. Be sensible—choose an earl's son and someday ye'll be a countess. Off wi' ye now, vixen! I'll ha' a word in private wi' Ada." After she left, he grated, "God's passion, women can be willful!"

"You'd have no respect for one who wasn't, Rob Kennedy."

"Aye, well, the other gets round me wi' her tears," he said, referring to his wife. "I suppose it'll cost me a visit tae England tae placate her." He gave her a sidelong glance. "Yer a fine figure of a woman, Ada—'tis a long time since we had a good grapple. Do ye think ye might be in need of company the nicht?"

Ada tossed her head so that her earrings swung provocatively. "I might," she admitted.

* * *

When Ada entered Tina's chamber, she found her before the polished silver mirror with her mouth open and her neck contorted at an odd angle.

"Let me have a look," Ada said, picking up a candelabrum.

Obediently Tina opened her mouth wide and pointed to the back. After a moment Ada said with relief, "It's a wisdom tooth having a spurt of growth because it's spring. Thank heaven you didn't let Butcher Bothwick pull it. A woman should keep her back teeth at all costs. It keeps your face young looking. Once your back teeth are gone, your cheeks fall in to age you terribly."

"Thank you, Ada. If I leave it alone, it should be gone soon?"

"If I were you, I'd be off to bed, and perhaps it will be gone by morning." Ada wanted what was best for Tina, but at the same time she had her own interests in mind. "Tomorrow is May Day."

"Beltane!" Tina said, hugging her arms in anticipation of the Celtic holy day. In daylight the villagers would dance around the maypole, but at night they would have revels and dance about Beltane fires—aye, and do more than dance!

Tina yawned and lifted a pretty shoulder. She shook out her bedgown and said, "Good night, Ada. I think I'll take your advice."

The minute Ada was through the door, Tina shoved the bedgown back beneath her pillow. "Not bloody likely," she murmured happily. Tonight was the night that the Gypsies returned to the Valley of Galloway.

Chapter 2

Degenerate Douglas! Unworthy Lord He!
Hush thee, hush, my little pet ye,
The Black Douglas will not get thee.

Thirty miles away at Douglas, the Black Ram lay stretched on the floor of the hall, casting dice with his brothers and some of his moss-troopers. The Boozer, his fierce wolfhound, sprawled at his feet before the fire. The flames turned Ram's swarthy face into planes of light and shadow.

Ramsay Douglas had saber-sharp cheekbones and pewter-colored eyes with heavy black brows arched above them, giving him the Devil's own look, and he'd the Devil's own temper when roused. Tonight, however, he seemed in a mellow enough mood as he lazily cast the dice.

The noise level in the hall was high but that was usual. The borderers were such a rough and rowdy bunch of lusty rogues, it always sounded like a brawl or a rape. A bagpipe skirled from somewhere on the walls, and Cameron, the youngest Douglas, was singing a bawdy song: " 'Hooray, hooray, the first of May, outdoor fuckin' starts today.' " The words then became even more grossly indecent, and two of his cousins joined in the chorus.

The Boozer stood up and stretched, thinking the company sufficiently drunk, it wouldn't be noticed if he helped himself to the leftovers littering the tables.

The massive wolfhound stood with great paws on the table, crunching a mutton bone with its razor-sharp teeth. A servitor tried to wave the beast from the board, but the Boozer laid his ears flat and growled deep in his throat.

The servant backed off with a filthy epithet, and the dog tipped over a goblet, then lapped up its contents before they had a chance to drip to the floor.

Gavin, every bit as dark as Ramsay, but handsomer and less dangerous looking, eyed his brother with speculation. "Would ye care tae raise the stakes to make this more interesting?"

"Why not?" Ram drawled.

With great audacity Gavin said, "Would ye put up Jenna?"

Ian and Drummond, captains of Douglas vessels, exchanged swift, apprehensive glances. The Black Douglas wasn't a man to share anything, let alone a woman who warmed his bed.

Ram Douglas lifted an amused brow. "Against what?" he asked.

Gavin's eyes glittered. "Against my falcon." He knew Ram admired his beautiful raptor.

Ram shrugged. "Why not?"

Gavin knew Ram had more confidence in his own ability than any man breathing, and he knew there was little chance of his outcasting his brother at dice. But it never hurt to try.

Gavin blinked as his brother Ram rolled a pitiful three, and he felt a rush of hot blood at his own good fortune. Then common sense took over, and he accused, "Ye lost on purpose, man."

Ram hauled himself to his feet and stretched. "No such thing—ye won fair and square. I wish ye joy of her. Well, I'm off."

Gavin Douglas looked puzzled. "I thought ye were tae bring the horses down from the mountains tomorrow."

"I leave at dawn," Ram said, "and there's still eight hours till dawn." He winked at Gavin and picked up his leather jack.

Ram's brother stared after him, then said to Cameron,

"He just lost Jenna tae me—I suspect it was done deliberately. Why the hell would he do that?"

Cameron's black brows smoothed from their puzzled
furrow as he remembered something. "The Gypsies! This
is the night the Gypsies return to Galloway Valley."

Tina changed into a warm green velvet riding habit and
slipped from the castle toward the stable. She looked up at
the tiny sliver of the new moon in the dark sky and shivered as she thought it would be a good night for a raid. As
she opened the stable door and slipped inside, her nostrils
quivered with the pungent odor of horseflesh, hay, and
manure that rose up in a miasma in the dim interior. Before she had taken three steps, however, she came face-to-
face with a dozen Kennedy men saddling their mounts.
The girl and the men looked at each other with dismay,
knowing they had been discovered in a clandestine activity.
"Oh, you're going on a raid!" Tina gasped. All her instincts
had told her they'd been planning a raid, but she had assumed they would wait until their father had sailed.

"Ye daft loon, of course we're no'," denied Donal.
"Where the hell are ye sneakin' off tae?"

She ignored the question. "I know you are riding out to
raid. None of you are wearing the telltale Kennedy tartan,
and the moon is just right!"

Donal mounted, and Duncan and the rest of the clan
members followed suit. "Tina, yer imagination takes flights
o' fancy. We're just riding tae Glasgow. Get back tae the
castle, lass, before ye get yersel in more trouble."

"Duncan, make Donal let me come with you! I'll do
exactly as I'm told. I want to help."

"Ye've never done as yer told in yer life," cut in Donal.

"I'm a Kennedy too!" she flared. "I want to come—I
want to help!"

Duncan bent low and said confidentially, "Tina, we're
off tae a whorehouse in Glasgow. How can ye help? Hold
up the lassies' skirts fer us, mayhap?"

She flushed at their crudeness, and they filed past her out into the dark night.

Valentina was relieved that the Kennedys were heading north to Glasgow. It was close to thirty miles, and the pace Donal and Duncan set would be punishing. She was riding east so there was no chance they would run into each other again.

Where the Gypsies made camp was about eight miles off along the banks of the River Ayr. Tina had no fear of riding in the dark save for concern that her beautiful mare might step into a badger hole, so she chose to canter over the rolling fells rather than gallop.

The hills were dotted with sheep and newborn lambs that had been freed from their winter pens to spend their first spring night outdoors this last day of April 1512. She could hear the river in spate at the moment, rushing headlong over rock and boulder, and not far off she heard the bark of a fox. It was the sort of night that was filled with promise and magic. The kind of night that made her glad to be alive with the wind in her hair and good horseflesh between her knees.

Tina embraced the night. Tomorrow with its threat of husband and marriage was a million miles away, but when it arrived she would meet it head on and on her own terms.

She saw their campfires first, and then the silhouettes of their caravans, long before she reached the valley's floor to mingle with the raffish band of dusky nomads.

A black stallion stood beneath the trees on the edge of the camp. His rider bent low to aid a young Gypsy girl mount behind him. Her red skirt fell back to reveal bare legs that she used seductively to grip the iron-hard thighs of the man in front of her. A deep thrill ran through Zara as her body came in contact with his. There was nothing about him that was not dark and hard. The line of his jaw was stubborn, and the set of his head was arrogantly proud atop the wide, powerful shoulders. He was clad in black from head to foot. His jack and thigh-high riding boots were made of supple black leather. Zara shivered, knowing the Black Ram was ruthless and dangerous. Of all the men she had ever known—and men were her business—he was the only one she couldn't rule in bed.

Suddenly he leaned forward, resting his arm on his saddle pommel, and watched intently as a young woman with flaming hair streaming about her shoulders rode into the camp. She rode astride, which was almost unheard of for a woman. She flung herself from her horse and ran laughing into the outstretched arms of a tall young Gypsy male: "Heath! Oh Heath, how I've missed you!"

Ram continued his slow, deliberate appraisal of the vivid creature as the man lifted her in the air and swung her about. "Who is she?" Ram asked, his voice low and intense, in no way trying to disguise his interest in the beauty.

"I don't know," Zara lied. "Probably someone's wife looking for forbidden fruit. In any case you'd better leave Heath's women alone unless you fancy a knife in your ribs."

Ram smiled to himself. Zara was clearly jealous, as she had every right to be, for the girl's looks were breathtaking, but her jealousy had better not make her bold enough to threaten him. "Would ye fancy following me on foot tae Douglas?" he asked silkily.

"What makes you think I'd follow you?" Zara hissed, but she knew she would and so did he, damn him to hellfire!

Heath and Valentina caught up on what had occurred in their lives since they'd last been together. The Gypsies had traveled as far north as Inverary in the Highlands during the summer and had wintered in Carlisle, in England, where the climate was not so inclement. They'd also spent time in the old capital of Stirling and the new capital of Edinburgh while king and court had been in residence.

Tina had a million questions for him, covering everything from the Earl of Argyll's Campbells to her own notorious kinswoman who was rumored to be the king's new mistress. "Is it true she was mistress to Archibald Douglas, the hated Earl of Angus?" Tina asked with a shudder. "No wonder she sought the king's protection."

"The Douglas name is never uttered without a shiver of fear, and yet I think Scotland has much more to fear from Argyll. He intends to swallow the Highlands whole."

"Heath, Douglas is less than thirty miles away. The whole of the border country is beneath their heel."

"Sweetheart, 'tis no bad thing that they're so strong. Since the king appointed Douglas the leading marcher lord patrolling the borders, England's learned it can't attack with impunity. This past winter I didn't hear of many raids between the two countries."

"Well, that is good news," she said, laughing. "We Scots can now resume our favorite pastime of raiding each other." She put her head on one side, the better to observe Heath's warm brown eyes. "You didn't answer my question about Janet Kennedy."

His beautiful white teeth flashed when he laughed. "To hell with Janet Kennedy! What about Valentina Kennedy?"

"The news is all bad," she teased. "I've a wisdom tooth plaguing the devil out of me, and the marriage noose tightens about my neck even as we speak."

His eyes twinkled. "You could always run away with the Gypsies."

"Someday I just might," she vowed passionately.

"Come on, Old Meg will give you something to soothe that tooth."

"Oh yes! She can tell me my fortune," Tina said with enthusiasm.

Old Meg's caravan was a small world within a world. The outside was painted a dramatic red and black, the inside cluttered with the curious trappings of her trade.

She told fortunes, cast spells, and dispensed electuaries for every complaint known to man. Her ceiling was hung with dried herbs that gave off odd pungent fragrances, and the walls were fitted with wooden shelves that held bottles, bowls, and boxes of strange powders, liquids, and dried animal parts. A polished brass lamp swung over a small round table, casting a red glow upon her mystic glass ball and tattered tarot cards.

Meg was a shrewd old party who had made herself rich by performing abortions on noble ladies. Her business was always briskest when they visited the king's court.

Meg gave Tina no greeting when she climbed the steps of her wagon, but mixed her a concoction to sup when told of the toothache. Heath was her grandson. His mother had died in childbirth.

"Meg, will you tell my fortune?" Tina asked hopefully as she sat down at the small table and sipped the steaming brew. Heath, who had to keep his head bent inside the caravan to avoid the ceiling, said, "I'll be at the campfire when you're done."

Old Meg, her mouth set in severe lines, went through the motions of placing her beringed hands upon the glass ball, but after a minute of silence she said, "The stars are not right tonight. I can tell you nothing."

Tina held her stare, her strong will battling with that of the Gypsy. "Meg, you know you can read the cards."

Meg compressed her lips. She disapproved of the relationship between her grandson and this spirited, spoiled girl. She had no reason to love the Kennedys. "Cross my palm with silver," she commanded, and held out her gnarled hand.

Tina placed three silver coins upon the none-too-clean palm and held her breath in anticipation as she shuffled the large deck of painted pasteboards Meg handed her. She closed her eyes and made a wish as she had been taught to do, then handed the cards back to the old professional.

The first card turned up was The Emperor, from the major arcana. Meg described the picture: "A dark, authoritative man sits upon a throne, the armrests and upper back made into rams' heads. In his right hand he holds the Cross of Life, the Egyptian ankh. On his right shoulder there is another image of the ram's head. Behind him are stark mountains devoid of scenery. The symbolism of The Emperor is earthly knowledge. This man is ruled by his mind rather than his emotions—he represents law and order. The stark mountains show his power and strength. He is unyielding and unbending in his judgments. He is a leader rather than a follower. He enjoys being in command and rules with an iron hand."

Meg turned over the second card. It was The Empress, also from the major arcana. Meg again described the card: "A beautiful woman is wearing a crown of twelve stars. By her side is a heart-shaped shield bearing the sign of Venus. Before her is a ripe field of corn, behind her are trees in full bloom. She is Aphrodite, goddess of human love. The symbolism of this card is fertility. Both sexes joined. It denotes a fulfillment of erotic needs. She represents heaven on earth, the Garden of Eden, the door that opens unto earthly pleasures and treasures."

Meg placed the Page of Swords, from the minor arcana, upon the table: "A youth holds a sword tightly in his hands. Clouds surround him. He has to prove his masculinity by fighting. He uses aggressiveness as a defense against self-doubt." Tina immediately thought of her brother David. She caught her breath as a second sword card turned up, for she knew they were the worst cards in the deck. It was the Five of Swords. "A man carrying two swords on his shoulder, another in his right hand looks with scorn upon two dejected figures whose swords are on the ground. The sky is filled with storm clouds. Here is a man who defeats others, who lives by the sword, who is insensitive and indifferent. The symbolism suggests you will lose something;

there will be a breaking of bonds and separation from loved ones."

Tina was relieved to see the next card was the Seven of Wands, but Meg made it, too, sound ominous. "All sevens imply change. The card indicates you must hold your own against unfavorable odds. You must take a stand and be adamant in the face of opposition, for only in change is there growth."

The Four of Cups was laid upon the small table, and Tina let out her breath thankfully. Meg continued: "A young man sits against a tree with his arms folded. A hand extends a cup to him, while three other cups sit upright in front of him. The young man is not reaching out for the cup extended to him, rather he is contemplating the offer. This card represents the love bed, pleasure, and irresistible sexual attraction."

Meg turned over the seventh and last card. Tina gasped; it was the Ten of Swords. Meg said nothing. Tina didn't need it described to her—she could clearly see it was a man lying prostrate on the ground with ten swords stuck into his back, while above him was a blackened sky.

Meg gathered the cards together quickly. "It has many meanings; everything looks black."

"Interpret the whole thing for me," Tina said, gathering her courage. "Will I get my wish?"

"Yes," said Meg without hesitation.

Tina sighed with relief. Though she had someone in mind for her husband, she had asked that there be no marriage for her this year.

"The cards speak for themselves. You will be involved with a dark man whose symbol is the ram. He will rule you. The Empress represents you. The dark man will bring you sexual fulfillment; you will be fertile."

At this point Tina decided none of it would come true because she would get her wish and her wish was "no marriage."

"The Page of Swords is a youth who is close to you. He

will be instrumental in starting trouble. The Five of Swords shows there will be fighting, struggling, bloodshed that will result in your being separated from your loved ones. The Seven of Wands confirms this change and warns you will have to stand firm if your will is to prevail, but the Four of Cups indicates you will receive an offer and the choice will be yours."

"And the last card?" Tina pressed.

Meg saw the dark male lying prostrate with the swords in his back. Her beloved Heath was dark. She pierced Tina with a fierce glare. "You will wish you were dead!" prophesied the old Gypsy.

Tina felt something move against her foot beneath the table and jumped. "Oh, what was that?" she cried, lifting aside the table cover and peering down. She saw a large tortoise with a great red jewel embedded in its shell. "Is that a ruby?" asked Tina with disbelief. "Aren't you afraid your tortoise will be stolen?" she asked, tracing her finger over the ruby.

The corners of Meg's mouth turned down in derision. "The jewel is cursed. Any who touch it will experience pain and sorrow."

Tina looked at Meg, and suddenly amusement filled her eyes. The Gypsy was doing her very best to fill her with foreboding. There were no such things as curses. Everyone was responsible for their own fortune or misfortune in this world. "You are a terrible tease, Meg. Thank you for the potion. The ache in my tooth is completely gone." She went to bid Heath good night so she could return to Doon before her absence was discovered. "Tomorrow night will you take me to see the Beltane fires?"

His teeth flashed. "What choice do I have? If I refuse, you will go alone." He lifted her into her saddle and she confided, "Father sails tomorrow. I'll be able to stay out all night!"

* * *

Ramsay Douglas thundered across the drawbridge at his castle, and the guard immediately drew it up and lowered the portcullis, preventing any other from entering. The guards had dubbed him Hotspur because he always rode hell for leather, even when he had a woman riding pillion.

Zara ran up the stairs ahead of Ramsay Douglas, lifting her red skirts high to display her bare ankles and shapely calves. Ram followed carrying a blazing torch that flared and sputtered, casting long shadows against the rough stone walls.

Suddenly another man holding a torch high stood at the top of the stone steps. He moved on with a lurch after acknowledging them with a curt nod. Ram placed his torch in the iron cresset outside his door, and Zara flew into the large chamber that she'd first entered the previous spring. As Ram lit the lamps, she turned to him with a provocative pout on her lips. "He hates me!" she said.

"Colin doesn't hate anyone. He's too soft and gutless for that."

"That was a look of disgust—I'm not blind."

He grinned at her. "That look was for me. My cousin disapproves of my wenching. He'd have me wed and breeding Douglas sons if he had his way, as would the rest of the clan."

She came close and slipped her arms up about his neck and whispered, "In this castle I suspect it's your way or no way."

He looked down at her with an almost casual glance. "Ye suspect right." Though the hour was late, he seemed in no hurry, and Zara was piqued. He continued his perusal of her person, of the small pointed breasts hardening beneath his glance, and the slanted eyes that gave her the look of her exotic ancestors. He touched the gold ring in her ear. "Did you lose the other earring I gave you, or did you pawn it?"

She gave him a provocative look. "It was the first real gold I ever earned. I shall keep it always—in a place that will do me the most good." She was speaking in riddles, and he had neither time nor patience for women's riddles. He pushed her away from him so that he could remove his leather jack. Her eyes widened when she saw he wore chain mail beneath it. His movements were so lithe, she hadn't guessed he was wearing the heavy vest; but the Black Ram had too many enemies to go about unprotected.

As he removed his linen shirt, boots, and leather trews, her eyes became greedy as they slid over the pure male splendor of him. In contrast Zara wore only two garments, skirt and blouse. Ram's deft fingers lifted the blouse over her head, and he said, "Let's have a look at you, then," holding her at arm's length.

The tip of her red tongue came out to slowly circle her lips as she lifted her red skirts beneath her chin and posed for him. His dark eyes lost their casual look as they focused upon her triangle of tight black curls. "Jesu," he breathed, "I thought I'd seen everything!"

The mate to her gold earring had been pierced and mounted at the tip of her mons. "This guarantees me more customers than I can ever accommodate. I am the highest-paid lay in Scotland, more famous than any courtesan. The king was enthralled."

Ram whistled. "The king? How do we compare in bed?"

She lifted off her skirt and flung it across the chamber. "The king is not without talent, but you most definitely have the longer . . . wind!"

He let out a whoop and lifted her high as if she weighed no more than a feather. He tossed her onto the great bed and dove after her, his fingers seeking the gold bauble.

" 'Tis exactly the right size for a man to pass through before he enters the gates of Paradise," she said, drawing her knees wide so the golden hoop dangled over her hot center.

"Then you've had inadequate lovers, my wild little

Gypsy. My shaft is far too thick, as ye can plainly see. . . .
However, if ye insist on playing games, I suppose I have
other appendages will fit through."

Chapter 3

Rob Kennedy had shrewdly guessed that his wife
would manipulate him into allowing her a visit to
her home in Carlisle. Her trunks were all packed
by the time he was ready to set sail at midday. The
five Kennedy offspring as well as the cousins from the
other branches of the clan went down to the firth to watch
them board the *Thistle Doon* and wave farewell to Lord
and Lady Kennedy.

Tina had had all night to think about her father's advice
to choose her own husband, and she had decided to send
him off with a tiny glimmer of hope. As they walked down
to the ship, she slipped her arm about his girth, and he
hugged her to him and again thought how like himself she
was.

"How do you fancy an alliance with the Hamiltons?" she
asked lightly.

He gave her a keen scrutiny. Was she hinting at the Earl
of Arran's heir? Jesu, James Hamilton, Earl of Arran was
the grandson of King James II and Lord High Admiral of
Scotland. "Are ye talking about Patrick Hamilton?"

"I decided long ago he's the most eligible of all my suit-
ors," she said, smiling up at him.

"Yer a canny wee lass. Invite him to Doon," he advised.

"The admiral has the king's flagship anchored a mile
away at Ayr, so Patrick won't be a stranger to these parts."

He grinned and hugged her to him. "I've nae doot ye'll have the young stallion eatin' out o' yer hand." He sobered and wagged an admonishing finger at her. "Just dinna let the laddie take gross an' filthy advantage o' ye, before ye bring him tae commit hissel!"

As the sails filled and the floodtide rapidly carried the ship out to sea every face showed signs of relief. Davie yawned behind his hand and Tina teased, "I'm amazed you dragged yourself out of bed to do your filial duty."

"Christ, I had tae see the back o' him wi' ma ain eyes. He's done nothin' but lecture me aboot carnal appetites o' the flesh. The old lecher makes me puke!"

Tina murmured to Donal, "David's not himself this afternoon."

"Davie is exactly himself. He's a vicious wee bastard at the best o' times," Donal said, thinking of the young prostitute David had abused at the brothel last night.

Tina didn't take Donal's criticism of her youngest brother seriously. When they were little, there had been a strong bond between her and Davie. The older brothers had never included him in their hell-raising because the birth of the two Kennedy daughters had separated him from them in age, and Davie had been relegated to playing with the girls. Tina, a few years his senior, had always protected him from life's knocks and disappointments. She'd always stood up for him against the others, but lately he had distanced himself from her and was bent on proving himself a man. To her he was still a boy, his slim build a long way from the brawn of the older, rougher Kennedy men. She would make an effort to stop mothering him.

Tina fell behind the others to walk with her sister Beth as the group of young people walked along the shore. Beth whispered, "I'm glad Mother didn't insist I go to England with her." She glanced shyly at the rugged-looking Andrew Kennedy, then blushed profusely.

Tina followed her sister's glance and smiled to herself.

"He never notices me," whispered Beth.

"That's because you never do anything to draw his attention," pointed out Tina. "Do something—do something right now!" Tina ordered.

Beth, afraid to, yet afraid not to, bent and picked up a pretty pink scallop shell and quickened her pace to catch up with Andrew. She summoned all her courage. "Lord Carrick," she said breathlessly, "see the shell I just found."

Andrew glanced down at the small blond girl and said absently, "Very pretty, dear."

Beth's steps faltered, and Tina came up beside her. "Men aren't interested in pretty shells, Beth."

"What does interest them?" she asked, wide-eyed.

Tina laughed. "You can always count on two things." But instead of blurting out *money* and *sex*, she said, "A man would get excited about a gold doubloon on the sand, or a moonlight swim with a naked lass."

Beth went white with shock.

Tina said, "Don't take everything so seriously. Men like to laugh. Listen to how rowdy they are. It takes a special talent to draw their attention from men's affairs and hold that attention. Let me show you." The light of challenge made Tina's eyes sparkle. She took off her shoes and stockings and kilted up her skirts to display a delicious length of bare legs, and the men moved toward her like steel filings attracted to a lodestone. When their remarks and suggestions became risqué, she kicked cold water over them, and Beth looked on in amazement that they didn't retreat because of the drenching they risked but instead became more daring in their antics, pushing and shoving each other like rams locking their horns over an ewe. Valentina managed to chase them away, like a queen banishing them from her presence. She sat down upon a rock to put on her shoes, stuffing her hose into her pocket.

"Tina, why don't I take supper in your chamber so we can spend the evening together?" Beth suggested hopefully.

Tina looked at her blankly. "Tonight is Beltane—I'm off

and away." Beth's face fell. "Come with me!" Tina invited generously.

"Heavens, no! Aren't you afraid?" Beth cried.

"Only a tiny bit, but that's what makes it exciting, like going to the graveyard at midnight or bathing in the waters of Black Loch naked."

"Kirsty said you were wicked," confided Beth, beginning to believe it.

"Did she?" Tina asked, sounding inordinately pleased. "I'd rather be wicked than frightened as a rabbit. There's nothing to fear. Heath's back. He'll look after me."

Beth flinched and wrinkled her nose. "That ragtag Gypsy?"

"That ragtag Gypsy is more man than any woman could wish for in her wildest dreams." But Tina admitted to herself, she was relieved that Beth didn't want to come. She brushed the lovely blond strands of hair from Beth's face and nodded toward the group of attractive red-headed men. "They'll all be gone tomorrow. They only came to bring their wool for export. I want you to dine in the hall tonight. Wear your prettiest gown."

By early afternoon, Hotspur Douglas had been in the saddle eight hours, and before dusk fell he would be in the Highlands in the magnificent Grampian Mountains. To cover this great distance in so short a time, he had taken an extra saddle horse and alternated between the two sturdy mounts. At five in the morning he had shaken awake one of his men and thrust the Gypsy girl into his arms with orders to return her to her valley. Then he had chosen two of his fleetest moss-troopers and told them that by dark tomorrow night, they would have the herd they were going to fetch, back at Douglas.

The wild, unbroken horses had been brought up in the northern forests so they could withstand cold and severe weather. They could run a dozen leagues without food. These sure-footed garrons were preferred by border moss-troopers who had to patrol endless miles of wild, wide-open rugged carse and moors. The Douglas stables boasted more than their share of blooded, well-fed stallions. Ram's favorite mount was a black brute that stood more than nineteen hands high. It amused him to call the animal Ruffian, a most misleading misnomer. He could vault into the saddle totally ignoring the stirrups, and many would-be imitators had come a cropper trying to master the trick, especially wearing heavy chain mail.

Ram Douglas had as sharp an eye for a horse as he did for a woman, and he soon cut the choicest mares and sturdy stallions from the herd. He left the foals with their dams to run free another year and laughed when the dominant stud stallion tried to attack him for stealing his mares. There was no way he was going to take him south to a possible gelding. Ram pulled a bullwhip from his belt and cracked it in the air whenever the stallion approached, and he shouted, laughing, "Get the hell away! If ye follow yer mares, ye'll lose yer balls!"

These Highland forests were alive with wolves, boar, and wild bulls, and Ram itched to hunt, but he promised himself not to indulge unless a beast crossed his path and threatened the herd. His instincts told him not to be absent from Douglas for any length of time, for it would be just like the bloody Hamiltons to pick this time to mount a raid, whoremongering cowards that they were.

When he returned, he would send his brother Gavin south to Castle Douglas with at least half the herd. The castle at the town of Douglas, which was often dubbed Castle Dangerous, was not to be confused with the massive stronghold of Castle Douglas, which lay deep in the borders, forty miles to the south.

When Beth Kennedy took her blue velvet gown from the wardrobe, Kirsty was alerted. "I think it best ye dine in yer chamber with me, since yer parents are no' in residence and the castle is full o' rough men."

For once Beth asserted herself. "I'm dining in the hall with Valentina tonight, thank you, Kirsty. She'll look after me."

Kirsty's lips compressed. She would be the length of the room away at the servants' table. Heaven only knew what topics that hellion Tina would introduce into the conversation.

Kirsty went down to the hall early so she would miss nothing that transpired tonight. Valentina arrived wearing a copper-colored outfit that made her even more vivid than usual. Kirsty was pleased to see that the men were not wearing their dress tartans to impress Mistress Honeypot, but she craned her neck to watch what Tina would do when Beth arrived. She was not best pleased when the two sisters sat down between Lord Carrick and Callum Kennedy. Respectable young women would have sat with their brothers.

When Ada took her seat at the servants' table, she saw immediately what was causing Kirsty's anxiety, and like a true adversary she decided to rub salt in her wounds. "I'm so glad that Tina has decided to teach Beth social intercourse."

Kirsty hissed, "I consider Valentina Kennedy no fit role model for my gently reared Beth."

With a straight face Ada said, "Oh Kirsty, let down your guard for one night. It's Beltane."

Kirsty gasped. "Filthy pagan ritual! How dare ye speak o' it in a godly household? 'Tis an excuse tae indulge in sinful antics of the nicht. Well, let me tell ye, madam, the carnal appetites o' the flesh shall no' inherit the Kingdom of Heaven."

"You think sex and church don't mix?" asked Ada with a laugh. "The holier the occasion, the fiercer the grapple. Did I ever tell you the tale of the Abbot of Aberdeen?"

"I willna listen tae such smut." She glanced at the steward and the other household servants at the table and saw they were enjoying her discomfort.

Meanwhile, Tina was enjoying teasing her dinner companions every bit as much as Ada was. With a straight face but mischievous flashing eyes, she said, "Andrew, why don't you tell Beth the interesting things you did on your visit to Glasgow last evening?"

Andrew darted a warning glance at Tina and wondered how she managed to look such a picture of innocence. "I'm sure she has nae interest in men's affairs," he said repressively.

"Oh, you are wrong, Lord Carrick. I am fascinated," said Beth, hanging on to his every word.

"Yer brothers showed us parts o' Glasgow I've never seen," he managed between mouthfuls.

Beth said, "I've heard there are a lot of poor hovels there, but I've seen some fine houses, and the ladies dress quite differently in town, don't you think?"

"Tell us about the house you visited, and how the ladies were dressed," Tina prompted.

"Ye'd no' be interested," he said repressively.

Beth put her small hand upon his arm. "Please?" she begged softly.

Andrew flushed as he recalled last night's debauch, then he put his hand over Beth's and gently explained, "Yer sister is a wicked tease. She knows we spent last night in a —an alehouse."

"Oh, how silly of me," said Beth, giggling. Tina joined in the laughter, then finally Andrew, and all was forgiven.

Down the hall the steward spoke up. "Mistress, would ye care tae attend the revels wi' me?" he asked Ada hopefully.

"Oh, I'm sorry, Jack, I already accepted Mr. Burque's offer," Ada said, casting a satisfied glance at Kirsty, for she knew the Scotswoman had lost her heart to the good-looking Frenchman.

"Burque? Yon prancin' cook? I thought ye'd be wantin' a more sportive companion on such a nicht," the steward derided.

"Mr. Burque is a chef," Ada corrected, "and you can take it from me," she said, glancing from the steward to Kirsty, "he can be exceeding sportive."

At the other end of the hall Valentina was plotting her getaway and wanted to be certain everyone was occupied when she rode out. She addressed both Callum and Andrew Kennedy. "You'll both be gone at sunup, I suppose? What are your plans for this evening?"

The men exchanged glances, and Andrew temporized, "Well, we did think tae visit Glasgow again."

"Oh, that's too bad. I thought perhaps you'd enjoy a stroll up on the ramparts to count the Beltane fires—unless there's time before you leave?"

Andrew spoke up. "That's exactly what I planned tae do as soon as we've finished here."

Callum scowled at him. "I'd like tae escort ye, Tina. It's very dark up on the walls. A lady needs a strong arm, an' I offer mine."

"You are both so gallant." Tina smiled. "I cannot accept, but Beth would like your escort."

Both men knew they'd been outmaneuvered and bowed to Lady Beth. "It would be an honor, mistress."

Kirsty's hand was at her throat as she saw Beth take both men by the arm. It was not customary for a maid to approach the head table in the great hall, but alarm made Kirsty ignore convention. "My lady, I will accompany ye, wherever it is ye wish tae go."

Tina looked the woman up and down coldly. "Don't overstep your bounds, Kirsty. I'm mistress here at Doon at the moment. I don't believe Lord Carrick would enjoy your forcing yourself upon him. I think perhaps the steward would be a better choice for you."

"But—but Beth has never been alone wi' men," she said angrily, as she watched her charge depart the hall.

"Then it is high time," Tina said. "There's safety in numbers, Kirsty. Besides, I don't really think little Beth will arouse their carnal appetites."

"Men don't need much arousin'," hissed Kirsty.

"Really?" Tina drawled, raising questioning eyebrows. "You must tell me all you know about men—sometime when you have a moment." Tina waved to Ada at the far end of the hall. It was her way of saying, "Don't wait up for me!"

Valentina had not ridden a mile's distance from Doon when Heath met her. He was dressed in soft doeskin breeches and was astride an animal every bit as expensive as Kennedy horseflesh. She whistled her appreciation. "Where did that come from?"

He grinned at her and laid a finger alongside his nose. "Ask no questions, sweeting. You wouldn't want to know."

"Could you get me a black mare with Barbary blood?" she asked eagerly.

"That's a tall order," he replied.

"But not impossible?" she pressed.

"No, sweetheart, not impossible," he admitted.

"Lovely! Where will we go tonight?"

"Wherever you fancy. Lead on." Before the words were out of his mouth, she was off on the wind. She had plaited her long copper hair into a thick braid that fell below her waist, and it soon began to unravel. Heath chuckled to himself and let her take the lead. She had a wildness in her blood, and he understood she needed this outlet.

The River Ayr was in spate, and once they crossed over the brig, they began to climb out of the valley. The Beltane fires would not be lit on hilltops, for then they could be mistaken for the beacon fires used as an alarm system for invasion and suchlike. Tina headed toward Muirkirk, a plain stretching between the counties of Ayr and Lanark, as this was likely the closest Beltane revel. As she topped the ridge, she saw half a dozen riders coming from the opposite direction and recognized they were Hamiltons from their bright blue tartan.

She quickly brought one leg over her saddle so that their

leader would not know she had been riding astride and hoped her velvet skirts would cover the fact that there was no side-saddle.

"Valentina!" Patrick Hamilton was both pleased and concerned to find her abroad this night. He dismounted immediately and came to her side. His men stayed back to give them some small privacy. Patrick Hamilton was dark and dashing, his tall slim back straight as a ramrod with the pride of clan in his bearing. He placed a possessive hand upon her knee. "I canna believe yer out without a groom, mistress. 'Tis Providence brought ye ma way."

The tip of her riding boot rested almost touching his hand upon her other knee. She let him know she could kick his hand away if she so chose. The last light was fading fast and wasn't sufficient for him to see her golden eyes, but where it touched her magnificent hair, it set it aflame. Patrick felt a strong desire to pull her down to him and ravish the mouth that teased so temptingly.

"I assume you are riding to visit the admiral," she said. "If you come to Doon for dinner on Friday evening, I'll get Mr. Burque to prepare your favorite, Patrick."

"Thanks, Tina, I'd be delighted. Ye know my destination, but I dinna know yours."

"You're right," she said laughing.

Just as Patrick was about to reach for the maddening creature, Heath topped the ridge. Patrick frowned at her escort's good looks and wide shoulders. "Ye ha' a groom after all," he said, sounding most disappointed.

"Good night, Patrick, I must be off. I have a most pressing appointment."

Hamilton had ridden five miles with Valentina Kennedy filling his senses before he remembered that it was Beltane, but as soon as the dark suspicion crossed his mind, he dismissed it. "She wouldna dare," he assured himself.

The Kennedys had laid their plans well the previous night and had even ridden out to the perimeter of the

Douglas lands they were about to raid. The Douglas clan was the richest in Scotland, their acreage vast, their herds too numerous to count. Donal and Duncan had conceived the idea and laid it before the other Kennedys when they brought down their winter wool. Without going close to the castle at Douglas, which was nicknamed Castle Dangerous, Donal estimated they could lift about two hundred cattle and four hundred curly-horned sheep from Douglas tenants, and the best part was that the Douglas clan would blame their bitter enemies, the Hamiltons, who lived not ten miles away in the same county, Lanark.

The Kennedys had agreed to divide whatever they were able to steal and leave immediately for their own holdings, which lay in half a dozen different directions. Donal would take his share to Castle Kennedy on Loch Ryan, which he hoped would be his when he married. He would also leave a few on his holding in Kirkcudbright, overlooking Solway Firth. It amused him that his peel tower at Kirkcudbright was only ten miles from the massive stronghold known as Castle Douglas.

Donal had given his men strict orders not to approach the castle, for he wanted no violent affray. This was to be a simple cattle raid under dark of night, and if their luck held, the Douglases wouldn't even know about it till dawn.

All went according to plan, with the Kennedys content to let Donal give the orders. All except David who had a few ideas of his own. It was Davie Kennedy's first taste of reiving, though he'd been anticipating the event for years, avidly listening to tales told at clan gatherings. He relished the brutish pleasure of wreaking havoc upon a rival. It was rumored the Douglases had an excess of ten thousand horned sheep, and this being the case, Davie reasoned their most vital crop was hay. Donal had ordered him to stand watch rather than rustle cattle and sheep, but he was boldly determined to play a more vital part in the operation. He set a torch to the hayfields, and the wildfire raced across the acres that hadn't felt rain in over a week.

When Donal smelled smoke and heard the flames begin to roar like the wind, he cursed violently. "What reckless whoreson set the fire?" he shouted. Already the Douglas tenants were running to the scene and had no doubt alerted the men of the castle. Fire at night was more terrifying than in daylight, and the Kennedys were able to drive off the sheep and cattle in the chaos and confusion it caused.

Duncan rode up beside Donal. "Davie was posted guard over yon. It must ha' been the little pisser."

"Christ's blood, I'll skelp the skin off his arse when I get back from Kirkcudbright."

David, elated with the successful destruction of the hayfields, moved on to the low cowsheds and haystacks against the very walls of the castle. The flames danced high, almost mesmerizing him, when suddenly the torch was dragged from his hand, brushing across his sleeve to set it afire. At the same time he was knocked from his saddle by something that felt like a thunderbolt.

The thunderbolt was a naked Gavin Douglas, who had been plucked from his bed and the soft arms of Jenna, his new wench. Davie Kennedy was lucky Gavin had no weapon to hand, or he would have been a corpse by now.

Gavin grabbed the raider by the scruff of the neck, rolled him in the dirt to extinguish his smoldering sleeve, and dragged him to his feet. His dark eyes widened as he saw the extreme youth of his culprit. He cursed that he'd only caught the runt of the litter, but as he peered about in frustrated fury, he saw none but his brother Cameron and other Douglas men whose first priority was to put out the fire before it destroyed the entire village of Douglas.

Gavin dragged his captive by the hair into the hall, which had suddenly come to life with men-at-arms and servants. As Colin Douglas limped into the hall, Gavin said, "I only caught one o' the bastards. The bloody Hamiltons are using bairns now tae raid us."

Colin saw the pallor of the fair-haired lad and said quietly, "I'll get ma bandages and dress that burn."

"Dress his burn?" Gavin shouted in disbelief. "I'll truss him on a spit in yon fireplace and roast his other bloody arm!"

Colin said, "When yer temper cools, ye'll realize Ram can likely ransom the bairn."

Davie decided he'd been called *bairn* once too often. Gathering a full gob of spit in his mouth, he shot it in Colin's face. Gavin backhanded him, bursting open his lip and felling him to the floor.

Gavin ran his hand through his tangle of black hair. "Christ's blood, Ram will ha' ma nuts fer this. Who was on guard?" he demanded, glaring at the men-at-arms. "Why wasna the alarm given at the first glimmer o' fire?"

"We thought it a Beltane fire," the mosstrooper said stupidly.

"Lazy lounging bastards—all ye are fit fer is drinkin', fightin', and fuckin'." Then as he rubbed the back of his neck, he glanced down at his own naked body and recalled what he'd been doing while Douglas crops burned. "Get him out o' ma sight. Lock him up downstairs." He glowered at the Douglas men. "Ye've two minutes tae get mounted. We'll catch them or see where the trail leads. When Ram gets back, one o' ye will swing for this." He rubbed his neck again, fervently hoping it wouldn't be him.

Chapter 4

Tina Kennedy was very excited about venturing out on Beltane. The chance meeting with Patrick Hamilton had heightened the excitement for her. Let the arrogant young lord wonder what she was up to!

She and Heath joined in the merrymaking wholeheartedly, leaping through the flames while the fire was small enough, then joining in the frenzied dancing when the bonfire was piled with brush and young trees and finally thick logs from oaks that had been felled and dragged from the forest to feed the Beltane fires.

It was the ancient rite of spring that all cultures had celebrated in·one form or another since pagan times, and Tina wouldn't have missed the exhilaration of this night for anything. By midnight, however, men and women, young and old, were either falling-down drunk or sexually aroused to the point where they tore off their clothes and copulated with any willing stranger.

Tina was visibly shocked, and Heath was quick to drag her away from the abandoned writhings. "It's time I got you back to Doon," he said firmly. As he lifted her into her saddle, she looked down into his warm brown eyes. "Is it always like this?" she asked in a distressed voice.

"Aye. Animals! They fool you by walking upright, don't they?"

She was subdued on the ride home, and Heath was thankful. He never forbade her nor read her a sermon about the things she wished to do. Rather, he let her experience everything and trusted to her own good sense whether she repeated the folly.

He stayed with her until she crossed the drawbridge of Doon, then turned his Thoroughbred and galloped south.

Tina stabled her mare in a rear stall, then quietly rubbed her down and covered her with a plaid. Suddenly the bailey was filled with horses, men, and herded animals. The cattle lowed, and about fifty sheep ran baaing into the stables, setting the dogs barking and the hens flapping.

Duncan's voice came terse and harsh to his men. "Get these bloody sheep tae the far meadow an' the cattle tae pasture by the river."

Tina walked from the rear stall just as Duncan lit the lantern. Her eyes were like saucers. "God's blood, you've been on a raid!"

"Fold yer tongue behind yer teeth. What the hell are ye doin' out here at this ungodly hour? Get tae bed, and keep yer mouth shut!"

Hands on hips, she was about to defy him when he raised his fist to her, and she saw he was in no mood to argue with a woman. Shrugging one pretty shoulder, she lifted her skirt and picked her way through the bleating menagerie.

Tina's blood was high, preventing sleep, so she arose at dawn and made her way to the kitchens, unwilling to wait until breakfast was served in the hall. Mr. Burque's face was tinged with green as he supervised the food preparation for scores of mouths while trying to keep his gorge from rising.

"Too much Beltane," Tina whispered knowingly.

"Too much whisky! It rots the gut as well as the brain. No wonder the Scots are thick-tongued!"

Duncan kicked open the kitchen door. "Christ, mon, when do we eat? Where the hell's the pot-boy wi' the ale?" he demanded before slamming the door.

Mr. Burque rolled his eyes. "Something's wrong— gravely wrong. Duncan is the best natured of all the Kennedys."

"They went on a raid last night," Tina whispered.

"That should put him in a benign mood. 'Tis a borderer's favorite pastime."

"I thought that was wenching," she whispered.

He shook his head very gingerly and said, "No, no, chérie, that is Frenchmen."

She stole a fresh pastry from the table and said, "I'll find out why he's in a filthy temper."

The Kennedys were merchants and Doon was no garrison, but they did have some men-at-arms. They sat morosely at the trestle tables in the hall. Usually their din was deafening, so Tina did not need to ask if something had gone amiss. "Well, this is a riotous company. Where's Donal?" she asked, suddenly apprehensive.

The pot-boy's hands shook as he filled Duncan's tankard, and as a result the ale sloshed over the rim. "Cursed lackey!" Then Duncan told her shortly, "Donal's away tae Kirkcudbright."

"Let me guess—Andrew went home to Carrick, and Callum to Newark." Tina grinned. "You divided the spoils and departed in six different directions. Duncan, that was brilliant strategy. Why are you fierce as a bear with a burr up his bum?"

Duncan looked at her bleakly. "Davie," he muttered.

"Davie?" she repeated, puzzled. "You think he'll rat on you out of spite for not taking him along?"

"We did take the little piss-ass."

Her throat tightened. "Where is he?"

Duncan flared, "Why are ye forever stickin' yer nose intae men's affairs?"

"He's been wounded," she cried, running toward the stairs.

"Tina!" Duncan's voice sounded anguished. "He didna ride back wi' us—he's missin'."

"Missing?" she echoed.

"Must ye repeat everythin' like a bloody demented parrot?"

"Ride out and look for him!" she ordered. "God's passion, I'll go!"

"We've been out lookin'—as close as we dare go. I think they captured him."

She was angry now. "Go and demand his return—threaten to pull their bloody castle down stone by stone! Who has him? Who did you raid?"

Duncan's mouth hardened, as if he couldn't get the name past his teeth. Finally he rasped, "Douglas."

"The Black Ram?" she whispered, and the color drained out of her face, leaving her lips bloodless and trembling. Her gaze encompassed all the Kennedy men, and none could look her in the eye. She was both appalled and afraid. "Do you realize what you've done? Challenged the Douglas might?" she whispered huskily. "God's death, why did you risk all? Our Kennedy motto is *Consider the end*. How could you be so brainless—so reckless?"

"The Hamiltons will take the fall fer this raid." Patrick Hamilton's devil-may-care face flashed before her eyes, and she groaned and sat down hopelessly upon a bench. "But they've got David," she pointed out.

"He's no' a redhead like the rest o' us. If he folds his tongue behind his teeth, they'll never guess he's a Kennedy."

"He's only a boy!" she cried. "You know what black-hearted bastards the Douglases are. They'll torture him. My God, Duncan, you must do something—anything!"

"We'll wait fer Donal. We'll lie low today. Davie won't open his mouth for fear Kennedy blood will stain the swords of Douglas. If we're no' careful, this raid may reap us more grief than spoils."

Valentina avoided her sister Beth for fear of alarming her. Every half hour she climbed to the parapets of Doon to anxiously scan the horizon for a sign of Davie or any other. Fear had a tight grip upon her as she paced back and forth. She knew a need to scream, yet her throat felt closed as if she couldn't scream if she tried. She had a very vivid imagination that was so graphic, it made her shudder at what they might do to Davie or to every Kennedy breathing if they set their black hearts to it.

The Kennedys had had no dealings with the Douglases in her lifetime because of the tragedy that had torn the two clans apart when she was first born. When her mother had come up from England to marry Lord Kennedy, his young sister Damaris had become her best friend. At the wedding Alexander Douglas had seen Damaris for the first time and he wanted her. A whirlwind courtship resulted in a quick marriage, the Kennedys thinking the heir to the title and fortune of Douglas a brilliant match. How wrong they had been!

While Damaris had still been a bride, her husband had poisoned her in a jealous rage. Tina shuddered, desperately hoping the hatred between the two clans would not flare up to destroy them. Perhaps David already lay dead. A sob escaped her as she said a fervent prayer to Saint Jude. If Davie was alive, escape was his only hope.

The bruise-colored clouds gathered above her head and cast an ominous pall over the whole countryside. She felt caged like a prisoner, completely attuned to Davie's condition. She knew if she didn't do something, she would go mad. She needed to be active to release the fear, worry, and dread that clutched her heart like a mail-clad fist.

She ran down to her chamber and rummaged about her wardrobe until her hand closed upon a lavender wool gown. Valentina was superstitious and believed any shade of purple was a lucky color for her. She concealed her knife inside one riding boot, then pulled on the other and her velvet cloak and went cautiously down to the stables.

When she rode out, Tina had no conscious destination in mind—she simply needed to free herself from the suffocating walls of Doon. She rode on and on, following a direct path eastward, never looking back, never slowing her pace. She was blind to the field of bluebells through which she cantered. She was oblivious to the intoxicating scent

that wafted upon the breeze. She was deaf to the screaming peewits and the baaing sheep. Tina's mind was obsessed with the plight of her brother. It blotted out all else.

Gradually it came to her where she was heading, and she
drew rein and looked about apprehensively. She had followed the River Ayr, and though she had never ridden this
far upriver before, she knew it led straight to Douglas. She
rode past burned and blackened fields, saw village people
rebuilding two burned huts, then rode out of the village
toward the castle, which sat apart, alone and brooding.

She knew she must somehow get inside, yet she knew it
would be futile to simply try to ride in. She would get no
farther than the guard on the drawbridge. Her thoughts
flashed about, quick as mercury. She pushed her fear away
from her and thought of Davie. The only certain way of
gaining entrance to Castle Dangerous was if a Douglas
took her inside. A plan came to her whose very audacity
made her tremble. She would stage a riding accident—her
own accident. She was a helpless woman, young and beautiful, surely the men of Douglas would come to her rescue.
She concentrated solely on making her fall look like a genuine accident. She tangled her reins in a gorse thicket,
loosened the girth strap so that her saddle slipped, then lay
down upon the ground, gathering her purple velvet cloak
about her body and flinging out her arm as if she had tried
to save herself. Then she screamed at the top of her voice,
closed her eyes and waited.

Almost immediately she began to wish she had not done
this reckless thing. The rainstorm that had held off all
morning dropped from the low sky in torrents. She lay still
as the deluge soaked through to her skin, making her
shiver uncontrollably. Tina knew it wasn't just the cold that
was making her shiver. Now that she had done this impulsive, reckless thing, she had nothing to do but lie there and
imagine what might happen to her in Douglas hands.

If she had been witness to the scene earlier, when Ramsay Douglas had returned to find his cattle lifted and his

hay and oat crops burned, she would have fled for her life. He had given his two brothers such a dressing-down that Gavin finally put up his fists and shouted, "I'll fight ye and be damned if it puts an end tae this harangue!"

Ram Douglas in full spate was not a pretty sight. His pewter-colored eyes glittered like hard diamonds, and his dark face looked as if it were chiseled from granite. They hadn't expected his return until well after dark. No wonder they called him Hotspur—he must have ridden a hundred and fifty miles without pause. Though he was hardened, the fact that he'd had little rest in the past three days added an extra edge to his vile temper. Next he turned his blistering tongue on the Douglas moss-troopers, denouncing them as lazy, drunken idlers who thought of nothing but their pricks. With a powerful arm he swept their tankards of ale from the table to the floor. "Not bad enough ye let the bastards lift the cattle an' burn the crops—ye let them escape! I couldha overlooked it if ye'd had a row o' stinkin' Hamiltons swingin' by their necks. I couldha overlooked it if ye'd retrieved the livestock—but ye couldna even find a clear trail! Maybe half rations will clear yer thick heads." He'd turned on his heel in disgust, his silver spurs striking sparks on the flagstones as he went himself to find the trail. Only his wolfhound Boozer had enough courage to keep him company.

He inspected the burned huts and told the womenfolk to take their bairns to the castle until their homes could be rebuilt. Then he accompanied a small group of his tenant farmers into the fields. "We'll replant wi' oats and hope for a second crop. Get seed from the castle stores."

They gave him a tally of the sheep and cattle missing, and he promised to replace the beasts.

"The sheep had all been sheared o' their winter wool, but it were stored in the sheds alongside the hay. It went up in smoke," a tenant told him grimly.

"I'll send the men-at-arms to repair the houses and re-plant the fields. They're on leave from patrolling the borders for a month. I don't want them idling about wi' naught tae do save drink and procreate," he said, grinning.

They watched him go, their hearts filled with gratitude. He had a black reputation for harshness, yet he was always more than fair to his Douglas tenants and their families.

The embers of his fiery temper were considerably banked when he saw with his own eyes that there was no clear trail and that the animal tracks went off in at least six different directions. Then the heavens opened, and he cursed the resulting deluge that would wash away all traces. Why the hell couldn't this rain have fallen before the raid to wet the oats and keep them from burning?

He was subdued as he turned his stallion's head toward Douglas and whistled for the Boozer to come to heel. The castle was in sight when suddenly the great wolfhound loped ahead of him to investigate a riderless horse that seemed to be tangled in a thicket.

Tina had never been more afraid in her life when a gigantic, hairy animal leaped upon her limp body. Her eyes flew open, and she discerned that it was a ferocious hound twice the size of any she'd ever seen. Immediately she closed her eyes and bit her lips to prevent a scream of terror from escaping. If the creature thought she was dead perhaps it wouldn't rend her limb from limb. Then she heard a man's deep voice cursing, and her body shuddered like a leaf in the wind.

"Heel! God's passion, what the hell have ye found here? Looks like a drowned rat." The man's voice was deep and resonant and sent a chilling shiver of fear down her back. She felt herself being lifted as if she weighed no more than a child, then without ceremony he threw her face-down across his saddle.

She risked a quick glimpse and couldn't believe how high she was off the ground. His horse was as oversized as his hound. She could have cried with chagrin at his cavalier treatment of her as her head hung down and her wet hair trailed down the stallion's long flanks.

As Ram untangled the reins of her mare, it screamed in fear as the enormous black stallion tried to bite it upon the neck. Ram smote the brute with his fist. "Nay, Ruffian—I'll admit 'tis a fancy piece, but ye'll no' mount it while I stand here taking a drenching."

Omigod, the brute is going to let his stallion ruin my mare, she thought wildly, and emitted a groan of despair. When they reached the bailey, Ram Douglas threw the reins of both horses to a groom. "Keep them separated," he ordered. "I'll no' have him waste his valuable seed on a piece o' cheap horseflesh."

"Looks like an expensive mount tae me, yer lordship."

"Did I ask fer yer opinion, man?" Ram asked shortly. He lifted the soggy burden from Ruffian's back none too gently and carried her through the massive studded doors of the castle. He carried her straight through to the hall where there was a roaring fire and deposited her upon a carved wooden settle.

He pulled off her sodden cloak and threw it to a servant, who spread it over a stool to dry, then the man knelt to remove his master's thigh-high boots.

Forcing herself to be totally limp with lashes lowered to her cheeks, she felt a strong, callused hand firmly take her chin and lift her face for his perusal. A flicker of recognition showed in Ram's eyes as the firelight showed him the lass had red hair. He'd seen her before, and he knew exactly where. His heart skipped a beat. When he'd seen her ride in to the Gypsy camp, he'd coveted her. Now here she was delivered up to him!

Tina opened her eyes slowly and put a trembling hand to her head. "Wh-where am I?" she asked. "Is this my home?"

Ram Douglas stared at her fiercely, afraid that she had sustained some terrible hurt in her fall. "This is Douglas Castle," he said as both his brothers came to investigate.

Tina tried not to shudder at the name, but she couldn't help it. The only thing she had control over was her face.

Her voice was unnaturally high-pitched and jerky from the threat of impending tears. The dark-visaged man who sat beside her was so broad-shouldered, he blotted out the rest of the room. He was clearly the figure of authority, and she knew instinctively that this was the man she must convince. She knew she must say something to confirm that she had received a blow to the head and wasn't in her right senses. She looked helplessly into Ram's glittering eyes and asked, "Are—are you my father?"

He was nettled at the insult. He found her unbelievably alluring, yet she thought him old. His voice cut through his brothers' laughter. "Christ, I don't deny the possibility of by-blows, but I'll be damned if I couldha fathered a woman grown. What's yer game?" he demanded.

"Who are ye, lass?" Gavin asked.

She looked at them blankly, and again her hand went to her head as if she were dizzy. "I—I don't know," she whispered.

Cameron, callous as only the very young can be, asked, "Is she a halfwit?"

"Nay," said Ram, more kindly now that he realized she had been hurt. "I've seen it in battle. She's lost her memory, but it'll return if she bides awhile."

Tina's golden eyes watched the beautiful curve of the man's mouth soften as he looked at her. She was momentarily mesmerized by his penetrating pewter gaze, and she sat absolutely still while his strong hands reached out to touch her body. He was checking her for broken bones, but suddenly she realized his hands were lingering upon her as if he were deliberately caressing her! Did he think her some groom's daughter he could tumble? She wanted to cry out that she was Lady Valentina Kennedy, but of course she could not. She had allowed men to kiss her before, but none had ever dared take the liberty of touching her body intimately as this bold devil had just done. His hands still lingered on her shoulders. She jerked away from him. "Don't!"

Colin came limping up and gave his cousins a black look. "Mistress, forgive these rough men. Yer soaked tae the skin. Allow me tae offer ye a private chamber wi' a bed and a fire where ye mun rest an' recover."

"Th-thank you," she said in a bewildered voice. She stood up, and indeed her knees were like butter. She swayed, and three pairs of Douglas arms reached for her. Ram was quicker than Gavin or Cameron, and he swept her high in his arms, gently enfolding her body against his hard-muscled chest. Her golden eyes were bright with tears and apprehension, her tempting, generous mouth inches from his own. Suddenly he was handling her much more gently than when he had carried her in from the rain.

Colin led the way, his crippled leg echoing oddly across the stone floor. Gavin followed.

Tina felt panic rise within her. If only one of the younger, less dangerous men had picked her up, she would be able to think coherently. She knew instinctively she would have a much easier time cozening them.

Ram's deep voice spoke intimately to her as they climbed the rough stone stairway. "When ye recall yer identity, sweetheart, send for me. If ye are no' known tae be a friend, perhaps yer a foe," he teased and gave her an audacious wink. He stopped at his own chamber door and handed her over to Gavin's waiting arms. "I'll change my wet clothes and look forward tae seeing more of ye later." His words were accompanied by a devilish leer as his pewter eyes dipped to her wet breasts—she could not mistake the double entendre.

Tina trembled in Gavin's arms, and he felt oddly protective of her. She was grateful to be relieved of *that* other one's presence. He was more swarthy than any Gypsy. His pewter eyes had had an arrogant gleam, his mouth a reckless slant that intensified his magnetism, yet everything about him was dangerously dark and hard and threatening.

"Who are you—and where am I?" Tina whispered, knowing he would be putty in her hands.

"I'm Gavin Douglas, and this older man is ma cousin Colin." The handsome devil grinned down at her.

Colin reprimanded his levity. "Stow yer foolishness, Gavin. The lass has injured her haid. This place is Douglas, mistress. Just north of the border country atween England and the cities o' Glasgow and Edinburgh." The rough stone passageway was cold, and she shivered uncontrollably in Gavin's arms. "I'll soon ha' ye out o' yer soakin' gown, lass," he said, grinning.

"Hoots, Gavin, ye've no' the brains ye were born wi'. Can ye no' see she's a lady? She must be frightened witless tae waken in the clutches o' Black Ram Douglas."

Tina jerked and stiffened. My God, that had been the infamous Black Ram!

They entered a most elegantly appointed chamber, one that had been decorated with the sure hand of a gentlewoman with taste and breeding. A cat that was curled in a chair awoke with a start and ran beneath it.

Gavin reluctantly put her down on the edge of the wide bed, and Colin limped over to a clothespress and brought her towels and a warm plaid.

A deep voice from the doorway said, "Don't stand there grinning like a gargoyle—the lass will think she's in a madhouse. Order a servant tae build a fire so she can get warm and have a rest."

Something inside Tina responded to that deep voice. His eyes told her that he found her special. As Gavin moved to the door, the tone of Ram Douglas's voice changed. "Ye can show me this prisoner ye took."

Colin said with disgust, "He's a bairn—wi' down on his cheeks."

"Then it should be child's play tae break him," Ram said.

Fury almost choked Valentina. She loathed herself for responding momentarily to his animal attraction. The cruel bastard had one count against him for throwing her over his saddle like a sack of grain. Two counts against him for

invading her body with his filthy hands. But in the moment
he'd spoken of breaking her wee brother Davie, a deep
hatred for the man had been born. It was a personal hatred, spawning a personal vendetta. If one hair on Davie's
head were harmed, she would settle the score with Black
Ram Douglas if it was the last thing she ever did in this
lifetime.

Chapter 5

The servants departed after building her a fire, and
a moment later she stripped off her woolen gown
and wet underclothes and hung them over the foot
of the bed to dry. She concealed the knife from her
boot under the mattress and took up a large linen towel to
dry her long red tresses. She noted that the towel was
finely woven from the best flax and embroidered with an
elaborate letter D. She tested the quality of the Douglas
plaid between her thumb and forefinger and felt an overwhelming distaste for the tartan's dark greens and blues.
Her pride forbade her to wrap herself in its warmth until
she heard a knock upon her chamber door. Then without
thinking, she grabbed the finely woven length of woolen
cloth and wrapped it about herself like a cloak.

Colin Douglas entered, balancing a tray upon his stiff,
almost useless arm. "Let me help you," she offered as a
rush of sympathy swept over her. This man was not nearly
so dark as the others. He had a square, honest, clean-cut
face, and his manners set him apart as being more civilized. She was curious to know what had ruined his once-

magnificent physique, but she had more breeding and sensitivity than to even stare at him.

"I've brought ye some broth an' bread. 'Tis rough fare, unfit fer a lady, but we're a household o' men without womenfolk, save fer servin' and kitchen wenches."

"Thank you. It smells good," she offered. "If there are no women here, whose chamber is this? The lady in the portrait?" she asked, indicating a painting above the fireplace.

"My brother Alexander's bride, Damaris. She's deceased," he said shortly, and limped toward the door.

Tina almost choked on her broth. "Don't burn yerself," he warned before he closed the heavy door.

Tina sprang up to examine the lovely face in the portrait. Her fingers reached up to trace the fine lace of what must have been her wedding gown. "Aunt Damaris," she whispered, "how unearthly fair you were." A lump came into her throat as she noticed how young and innocent the girl must have been.

From a shadowed corner of the room, the spirit of Damaris focused on the young woman with flaming hair and whispered, "Sweet Mary, you must be my niece, Valentina Kennedy!" She hovered between Tina and her own portrait, more agitated than she had been for fifteen years. "Begone! Begone from this place," she cried, then she was filled with a great sadness because she knew she could not communicate with the living, breathing Valentina.

"What did the degenerate Douglas do to you?" asked Tina, overwhelmed with pity.

"Don't you know Alexander poisoned me? My own husband whom I loved more than life? He accused me of lying with his brother Colin. He struck me." Damaris's hand went up to her cheek, still feeling the blow after fifteen long years.

Tina picked up a hand-painted porcelain powder bowl and matching toilet articles standing upon the mantel. "These were your things," Tina said in wonder. She moved across the chamber to touch the heavy, silver-backed hair-brushes and the brocaded bedhangings. "It's so strange—it's almost as if I can feel your essence in the room," Tina said.

"Oh God, I hope so, my dear. Get out, get out while there is still time!"

Tina closed her eyes and lifted the stopper of a crystal perfume bottle to touch her cheek. "They say you were murdered here, but all I can feel is love and warmth. You must have suffered unbearably, and yet I sense only your happiness in this lovely room."

"I *was* happy—happier than I'd ever been in my entire life—happier perhaps than a woman has a right to be—before that fateful day. Love is blind. Don't let the Douglas blind you, Valentina!" Damaris passed an invisible hand over the garments hanging to dry. "Quickly, put on your clothes and depart."

Tina reached out her hand to touch her undergarments and was amazed to find they were already dry. She unwound the plaid from her body and donned her under-clothes. Ada had sewn every stitch of them, and they were exquisite. She fingered the delicate mauve frills embroidered with violets and was willing to wager she had the most beautiful lingerie in Scotland. *Lingerie* was a French word that Ada had picked up from Mr. Burque.

"Hurry, Valentina!" Damaris placed an urgent hand upon Tina's shoulder. Tina felt a sudden chill and hurried into her undershift.

When Ram Douglas inspected the youth his brothers had captured, he laughed outright. "Christ, he's still on mother's milk. What's yer name, laddie?" Ram asked the pale young man incarcerated in the dungeon, one floor beneath the hall.

David Kennedy gathered a full gob of spit and aimed it at the Douglas. "Piss off!"

Ram grimaced. "A length o' hemp about yer throat will choke the spit from it."

"Hang me an' be damned tae ye!" flung David.

"Bloody little bantam cock!" Gavin said.

"Bravado—he's scared shitless," Ram said, "whistling past the graveyard."

"I'm scared o' no fuckin' Douglas!"

"Then it's brainless ye are, laddie," Ram said cheerfully. Then to Gavin, "I'll give the Hamiltons a chance to ransom him. If they're tightfisted, I'll hang him."

Upstairs, Tina reached beneath the mattress to retrieve her knife when without warning the chamber door opened. She whirled about to face her intruder, her golden eyes flashing annoyance, then fear. "Don't you knock, sir?"

Ram Douglas slanted a black brow. "In my own castle?"

"Yes, in your own castle, before you enter the chamber of a lady."

"Lady?" he questioned. "Then ye remember who ye are?"

"N-no." She again reached for the hated Douglas plaid to cloak her undergarments from his bold, dark eyes. The warm fire had dried her sodden hair, and it fell about her in radiant abundance. Tiny gold-red tendrils framed her face and Ram's fingers itched to touch the tempting mass. She spoke from nervousness. "I remember I was out riding —I remember a torrential rain—I remember your hands upon me," she accused.

"Aye, well, that's something no woman could forget."

Her temper almost choked her, temporarily blotting out her fear. He thought himself God's gift to women! He was so deadly dangerous, however, she knew she must not anger him. She bit her lip and managed a faint smile. "I'm sorry, my lord, to intrude like this. As soon as I remember where I live, I will leave. 'Tis the most maddening thing— my name is on the tip of my tongue, then it escapes and eludes me."

His eyes ran over her as if he were assessing her fine points. His eyes lifted to her mouth, fell to her breasts now concealed by the plaid, then lifted to her eyes. She bit back a cutting remark, but she might as well have uttered it because his eyes filled with amusement. "If worse comes tae worst and ye never recall yer name, I'll just keep ye." He laughed. "Don't look so outraged, lass. If ye don't get total recall by tomorrow, I can soon learn who ye are."

Tina sensed danger immediately. "How?" she asked blankly.

He stepped closer, and his fingers closed over a tempting tress of molten copper. "I've seen ye before."

The statement left her terrified. Where on God's earth had he seen her? She'd never laid eyes on him before. She'd remember that face for a lifetime. "Wh-where?" she asked warily.

"In a man's arms," he said cryptically.

She thought that impossible. "You mistake me, sir."

"Impossible—I could never mistake ye," he assured her. More than anything else in the world, he wanted to taste this woman, and since Ram Douglas usually did whatever he wanted, he threaded his fingers into the crackling mass of flaming curls and lifted her mouth to his. A static spark jumped between them, producing a little shock.

"Oh, let me go, sir! I am unused to men," she gasped breathlessly.

"Ye delude yerself," he said flatly. "I think yer very used tae men. A husband perhaps—lovers, of a certainty."

"How dare you say such a wicked thing?" Tina demanded in outrage.

"Because ye had no trouble arousing me." His strong, brown hand tore the plaid from her breast. "Yer underclothes are designed tae bring pleasure tae a man's eyes. They reveal the swell of yer breasts, emphasize yer tiny waist, tempt a man's fingers tae undo the ribbons and remove yer frilly laces—like so." In the space of a heartbeat he undid a ribbon and actually opened his palm to cup her breast.

Valentina was shocked to her very soul. She raised her hand to slap him full across the face, Douglas or no Douglas.

He caught her hand before it connected. "Ye must be exclusive. I like that." He grinned.

She snatched back her hand and whirled away from him, then gathered the plaid high about her neck and clutched it desperately. "Please leave me in peace so I may dress and come downstairs."

"Don't ye like this luxurious chamber?" he mocked.

"Yes, it's lovely—she's lovely," Tina said, indicating the portrait of Damaris.

"The Kennedy bitch!" She thought she saw a look of pain in his eyes before he spat.

Valentina felt as if he had slapped her in the face. "If you hate her so much, why haven't you removed it?"

Ramsay Douglas laughed, but there was no mirth in that laughter. "Don't think we haven't tried. When the painting is taken down, all hell breaks loose in the castle until it's back in its place. The bitch haunts us," he said quite matter-of-factly.

She laughed derisively. "Oh come—the infamous Black Ram believing in ghosts?"

His eyes narrowed and gleamed with their strange pewter shade. "Ye know me, wench?"

"C-Colin told me your name. He said it with such reverence, I assumed you must be a god at the very least."

"A god?" he snorted. "Perhaps an archangel," he conceded.

Valentina laughed and her eyes sparkled, her fear momentarily forgotten. "Well, at least you have a sense of humor."

"Ye too," he conceded. "Perhaps we are alike in other ways."

"I don't even know who I am, or who you are for that matter," she replied coolly.

"Yer a woman, I'm a man. It might be rewarding tae find out," he said, stepping closer. If he touched her again, Tina thought she might faint. There was a sound at the door, and impatiently Ram flung it open. It was his wolfhound.

"Oh, please don't let him in," she begged, retreating to the fireplace.

"Never fear, he won't enter this room. The specter keeps him at bay."

"You are serious about her spirit haunting this castle?"

"Aye," he said grimly. "My cousin Alexander brought her here as a bride over fifteen years ago. She was a whore, like all the Kennedy women. She had two brothers at each other's throats over her. Alexander poisoned her, then took a dive from the parapets."

Tina's cheeks colored with anger at his offensive words. "Perhaps it is the evil shade of the poisoner Alexander who is condemned through eternity to haunt the halls of this cursed castle."

"His phantom stands ever at my shoulder warning me against marriage. Wives are like spiders—once they are mated, the female slowly devours the male."

Valentina shuddered. She knew she must get away from this dangerous man. Women were obviously less than dirt to him. "My lord, I beg you will allow me to finish dressing and also allow me the freedom of your castle. I know my memory will come back to me if I walk about—perhaps get some fresh air—take a look at the spot where I fell. Perhaps seeing my horse will jog my mind so that all will fall into place."

He waved an arm. "Feel free tae explore my cursed castle, if yer no' afraid of bogles."

" 'Tis the living I fear," she said pointedly.

"Touché, my lovely vixen. 'Tis obvious ye would be rid o' me." He smiled cruelly. "I'm off for an interesting encounter wi' my nearest and dearest neighbors, the Hamiltons. I invite ye tae sup wi' me when I return."

"Thank you," she said faintly. She leaned her head against the door weakly after he'd gone. He'd called her vixen—her father's name for her.

"Never be alone with him again," warned Damaris.

Tina walked to the fireplace, threw off the despised Douglas tartan, and put on her lavender-wool gown. She looked up at the beautiful pale girl in the portrait and whispered, "Damaris, help me find Davie. We must get away. All hell will break loose when he learns it wasn't the Hamiltons who raided."

"I seldom leave this chamber. 'Tis the only way to avoid Alexander," whispered Damaris.

Tina retrieved her knife and carefully slipped it up the sleeve of her gown.

"Mary and Joseph, whatever are you doing with a knife? I suppose I have no choice but to come with you. I must do all I can to protect you. You must be a very reckless girl," Damaris lamented.

Tina climbed upon a chest beneath the high window slit. After a few minutes she saw the powerful figure of the Black Ram heading toward the stables, his moss-troopers at his heels. She sighed with relief knowing they were no longer under the same roof. Before she crept quietly from the chamber, she picked up the Douglas plaid and covered her bright hair.

Her heart was in her mouth as she made her way with stealth along the passageway, then she forced herself to walk casually as if she had nothing to hide. For the moment she hoped to avoid the hall where men-at-arms tended to gather in inclement weather. From afar she saw servants and members of the Douglas clan, and she was thankful they wore plaids as she did. The moment she saw stone steps leading below, she slipped down them. The air had a distinct damp and musty smell here below ground that was mingled with the sickening odor of rushlights burning mutton fat.

She passed through a room filled with barrels and kegs of ale and wine. Scufflings and squeaks came from the shadows, and she stopped dead in her tracks as she realized what creatures caused them.

"The rats can sense me," Damaris said. "Don't be afraid."

When Tina realized the rats had fled, her courage returned, and she ventured down a narrow, whitewashed passageway. Here were empty cells with barred doors, similar to the ones beneath Castle Doon. When she looked through the bars of the fourth door, she gasped as she saw her brother nursing a bandaged arm.

She put her fingers to her lips and didn't speak until they were only inches apart. "You're wounded. What did they do to you, Davie?"

"They burned me!" he lied.

"Give him the knife," Damaris urged.

"What the hell are you doing here, Firebrand? Are ye here tae ransom me?"

She shook her head. "They don't know who we are, and we must get away before they find out. There isn't much time, Davie. That bastard Douglas has gone to the Hamiltons to demand ransom for you. I can't unlock the cell, but here's my knife, Davie."

As he grasped the haft, he said, "When the moss-trooper brings me food, he'll be a dead man if he doesn't unlock this door."

"Don't kill him unless you must, David—there's been no bloodshed yet," she urged.

He held up his arm grimly. "Someone will pay fer this."

"I've done all I can. I'm leaving before the Douglas returns."

"Done all ye can?" he scoffed. "Fire the castle afore ye leave—raze the bloody place tae the ground!"

"God's passion, keep your voice down. I just want us

both out of here with our lives!" Her heart was hammering as she retraced her steps and walked a direct path to the hall.

The spirit of Alexander Douglas sensed the presence of Damaris immediately. He left the small group of men-at-arms who were casting dice and approached the two beautiful women, one flesh, blood, liver, and vibrant with energy, the other ethereal and hauntingly remote. "Damaris, beloved, who is this ye guard so carefully?"

Not by the flicker of an eyelash did the lovely wraith acknowledge that she had seen or heard him. Alexander sighed. For fifteen years he had begged that his bride listen to his denials, but he had begun to conclude that though he saw her apparition, she could not see his.

At first he had tried to communicate with the living, consumed by the need to exonerate his name and honor, but it had been impossible. The horses in the stables were aware of him, and Ram's wolfhound had seen him so often, he'd begun to wag his tail when Alexander approached, but Damaris always acted as if he were invisible. He suspected that she saw him and heard him well enough, but she believed the lies that he had poisoned her and like all females was too pig-headed and stubborn to listen to his pleas.

As she glided past him, his breath caught at her loveliness. She was still exactly as she had been that fateful night over fifteen years ago. Her blush-pink nightgown with its trailing sleeves emphasized her delicate beauty. Her skin was like porcelain and her hair like silken strands of moonlight.

Alexander was heartsore that his beloved Damaris was lost to him, yet he was willing to exist through eternity if he could see her like this and know they were together at Douglas. He still clung to the hope that someday she would look at him, smile at him, or even curse him—anything that would indicate she was aware of his spirit's existence.

Tina knew the moss-troopers were staring at her. She shrugged her shoulder and removed the dark green plaid. Then she picked up her purple velvet cloak from the wooden settle, wrapped it about herself, and pulled the hood close.

Colin Douglas moved slowly across the hall toward her. "Are ye leavin' us, mistress?" he puzzled.

"No, no. I thought I'd walk about the castle now that the rain has stopped. Lord Douglas suggested that seeing my horse might bring all back to me. I promised to sup with him when he returns from Lanark." She bit her lip. She knew immediately that she had made a slip. Her own knowledge provided the information that the closest Hamilton castle was at Lanark, less than ten miles north. But it went unremarked by Colin Douglas, who must have assumed Ram had mentioned his destination, and the blush that colored her cheeks began to fade. A pulse beat in her throat as she tried not to quicken her steps outside.

Damaris did not want to accompany her niece inside the stables because her presence always made the horses skittish. She knew that Tina would get away safely, and she was grateful she had had a chance to see the lovely creature. She kissed Valentina's brow and whispered, "Goodbye—please never return."

Tina's hand came up unconsciously to brush back the hair from her brow, then boldly she walked to her mare and led her from the stable. The saddle had been removed, but luckily the bridle had not.

Tina vaulted onto the mare's back and dug in her heels. She didn't think anyone would ride after her to bring her back. The men of Douglas were likely glad to be rid of the strange female.

It was full dark before Tina clattered over the drawbridge into the bailey of Castle Doon. A grim-faced Duncan was awaiting her by the time she climbed the stairs to the elegant living quarters. He grabbed her unceremoniously and shook her until her teeth rattled.

"Do ye ken how worried I've been the day? Yer a right thoughtless bitch, Tina! Ye knew Donal wouldn't be back till the morrow, so ye went runnin' off tae yer stinkin' Gypsy friends! Do ye even care I ha' all the worry an' responsibility on ma shoulders?"

"Don't you dare be fierce with me, Duncan. I went to Douglas to rescue Davie! I've just ridden thirty miles—I'm exhausted."

"Are ye insane? How many times must ye be told tae stay out o' men's affairs?" He ran his hand wildly through his flaming hair in an effort to keep from striking her. He breathed deeply before passing sentence. "I'm goin' tae recommend Donal give ye a beatin'."

Tina was dead on her feet, and giddiness made her flippant. "It'll give him practice for when he weds Meg Campbell."

"Donal has more sense than tae wed a lass who needs beatin'. Meggie is obedient and gentle. She's no' a curse tae her menfolk. Father lets ye get away wi' murder. Ye twist him aboot yer finger. Meggie canna do that wi' Archibald Campbell."

To be fair, Valentina saw his point now that he made it so graphically. She only knew one man as coarsely dominant as Archibald Campbell, and that was Archibald Kennedy, Earl of Cassillis and head of their own clan. Perhaps it was the name Archibald that made them so unpalatable.

A great shout went up outside, and hope sprang into Duncan's eyes. "Mayhap it's Davie."

"Of course it's Davie," Tina said, shrugging a pretty shoulder. "Haven't I been telling you I went to rescue him?" She quickly closed her eyes and crossed herself, praying that it was so.

When Duncan saw the state his young brother was in, he carried him to his bedchamber and undressed him. He sent for Ada to tend the lad's arm because his pain was almost unbearable.

"Get me whisky, Duncan," Ada bade, assuming the role of female authority. While a servant was dispatched for a full jug, she examined the soiled bandages.

"It must have been Colin who dressed your arm. He's the only Douglas who is half civilized," Tina said.

"Aye, the cripple," Davie said, gritting his teeth in front of the women.

Ada took the whisky from the servant and told Davie to drink up. He grinned at her and took a long slug of the fiery liquor. "He shouldn't have put grease on it. I'll have to wash it off," she said regretfully. "Do you think you're up to it, David?"

He took another long pull on the stone jug and began to laugh. "When the Douglas asked ma name, I spit on him an' told him tae hang me an' be damned, so I think I can suffer your ministrations."

"One day your temper will be the death of you!" Tina said.

"I dinna ha' a temper, and I'll knife anyone who says so!"

Duncan grinned. "And here was I thinkin' Flamin' Tina had all the Kennedy guts."

"And so I have. You would have been proud of me if you'd seen my performance."

David had consumed half the jug of whisky and couldn't stop laughing. "The Douglas said if the Hamiltons were tightfisted, he would hang me. I'd like tae ha' seen his bloody face when he found the bird had flown. I bet it was blacker than the hobs o' hell!"

"Tina, help me with this bandage—it's stuck to his arm," Ada implored.

As Valentina saw the extent of the ugly burn, she was furious and called the Douglas every foul name in her extensive vocabulary.

David laughed between long mouthfuls of whisky all the

while Ada bathed the arm. Then she took the jug from him and ordered Duncan to hold him securely. Before Davie was aware of what she did, she poured the last half of the fiery liquor over the burn.

David screamed and passed out.

"I had to do that. If that arm starts to fester, he might lose it," she said plainly.

Valentina's face was white. "I never really knew what hate was until today. Ada, I hate Black Ram Douglas with all my heart and soul, and I pray God I never, ever see his ugly face again."

"Get her tae bed," said Duncan. "Sufficient untae the day is the evil thereof."

Chapter 6

Tina did not get her wish. The moment she succumbed to exhaustion and fell into a deep sleep, she was back at Douglas, an unwilling prisoner of the Black Ram. He was The Emperor sitting upon a throne decorated with carved ram's heads. As she lay at his feet clutching a dark green plaid over her nakedness, she was aware that he had the power and strength of ten men. He was unyielding and unbending in his judgments, and he ruled with an iron hand.

Across the room Butcher Bothwick stood before a steaming caldron, his instruments of torture displayed upon the wall behind him. He held her brother David in a grip of iron.

"Guilty! Hang him!" ordered the Black Ram.

"No! Please!" begged Tina, crawling to his feet, which were booted and spurred with spiked ram's horns.

"Arise! Disrobe!" ordered the Black Ram.

"Never!" cried Tina defiantly, her golden eyes blazing her fury.

The Black Ram raised his thunderous brows to Bothwick, who plunged David's arm into the vat of boiling oil. The boy screamed in agony.

"Obey me, and the torture will stop!"

Slowly Valentina arose and let the plaid fall to the floor. She stood before him naked, trembling with loathing and fear. She knew she must not let him see either the loathing or the fear. Pride straightened her back and lifted her flaming head high. Her breasts thrust forward impudently, her rouching nipples drawing his eyes, which were devouring her with animal lust. He held out a commanding hand: "Come!"

She hid her seething emotions behind a cold mask as she drew close to the cruel monster. His callused fingers brushed the flaming triangle of curls upon her mons, and he leered, "Firebrand."

She shuddered as he lifted her upon his knee and placed a large ruby in her navel. "The jewel is cursed," he told her cruelly. "Any other who touches you will die." The palm of one hand opened, and she gasped aloud as it cupped her bare breast; his other hand moved down her thigh, and he whispered hoarsely, "Open for me."

Her mind refused to believe he meant her to open her legs, then suddenly he was holding a golden chalice filled with bloodred wine. "Open for me," he repeated coaxingly. She was relieved that he meant her to open her lips, but as she drank from the goblet, she realized with horror that the wine was poisoned.

Valentina sat bolt upright in bed and cried out. As she sat shivering, it was a long time before she realized she had been having a nightmare and that in reality she had never sat naked upon the Black Ram's knees while he fondled her and took pleasure in feeding her poison.

She slipped from bed and lit a candle to dispel the darklings; then on her knees she gave a quick thanksgiving for their deliverance. When she recalled Old Meg's tarot cards and her tortoise, she got back into bed and hugged her knees. Safe and secure in her own bed, she began to laugh. She savored the victory she and David had won over Ram Douglas, and warmth crept back into her limbs as she exulted over the impotence he would experience when he discovered his pigeons had flown the coop.

Tina's first stop in the early morning was David's bedchamber, where she discovered that Duncan had slept there to keep an eye on Davie. They were relieved that he was looking considerably healthier and that most of the pain had left his arm.

"Duncan," she said in a coaxing tone, "I don't believe it would be politic to tell Donal about what I did yesterday. In fact," she said, giving David a speaking look, "why even tell him that Davie was caught, since everything worked out so beautifully? He'll rant and rave and read us a sermon cataloguing all our shortcomings, and before you know it Beth will be in tears, the maids will be embroidering the tale, and that Kirsty will have a face like a pikestaff and will make a point of letting Father know you went raiding as soon as his back was turned."

David pressed, "She has a point, ye know. The raid was a success. Why spoil it fer Donal?"

Duncan eyed his uncontrollable young siblings. "If ye stop in bed all day," he told Davie, "and ye dinna leave Doon tae go gallivantin' God only knows where," he told Tina, "I'll think on it."

"Duncan, we promise to do whatever you say. We won't give you the slightest trouble," she vowed.

"Trouble is yer middle name, Valentina Kennedy, as half

Scotland already knows and the other half will discover before yer twenty!" Duncan said.

"Wheesht, man, when ye flatter her like that, there's no living wi' her, Duncan!" said Davie.

With a light heart, Tina flew downstairs to the kitchens. She sat herself on Mr. Burque's worktable, a favorite perch whenever she wanted to beguile the attractive Frenchman. "Mr. Burque, I need your assistance. I've invited Patrick Hamilton to dinner tonight, and I need you to serve something superb. And please, my dearest Mr. Burque, make it something that doesn't wear horns."

He chuckled. "Chérie, a Scot doesn't feel he's been fed unless he's served mutton."

"Patrick is the Earl of Arran's son. He's not quite as coarse as last week's visitors."

"Then I suggest smoked salmon followed by grouse. I'll make the skin brown and crackling, just the way you like it."

"I don't know—men always eat game with their fingers," she said doubtfully.

"Then I'll provide rose-water fingerbowls and napkins," he suggested.

"Mr. Burque, I said he wasn't coarse, I didn't say he was refined!"

"Donal will be back today. Just to be on the safe side, chérie, I think I'd better do a rack of lamb. It's in your best interests to have him in a mellow mood, *n'est-ce pas*?"

Tina was not worried that Mr. Burque was privy to Kennedy business. He knew enough to keep his mouth shut about her secrets. "Last time Patrick Hamilton was here, he went mad over your *pâté en gelée*. Could I impose upon you to make it again, Mr. Burque?"

He cast her a provocative glance. "Beware! It will make him very frisky!"

"Oooh la-la, promise?" Tina giggled.

* * *

Ram Douglas would not have taken the word of a lying Hamilton for all the whisky in the Highlands, but something about the gatehouse guard of Lanark Castle rang true. He told Douglas that he was the highest-ranking Hamilton in residence. Patrick and his men were at Ayr, where his father had anchored the king's new flagship. The Earl of Arran's younger sons were on border patrol, and the rest of the Hamiltons were at Hamilton Castle, much farther north. Too, the deep-seated rivalry between the two clans was so ingrained, a Hamilton would have found it impossible to cower inside his castle while a Douglas with half a dozen moss-troopers sat without. The challenge would have been too insulting, too provoking, too damned deliciously tempting to pass up.

On the ride back to Douglas, Ram pondered who but the Hamiltons would dare lift his cattle. The English would never get this far north because even when he and his moss-troopers were on leave, other borderers guarded the marches. His brow cleared. When he got back, he would soon persuade the lad languishing in the dungeon to enlighten him. He'd never seriously considered hanging the young devil, but he was ready to give his head a damned good bashing against the stone wall of his cell.

That decided, Ram's thoughts turned to the fiery beauty who awaited his return. His loins tingled, and his shaft began to fill just thinking about her. Had she seen him at the Gypsy camp and decided to try her luck at snaring him? Women tended to throw themselves at him when they learned he was a wealthy, powerful Douglas. He hadn't wholly swallowed her tale of memory loss. He smiled. She was up to some female mischief, and he was willing to join her in whatever game she wanted to play. He'd had little sleep in the last few days and was ready for bed in more ways than one.

His mouth went dry at the thought of undressing her. He'd never realized it before, but lacy undergarments that both concealed and revealed the delicious curves of a woman's body were erotically arousing. Ram Douglas licked his lips in anticipation.

The hallful of hard-bitten Douglas men looked very sheepish indeed as Ram read the riot act. "Christ's holy wounds, to be outfoxed and duped by a bairn!" His brothers hung on to their tankards, knowing his fondness for sweeping them from the table in his rage. "Did ye lend him a horse and pack him a bag of oat cakes for his ride home?"

"Logan's bad wounded," Gavin said. "He was a vicious wee bastard."

"Ye didna even strip him tae see if he had a knife concealed," he said with contempt. "The Boozer here wouldha made a damned sight better guard. Ye make me spew!" He ordered a servitor. "Ye can take food tae my chamber— enough for two." He looked at Colin. "Where's the girl?"

"Overwhelmed by Douglas hospitality, she fled while her virtue was still intact," he said sarcastically.

Gavin shrugged helplessly and tried for a light note. "She must ha' come tae her senses and bolted when she realized she was in the evil clutches o' Douglas."

Cameron ventured, "Let me pour ye a dram o' whisky."

"Stay back," Ram warned, picking up a jug of whisky from the table and taking it with him. "Tonight I dinna trust myself!"

He threw off his leather jack and poured whisky into the first thing that came to hand—a silver goblet wrought with Celtic patterns. He tossed off the liquor in one mouthful. Its heat warmed his throat and blossomed in his chest. He braced his arms on the mantel, then pressed his forehead against them and gazed down into the flames. It was a few minutes before he realized how good it felt.

The wolfhound sat beside him and leaned into his leg. Absently he reached down to ruffle the dog's shaggy head. The minute his hand stopped, the Boozer lifted his paw and prodded him, a tiny wheedling whine emitting from the animal's throat.

"Oh, all right, for Christ's sake! Don't cry about it." He unbuttoned his fine linen shirt and threw it on a chair. As if that were a signal, the wolfhound stood on his hind legs and placed his front paws on Ram's shoulders. As they stood eye to eye, a low growl gathered in their throats, and then they were rolling together on the floor, each trying to pin the other down, ferocious as a pair of wild beasts, pitting their strength and wits against each other.

Ram grabbed two great handfuls of hair and had his opponent on his back for about three seconds, but the flailing legs and sharp, nipping teeth soon reversed their positions. The minute the Boozer had Ram on his back, his great tongue came out to wash his master's face. Ram doubled over with laughter, and the dog lay down beside him, paws in the air, belly shamelessly exposed, knowing Ram would scratch it for him until he was in ecstasy.

When the servant brought the food, he knew enough to knock. "Enter," called Ram with an amused eye on Boozer. The dog was immediately on his legs, hackles raised, body rigid with warning. He knew better than to play the puppy when any but Ram was about.

Ram Douglas sighed with regret as he saw the tray set for two. He put the second plate on the floor for the wolfhound. "To lowest hell wi' all women," he said, "especially redheads." Then he gave his full attention to his meat and his whisky. Two hours later, as he watched the play of the firelight on the wolfhound's silvery pewter coat, his eyes closed and the silver goblet rolled from his nerveless fingers.

He descended into sleep and began to dream. He was astride a tireless garron, facing into the wind. He'd been in the saddle twelve hours on border patrol, and Castle Douglas just beyond the River Dee called to him to come home. He wasn't tired, he was alive with anticipation. As the massive fortalice shadowed by moonlight rose before him, he suddenly knew what drew him so irresistibly. It was the woman. At sight of him, her face was filled with joy. Her flaming hair tumbled about her in a fiery mass. His heart overflowed with happiness because he knew she would always be there to welcome him, day or night.

He vaulted from the horse and ran up the stone steps to lift her against his heart. She laughed up into his face, clinging to him, inviting his touch, inviting his kisses, inviting his body to claim hers. Then suddenly he was naked, carrying her to his wide bed. He was fully aroused and taut and could not think beyond her body. He knew if he did not soon see and touch the blazing red curls between her legs and burn himself in her fire, he would die of need.

She wore the most erotic garment he'd ever seen. It was pale lavender, embroidered with flower petals that cupped her breasts. The centers of the flowers, however, were her nipples that burst through slits in the sheer material. Filmy panels floated from the navel down, and each time his hand lifted one of the silken panels to reveal her treasure, there was another to impede and frustrate him. His callused hand ripped the garment from her body with one brutal tear, and he buried his face against her fragrant satin skin. "I know who ye are," he whispered huskily.

"Who?" she begged.

"Ye are my woman," he shouted exultantly, ready to plunge in and drown in her. Suddenly the chamber door was flung open, and the handsomest man he'd ever seen challenged, "She was mine first." He sprang from the bed to face the Gypsy, who was as swarthy and naked as himself. They faced each other with knives, eager for the fight that would give the victor the undisputed prize. Through his teeth he snarled, "Ye may have been first, but I shall be last." He plunged in the knife, and blood covered his hand, wet and sticky. His eyes flew open, and he realized it was just his hound licking his hand. He arose and went to bed, laughing at himself ruefully. Perhaps if he fell asleep again he could call her back in his dreams. As he drifted off he distinctly heard her voice: *"Well, at least you have a sense of humor."*

The next day, however, his sense of humor deserted him completely. He usually had a hard head for liquor, but this morning it felt like a cord was knotted about his temples and being slowly tightened. One thing, however, was glaringly clear: The escape of the youth and the visit of the beautiful vixen were directly linked. Had her vivid beauty blinded him—addled his brains? He was astounded that he had not guessed her purpose the moment he discovered her lying in his path. She had made fools of them all! The rest of the Douglas men had been as obtuse as himself. Anger at the youth who had stabbed one of his men and anger at himself put him in a savage mood. The knowledge that he had been bested by a woman poured oil on his fiery temper. The face of the Gypsy rose up from his dream. Ram's mouth hardened and set in grim lines. Of one thing he was sure. Deadly sure. Before the sun set, he would know her name.

Chapter 7

When Donal arrived back at Doon, he was in high good humor. Castle Kennedy was partially stocked now, and his mind was busy with plans for the future. He would talk his father into giving the peel tower and lands at the mouth of the River Dee to Duncan in exchange for sole ownership of Castle Kennedy at Wigtown. The castle would be more fitting for a bride, especially a Campbell bride and daughter of the powerful Argyll. He'd finish stocking it with milky herds of cattle

and curly-horned sheep, supplemented by what he could
lift in another raid, perhaps from the massive Castle Douglas itself next time. Then he'd propose to Meggie and carry
her off to Wigtown with Argyll's blessing. The buxom
wench who'd warmed his bed at Kirkcudbright last night
played only a small role in his decision. 'Twould only be
politic to keep his whore separate from his wife.

Just as dawn began to pinken the sky, Ram Douglas led
his favorite mount, Ruffian, down to the river. He removed
the bridle and left the choice to the horse. Ram, however,
stripped and plunged into the frigid, fast-flowing waters
without hesitation to clear his head and keep an icy edge
upon his temper. He knew it would be late in the day
before he extracted the information he needed, and he
didn't want to vent his spleen in an explosion with his family.

He'd take no moss-troopers with him this time. He
would extract a personal revenge. Ruffian enjoyed his bath,
blowing the water from his nostrils, then dashing up the
riverbank to roll ecstatically in the sweet green grass of
spring.

Ram banked the fires of his fury and went about his day
with slow deliberation. At the noon meal his brothers and
Colin eyed him with speculation. They knew him for a man
of action. Quick anger followed by swift retribution was
ever his way; he had not earned the sobriquet Hotspur for
his sweet temper.

In the early afternoon he took one of his favorite swords
down from the wall, cleaned and oiled it lovingly, then
polished its silver sheath. It was a flat, broad, double-edged
claymore with a heavy, blunt handle, worn smooth over
years of use, that fitted his palm to perfection. Then he did
the same with his favorite dagger, whose hilt was a heavy
silver ram's head with curled horns. He stood naked before
his mirror contemplating what he would wear. His arms,
legs, and chest were furred with black hair. He usually fa-

vored black from head to toe, for with his swarthy face and long black hair it had an intimidating effect.

Today, however, he took up his Douglas plaid. The short kilt rode on his hipbones, exposing muscular thighs. He eschewed a shirt and instead draped the plaid across one massive bare shoulder and fastened it with a brooch boasting the clan's ancient device, the Bleeding Heart of Douglas. He fastened his sword about his hips and stuck the dagger into his wide leather belt. From only a short distance the dark greens and blues of the Douglas plaid appeared black.

As he observed his reflection, his were not the only eyes that looked upon him. The spirit of Alexander Douglas was restless and alert. The very air of the chamber was charged with raw animal power, barely held in check by the Black Ram. With his long black hair falling to his wide shoulders, he looked exactly as his wild ancestors had looked, and Alexander knew that only an extremely thin layer of veneer covered a savage, primitive nature. He was as uncivilized as the first Douglas had been centuries ago. Alexander was filled with dread, for he feared that Ramsay was tainted by the fatal Scot weakness—a preference for fighting each other rather than a common foe. This very castle harbored evil and hatred for Douglas against Douglas. There had been enough bloodshed and sorrow in Castle Dangerous, in every Douglas castle for that matter, to stain the stones throughout eternity. The Douglas reputation for ruthlessness was legend. Mothers threatened their bairns with punishment by the Black Douglas only as a last resort. The fact that Ram was nephew to the all-powerful Archibald Douglas, Earl of Angus, only added to the dread in which he was held. Angus's favorite pastime was hanging felons. He was rumored to have a degenerate capacity for cruelty, and when he rode forth with his escort of one hundred clansmen at his heels, all obeyed the order, "Make way for a Douglas!"

Hotspur needed no saddle. Ruffian's glossy black coat

reflected the last rays of the afternoon sun before it sank behind the mountains. Ram Douglas knew exactly the picture he created astride the stallion, which stood an impossible nineteen hands high. He held the reins lightly, guiding the animal with his bare knees.

When Zara saw the Black Ram gallop into the Gypsy camp, her heart leaped inside her breast. Was his need for her so great that he came before the last twilight of late afternoon deepened into dusk? She ran to him before he had time to dismount, her dark eyes greedily running over his bare thighs, lingering upon his wide, furred chest, then up to the dark face whose intensity made her shudder.

Her teeth flashed, and her eyes could not conceal her pleasure. "My lord, I am flattered that you came before dark of night."

"You have something I need. I have come for it," he said simply.

Prideful as a cat, she led him through the camp toward her caravan. Zara threw pitiful glances toward the other Gypsy women who were starting cooking fires for the evening meal. In truth, she felt more triumphant than the night she had managed to snare James Stewart, King of Scots.

Ram Douglas halted as he saw a Gypsy man leading a string of horses from the river. He did not need to examine the animals to see that they were prime quality. At the moment, it was the male who received his piercing scrutiny. The two men faced each other, their thoughts hidden behind careful masks, but the challenge of their stances revealed the raw animosity they felt toward each other. Ramsay tasted bloodlust on his tongue. He would have relished pressing his knifepoint into the Gypsy's throat to make him utter the name he needed to know, but he knew he would be able to extract that from Zara. Tonight he could not spend his fury on the Gypsy; he was saving it, holding it in check for a deadlier enemy. He promised himself, however, that at its appointed time the smoldering emotions each provoked in the other would burst into violence and probably climax in death.

Ram took a firmer hold upon Ruffian's bridle as he felt the stallion respond to the string of mares. The two men disengaged their eyes, and Ram passed through the camp to Zara's painted wagon. He fastened Ruffian securely where the animal could graze upon the clover-rich grass and climbed the three steps that took him up inside the caravan.

Most of the room was taken up by her bed, and as Ram's eyes adjusted to the darkened interior, he saw that already Zara lay back upon the covers.

"Light the lanterns for me," she begged, her ragged voice revealing her need to see the magnificent male torso the dimness hid.

The red glass chimney of the lantern illuminated the caravan with an erotic glow, and Zara's eyes dilated with pleasure as the light played across the planes of the strong face, wide shoulders, and bared thighs of her unequaled lover. Her nimble fingers tore off her top to display her small, round breasts, as hard and deliciously tempting as apples from the tree in the Garden of Eden.

She spread her knees wide apart, then her quick brown fingers went to the hem of her scarlet skirt and she inched it slowly up her bare legs until she was naked to the waist. The corners of her mouth went up with delight when she saw Ram's erection lift the folds of the dark Douglas tartan. She quickly lifted off her skirt over her head and caught her breath in wonder as he slowly removed his plaid.

She worshipped him with her eyes, knowing that when he joined his body with hers, she would be filled with his strength, his power, his force. Damn him, he seemed in no hurry in spite of the evidence of his readiness for her. He stood still, looking down at her, making no move whatsoever to join her on the bed or reach for her.

She gazed up at him almost mesmerized. The sheer

brawn of his thews and sinewed muscles caused a painful ache from the pit of her belly all the way down between her legs. Her need for him built inside her until it erupted into her throat and she wanted to scream. She came up onto her knees and crawled to him as he towered there at the foot of the bed. Her eyes became fixed upon his male center with its thick, rigid shaft and proud vermilion head. The tip of her tongue circled her red mouth, and she moved close enough for him to feel her warm breath as she blew upon him lightly to tease, to tempt, to lure, to stimulate the virile, lusty border lord to expend his brute force upon her. Her lips opened to take him.

When she was only a fraction of an inch away, she asked, "Is this what you want from me, my lord?"

"No," he said, lifting her to stand before him on the bed.

She threaded her fingers through the crisp dark pelt of his chest and clung to him seductively. He peeled her body from his and held her off momentarily; then very deliberately he reached down to unfasten the golden circle from her mons. She moaned as his hands came into contact with her sensitive female cleft, and the backs of his fingers brushed her tiny curls aside to unhook the golden wire that pierced her female flesh.

He fastened it into her ear and lifted her so that she could clasp her legs about his waist. The tip of his tongue traced the outline of her lips, and she closed her eyes as she felt his intimate gesture arouse her further. The head of his shaft brushed her bare buttocks rhythmically as his massive ribcage moved her up and down with every breath he took.

His fingers stroked her breasts, encircling over and over the hardening nipples until they stood at attention, making her ache above as she did below. Then his hard mouth finally took hers, and she opened her lips eagerly, needing the thrust of his tongue inside her as much as she needed the thrust of his shaft.

She tasted the texture of him and caught the scent of his

special maleness. Her fingers tangled in the black night of his hair, and she felt she would scream if he aroused her further or die if he did not soon give her release. He lifted his mouth from hers and his hands lightly caressed her back. "Is the Gypsy your brother?"

Every sense was filled with Ram Douglas, so it took a moment for her thoughts to organize themselves. "No, Heath is not my brother."

"This Heath—is he your sometime lover?"

She puzzled over the questions, not wanting to talk. "No, no. He has no desire for me, no claim upon me at all. Do not worry, my lord."

"He prefers redheads," said Ram Douglas.

Suddenly she knew. Zara knew exactly what he wanted —precisely how he would go about getting it—and yet she did not care. She wanted something from him, and if she could, she would make him pay the price in full. She untangled her slim brown legs from his body and stood upon the bed. "I told you, my lord," she said playfully, "I do not know her name."

Ram Douglas smiled inwardly. By her denial, she had just told him she knew the girl's name as well as she knew her own. It would be child's play to coax it from her. He could be a most persuasive man when he put half a mind to it. He spread himself across her bed and pulled her down on top of him. He slid his hard shaft into her hot, wet cleft and rubbed it back and forth in a most seductive and tantalizing manner.

Zara reached down between their bodies and tried to guide him up inside her. Ram's hand slid down to cup her and form a barrier. Holding her whole mons in his warm, strong hand, he squeezed and massaged her expertly. "I really don't know her name," she gasped stubbornly.

His hand came up to grasp her chin, and as his mouth lifted to take hers, he growled, "Hush." His kisses were like heaven. His mouth was so firm and so demanding, she gave herself up to him totally. He rolled her onto her back and held her captive between his muscular thighs. He was torturing her, and he knew it—damn him to hellfire!

"I—I think her name is Tina," she whispered. The name meant nothing to Ram, but he rewarded Zara for the scrap of information. He braced himself above her on his arms, then thrust deeply inside her. She cried out her pleasure, digging her nails into his massive shoulders. He thrust savagely three times, filling her completely until he was buried to the hilt. Then suddenly he withdrew and said, "Let's go outside now that it's darker. This small caravan makes me feel trapped."

Zara knew it was a cruel game he played. She knew also that before he was finished with her, she would give him the rich lady's name. Hellfire, Ram Douglas would arouse her to the point where she'd give him her soul if he asked for it!

She wrapped a shawl about her body and slipped outside. Ram followed her naked. He was one of those men who enjoyed being naked. He was totally at ease without his clothes, never feeling threatened or vulnerable, as others did when they were bare. It was the animal side of him. It felt natural, and like most animals he was well furred.

He took her to the riverbank and laid her back in the long, cool grass, stroking the most vulnerable, intimate places of her straining, healthy young body. He kissed her temples, her eyelids, her high cheekbones, and then he hung over her in the moonlight with his hungry eyes upon her mouth. The tension built until it was unendurable. "She lives west."

Ram's fingertips traced a line from her taut nipple, straight down across her belly and directly to the swollen bud high in the slit between her legs. He took it between his finger and thumb, rolling it gently, then squeezing it rhythmically, keeping time with her heartbeat.

Zara's hand reached out to cup his heavy sac, and she used the same technique on him, gently rolling his balls one against the other to arouse him to where he might lose control. Her fingers closed around his thick shaft, and she manipulated his foreskin up and down with expertise. She knew every trick. It was her business to know what pleasured a man, what aroused him to madness, and what made him beg for mercy.

He plunged two fingers deep inside her, and she arched up into his hand. Then he straddled her, withdrawing his fingers and replacing them with his long, hard manroot. He thrust to the hilt, knowing he was filling her as only he could.

She was almost incoherent now, rising and falling with his deep thrusts. Suddenly he withdrew and whispered, "Sweetheart, I think it was better in your caravan after all."

Dear God, she hadn't known there were any more mountains left to climb! He had taken her to the peaks over and over, only to let her fall back into the valleys without ever reaching the summit. She knew she could not bear to have him start again. "Lady Valentina Kennedy!" she cried.

He plunged down savagely, knowing exactly how many deep thrusts would bring her to the point where she would let down her love juices and enjoy a merciful release. He waited patiently for her to come down from the dark side of Paradise to a place where she was aware of their surroundings. Zara became aware of more than that, however. She knew he had not ejaculated. She knew he was still hard and throbbing, still unsatisfied, and she knew that that was what his perverse body wanted at that moment.

She knew also that his mind had left her the moment she had uttered the name. She reached for her shawl, and he picked her up as if she were made of thistledown and carried her back to her caravan. He laid her gently upon her bed, donned his plaid, and left without another word.

The bloody Kennedys! They'd once been kings of Carrick. This western seacoast had more than two dozen Kennedy lairds. His eyes raised to the hills, which had seen some of the grimmest scenes of clan warfare and feudal savageries. The Kennedys were as awkward and troublesome a bunch as history had ever thrown up!

He rode toward Castle Doon at almost a leisurely pace with slow deliberation. Finally he allowed his mind to focus on the woman. So that was Flaming Tina Kennedy. He should have guessed. In actuality he was shocked that the beautiful wild creature he had seen was a lady of noble birth. He was doubly shocked that an unmarried lady was allowed the freedom of a Gypsy camp, the freedom to ride about the countryside unescorted, the freedom to come and go, obtaining entrance into castles where she could be raped or worse. Of course he did not delude himself that she was a virgin. She was a honeypot. Her reputation was legend. He'd heard her name on the lips of men at court, on the lips of his friends, the Gordons and the Campbells. He'd heard her name deep in the borders and in the Highlands. He'd heard her name in Glasgow and Edinburgh and Stirling. Her name was mentioned every time men spoke of beautiful women, of willful women, of women they would like to bed, of women who would make magnificent mistresses. He clamped his teeth until his jaw looked and felt like a lump of iron. She was just another Kennedy bitch!

Chapter 8

The dinner at Castle Doon had been enjoyed by one and all. Donal was so pleased with himself, he pummeled Duncan's broad back with his hamlike fist each time he passed him. Duncan was pleased that for once he had taken Tina's advice to shut his mouth, and as a result matters had not blown up in his face.

David was pleased that his arm was healed enough to leave off the bandage. What scar still remained from the burn was a testament to his daring deeds on the night of the raid.

Beth was pleased that her sister Valentina had taken the trouble to help her select a gown for dinner and that her brothers for once were as amicable as three red fox pups.

Ada was more than pleased that when Lord Hamilton arrived, he had had his second-in-command with him, who seemed as gallant and polished as a Hamilton—indeed, she suspected he was a by-blow of the Earl of Arran himself.

Kirsty was pleased that Mr. Burque had stared at her for a full minute tonight. It could only be due to the padding she had courageously stitched inside the bodice of her gown. Apparently a little enhancement had gone a long way in gaining her the attention she craved. Mercifully, she had not yet discovered that one of her new titties had slipped around to the back of her gown.

Lady Valentina Kennedy was more than pleased that Patrick Hamilton had arrived early and had never once taken his dark blue eyes from her. He was attentive, witty, intrigued, and very clearly smitten. In the past they had exchanged many glances, many teasing sallies, many dances, and many touches and light kisses, but she had never singled him out from her other admirers for special attention until lately. Tonight there was something in the very air that told them both they would get to know each other more intimately. All was conducive to forging the first links of a liaison. Her brothers were friendly and affable tonight, almost treating him as one of the family, and best of all her parents were not in residence.

The food had been nothing short of superb, and the wine and whisky had flowed freely. The evening itself was romantic. The spring air was almost balmy, fragrant with the scent of bluebells and gorse. The moon and stars hung brilliantly in a black velvet sky.

Tina took Patrick up on the parapets of Doon to observe the savage beauty of the sea, but he was both annoyed and disappointed that her woman, Ada, chaperoned them. Valentina's hair was blown into a red cloud by the night wind, and it billowed about the shoulders of her white silk gown. Patrick was so close that her fragrance stole to him, filling his nostrils with the mingled, heady scent of hyacinth and woman as she threw out her arm: "This view is never static. The ebbing tides and the rolling mist see to that."

"Beautiful . . . breathtaking," he whispered in her ear, and she knew he was paying homage. He slipped his arm about her waist, defying her woman to make some objection. He stiffened as Ada approached. He was ready for her. To his amazement she suggested, "Valentina, why don't you take Lord Hamilton to see the pear trees in the orchard? The blossoms are so profuse, you'd swear the branches were covered by snow." She smiled at Patrick. "My lord, if you send your man up here, I will show him the sea and entertain him so that the next two hours will not drag endlessly for him."

Patrick could have kissed the woman. She couldn't have made it plainer that she was allowing him two hours of uninterrupted privacy with her charge. Tina flashed him a provocative smile. She removed his arm from her waist and clasped his hand, then together they descended the castle stairs. He had a quiet word with his man, directing him to the parapets, and then he and Tina went out into the castle garden. Once there, she took back her hand, then quickened her steps to carry her deep into the orchard, glancing back over her shoulder to lure him after her.

The moon bathed the blossoming trees with a pale, delicate light, and her silk gown was like a splash of whiteness beneath the fragrant pear blooms. His long stride soon closed the distance between them. "I'm having a most enjoyable evening. Will ye allow me tae come again?"

Tina shrugged a beautiful shoulder. "Perhaps."

He took a step closer. She did not retreat. "If I invite ye tae Lanark an' Hamilton, will ye come?"

Tina ran a provocative tongue over her top lip. "Perhaps."

Patrick was quick to catch on to her teasing replies, and he framed his next question accordingly. "If I kiss ye, will ye kiss me back?"

Her lips made a little moue. "Perhaps."

He closed the distance between them, then placed his hands on either side of her small waist and drew her toward him. The piquant fragrance of pear blossoms mingled with her delicious woman's scent. He had become aroused the moment they were alone together, and her teasing, come-hither glances to lure him after her had painfully hardened him. Now as he dipped his head to taste her, his manhood reared and bucked and then began to throb. He felt the throbbing all the way to his eardrums. He kissed her softly, tentatively, molding his lips to hers. His pulse quickened when she opened her mouth slightly beneath his in a most inviting way. He lifted his mouth from hers and murmured huskily, "Sweetheart, when ye say *perhaps,* do ye always mean *yes*?"

"Perhaps," she whispered, but when he again lowered his mouth to hers, she slipped away playfully and ducked beneath a heavily laden bough. He did not hesitate to pursue and capture her. This time he brought her body close to his and pressed her against his hardness. "Little wanton, ye know what ye do tae me," he said raggedly.

"What?" she asked innocently, her eyes brimful of mischief.

Patrick Hamilton was a very experienced man with ladies of the sporting variety, and up until tonight he had always had a strict code of behavior toward unmarried girls of high birth. But Flaming Tina Kennedy was a force to be reckoned with. More than any female he'd ever desired, either whore or virgin, she made a man think of bed and fucking.

He decided to break his code of behavior. He bent his lips to her ear and whispered, "Ye are cockteasing."

Tina had to stand on tiptoe to put her lips against his ear. "Am I good at it?" she whispered outrageously.

"Damned good!" he said aloud. "I think ye've had lots of practice. Is it true ye've turned down six proposals?"

She laughed up into his handsome face. "Six marriage proposals, but scores of indecent proposals."

He laughed at her candor, then exhaled a slow breath of desire. Though her interest in him was undisguised, he feared she would not succumb to his wiles. "Ye know exactly how tae twist men about yer fingers. Ye refuse a proposal and twist them tighter."

"Not guilty, Patrick. I truly didn't want to wed any of them."

He slipped an arm about her, then took her chin in his other hand and held her so that he could look deeply into her eyes. "What about me, Tina?"

"You have a most comfortable pair of arms, my lord."

He smiled, knowing she would make him spell it out in plain language. "Do ye think I could make Lady Kennedy become Lady Hamilton?"

"Patrick, I must be totally honest with you. I told my father flatly I did not wish to be married. He told me in no uncertain terms that I must marry. He advised me to choose while the choice was still mine. The alternative would be a forced marriage, chosen either by Archibald Kennedy or the king."

She was easily the loveliest woman he'd ever held. Too, she had a most exciting quality about her, as if she were ready to kick over the traces, and more than anything on earth he wanted to be the man to teach her the mysteries of her own sexuality. "Sweet, are ye telling me that I am yer choice?"

"I am telling you that I am in no hurry to marry, but that I should like to be wooed. I am telling you that perhaps I would enjoy being your sweetheart. Then, if we find that we love each other, we could be betrothed. I'm told that leads to marriage." The look in her eyes held all the fatal power of destruction.

He groaned and covered her mouth with his, this time kissing her deeply. "Tina, I'd be unwilling tae wait that long for ye."

The man on guard at Doon's gate tower saw the lone rider in the dark plaid and raised the portcullis. He shook his head and laughed to himself, for obviously it was another suitor for Valentina. The torches on the gatehouse showed the dark head of the clansman and the dark greens of the tartan, and the guard guessed that it was either a Campbell or a Gordon. Both men were heirs to powerful earldoms, and he wished he could be present when the man riding in discovered that the heir to the powerful Arran and cousin to the king already had his feet under the table.

Ram Douglas rode up to Doon Castle and across the drawbridge with cold deliberation. God help any who stood in his path. A young Kennedy groom came forward to take his horse, but one look at the enormous beast stopped him short. He saw that the black devil was savage and ready to attack anyone who approached with teeth and hooves. The groom ran back into the stables.

The Black Ram dismounted and tethered Ruffian securely. He strode into the castle as if he owned it. No one even considered stopping him. He had all the arrogant poise and confidence of a man who knew his own power. He walked a direct path to the great hall. The servants moved back to make way for him.

"Donal Kennedy." His voice was deep, resonant, and commanding.

Donal looked up from his leather tankard, and Ram Douglas saw the burly figure, the full-bearded face, the piercing eyes. He saw those eyes widen in recognition.

There was no mistaking the swart darkness of Black Ram Douglas. Holy Christ, how had he found out? Donal's claymore was at the ready, but he never even got the chance to unsheath it. Ramsay swung his weapon high with both powerful arms and brought the flat of the broadsword down full force upon Donal Kennedy's head. It felled him instantly. He dropped like a dead horse.

Duncan Kennedy stared in disbelief at the scene that met his eyes as he came into the back of the hall from the kitchen. He saw his brother go down, and even from behind he knew a dreaded Douglas when he saw one. He drew his dirk and launched himself from behind.

The Black Douglas had the eyes and ears of a hawk. He did not need to turn around to know he was being assailed. His elbow smashed into Duncan's belly, doubling him over; then the heavy hilt of Ram's knife came up under Duncan's chin with an uppercut that knocked out a tooth and embedded it in his tongue. Blood was everywhere.

Davie was in the solar plucking out a tune on a lute when he heard the commotion. He thought that most likely Donal had had too much to drink and had picked a fight with Patrick Hamilton. Not wanting to miss the fun, he ran down the winding stone staircase that led to the hall. His face turned ashen as he saw the fury of Black Ram Douglas. The intruder snatched the lute from David's hands and smashed it against the wall. The wooden, pear-shaped body splintered away, leaving a jagged neck with its fretted fingerboard. Ram jabbed it into Davie's throat as he growled, "Vicious young bastard!"

In spite of his damaged mouth Duncan had cried the alarm, and now red Kennedys were gathering from every direction. Ram grabbed Davie with one powerful arm and wielded his sword with the other. None dared to make a move against him. Ram knew he had timed his one-man assault perfectly. Every last Kennedy had been drinking heavily, and there was none to challenge the Douglas might.

Ramsay's voice rang through the castle: "Restore my cattle, or face the consequences! If it's reiving ye want, it's reiving ye'll get!" he promised with relish. Before he came to Doon, he'd had a notion to take back his young prisoner and hold him for ransom, but now with great contempt for the cowardice of a clan who would raid knowing another clan would be blamed, he flung David Kennedy away from him and watched dispassionately as he hit his head against a fireplace and sank to the flagstones.

Ramsay turned to leave, disappointment surging inside him that there were not more of them to put up a fight. He still had a hot ball of fury burning inside his gut that needed an outlet. He flung open the heavy studded door and heard the seductive laughter of a woman very sure of her prey. A couple were kissing before they came inside.

Douglas stood to one side to let them enter and stared directly into the eyes of Patrick Hamilton. "Christ's passion!" he swore, his pewter eyes glittering with hatred. "The bloody rotten Hamiltons in cahoots with the cowardly Kennedys!" He spat on the floor to rid his mouth of the taste of their names.

Patrick Kennedy had no idea what Douglas was talking about, but it made little difference to him. Here was his hereditary enemy. They'd lived their entire lives at each other's throats. Their castles were built almost nose to nose, and the two clans were bitter rivals because of territory, ambition, and the ruthless power-mongering of Archibald Douglas, Earl of Angus, and James Hamilton, Earl of Arran. Even the king knew better than to put them on border patrol at the same time, and he was forever at them to sign a bond of friendship or at least declare a truce.

"Step inside, man," invited Douglas.

"Ye scurvy, uncouth bastard, how dare ye act like an uncivilized savage afore a lady?" Hamilton demanded, drawing his rapier. "This is a godly household!"

"Man, yer so self-righteous, I wonder it doesna choke ye!" spat Ramsay. Both men stepped into the hall to give them more room for their quarrel. "Join yer fearsome partners in crime. They fair had me quaking in my boots," invited Douglas.

Hamilton gazed about the room in disbelief. "Where are yer men?" he demanded.

"I came alone," the Black Ram said insolently.

"Yer vaunty boasting makes me spew!" roared Hamilton.

"Ye need guts before ye can spew!" taunted Douglas.

"It will give me pleasure tae rid the world o' one more maggot-blown Douglas," snarled Hamilton.

"Ye crawling louse—I ha' better things than ye crawling in ma body hair!" spat Douglas.

Valentina had followed the two men inside. She ran to Donal with her heart in her throat, thinking him dead. When she saw he was unconscious, she was angry and assumed he'd drunken himself into oblivion just when Doon needed defending.

Duncan, covered with blood, was still trying to stanch the flow of the severed artery in his tongue. Tina ran to David's side. He too was bleeding from a gash on the head. "Let me help you, Davie!" she cried.

"Get the hell away from me!" he snarled, shamed that she treated him like a puling bairn.

She stared about the hall at the servants and the Kennedy clansmen and wondered wildly why they did naught, save watch and listen to Patrick Hamilton and Ramsay Douglas circle each other exchanging insults. Her pulses raced, her heartbeats quickened. Suddenly she felt no fear, only a mounting excitement that she was witness to the confrontation of two deadly enemies. As they circled each other warily, she saw how proud Patrick Hamilton looked garbed in elegant black with the white linen ruffle at his throat. He was tall and slim and moved with the grace of a black panther. His deadly rapier blade glinted in the torch-light, and she knew his reach was longer than that of Douglas.

Then her eyes were drawn to the Black Ram. She had never seen a naked man before. His plaid did little to cover his nakedness. Instead it revealed and emphasized his magnificent torso. He was not as tall as Patrick, but his shoulders were broader by far, with the powerful, sleek strength of a swordsman.

Her mind flashed about like quicksilver. Part of her felt guilty because she was enjoying the spectacle. Then she saw with disbelief that the two men were smiling, and she realized with a shock that they were relishing it more than she. She caught her breath on a half sob as the two enemies lunged at each other, but instead of the blood she expected she saw the double-edged Douglas sword snatch the deadly rapier from Hamilton's grip. It flipped into the air, and Douglas neatly caught it in his left hand.

Hamilton, unarmed, tore off his doublet and challenged Douglas. "Throw aside yer weapons and fight me wi' yer fists!"

Douglas was guilty of many things, but stupidity was not one of them. Unarmed he would have been jumped by a score of Kennedys. He slammed his broadsword into its scabbard and advanced upon Hamilton with the man's own rapier. Patrick had the good sense to back away.

"Bad enough ye raided my cattle, but tae aid an' abet the Kennedys tae do likewise, lured on by yon red-haired bitch in heat, is unconscionable, Patrick man."

His foul accusation was totally unfounded, but when Tina tried to defend Patrick, both men totally ignored her. Douglas backed his prey clean across the hall, then with a swift downward slash he slit the white linen shirt and carved a crude letter D on Hamilton's breast.

"You swine!" screamed Tina. "You're doing this because I bested you. How did you learn my name?"

" 'Twas a simple thing tae sniff out—yer reputation as a wanton stinks to high heaven."

Patrick Hamilton tried to control her, but she'd heed no man at this moment. "Before I'm done, I'll see you in hell-fire!" she screamed.

"Most likely," Ram acknowledged with a courteous bow. Then he dismissed her and swept Hamilton and the Kennedy men with a look of blackest contempt. "Yer no' fit tae clean the shit off ma boots." He strode from the hall looking to neither right nor left. Turning his back on all that company showed he was fearless.

Valentina looked down at her white gown and saw it spattered with Patrick's blood and smeared with David's. In that moment she knew a need to see Douglas blood spilled. She cried out to the men in the room, but they were already screaming abuse at one another and exchanging brutal blows. Heedlessly, she ran outside after Black Ram Douglas. His hand was about to untether his devil-horse. "Coward! Whoreson coward!" she cried.

He turned to face her, his eyes raking her from breast to hip. "Ye mistake, mistress. 'Tis all Kennedy men who are cowards, just as all Kennedy women are whores!"

She flew at him and struck him full in the face. Her breasts heaved wildly with her agitation as she screamed, "You don't have the guts to strike me back! You don't have the guts to defend yourself against a woman. You don't have the guts to lay a finger on me!"

A muscular bare leg shot out and knocked her to the ground. Then Lady Valentina Kennedy found herself in a shameful position she'd never experienced before in her life. Ram Douglas was on top of her, imprisoning her body between his muscular thighs. As she struggled wildly, her hands came in contact with his massive hirsute chest, and her eyes saw clearly his shameful male parts. As he straddled her they were shamelessly displayed only inches from her face. She was acutely aware of the heady, disgraceful, masculine scent of him.

He clenched his fist on a handful of turf and was sorely tempted to grind the dirt into her beautiful face. He mastered the impulse as beneath his dignity. He did not need to use his brawn on the little wanton. His contempt would show his superiority. "How many men have ye rolled in the grass?" Ram Douglas got to his feet. He was secretly impressed that she had shown more courage than the Kennedy men. He hid his response to her passion and fire behind a contemptuous look of scorn to show he despised her. He drew away from her as if contact would contaminate him. He gave her one last insolent look that almost scorched her skin, then vaulted onto the back of his black devil-horse.

Tina struggled to her feet, impotence feeding the fires of her anger and hatred. She cried out into the night, "I swear that someday the positions will be reversed! I shall be armed, and you will be weaponless, but I vow to you that I shall use my weapon!"

When Tina went back inside, she saw Patrick and the clansman who had attended him exchanging blows. Ada looked on helplessly. She'd spent a most rewarding evening with the Hamilton moss-trooper in the privacy of her cozy chamber and wondered why men always ended up shouting and brawling by midnight.

Donal was staggering about. Though now conscious, he was still groggy and very much confused about what had taken place at Doon tonight. Tina's eyes caught sight of her pretty lute smashed to smithereens, and suddenly she was overwhelmed. She picked up the forlorn neck with its dangling strings and broke down in tears. She brushed them away impatiently with unclean hands, smearing dirty rivulets across her cheeks. "Why do they ruin and destroy everything they touch?" whispered Valentina.

"Because they're men," explained Ada, ushering her off to bed.

The moment she was alone in her chamber she remembered Old Meg's tarot cards.

She had met The Emperor, the dark man of authority who sat upon the throne decorated by ram's heads. She saw the Five of Swords in her mind's eye. Just as Meg had foretold, he had come with his swords and defeated all. Her mind refused to go further. It was all ridiculous nonsense. Her future could not possibly be affected by some silly pasteboards laid out by an old Gypsy!

Chapter 9

During the following week the Kennedys of Newark, Dunure, and Carrick were raided, along with the Hamiltons of Lanark, Dunbar, and Midlothian.

Naturally Black Ram Douglas was the prime suspect, but there were many who doubted that it was possible for one man to hit so many far-flung castles within the same week.

Ramsay Douglas had decided to join in the game and to teach the other players how to go about the thing with a vengeance. When he hit, he hit hard, and he hit where he knew it would stir up a stink as foul as a cesspool. At each of the Kennedy holdings he left cattle that belonged to the Hamiltons, and likewise he deposited the famous Kennedy sheep upon Hamilton property.

The Kennedys of Doon, however, were not touched, and it was a week before they realized their herds were mysteriously multiplying. The head of the Kennedy clan, Archibald, Earl of Cassillis, was renowned for owning the finest horseflesh in Scotland. Some he bred, others he imported from Ireland, Flanders, Spain, and Morocco. He supplied the royal stables, both at Stirling and Edinburgh, with the very best. Ram Douglas, with his brothers Gavin and Cameron, lifted every horse at Cassillis. It was a major undertaking that required planning, cunning, nerve, and speed. The brothers relayed the horses to their Douglas cousins, Ian, Drummond, and Jamie, who in turn passed them on to Douglas moss-troopers, who planted them in the stables of both the Kennedys and the Hamiltons.

There was one particular mare, however, with which Black Ram Douglas could not bear to part. He had been looking for a worthy dam for Ruffian's offspring, and the moment he saw the glossy filly, he knew he had found her.

She was tall for a female, with extremely long legs. Her neck also was long and graceful, yet her chest was deep, and he knew instinctively she would prove to have long wind. In the dark she had looked black, but when he examined her more carefully back at Douglas, he saw she was an unbelievable shade of purple damson. Just by looking at her, he could tell her bloodlines were royal and that she was part Barbary or Arabian. Her face was exotic, with large eyes, and if he wasn't mistaken, she had been bred with one less vertebra, so that her tail went up high at the least excitement.

He tucked her away in a small meadow at Douglas with one of his most trusted herdsman-tenants. Then Ramsay's perverse humor prompted him to further mischief. It was no secret that the wealthy Kennedys of Doon were thick as thieves with the Campbells of Argyll and that the clans would soon be united in marriage. This was clearly a power-move by the ruthless Argyll. The Campbells already held and ruled the Northwest, and the Kennedy alliance proved their greedy eyes had turned south.

Douglas knew the Campbells had culled about sixty young bulls from their famous herds of shaggy, short-legged Highland cattle with their great spread of horn and had brought them to the spring cattle auction in Glasgow. Lifting the cattle was child's play for the Douglas reivers; the tricky part was depositing them on Donal Kennedy's doorstep without being observed. Black Ram Douglas's men used the ancient border trick for sneaking undetected upon a castle: they covered themselves with cowhides.

By the time the violet fingers of dawn turned the sky an ominous dull pink, panic had set in at Doon. How in the name of all that was holy were the Kennedy brothers to explain their possession of hundreds of cattle and sheep that belonged to their neighbors, to say nothing of their Kennedy chief's horses and Argyll's prize bulls?

The scene at Douglas was as different as chalk from cheese. Though the promised storm was gathering by late afternoon, a holiday atmosphere prevailed. By way of celebration for a most successful and satisfying week, the Douglases had invited the Gypsies to their castle to entertain them till dawn.

With his wolfhound at his heels, Ramsay Douglas cantered Ruffian out to the meadow where he had hidden the beautiful new mare. When they came within half a mile, the stallion's nostrils began to quiver as he scented the female he would serve. Ram had not used him on the raids because a horse that stood nineteen hands high was instantly recognized. As a result, he was difficult and mettlesome. Ram removed his bridle, then sent him thundering into the meadow with a slap across his rump. He secured the tall gate and stood for a few minutes watching the biplay of the two magnificent animals. "Tonight every Douglas celebrates," he called into the wind. "Wear off some o' that energy that makes ye so damned bad-tempered." He laughed as the mare kicked up her heels and raced about the meadow as if the demon of darkness were after her. Ruffian took up the relentless pursuit, teeth bared and eyes rolling. "I think ye've met yer match. By morning, she'll have ye quivering on yer legs, man."

By the time Ram and Boozer walked back to the castle, the Gypsies were setting up their wares in the bailey. The great wolfhound scattered a troupe of trained miniature dogs, then started nipping at the heels of their Welsh ponies until all was pandemonium. With a quiet word Ram brought the wolfhound back to his side and took him upstairs to his chamber. While he bathed and changed into doeskin breeches and linen shirt, the dog rolled on his back in a disgraceful display of love and affection. Ram ruffled the shaggy pewter head. "Yer a fraud. Ye think yer quite a perilous character, and ye expect me tae keep yer secret." The great wolfhound was such a contradiction. Capable of tearing the throat from a man, a soft word from Ram turned him to jelly. "Don't worry—I'll keep yer reputation intact," he promised as he reflected whimsically on whether the dog had taken on his own personality. He'd never know, for there was none to give him a soft word.

The Gypsies set up their wares on colored blankets both outside in the bailey and in the great hall. They sold and bartered everything from tawdry paper flowers to knives of finest Toledo steel. They had the knack of being vivid, dramatic, and exotic, and their displays cleverly appealed to all tastes and all ages.

The children were attracted by the straw dolls and tin whistles, the women by the ribbons, beads, and love potions, the men by the leather belts, knives, and luck charms set into amulets. Their love of life and zest for living were infectious. They made their own music with fiddle, tambourine, and lute, which fired the blood and inspired both men and women to set their feet to dancing. Whenever the Gypsies entertained, it was guaranteed the very air would be charged with excitement and laughter.

Ramsay sent the servants scurrying to the cellar for barrels of ale and kegs of whisky, sniffing the air with appreciation. "Kennedy lamb and Hamilton beef smell better than our own when spitted and roasting," he told a grinning Gavin. "Let's bring down old Malcolm," Ram suggested.

"The mad laird?" asked Colin with disapproval. "He's better off in bed."

"The hell he is!" disagreed Ram. "He's condemned tae that bed fer the rest of his life now his legs are gone. Gavin man, fetch that chair we fixed wheels on last year, an' I'll carry him down."

" 'Tis not just his legs are gone—he's a ravin' lunatic. 'Twould no' be kind."

Ram understood how sensitive Colin was because of his own affliction, but he overruled him. " 'Twould no' be kind tae exclude him like a bloody leper!"

"He won't thank ye. He never had a kind word for anybody in his life, even before he went off it," said Cameron.

"He takes his pleasure by cursing everything and everybody, but I know for a fact he wouldna be a Douglas if he didna enjoy the whisky and the Gypsy dancers. Maybe I'll buy one of the wenches fer his bed tonight," said Ram.

"Maybe ye'll buy one fer the cripple while yer at it," flared Colin. "We all know Black Ram Douglas never had tae pay fer a woman in his life," he sneered.

Gavin arrived with the old wooden chair. "What the hell's burnin yer arse?" he asked Colin.

"Flames about this high," taunted Cameron, holding his hand a scant two feet from the floor.

Colin relented. "I suppose I felt sorry fer myself all week, missin' the sport."

Ram thumped his shoulder. "There's nothing tae stop ye tonight, man. There's everything from a cockfight tae a knife-throwing contest. Ian, ride down tae Douglas village and tell everyone they're invited—not just the lasses, mind. Drummond, tell all the kitchen wenches they can have the night off. I'll go and fetch Mad Malcolm from his tower room."

There wasn't a woman at Douglas who didn't look forward to having her fortune told; there wasn't a man who didn't anticipate the late hour when any woman with a shred of respectability retired from the bacchanalia of the hall and the dusky-skinned Gypsy girls danced naked.

Two slim Gypsy youths were performing acrobatic feats on the backs of half a dozen white ponies while the little dogs with ruffs around their necks ran in and out of the riders' legs. Ram was drawn to them. He was dying to try his own skills. He recalled he'd wasted many an hour of his own youth practicing such daring feats of dexterity. His moss-troopers egged him on, challenging him to duplicate the supple acrobatic leaps of the young Gypsies.

When they wagered their silver that he would come a cropper and fall off in less than a minute, he had to prove them wrong. He selected his pony carefully, choosing one that was not on too short a rein. He knew that man and beast must not be mismatched. His eye soon singled out the animal with the steadiest rhythm, and vaulting onto its back, he rode astride for a few moments to accustom himself to its gait. Slowly he pulled up his feet until his palms and his soles rested on its broad back; then finally he stood tall with his arms stretched out to the sides and rode with ease, circling the bailey.

The cheers that went up were deafening, not only from his own men but from all the people of Douglas and from the Gypsies themselves. Ram chuckled to himself. There was nothing to it really. It was simply a matter of agility and balance. The trick of course was to summon enough courage to try it. He vaulted to the ground and back up again, then he did the same on the pony's other side. He reflected that here was the secret of success in any venture, whether it was a small cattle raid or a war battle: the courage to take a chance, while at the same time having confidence in your own ability to accomplish what you set out to do. It worked every time!

Men were setting up a target butt for the knife throwing

when suddenly lightning flashed, thunder rolled, and large
raindrops began to spatter the bailey. Everyone dashed inside to the great hall, laughing and jostling one another.
The barrels of ale were rolled inside, and six men lifted the
heavy wooden butt they'd set up for the knives and carried
it indoors. It put an effective stop to the cockfights, but the
whole troupe of trained dogs ran inside with the throng,
sniffing around the sizzling spits and initiating the legs of
the stools.

At first, Mad Malcolm brandished a wicked-looking
walking stick at any who approached his chair, but Colin
kept his leather horn filled with whisky, and eventually the
old laird was seen tapping on the flagstones, keeping time
with the music.

Occasionally tempers flared over possession of a castle
wench or a Gypsy girl, but the high spirits of the men
prevented the scuffles from degenerating into full-scale
brawls. Gavin Douglas couldn't keep his eyes off a beautiful young Gypsy until he noticed with annoyance that
Jenna was flirting outrageously with an extremely well-fa-
vored Gypsy male. When the knife-throwing contest began, she urged the Gypsy to show off his skills and tossed
her tawny head when she saw Gavin was watching her. The
men of Douglas and their moss-troopers were trained in
the expert use of many different weapons from swords and
dirks, bills and spears, to hagbuts and longbows. The Gypsies, however, used only knives and were highly profficient,
so there was no shortage of contestants who lined up to pit
their skills against the Gypsies.

Not a single contestant from either side missed the target, and there were quite a few men of Douglas who had
no trouble hitting the bull's eye with the same regularity as
the Gypsy men. But when the ringed target was removed
and replaced by one with small red stars forming intricate
patterns, the ranks soon thinned.

Heath had a matching set of eight balanced silver knives
that he used on these festive occasions when they earned

money entertaining the nobility. Gavin Douglas was determined to match the Gypsy's skills and gathered knives
from the moss-troopers. Because he had to prove himself
to both the beautiful young Gypsy girl and to Jenna, his
performance matched Heath's, and he hit every single red
star. He was gratified by the deafening cheers of the men,
who all seemed to be pulling for him.

Heath flashed his white teeth in a good-natured grin and
held out his hand to the audience. The beautiful young
Gypsy girl stepped forward without hesitation, and Heath
positioned her before the target, her head high, her arms
and legs spread wide. It was an act the couple had performed many times.

Every breath was caught and held as Heath took the first
dagger blade in his hand, pointed the hilt toward the un-
flinching girl, and let it fly through the air. It thunked into
the wooden target three inches from her left ear. The
crowd gasped as another knife found its mark three inches
from her right ear. The next two knifeblades struck the
target between the spread fingers of her small brown
hands, and the crowd broke into applause. The knives that
struck either side of her waist were an inch closer to her
body than the others had been, and the crowd roared its
approval. The seventh dagger entered between her legs,
pinning the scarlet material of her skirt to the target. The
knife's haft protruded from between the girl's legs like a
suggestive phallic symbol, and every male watching
achieved an erection. The climax of the performance followed quickly. As Heath's final knife left his fingers, his
beautiful target bent double from the waist and the wide
eyes of the audience saw that the last dagger had entered
the target exactly where her heart had been.

Tension filled the air as all eyes swung to Gavin Douglas,
but before he could take up the challenge, the beautiful
young Gypsy girl held up her hands, laughing prettily, but
refusing to be the target for the handsome young Scot.
Gavin grinned good-naturedly, extremely relieved that the

challenge was over. Jenna touched his shoulder. "I'll be your target, Gavin," she offered bravely.

He looked down into her clear green eyes and wondered what in the name of God he'd found attractive about the young Gypsy girl. "Sweetheart, I canna let ye do that, but I've other weapons I wouldna mind testing." As Gavin slipped his arm about Jenna, he cast Heath a look of triumph, feeling he had definitely taken the prize even though he'd lost the contest.

Ramsay Douglas stepped forward to take up the challenge. His pewter eyes glittered coldly as they fixed upon Heath's darkly handsome face. "I'll use your knives since they're perfectly balanced," his deep voice said decisively.

Heath's warm brown eyes crinkled at the corners as he accepted the challenge. He gestured toward the fine silver-handled weapons. "Be my guest, if you can find anyone brave enough to be your human target."

"There's someone here with enough courage," Ram said calmly.

"Who?" Heath asked with a smile, as no one stepped forward.

"You," Ram said simply.

The smile left Heath's face as the men took each other's measure like two dogs with their hackles raised. Heath was aware of Black Ram Douglas's other nickname, Hotspur, that sprang from his volatile temper and low boiling point. In these parts he enjoyed a larger-than-life reputation for breaking women's hearts and men's jaws, but Heath looked beneath the surface, realizing this man was intense, complex, and intelligent as well as strong and poised for an eruption. Apart from this, there was an unknown quality about him. Gypsies were hot-blooded and admitted it freely; Heath wondered if Ram Douglas was the same, or if he was cold-blooded. He was about to find out.

With a nonchalant bravado he did not quite feel, he handed over the knives and stepped in front of the wooden target. Douglas picked up the first knife and fixed the

Gypsy with a piercing look. The weapon was an age in coming, and Heath realized it would be a battle of nerves. Douglas was testing him to try to learn his breaking point. Heath was puzzled. He knew this level of rivalry between two men was only ever about a woman, yet he was almost sure that woman was not Zara. Douglas had too fine an intelligence and was too blood-proud to be jealous of a Gypsy harlot.

Heath did not flinch as the first two knives thunked into the wood beside his ears; he knew Douglas had enough confidence in his own ability to stretch the game to its limits. Heath realized it would be the last two daggers he must worry about, but he was relieved to find he still had all his fingers after the second pair was thrown.

The third set of daggers came so close to his body, they nicked his shirt at the beltline. It was a clear reminder that Douglas had him at his mercy. Heath's mouth went dry as he thought about the next knife. This hostility between them was definitely a cock-and-balls thing. Heath prayed that Ram Douglas's pride was stronger than his acrimony. How easy it would be to emasculate him, then claim it was accidental—but then, all would think his prowess with a knife somewhat inferior.

Heath wanted to flash him an insolent devil-may-care sneer, but his lips seemed to stick to his teeth. It was Ram's mouth that curved into a wolf's grin as the dagger left his fingers and embedded itself snugly against Heath's balls, bruising them deliberately.

So far, Douglas had won and both men knew it. But they were more alike than either knew. Built into both were seeds of self-destruction. The whole point of the challenge came down to the last knife, yet the conclusion was far from inevitable. At that moment it was as if they stood alone—no other beings existed in the entire universe. Each man had a decision he must make regarding his enemy.

Heath asked himself if Ram would aim for the heart or throw the knife above his head. Ram asked himself if the

Gypsy would drop the top half of his body or defy him by remaining erect.

Their eyes locked together for endless minutes as each man made his fatal choice. Heath found suddenly that he could smile. As he did so, his head lifted with pride. At the last split second the Black Ram knew the Gypsy would not move a muscle. The dagger parted the Gypsy's hair, cutting off a lock and pinning it to the wood behind him.

A great roar of approval went up from the clan and the moss-troopers, showing that they believed Douglas the clear victor. But Ram and the Gypsy male knew otherwise. Both knew who had given way at the last moment. And yet it was a moral victory for Ram Douglas. He alone knew he had not given in to the bloodlust that would have branded him a coward in his own eyes.

As the night progressed, the noise level increased. The music came louder and faster. The shrieking laughter, stamping feet, and barking dogs made it necessary to shout every word. The amount of food and drink consumed would have fed an army for a week, and the entire castle rang with the unrestrained mirth of men and women who knew how to abandon themselves to the moment.

The spirit of Damaris was extremely restless. At first she kept to her chamber, but the laughter and the Gypsy music finally lured her to the hall. As she surveyed the celebration, she reflected how shocked she would have been at such abandoned behavior when she first came to Douglas, but after roaming the castle for fifteen years, she understood and accepted that they had a hungry zest for life. She sighed. 'Twas what had attracted her to Alexander in the first place. Ramsay had a love for music and a passion for heroic literature that he kept hidden. He was so like her dead husband, it frightened her. They were both so dour, grave and curt on the surface, but underneath they loved colorful spectacle and had a distinct flair for extremes. She watched one or two Gypsy women laying out tarot cards

and listened as they told fortunes. Damaris smiled sadly.
All that the young girls seemed interested in was snaring a
man. Had she been like that? Once she had laid eyes on
Alex Douglas, she admitted, he was all she had ever
thought about. She had grown up amongst a clan of redheads and garnered a lot of attention because she had
silken blond hair and not a freckle in sight. Alexander
Douglas had been the darkest man she'd ever seen. So
dark, it gave her shivers just picturing him. He had seemed
just as wildly attracted to her paleness. How ridiculous to
choose a lifetime mate on the basis of coloring! And yet
when you thought about it, vivid coloring was what made
certain individuals stand out from the crowd. It was the
first thing you noticed about them. There were millions of
ordinary drab people, and then nature would produce
someone so darkly beautiful, they looked sinful. Someone
with the opposite coloring like herself, with milk-white skin
and silvery-gilt hair, looked pure and angelic. Then there
were vivid creatures like her niece Valentina, with startling
golden eyes and a mass of molten, flaming hair at which a
man wanted to warm his hands. She and Alexander had
been fatally attracted, and the day Tina came to Douglas,
she had feared the same thing would happen between her
and Ram. Fortunately, sparks of hatred had been kindled,
so she need never worry on that score.

The specter of Alexander watched her from the shadows
of a deep window embrasure. How ethereal she looked!
His heart ached with longing as he remembered the first
night they had shared a bed. Her limbs, so exquisitely pale,
contrasted shockingly against his swarthy black-haired legs
and chest. It had seemed a desecration to join their bodies,
to mate, almost like a devil ravishing an angel, and yet
their wild attraction for each other had aroused them to
such need, such peaks of desire, he knew he must wed her
so they could share a bed every night for the rest of their
lives.

Alexander could not help himself. He drew near to his love. "Damaris," he breathed.

Her apparition began to fade, then was gone.

"Damaris!" he called urgently, but he knew it was quite pointless. She would never acknowledge his presence.

Old Meg the Gypsy, however, said, "Who is there? What do you want?"

"I'm Alexander Douglas! Can ye see me? Can ye hear me?" he demanded.

The old woman stood up and put out a gnarled hand, feeling the texture of the air about her.

"Ye canna see or hear me, but ye can sense me, can't you? God, if only I could communicate with ye. Damaris is ma wife. I didna kill her! Come with me—I'll show ye her portrait."

Old Meg's eyes swept around the hall searching for something. She did not quite know what she sought. She closed her eyes and let her other senses, including her sixth sense, have full rein. She circled the hall slowly, her shrewd eyes missing very little. She paused beside Mad Malcolm. He brandished his stick. "Filthy Gypsy—away wi' ye!"

Old Meg recoiled, not at his words but at the evil she felt surrounding him. Something from the long-dead past stirred in her memory. She'd had an unwitting hand in a poisoning here at Douglas. At the time she had put it from her mind—she had no reason to waste her pity on a Kennedy. She had a nodding acquaintance with evil. She'd been exchanging poison for obscene amounts of silver for years. She lived by the Gypsy code of "no guilt."

Colin Douglas refilled Malcolm's drinking horn and cast Meg a helpless apologetic look, then he tapped his fingers to his temple in the age-old sign that conveyed madness. Meg stalked off. She was in a mood to prowl about a bit. Alexander stood at her shoulder at the bottom of the staircase. He tried to "will" her up the steps but learned that her willpower was every bit as strong as his own. Discouraged, he withdrew up the staircase. Old Meg followed.

Alexander halted outside his wife's chamber. Ever since his death, he had never entered, never violated her sanctuary. Meg, it seemed, had no such scruples. Her gnarled hand turned the doorknob, and she went inside and stood transfixed before the painting of Damaris.

Alexander said, "The portrait-limner did a credible job, but she was beautiful on the inside as well."

"Get out!"

Alexander whirled about, joy radiating from him like the rays of the sun. "Damaris—ye *can* see me. Fifteen years ye've looked through me, but I never gave up!"

"Fifteen years should have conveyed how I feel, you pig-headed spawn of the Devil!"

His eyes shone with happiness. "Yer angry wi' me."

"Angry? There's the understatement of the century! I hate you, I loathe you, I detest you, I abhor you!"

"I love ye, Damaris," he declared.

"I curse you!" she vowed, then vanished.

Old Meg reached up her fingers to touch the girl in the portrait. She could feel the very air in this chamber was charged with emotions, all conflicting. The memory came back clearly now. So this was the Kennedy girl who had wed a Douglas—an explosive, deadly combination. Both clans were insufferably blood-proud.

"Don't touch that portrait, or all hell will break loose," ordered a deep voice of authority.

Old Meg turned to see an angry Ram Douglas. Zara hovered in the corridor, assuming Meg had been caught stealing.

"A double murder will leave its imprint until justice prevails," Meg said.

" 'Twas a murder-suicide. They got justice. The bitch was unfaithful. Alex Douglas killed himself before the Kennedys could get their vengeful hands on him. Get downstairs before I hang ye fer theft."

Her lip curled with contempt. As if it were yesterday, she recalled selling the poison to this man who stood before her so arrogantly. He had been a wild and willful youth of only about sixteen, but shortly thereafter Lord Alexander Douglas lay dead and the Black Ram was the new lord and master. "Have a care for yourself, Ramsay Douglas. Visitants from the other side have such power, they could strike you down for the lies you perpetrate."

Ram laughed derisively. "Go on, call up the dead—command them to materialize. Yer supernatural powers underwhelm me, old woman!"

"I claim no supernatural power, but I do have the second sight." Her eyes flickered beyond the door toward Zara. "Debauch yourself while there's darkness left. 'Tis the last time you'll be permitted to waste your seed."

Her implication was marriage or death, and he wasn't sure he didn't prefer the latter. "If yer hinting at my being leg shackled, yer second sight is playing tricks on ye, old woman. 'Tis yer own shackles ye can see when I lock ye up. Begone from this place, while ye've breath left in yer body."

Meg's eyelids covered the windows of her soul. It was not politic to threaten this man. He would not cavil at one more murder.

Chapter 10

Ram Douglas could not close his eyes even long after he'd sated himself. Zara slept beside him, curled into a ball like a sleek cat replete with a fortnight's ration of cream inside her. He smiled grimly into the darkness. The mere hint of a suggestion of marriage had robbed him of sleep. Deny it as much as he liked, the truth was he was a coward with no guts for marriage.

Wedding bells were the death knell for love. Love was a myth in itself, perpetrated by females and poets. He'd never seen a happy union in his life. Lord Alexander Douglas and Lady Damaris Kennedy had had everything going for them. Their union had joined two of Scotland's greatest clans. Not only that, but both of their great-grandfathers had married daughters of King Robert III, so their marriage linked them with the royal house. How long had it lasted—twelve days? A fortnight?

His mind strayed to his mother and father. There was a union made in hell. They'd lived at the top of their lungs, not caring if the whole world knew of their savage exchanges. How many nights had he comforted Gavin and Cameron as they crawled into his bed shaking? His mother was a Ramsay, giving as good as she got. Threats, fights, recriminations, betrayals, beatings. He had been ten when she left. She'd taught him the hypocrisy of the sanctity of marriage.

His relentless mind moved on. The biggest sham in Scotland was their king's marriage. James IV had a weakness for women, and Scotland thanked God for it. His father had been a raving homosexual who had failed to keep his minions in his bedchamber but allowed them in the council chamber. His ruling chiefs could not stomach such a thing; sodomy was not a Scots vice. Archibald Douglas, Earl of Angus, had led the men who had dragged the king's catamites out and hanged them. Ram's thoughts shied away from examining his uncle too closely and returned to the king's marriage. James had avoided the matrimonial trap until he was thirty, then for the weal of the realm and to beget heirs, he'd been persuaded to wed fourteen-year-old Margaret Tudor, Princess of England.

Their marriage was a nightmare. The princess had a flat, pudgy face like a lump of dough and a stodgy body to match, yet she was highly sexed. James himself had once confided to Ram that he feared impotence when he had to bed her. Though they'd now been wed over eight years, every pregnancy had ended in a dead child. The queen had just produced another puny bairn, so there still might be no heirs to the throne. Even a sanctified marriage was no guarantee of heirs. Marriage in fact was a guarantee of naught save misery!

Ram reflected that he was past thirty, and he knew it was his duty to produce strong Douglas sons to inherit the land, titles, and wealth and to keep the clan powerful. One of these days he'd have to hold his nose and take the plunge. When the time came, he'd yield to expediency. He'd listen to his head and choose the wife who would bring him the most wealth and power. He could listen to his blood when he chose his mistresses, and if worse came to worst, there were ways of ridding yourself of an unwanted woman.

Valentina Kennedy's day began splendidly. Ada brought her a breakfast tray with the most divine-smelling, freshly baked French bread. The first strawberries of the season sat in a compote of clotted cream. Mr. Burque had followed Lord Kennedy's orders to serve everyone at Doon with porridge, but he had provided a jug of sweet golden syrup to make the oatmeal palatable. Tina picked up the fruit but pushed away the fluffy eggs surrounded by thick cured ham.

"I'll join you," Ada said, picking up the plate. "If I have to suffer your brothers' company through one more meal, the back of my skull will fall in. Their tempers are ready to explode."

"Isn't it wonderful that for once trouble has passed me by?"

Ada laughed, but at the same time she felt sorry for the lads. "Poor buggers, how the hell are they to hide two hundred shaggy Highland cattle amongst our own herds of red and white Ayrshires?"

"That's their problem," Tina said, throwing back the covers.

Ada gave a little gasp as a man climbed in at the open casement. "Heath! God's nails, you scared me."

"Liar." He grinned, spanning her waist with his strong brown hands and lifting the woman for a kiss. "There isn't a man breathing scares you!"

He occupied the spot Tina had just vacated and pulled the breakfast tray toward him. " 'Tis a bonnie day for a ride," he told Tina, his rogue's eyes sparkling.

"Heath, you didn't!" she squealed with excitement. "Close your eyes while I put on a riding dress."

The moment he'd denuded the tray of every last morsel, he swung his leg across the sill. Tina prepared to follow him. "Use the stairs, Firebrand—you're a lady, not a Gypsy," he said.

"Praise God one of you remembers," Ada said, rolling her eyes.

Heath had the mare tethered down by the river, away from the castle. As she approached, Tina thought she'd never beheld such a memorable picture in her life. Above, thrushes and yellow hammers flitted in the hazels. She walked across a carpet of moss and ladyferns and slowly held out her hand to the graceful mare. The animal pricked its ears forward, staring at her intently; then catching her scent and accepting her, she lowered her head, blew through her nostrils, and allowed Tina's hand to rest upon her velvet nose. "Oh, her lines are superb, her color indescribable!" Tina exclaimed with awe. "Wherever did you manage to find her?"

"At the horse fair in Paisley," he said with a straight face. He took a paper from his shirt. "Listen to me, Tina. It's important that you have this bill of sale to prove ownership—she's had one or two owners recently."

She glanced at him knowingly and took the paper. "Her name must reflect her color. Her coat is the hue of damsons or aubergines—let's see, Heliotrope doesn't sound right. I know, I'll call her Indigo!" She took a few steps back to observe the animal's lines. Behind Indigo, the water cascaded over the rocks into a deep pool surrounded by bog-myrtle and marsh marigolds. The morning sun filtered through the trees, making a nimbus of light about the purple equine, turning it into some mythical, magical creature from the Arabian nights. She looked at the paper again. "Did you really pay this much for her?"

His teeth flashed. "I won her in a knife-throwing contest."

"I believe you; thousands wouldn't."

He lifted her to the mare's back. "I know you are far too impatient to take her to the stables to be saddled. Just be careful," he admonished, "and don't lose that paper."

Valentina discovered Indigo had a sensitive mouth and responded beautifully to the slightest pull on the bit, but when given her head she could run as fast as the wind. They rode along the banks of the River Doon all the way into the seaport of Ayr. Tina wanted to see how the animal reacted on the streets of a busy town.

Something was causing a stir down at the quay. Curious, she rode through the crowd that had gathered. Suddenly her heart, which had been so high, plummeted to her feet and her spirits sank to the pit of her stomach. The *Thistle Doon* rode at anchor badly damaged. She now boasted only half a mast, and her taffrails had been blown away by what must have been cannon fire.

Tina dismounted hastily as she saw her mother being helped into a litter. "Mother, whatever happened?" she cried.

"Tina, thank God!" thundered Rob Kennedy, taking a firm grasp of her arm and propelling her some distance from the litter. "The bloody woman will drive me tae violence if ye dinna get her outa ma sight." His face was purple with choler.

"What happened?"

"The bloody English is what happened! They attacked

ma ship, stole ma precious wool, almost sank us. I've been limpin' home fer days, an' all the bloody woman has done is cry!" He cast a scornful look down the quay. "I tell ye, lass, nothin' good ever came up from England. Deliver me, there's a good lass."

"I'll take her home and see to her needs," Tina said, and for once her heart went out to the gentlewoman's plight.

" 'Tis a curse tae be wed tae a woman who expects ye tae dance attendance on her. I've dispatched a rider tae fetch Archibald Kennedy, and I see Arran is here. I've a complaint or two fer the bloody admiral. The king must be informed that the English are attackin' our ships, and all the pathetic woman can do is weep an' wail an' gnash her teeth!"

Tina thought she would scream at the slow progress of the litter, but she firmly squelched her impulse to ride hell for leather into Doon to tell her poor beleaguered brothers that not only was Lord Kennedy home, they could expect the chief of Clan Kennedy to descend upon them shortly.

She patiently listened to her mother's tale of woe, gently helped her from the litter, summoned Duncan to carry her up to her chamber, ignoring his look of desperation, and began to feel positively virtuous for the sacrifice she was making. She ordered the servants to plenish the room, and she bathed her mother's pale face with rosewater, removed her shoes, and asked softly, "What can I get you?"

"You can get me Beth," Elizabeth said in tragic tones. "Valentina, you are not the most restful person for an invalid. Just looking at all that flaming hair and vulgar vitality is exacting a toll upon what little strength I have left."

"I'm sorry," Tina whispered, quickly lowering her dark lashes to mask her hurt. "I'll get Beth and ask Mr. Burque to make you some chamomile tea."

"Yes," her mother said rather petulantly, "but have Ada bring it to me, if you please."

When Lord Kennedy arrived home, his mind was so preoccupied, he saw naught amiss at Doon. His three sons

met him at the door rather than waiting to be summoned.
They did not want to further exacerbate Rob Kennedy's
temper.

When Tina joined them in the hall, her father was alter-
nately describing the harrowing sea venture and raining
curses upon the English. His Scots was so thick, she could
hardly comprehend his words until he said all too clearly,
"Arran an' Archibald Kennedy will be here the nicht. Tina,
direct yon peste Mr. Burque tae prepare somethin' fittin'
fer two earls o' the realm."

She saw her brothers exchange trapped looks.

"Tell Elizabeth tae prepare guest chambers. Davie, see
there's room in the stables—they'll both ha' their men wi'
'em."

David slunk out like a rat deserting a sinking ship. Donal
cleared his throat as if he were about to make a clean
breast of things. Tina shot him a warning glance and said,
"Mother's in bed."

"God damn an' flay the woman! What use is she tae a
mon?" he choked.

Tina said, "I'll give the servants their orders. Everything
will be ready for them. Mr. Burque is ever prepared, no
matter how many descend upon us."

"There's ma lass," he said, thankful that one of his offspring could be counted upon. "I want ye at the table the
nicht, sittin' smack atween James Hamilton an' Archibald
Kennedy. Ye can cozen them intae givin' me their full support when I take ma complaints tae the king. Neither o'
them can resist the blandishment o' a beautiful lass."

She glanced at Donal, now feeling just as trapped as he.
"It must be catching," she muttered to herself.

Though he had farther to come, Archibald Kennedy,
Earl of Cassillis, was the first to arrive. He had twenty of
his men at his heels, all armed to the teeth. David had the
presence of mind to keep them out of the stables by having
a dozen grooms and stableboys on hand to receive their
horses in the bailey as soon as they dismounted.

Valentina took a deep breath and came forward with ale on knees that felt like butter. Archibald Kennedy was so coarse in appearance, he made her father look refined. He had once been barrel-chested, but with age all had slipped into a heavy paunch. It seemed a miracle his short bowlegs supported his girth. He seemed to have no neck—his wide florid face, marred by broken veins, sat directly upon his shoulders.

His men drank off their ale, but he grabbed the goblet from Tina, sniffed it loudly, then flung its contents to the back of the fire. "Wheest, lass, what's this muck?" he demanded, fixing her with a small beady eye. Rob came forward with the whisky, and Tina thought, well, so much for being unable to resist me!

"There's no need tae tell me—ye've been raided. Yer no' the only one, Rabbie. Every Kennedy has been systematically raped, frae Newark tae Portpatrick. When we find the culprits, there'll be the biggest reivers' battle ever fought. We'll gibbet the lot! The whoresons lifted all ma prime horseflesh, an' one in especial was earmarked fer the king!"

Rob looked up sharply at Donal. "We've no' been raided? Weesucks, we're overrun wi' horses an' cattle."

Archibald's beady eye became instantly suspicious. "Is that a fact? I'd best ha' a look aboot Doon. Yer meadows did seem uncommon full o' beasties when we rode in!"

Rob Kennedy's face turned purple with choler, but Donal's ruddiness vanished completely.

"Are ye accusin' me, Rob Kennedy, Lord o' Galloway, o' liftin' cattle frae ma ain kith an' kin?" he demanded.

"We'll see!" said Archibald, snatching up his riding whip and gauntlets from where he'd flung them on the oak table. The two Kennedy lords elbowed each other as they exited the castle, but wide as the doorway was, it could not accommodate two such broad individuals at the same time. Tina noticed it was Archibald who took precedence. She heard Donal mutter to Duncan, "I'll lay ye ten tae one they're the earl's horses."

Tina followed, unable to resist observing what could very well be the doom of Doon. Rob Kennedy's eyes bulged as he saw that every stall held at least two animals. The stablehands and Archibald's men fell back to watch the fireworks.

"Ye filthy, thievin' rogues! Here's the proof these are ma horses. This Barbary mare was fer King Jamie hissel!"

Rob Kennedy felled his son Duncan with one powerful blow, though Duncan topped him by a full head. Donal had wisely stayed beyond his reach. "Ma ain sons are a curse tae me! What a' pox have ye been doin'? The minute I'm off tae sea, ye whore aboot the country, disobey ma orders, squander my siller, and now ye've lifted the earl's horseflesh. 'Tis like bitin' the hand that feeds ye, tae rob yer ain!"

Tina had to do something. "My lord earl, you are mistaken about this particular mare." She fished the paper from the leather purse at her belt. "I've a bill of sale to show she was purchased at the horse fair in Paisley. She's mine, and you can see I paid a fortune for her."

Archibald Kennedy snatched up the paper, and his rage doubled. " 'Tis a conspiracy! Yer lass is the biggest liar o' the bunch!"

"Why, ye bandy-legged bastard, ye'd best keep a civil tongue in yer haid when ye speak o' ma daughter Tina!"

"Ye maggot-blown bladder o' lard, I'm the haid o' Clan Kennedy—I'll see ye hanged fer yer crimes afore this day is done!"

A great clatter of horses echoed round the bailey as James Hamilton, Earl of Arran, Lord High Admiral of Scotland, with twenty men at his heels, arrived. Before he dismounted, he was hurling accusations. "Christ's blood, I've worn ma nag's legs down tae its fetlocks ridin' about my holdin's this week. Ma sheep an' cattle hav' been disappearin' like snow in summer, an' here are the bloody culprits holed up like a skulk o' foxes!''

Archibald Kennedy, also an earl of the realm, decided to take exception to his words. ''Yer no' insinuatin' the Kennedys have dirtied their hands wi' yer vermin-ridden sheep, are ye, Jamie boy?''

Arran's dark, thin face was stiff with outrage. His eyes were narrowed to slits, and his pinched lips had disappeared altogether. Tina groaned inwardly. Just when she had Patrick Hamilton eating out of her hand, their families were determined to start a feud. Still, she mused wryly, if Patrick was going to look like his father in later years, perhaps it was just as well.

Rob tried to speak up, but Archibald was ahead of him. He waved Tina's bill of sale in his hand and said, ''Everything on four legs on Kennedy land has been bought an' paid for, an' we've the papers tae prove it, which is more than ye can say, Hamilton! And while we're talkin' plain, our red hair may make us resemble foxes, but we're all legitimately born here. We dinna ride about wi' a passel o' bastards at our back!''

Tina bit her lip at Archibald's hypocrisy. Both he and her father had their share of by-blows.

''We'll no' stop here tae be insulted. We'll ride tae Edinburgh and lay our complaints afore the king,'' Arran shouted.

Rob spoke at last. ''An' while yer at it, ye can report that yer doin' such an *admiral* job as *admiral*, the bloody English are attackin' our ships the minute they sail outa the Firth o' Clyde!''

Arran dismounted, completely distracted for the moment. ''I saw yer ship—I'll need a full report. Don't keep us standin' aboot out here. Yer hospitality is as lackin' as yer wits.''

Valentina closed her eyes at the thought of having to sit between these two men, who had taken on the characteristics of two bristling boars. In the hall, the Kennedys closed ranks, as any clan worth its salt did in times of trouble. The Kennedys of Cassillis and of Doon presented a solid flank to the Hamiltons.

No sooner were the servitors carrying in the first course of Mr. Burque's culinary efforts than a great uproar of shouting and brawling was heard outside. Archibald Campbell, Earl of Argyll, strode into the long room. The escort at his back, all Highlanders, looked savage as prehistoric men. Campbell was blue-jowled, hard as granite, and foul-mouthed. "Firkin' borderers!" He spat a gob of phlegm onto the flagstones. "I come in good faith tae sign the betrothal document, an' I find ma own Highland cattle that went astray last week. So the Hamiltons and the Kennedys are up each other's arses! Looks like a treasonable plot tae take ower the whole south!" His fierce eyes beneath his bushy brows challenged every last one seated on the dais table. When his eyes fell on Donal, he recalled his original mission. "Whoremonger! Ye ha' taken gross and filthy advantage of ma foolish daughter." He flung out his hand toward the entrance to the hall, and Tina and Donal both realized that Meggie must have accompanied her father. They arose in unison and hurried out to find her.

"Ye've foxed and duped, cheated and defrauded Argyll fer the first and last time!" he roared. "I'll seek damages fra' the crown, and if ma Meggie has a bairn in her belly, yer son will swing frae the turrets o' Doon!"

Meggan Campbell, covered with shame, shrank into a corner of the passageway outside the hall. Donal slipped a protective arm about her, and she buried her face against his powerful barrel-chest. "Dinna fash yersel, Meggie. I'll put things right. I'll tell the truth and confess all."

Tina swept him with a scornful glance. "This calls for more than the truth! This calls for a magnificent lie! This lot will swallow lies a hell of a lot faster than the truth."

Meggan was trembling, and Donal could not persuade her to come into the hall, so Tina said, "You go up to my chamber, Meggie. As soon as I can get away, I'll bring you some comfits from Mr. Burque's kitchen. Donal, stand beside me in the hall and back up whatever I say."

When the beautiful young woman stood in the center of the hall and raised her hands for silence, she drew every eye until finally the men left off their curses and threats while they drank in the flaming hair and proud breasts. "My lord earls, we have all been the victims of a ruthless freebooter. My brothers are too ashamed to acknowledge how easily they were gulled in my father's absence. You all know the name of the cattle thieves who've made merry hell in the borders for centuries. Their clan has made it their business to keep the rest of us at each other's throats —made it their business to keep the throne and the kingdom weak to their own advantage. No wonder all men shudder when they hear the name Douglas! 'Twas Black Ram Douglas sold us Campbell longhorns, Hamilton sheep and Cassillis horses, and provided us with bogus bills of sale. He knew Donal was needing to stock Castle Kennedy in Wigtown before he wed with Meggie Campbell."

Arran took up the denigration of the Douglas name, and inside five minutes every man in the vast dining hall took up the cry and was banging his tankard or his sword hilt on the table.

Donal felt the sore spot on the top of his head where Douglas had brought down his broadsword. Christ, women were natural-born mischief-makers! A simple man didn't stand a chance against a clever woman. He thanked God for his Meggie.

Before Tina left the hall, she was amazed that for once they were all in agreement. They would all go to the king in Edinburgh to lay the blame at the door of Douglas. Donal cast Tina a look of alarm. She shrugged one pretty shoulder and came to a quick decision. She wasn't going to be left behind to face Black Ram Douglas when next he came hotspur to Doon.

Every Kennedy servant would be occupied this night, plenishing chambers and serving food and drink. Only the earls and Meggan would be provided with rooms, of course. Their men would bed down wherever they could, either in the hall or in the outbuildings surrounding the bailey. The stables were so overfilled with horses that stableboys were working around the clock to shovel out the piles of manure. The men-at-arms were so toughened, especially those from the Highlands, that if there were no shelter, they simply dug themselves a hole in the ground, no matter the season.

In the kitchen Tina found Ada making up a tray for her mother. "Damn it, I've missed all the fun."

"God's nightgown, it was like a scene from the Hobs of Hell where they house all the lunatics," Tina said. "You warned me how coarse and uncouth men were. They are bad enough one at a time, but en masse they are unbearable, unreasonable, unruly, and unsavory. When Archibald Kennedy arrived, he made Father look refined. Then when Archibald Campbell crawled in, he made the others look like gentlemen!"

Ada laughed. "When I've taken this up to your mother, I'm going to leave her in Beth and Kirsty's capable hands and slip down to the hall for a bit of fun."

Valentina shuddered. "Better you than me. I'll try to soothe Meggie Campbell. No wonder she wants to marry Donal. He must seem like a bloody prince after living with Argyll at Castle Gloom. Oh Ada, before I forget. I want you to talk Father into taking me to Edinburgh with him."

"And how in God's name am I to manage that?" Ada demanded.

Tina winked. "Oh, you'll think of a way, love."

The hour was extremely late when Rob Kennedy extricated himself from his unexpected guests and climbed the stairs. In the passageway outside his wife's chamber, he was pleased to encounter Ada. He undid the laces of her gown and fondled her lovely breasts as they came spilling out. "Lass, lass, I'm in sore need o' a real woman."

She slipped her arms about his neck and rubbed against his hardness. "Valentina wants you to take her to Edinburgh, instead of your wife."

He whispered, "Elizabeth will have a rapid recovery if she thinks she's goin' tae the queen's court."

Ada pressed against him. "I could come with Tina to do for her—and do for you," she promised.

"How will I manage it, Ada? Ye know what Elizabeth's like."

Ada laced up her gown and reached out to unlatch the door. "Order her to go, and leave the rest to me."

As Ada approached the bed to trim the candles, Elizabeth sighed and sat up. "Rob, how can you disturb me at such an hour?" she asked reproachfully.

"Ada's come tae pack fer ye. We leave fer Edinburgh at dawn."

Ada shot him a withering glance and said, "Lady Elizabeth is in need of peace and quiet after her terrible voyage."

"I need a woman's influence at court," he insisted.

"It's high time Valentina took on some of these responsibilities," Ada suggested.

"I'm traveling wi' Arran, Cassillis, and Archibald Campbell. It would no' be fittin' fer an unwed lass."

Elizabeth felt a relapse coming on at mention of the company she would be expected to keep.

"If I came along to look after Valentina, it would be quite proper," Ada said firmly.

"Yes, Rob. Valentina can go in my stead for once. It will give me a chance to spend time with Beth."

"I suppose I could manage," said Rob grudgingly. "Wheest, woman, ye always get yer ain road." He followed Ada outside the door and whispered, "Can I come up later?"

"You'll have to wait until Edinburgh," she said firmly, removing his hands from her breasts. "I promised Archibald Kennedy a bit of a romp. I'll mollify him over the horses he lost." She winked.

He slapped her across the bottom, sighing with regret. "So long as yer doin' this fer me—keep it in the clan, mind!" he admonished.

Ada blew him a kiss. He had nothing to worry about; even she would be hard pressed to tackle Archibald Campbell, Earl of Argyll.

Chapter 11

Ramsay Douglas received the king's messenger with resignation. At the beginning of the month, when he and his men came on leave, he should have reported to James, but once they arrived back in Douglas, the hunting had been excellent and lambing time was upon them—no small undertaking when you grazed ten thousand horned sheep. Too, other things had occupied him, the wild horses from the Highlands, the Gypsies, then the sport of the raids. Time was drawing close for the Border Wardens' Court, when the Scots who patrolled the marches met with their English counterparts and disputes were discussed and resolved.

The king must wish to advise him regarding this formal, seasonal meeting, he decided. He may even wish to attend. James Stewart was a king who ruled his country with a stern eye and a strong hand. The king's law prevailed everywhere, except in the wildest borders and the remote Highlands.

As Ram gave his servants orders to pack his finest clothes for court, he told Gavin to pass the word to the rest of the Douglases and to the moss-troopers. He walked down to the meadow taking note of the scent of broom and the golden gorse. It was a far cry from the filthy vennels of Edinburgh, yet he was ready for a change.

He was an adaptable man who fit easily into any background, squeezing the most life had to give from his days and his nights. A curse fell from his lips as he saw a solitary Ruffian cropping the thick clover. "Did ye have tae be such a savage brute she jumped the hedge tae get away from ye?" He mounted the stallion and searched for over an hour for the lovely mare with a sinking feeling inside him. He was truly disappointed that he had lost her, for already he had been picturing the exquisite colts the pair would have produced.

Edinburgh was only thirty-five miles as the crow flies, but the rugged Pentlands stood between Douglas and Auld Reekie, as the capital was called. Ram Douglas with his full complement of forty moss-troopers rode in their leathers, armed to the teeth. They met with no trouble on their journey since any who encountered them gave them a wide berth.

They watered their horses in the reed beds of a loch, startling its mallards and wild geese, and then in the distance they saw the long, smoky skyline of Edinburgh. The city was walled, and they entered through the archway called the West Bow. They clattered past St. Giles, where The Maiden was set up at the Market Cross. It was a delicate piece of machinery, to be sure, with its great knife counterbalanced by a heavy weight, designed to chop off heads. It always seemed to give his men a raging thirst, for they could never get beyond the alehouse on the corner.

Inside, one of the patrons unfortunately was wearing a bright blue and red plaid that looked suspiciously like the Hamilton tartan. Two Douglas moss-troopers picked him up bodily, tankard and all, and flung him into the cobbled high street. Ram allowed them an hour before he called,

"To me!" He showed no mercy for his man who had just lifted a barmaid's skirts and laid her across the table. If he hadn't been able to get himself a piece of mutton in an hour, it was his own fault.

As they stepped outside the alehouse onto the long, busy street that stretched uphill to Castle Rock, there seemed to be a preponderance of Hamilton moss-troopers. Ram frowned, then his brow cleared. The king must have summoned Patrick Hamilton and his other border lords. Ram eyed his men, trying to keep the wolf's grin from his face. "What do ye say, lads? Shall we cleanse the thoroughfare?"

A cheer went up followed by cries of "Way fer a Douglas! Make way fer a Douglas!" None hearing it could repress a shudder. It had been an ominous cry for three centuries. They fought and brawled their way to the very gates of Edinburgh Castle, surely the most bloodstained fortalice in the world. The Hamiltons gave almost as good as they got, so that by the time the high west gate, separating the castle from the city street, clanged shut behind the Douglases, there was not a moss-trooper of either clan who wasn't sporting a black eye, a bloody lip, or a busted hand. Needless to say, they were thoroughly enjoying their visit to the capital.

Bathed, shaved, and resplendent in skintight hose and velvet doublet, Ram Douglas joined the throng of ambassadors, diplomats, bishops, petitioners, and courtiers who daily sought audience with James Stewart. The king was handsome and athletic, though he was nearing forty. His dark auburn hair fell to his shoulders, and his hazel eyes, though warm and friendly, were exceedingly shrewd. He eschewed sitting upon his carved throne but preferred to mingle with his people, both here at court and outside in the streets of the city. He was much loved by his people. He could tend a sick man, apply a leech, play a practical joke, or couch a lance with his knights.

James spotted Ramsay Douglas immediately. His

swarthiness set him apart from other men. James did not acknowledge his presence immediately, however, so that he could observe his behavior when he came face to face with Patrick Hamilton. James was mildly surprised when the two borderers ignored each other; then his mouth tightened as he saw Hamilton's swollen nose and the raw gash on Douglas's cheekbone. Apparently this wasn't their first encounter here. He had overlooked their feud, excusing their incompatible personalities. He decided he would put up with it no longer. He understood them only too well. War rather than peace was their normal condition. It was right and proper to be a fighter for just causes, but in times of peace they became rogue animals.

He dismissed everyone from the reception room except for his two border lords, and still they ignored each other. James smoothed his down-curving moustache thoughtfully. "Let's sit down," he said, indicating padded chairs around a carved refectory table.

"I'll stand, sire," Douglas replied.

"Ye'll sit!" the king said with authority.

Ram sat with his back toward Patrick Hamilton.

"Wine?" offered James, serving them with his own hands.

Hamilton shook his head, refusing to drink with Douglas.

James exploded. "Goddamn it, I don't ask that ye love each other! Clan feuds are no' a way of life—they are an evil. An evil I intend tae eradicate!"

Neither of his lords was cowed, but they were warned. The king was noted for his quick bursts of temper that were soon over and served to clear the air. He never held a grudge. "Ye can vent yer spleen on the enemy, not each other. Ye are *both* indispensable tae me in the borders. The minute ye went on leave, a Scots warden was murdered by an English warden," he told Douglas.

"Who?" asked Ram, his dark brows drawing together.

"Kerr," said the king, "murdered by Heron of Ford."

Ram shook his head. "The Kerrs and Herons have lived within spitting distance for decades with only the border between them. They've always been mortal enemies—it was bound tae happen. I'll hunt Heron down, sire."

The king slammed his fist on the table, making the wine goblets dance. "Ye'll no' hunt him down. It is clearly a case for the Border Wardens' Court. Ye will attend and resolve this dispute."

"When I patrol the borders, sire, there is little trouble because I dispense justice, not mercy," Douglas said fiercely.

Patrick Hamilton spoke up. "Sire, when old Henry Tudor was King o' England, we could expect redress occasionally. That's all gone by the board now that the spoiled boy-king sits on the throne."

"Ye dinna need tae paint me a picture o' Tudor's shortcomings. I married his sister. They're like two peas from the same worm-eaten pod. Both are shallow, greedy, vain, immature, petulant, and demanding. These are their virtues."

Ramsay's mouth lifted in a rare smile.

Christ's holy wounds, thought James Stewart, if I sent Black Ram Douglas to Whitehall, he would serve as such a dire warning to that overblown bairn Henry VIII, he might even die of fright.

Patrick Hamilton opened his mouth to speak, but James held up his hand. "We'll take it to the Border Court first." He dismissed the subject and proceeded. "Tonight we will have music and pipers, and tomorrow night there is a play for entertainment. See that ye keep yer swords sheathed and yer men under control."

Ramsay gave his moss-troopers leave to go abroad in the city, knowing that if Hamilton's men were housed at Edinburgh Castle, it would be the only way to avoid brawls and knifings. For a moment he envied them their adventure into the notorious windy city. It was dark as pitch in that labyrinth of vennels, or narrow passageways between tall timbered houses. They stank of damp and piss, cats and rotted rubbish. If you set a foot wrong after a rain, it squelched in filth up to the ankle, yet the alehouses were filled with song, good food, and merry company; the brothels and gambling houses were colorful and filled with laughter and good sport.

Ram entered the banqueting hall at Edinburgh Castle. It was long, low and dark, with small slit windows set high in its rough-cast walls. Though the floor was flagged, it was uneven, and a deep runnel ran across it, intended as a urinal when it was built. So much smoke blew back down its chimneys, the ceiling had to be whitewashed between the beams every month. No expense had been spared to make it habitable. The walls were covered with Flanders tapestries, the floor with woven silk rugs from Damascus, the mantels with French velvet. The dining tables were laid with silver plates, cups and chalices, Venetian crystal bowls, and silver with ornate Celtic patterns. Dominating the room was a thirty-foot banner of the tressured Red Lion of Scotland on its field of gold.

Janet Kennedy appraised the swarthy Douglas, who wore black velvet, startlingly relieved by his crest, the Bleeding Heart of Douglas, embroidered in crimson. She stepped intimately close to him and touched her finger to the raw gash upon his cheek. She was amused that he did not flinch. "That's what comes of having saber-sharp cheekbones." His shoulders were so broad, they looked padded, yet she knew otherwise. She'd seen him naked once, swimming in the sea at Tantallon, which belonged to Archibald Douglas, Earl of Angus. She knew that his uncle preferred him to his own son and often lamented that the earldom would be passed to the wrong Douglas. She allowed herself the indulgence of imagining Ram naked. She could still remember the drops of salt water clinging to the dark pelt of his chest and groin. But it was something else about him that made her pulse accelerate and her breath catch in her throat. One glance told a woman he was dangerous. She'd never tame him if she tried for a hundred years. His pewter eyes made a woman feel she was inherently shallow and vain and that all her blandishing cajolery would get her a fuck and nothing more.

"Hello, Janet," he said, his eyes boldly dipping into her décolletage to stare at her scarlet-painted nipples.

The king, who adored beautiful women and had a particular weakness for redheads, came up behind Ram and said, "I thought I told ye tae keep yer sword sheathed." He then passed on to the dais table. For appearances he would dine with the queen, but after dinner he usually left the board to his heavy-drinking lords while he indulged vices more to his taste.

Janet laughed up at Ram. They knew each other quite well, since she had been Archibald Douglas's mistress for some years. She was indeed beautiful tonight, yet inexplicably it annoyed him that she reminded him of Valentina Kennedy.

"I've risen in the world since last we met," she said lightly.

"Indeed? Tae go from a Douglas tae a Stewart is a step down, in my opinion."

"Christ, you're still the most arrogant bastard in Scotland!"

He brought her fingers to his lips. "Yer silver tongue is no doubt what attracted a king." He bowed and passed on down the room. He turned the head of every woman in sight. He deliberately avoided the Countess of Surrey, who had come from England with Margaret Tudor. Lady Howard had six daughters at court, known as the queen's sluts of honor, and she was never without that speculative look of a huntress. He had no patience for a woman who was obtuse enough to think a Douglas might take an English woman to wife. The Kennedys might have lowered their standards and even the royal Stewarts, but Douglas blood was the finest in Scotland, and they'd never taint it.

He could not, however, avoid Queen Margaret. She

beckoned him the moment she spied his dark countenance. She had only four interests in the world: jewels, clothes, rich food, and sex—not necessarily in that order. She was in the market for lovers and no longer even paid lip-service to discretion since the king had made no secret of the fact that he would welcome a horning from any of his nobles kind enough to oblige.

Ramsay graciously accepted her invitation to partner her for dinner, and he caught the amused glance James bestowed upon him. She cast Douglas a babyish glance of helplessness so that he would pull out her chair. She spoke in a childish voice that might have been provocatively arousing in a young girl, but Margaret looked middle-aged and because she could not curb her appetite, her figure was dumpy. She spoke of fashion, rudely pointing to the clothes of various women in the banqueting hall. She rabbited on, exhausting both the subject and those close by who were forced to listen. When she was finished with a subject, there was no further contribution to be made or detail added.

Ram's eyes traveled about the hall, mentally noting the attractive women, most of whom had been mistress to the king at one time or another. Marion Boyd was the mother of the king's eldest illegimate son, Alexander. Isobel Stewart, the king's own cousin, had borne him a daughter he'd called Jean. He had other bastards—Catherine, James— and Ram remembered a dark-haired baby girl that James and his beloved Margaret Drummond had made together. Margaret Drummond had been the great love of James Stewart's life. It was even rumored they had secretly wed. She had been exceedingly beautiful with her black hair and creamy, flawless skin. Ram wondered cynically how long it would have lasted if the girl hadn't been poisoned. It had supposedly left the king brokenhearted, yet he had managed to console himself with the aid of endless courtesans like Janet Kennedy.

Suddenly, Ram became aware of a hand upon his knee.

It trailed up his thigh slowly in blatant invitation. He looked down at Margaret in disbelief. He was tempted to let her reach her goal and learn the unflattering truth that he remained flaccid and unaroused, but he found the invasion so distasteful, his hand closed about her fingers and firmly lifted her hand until it lay in her own lap. Margaret looked up at him with hurt bewilderment. He held her eyes with a scorching look of anger and pressed her hand to her woman's hot center. He deliberately used her own fingers to rub her until her eyes became dilated and glazed, her mouth slack with need. Once she was fully aroused, he swiftly let go of her hand and resumed eating. Thirty seconds later Margaret was on her feet, begging to be excused. She would have to finish what the wicked Douglas had begun.

Ram moved over to sit beside James, with whom he had much more in common. The king was intelligent, curious, high-spirited, warm-hearted, and generous. He could discuss ships, trade, crafts, politics, or alchemy. His latest passion was building up a creditable fleet in the royal shipyards along the River Clyde.

"Ram, I wanted to talk to ye about mounting cannon on your mercantile vessels to convert them to warships."

"My ships are already armed, sire."

The king raised his eyebrows. "Without my authority?"

Ram shrugged. "I've letters of marque against the Portuguese. My ships must be able tae defend themselves when I take my wool tae Flanders. I've ten thousand sheep, ye ken."

"So it is feasible tae convert mercantile ships? Over two-thirds of Scotland's vessels are the property of my subjects. We keep England, France, Flanders, and the Low Countries supplied with fish, wool, and hides. How many ships do ye have?" asked the king.

"I have only three vessels, sire. I could use more. One is here at Leith, the other two are anchored where the River Dee empties into Solway Firth."

"Castle Douglas is on the Dee. Can ye sail clean up tae the castle?"

"Only with the smallest ship, sire, but we get close enough," Ram said. "Angus has ships, of course."

"Do his vessels bristle wi' cannon?" James challenged.

"Ye'd best ask Angus."

"By the Power, yer a canny bastard," James said with a grin. Though technically the king's authority was the highest in the land, if there was a power behind the throne, it was Archibald Douglas, Earl of Angus. If ever James was absent or disposed, Angus was acting Regent of Scotland, but where the king was loved, Angus was feared. "I expect sometime tomorrow he'll be returning from Stirling," James said, and was amused at the look that came into Ram's face. "Ye chafe under Archibald's authority." James laughed. "I didn't think there was a man breathed who put fear into ye."

Ram grimaced. "I don't fear him—I fear myself and the injury I may do the bloody dictator one day."

The king shook his head with forbearance. "Douglas men are all savages, yet I know that Archibald loves ye above every other Douglas, and only wants what's best for ye."

"Or what's best for him—not always one and the same thing, sire," Ram pointed out. Though they were discussing the iron-fisted authority of the Earl of Angus, Ram did not make the fatal mistake of underestimating the king. There were times when he was easygoing and intimately friendly, but his word was law, and he would assert his authority if it meant hanging every last one of his hardened Scots lords.

The next day brought not only Archibald Douglas and his son, the Master of Douglas, with two hundred men at their back, but a veritable horde of disgruntled nobles, each vexed and querulous and all clashing one with another. The king received them en masse, saw his error immediately and brought the audience to a close, banishing them to the bowels of Edinburgh Castle until they could be summoned one at a time in strict pecking order.

This was enough to make them sink their teeth further into each other's throats. When James summoned his admiral, James Hamilton, Earl of Arran, first, it immediately plunged Archibald Campbell, Earl of Argyll, into a black temper. He raged that though Arran was in charge of Scotland's navy, that merely amounted to one new flagship and a ragtag of dubious floating arks.

The king asked Arran about the seaworthiness of his new flagship, the *Great Michael*, then went on to tell him he intended to keep the shipyards busy building vessels from now on. The admiral eyed him, wondering if Rob Kennedy had been before him with his tale of the English attacking his ship. He kept his mouth shut about the incident and instead launched into a complaint about his cattle being raided. James raised his eyebrows and assured him he'd get back to him when he got to the bottom of it.

When Archibald Campbell rolled into the presence chamber, James knew better than to expect a courtier. Only a trained ear could understand his thick Highland burr, and when he spat on the velvet carpet, James forced himself to remember the invaluable service this powerful earl had recently rendered in destroying the rebellious MacDonald, who had declared himself Lord of the Isles and become a traitorous law unto himself.

"I'm no' best pleased yon whoreson Arran takes precedence o'er me in yer favor, Jamie!"

"No such thing, Archibald. You are invaluable to me. Are you not Master of the Royal Household?"

"A tinpot empty title, Jamie, when stacked against Lord High Admiral," he said bluntly, and spat again.

James sighed. Argyll was a canny old bastard; land greedy to boot. The king's other nobles feared Argyll's growing might, feared that before he was finished, he'd have the whole of the western Highlands under his thumb. Still, it was the only way to keep rebellion down, so James knew he must keep Archibald Campbell loyal. "Governor," James said. "Governor General of the Northwest. I think that would be in order."

The old chief grunted with satisfaction, was about to spit, saw the king's forbidding eye upon him, and changed his mind. "Governor general," he beamed. "Now that's summat like a royal post," he said with satisfaction.

"Now then, Archibald, what's this complaint you've brought me?"

"Firkin' Kennedys raided ma prize longhorns! Yer permission tae hang the bastards frae their ain trees?"

The king wasn't amused. "I thought your daughter was betrothed to Donal Kennedy. I'm in favor of such a marriage bond."

"The governor general's daughter wed tae a bloody Kennedy?" he asked in outrage.

The king tried to hold his patience and failed. "It's gone straight to your bloody head, Archibald. I can have it off you in a minute!"

"Ma haid or ma new office?" asked Argyll, in a heavy attempt at humor.

"Christ, not only do I have Kennedys and Hamiltons at each other's throats, now I have Kennedys and Campbells! Settle yer differences, man! Ye'll sign a bond of marriage and a bond of friendship. And ye'll do it before ye leave."

Argyll eyed Jamie, saw he was adamant and would brook no refusal, so he immediately acquiesced. "When the daughter of Argyll weds, it should be in the capital. The Highlands are too far off fer Scotland's nobility," said the canny Scot.

James shook his head at Archibald Campbell's audacity. "Stirling," said the king. "They can be wed in the chapel royal. I think even ye will agree it is a signal honor fer the Royal House of Stewart to offer the hospitality of Stirling." James looked at Argyll fastidiously. "Have ye no other attire save sheepskins?"

Argyll drew himself up with pride. "That I ha', Jamie. It shall be bearskins the nicht!"

James Stewart rolled his eyes heavenward, not really expecting help from that quarter, and gave audience to the next noble.

Archibald Kennedy, Earl of Cassillis, heaped every crime in the book upon the shoulders of the Hamiltons and the Campbells, then started afresh upon Clan Douglas.

"Christ Almighty!" swore the King. "Now ye're dragging another clan into it! Wild accusations are useless, Archibald. I need proof."

"Yer Grace, the Barbary that was meant fer ye was ridden tae Edinburgh by ma niece, Lady Valentina Kennedy. Black Ram Douglas sold it tae her and forged a legal bill o' sale. I'll show ye the horse, sire—it's in yer ain stables."

The king's eyes narrowed. "Make no mistake, Cassillis— I shall countenance no clan feuds. If I investigate the matter of raiding and find any of you involved, I'll hang the lot of you." Cattle reiving, then demanding mail for the beasts' return, had been a way of life until he had clamped down on it with an iron hand and added robbery to murder, arson, and rape—the criminal offenses that were pleas to the crown and judged by the king. "Ye can send in Rob Kennedy," the king said wearily.

James was thunderstruck when he heard Robert's tale of attack on the high seas. While his bloody earls were savaging each other, the English had committed what amounted to an act of war. "Too bad I didn't have the good sense to fetch ye in first, Rob. My governor general and my admiral are haggling over sheep and cattle while Scotland's ships are being attacked and destroyed. When my borders and my ships are attacked by the enemy, I need unity in the realm, but unity is abhorred by all!" He crashed his fist upon the black walnut table, making the inkwell and sandcaster dance about. Men often said the king was gifted with the second sight, and he often wondered himself if it were not so. For a long time now he had known an inner urgency to build warships and amass a navy. He had built the *Lion,* the *Margaret,* and the *Michael* with seasoned oak from Fyfe, but he had the feeling now that he would need many more vessels and men with experience to sail them.

"Thank you, Rob, for coming to me directly with this news. Nothing good ever came out of England." James thought of his dumpy wife the moment the words were out of his mouth, and inevitably Rob Kennedy thought of his. "I hear that Lady Valentina accompanied ye. I shall be delighted tae make her acquaintance."

"Thank ye, Yer Grace," replied Rob, wishing he had left her at home where James's roving eye could not fall upon her. Then James smiled and added, "Janet will be delighted tae have her kinswoman here for a visit." The king looked appreciatively at Rob. "The Kennedy women are said tae be the most beauteous in the land with hair like fire."

"Oh aye, my Tina's a firebrand, sire."

"We are tae be entertained by a play tonight. I hope ye and yer daughter will join us."

Chapter 12

The firebrand was almost without breath at the moment as Ada pulled mercilessly upon the strings of her corset. Although they had been at court less than a full day, both women were aware of the contrast between Tina's gowns and the costumes displayed by the courtiers.

Men's doublets were now wide at the shoulders with

padding, the sleeves slashed with silken undershirts plucked through the vents. The women's gowns were quilted and embroidered, and the queen's were decorated by dangling jewel egrets. Bodices were so low in the front, they were shocking, and so high in the back, they were wired so that the high collars were like frames for the face.

The fashion that Valentina had immediately fallen in love with and that Ada had already copied for her was a frilled and pleated creation worn under the chin like a small plate and called a ruff. Ada's needle had lowered the neckline on Tina's most vivid gown, an emerald green velvet, and when she fastened the snow-white ruff and brushed out her silken mass of flaming copper hair, she hoped she would not look too gauche.

Tina shared a chamber with Meggan Campbell, and when the two girls entered Edinburgh Castle's long, dim banqueting hall, they were vastly relieved to see Donal Kennedy and Patrick Hamilton walk a direct path to claim them. Meggan clutched Donal's hand almost desperately, and the couple sought a quiet corner where they could talk.

Tina smiled up at Patrick with genuine pleasure. "I'd no idea you were in Edinburgh."

"Nor I you," he said, his eyes telling her how lovely he found her, his brain giving thanks that his nose was no longer swollen.

Tina placed her hand upon his arm and bent toward him confidentially. "Your father descended upon Doon accusing us of cattle rustling, and then my father accused yours of not keeping the seas safe. It was like a circus, especially when the clowns arrived. The upshot was our families rushed to the king to lay their complaints and have him settle the disputes. I was afraid we'd never be allowed to see each other again."

He covered her hand and squeezed it. "Sweet, I think I would die without ye."

She withdrew her hand and slapped him playfully. "Flatterer!" Suddenly she felt nervous. The hall seemed to be filled with Douglas men, easily identified by their dark dress tartan and their Bleeding Heart crests. Two of the dark-visaged fellows were openly staring at her now, and she felt her cheeks suffuse as Patrick said curtly, "Keep yer eyes tae yerselves!"

She whispered, "The ugly fellows seem to be everywhere."

Patrick told her, "The earl rode in today—afraid tae move without two hundred at his back."

Her eyes danced, but she whispered a warning: "For God's sake, Patrick, have a care for your tongue. The Earl of Angus is all-powerful and ruthless."

"I'm no' afraid of Archibald Douglas," he said with reckless bravado.

Tina shuddered. "The name Archibald turns men into monsters."

"Where's Meggan?" demanded a rough voice. The piercing eyes of Argyll bored into her so that she did not dare to lie. "She's with my brother, my lord earl," Tina managed.

To her vast relief he grunted and replied, "That's good. I dinna want her flauntin' hersel aboot the hall until she's raped." The narrow morals he set for his daughter in no way applied to himself. He leered down the front of Tina Kennedy's gown and in a coarse whisper that carried said, "Yer bonnie enough tae make an auld man scorch." Then he thumped Hamilton on the back. "Careful ye dinna receive a hornin'!"

Tina's cheeks flamed, and Patrick flushed. "Old lecher! No lady is safe from his coarse tongue."

"See what I mean about the name Archibald? Meggie Campbell is incapable of flaunting herself." Her eyes lit with amusement again. "While I . . ." She let her words trail away, and Patrick finished her sentence. "While ye attract every man from sixteen to sixty. Damn, the hall is crowded tonight. As soon as the meat is ready, there will be such an undignified rush for seats, I think I'd best go and secure ours, or we'll find ourselves below the salt."

"That would never do for the admiral's son." She laughed.

"Nor his betrothed," he murmured low.

Her eyebrows rose at his presumption, but she was far from displeased that he was beginning to commit to a serious relationship. Suddenly she stiffened as a pair of very possessive hands squeezed her waist and a beautifully modulated voice said from behind, "Honey love, slip away before the play is done, and I'll join you in bed as soon as I can get away."

With an angry retort upon her lips she swung about and looked into the face of an extremely handsome man with dark auburn hair and beard. The king's hazel eyes widened as he realized the lady was not his mistress, Janet Kennedy. "I beg yer pardon, my lady. I mistook ye for another."

At that moment the other radiant redhead appeared at his elbow, and the women's resemblance was so marked that they all laughed and knew each other's identities immediately.

"You could only be Lady Valentina Kennedy," the king said, kissing her hand.

"And you could only be the king." She curtsied gracefully and with mock innocence asked, "Your Grace, does that mean your invitation is withdrawn?"

His hazel eyes held warm admiration mixed with the secret amusement they alone shared. "Nay, it is an open invitation that will stand through the years." James introduced her to Janet, who was thicker than Tina through the middle, but no man's eyes would ever notice with her nipples deliciously exposed and painted red like two ripe cherries. James excused himself to join the queen on the dais and murmured to Janet, "Later."

A pair of pewter eyes across the room had watched as the king laid familiar hands upon Valentina Kennedy. It merely confirmed what he had always known—that Ken-

nedy women were whores, he thought with contempt. As
the tall, slim figure of Patrick Hamilton claimed Tina Kennedy, Ram Douglas felt pity for his enemy. He'd be wearing horns before he was even a bridegroom. He had no
idea he was the third man to think of a horning within
minutes of glancing at the honeypot.

Janet joined her Kennedy cousin and Patrick Hamilton,
surprised that coarse Rob Kennedy had bred such a dazzling creature. She remarked upon it: "The contrast between the men and women of Clan Kennedy never ceases
to amaze me."

Tina's eyes swept over her brother Donal's barrel-chest
and sparse carroty hair, then they passed over her father's
coarse, ruddy person and on to the Kennedy chief, Archibald, Earl of Cassillis. She repressed a shudder and smiled
at Janet's radiant beauty.

Janet said, "I remember your aunt Damaris at her wedding. I was only a young girl at the time, but I was quite
overcome with envy for her delicate beauty and for that
sinfully handsome Alex Douglas."

Both women thought of Damaris's death, and Janet, on
a sigh, said softly, "He was a man to die for."

Tina almost said something about the degenerate Douglas men, then bethought herself that Janet had been mistress to the Douglas chief and shuddered instead.

Patrick put an arm about her shoulders. "Surely yer not
cold in this crowd?"

She arched her brows at his familiar hand, and he removed it with a murmured apology. He knew better than
to treat her like one of the easy ladies of the court.

Janet and Tina had instantly decided there would be no
rivalry between them. They were fast friends upon the
briefest acquaintance, and Tina spoke quite intimately with
Janet, who filled her in regarding half the people at court.

"Is it true that the king wears an iron belt of remorse
because he feels guilt over his father's death?" Tina asked.

Janet's lips tightened momentarily. " 'Tis true, though I

rail against the obscene thing. 'Tis so heavy, it would cripple any other man." She leaned closer. "I do talk him out of wearing it to bed since I've been with him. Hell's teeth, 'tis penance enough to have to live in Edinburgh Castle and be wed to Margaret Tudor!"

After the meal, while the court remained seated at table, the play began. Valentina was caught up with the novelty of it all, when suddenly the gnarled Argyll, resplendent in his black bearskin, confused the actors with reality and joined the argument and the swordfighting. The king and the more sophisticated of his courtiers were helpless with laughter until it became apparent that Argyll was going to dispatch the actors with his mighty swordarm.

The Earl of Angus directed his son, young Archibald Douglas, to get Argyll under control and explain matters to him, a formidable task that the faint at heart would not attempt. Douglas did a creditable job of controlling Argyll, and the assembly applauded him with many a ribald comment about Lord Bleary.

Janet said, "There is something splendid about Douglas men." She was not looking at the young Master of Angus, however, but at his powerful father, the highest earl in the land. Valentina could see she was still half in love with him.

Janet sighed and arose. "It is time for me to withdraw, I think. I shall look forward to seeing you tomorrow. Perhaps we could ride together."

As the tables were cleared away for dancing, Patrick Hamilton presented Tina to the queen. Though her face and figure were heavy and plain, her gown was not. It was black velvet, embroidered all over with white silken Tudor roses whose centers were diamonds, pearls, and rubies. As Tina went down before her, Queen Margaret looked her over, saw no array of jewels, and decided she was no rival. She chose to overlook the fact that the girl's face and hair were adornment more radiant than any jewels.

"Lady Valentina, how sweet of you to honor me by wearing my green and white Tudor colors."

Tina had not been aware of it until the queen pointed it out. The queen continued, "Your dear mother is English, of course. That is why you have such pretty manners and a cultured voice. This is Nan Howard," said the queen, introducing her lady-in-waiting. Beside the queen's sallowness, the Howard girl looked like a flower from an English rose garden. She was all lovely round curves with golden hair and blue eyes, yet the look she cast Tina was most unlovely. It was sullen, in fact, which was puzzling until Valentina saw her glance at Patrick Hamilton with accusation in her eyes.

Tina was almost amused. She negligently shrugged one pretty shoulder before she turned away from the girl to be introduced to her father. Lord Howard, Earl of Surrey, was acting as ambassador to Scotland at the moment. He was a close confidant of the queen and acted as secret liaison between Margaret Tudor and her brother Henry, the new all-powerful king of England. Howard's daughters had inherited his blond hair and fine English skin, which gave him a youthful appearance, belying his almost fifty years.

Howard raised Valentina's fingers to his lips and made her an elegant leg. Though dressed in the height of fashion, his clothes were in impeccable taste. The contrast between Howard and the Scots nobles clearly showed he was from a more civilized culture. He was no fop, however. He had a military bearing and had commanded forces for the old Tudor king when he was alive. "Lady Valentina, may I tell you that you are more breathtaking than your mother? In my youth I spent time in Carlisle, and I admit freely that Elizabeth broke my heart when she married Robert Kennedy."

Tina rewarded him with a smile, thinking how nice it would be to have a father with such polished manners.

"Will you save me a dance, my lady? I intend to give these younger men a run for their money."

Farther down the hall, Ramsay Douglas praised his cousin Archibald in front of his father, the Earl of Angus, in hope of raising his uncle's opinion of his own son. "That took both courage and diplomacy," Ram said.

The rash Master of Douglas replied, "It felt good tae ha' control of Argyll, even if only fer a few minutes."

Ram made no comment but thought it showed a lack of self-control to display his lust for power quite so openly. Still, his father was so dominant, it was hard to get out from under his shadow. Though aging, Angus still ruled the whole Douglas clan, not just his son, with an iron fist. Ram smiled wryly. At least a dozen women had their eyes upon them as they stood talking, and he knew that if he spurned their offers, they would gladly settle for the powerful Earl of Angus, despite his age.

As the music started for the dancing, Ram said low to his cousin, "Here comes the queen. I would rather avoid her advances."

"What do ye mean, man?" asked young Archie.

Ram cast him a cynically amused glance. "She seems tae have developed a craving for Douglas flesh." Ram saw raw speculation come into his cousin's eyes.

"By God, I'll ha' at her!" he said aggressively, and Ram suppressed a shudder, thinking it would take a great deal of either fortitude or ambition to ride that gray mare. He was cynical enough to wonder if his cousin acted on orders from his father; then his cynicism went one step further, and he wondered if Angus had pushed Janet into the king's bed for his own devious purpose.

Patrick Hamilton led Valentina Kennedy onto the floor for the slow and sensual pavane. She concentrated on the gliding steps, carefully keeping pace with Patrick, who had obviously danced at court before. There were many elegantly gowned ladies dancing, and Tina did not wish to appear unsophisticated before that polished assembly.

As the slow measure advanced, she gained confidence and began to enjoy the music. Everyone changed partners as the men circled one way and the ladies the other. Valentina was shocked to find herself face to face with Black

Ram Douglas. His pewter eyes went insolently up and down her person, as if he were measuring her with his own personal yardstick and found her lacking in every way.

Here was a very different Ramsay Douglas from the uncouth wretch in thigh boots and leathers. He wore a jeweled codpiece, begod! It drew her eyes, then she could have died when she felt herself blushing. Suddenly all her fine confidence dissolved. She felt young and awkward and very countrified. He was so damned elegant, so arrogant and utterly sure of himself. She remembered with deep humiliation how he had straddled her in the grass, and suddenly she could not bear the thought of his hands touching her again. She gathered all her courage, lifted first an elegant bare shoulder, then her chin, then deliberately walked off the dance floor.

Hotspur's jaw clenched like a lump of iron at the insult. All Douglas males were blood-proud, but this particular Douglas was nine-tenths pride. He knew a murderous urge to pursue her, to put his hands about that slender neck below the pretty ruff and snap it. His rage blinded him to the open invitation of other women, and he left the hall and went alone to his bed that night.

Patrick Hamilton saw Valentina depart and hurried after her. He caught up with her outside in the chilly night air. "Tina, are ye feeling unwell?"

"I needed fresh air," she temporized.

"The smoke from the candles is enough tae choke a strong man, but there's a cold wind off the North Sea tonight." He moved close to slip a warming arm about her shoulders.

"Patrick, I walked off the dance floor because my next partner was to be Ramsay Douglas."

She felt his hands tighten into fists, and he demanded, "He hasn't made advances toward ye, has he?"

"No, no. We cannot tolerate each other." She shivered. He drew her against his body. "Let me warm ye," he said thickly. Her scent stole to him, and the wind blew a tress of her hair against his cheek, arousing him instantly. His lips sought hers, and as their mouths fused, he lengthened and hardened with a dizzying need. "Tina, Tina, come tae my chamber. . . . We can be snug up there."

She pulled away from him. "Patrick, you know I cannot."

His raging desire made him ignore her refusal. He pressed her urgently. "We'll soon be betrothed—let me love ye, Tina?" His insistent lips came down upon hers again, and his hands pulled her hips against his hard sex.

Valentina knew she must leave him before he lost control. She was not ready for this yet. The court might be amoral, but she was not. "Patrick, let me go! We both know what would happen if I came to your chamber."

Christ, he could see her in his bed, feel her beneath his hard body. Talking about what would happen sent the blood beating in his temples and his cock. She pried his hands from her hips and said, "In the morning I would hate myself, and I would hate you too. I must find Meggie Campbell and go up now."

Patrick groaned. Donal Kennedy was likely fucking Meggie Campbell's brains out at this moment, but of course he couldn't say such a thing to Lady Valentina. He had to let her go back inside alone because it would be a few minutes before he could even walk.

Nan Howard saw Valentina Kennedy return to the hall without Patrick Hamilton. She took hold of her sister Kat's hand and went outside to look for him. She didn't have to go far before she saw his tall, slim figure in the shadows. She went forward to him, while Kat hovered behind her. She was shorter, plumper than Tina, but oh so much more willing. "Patrick," she said in her little girl voice, "have you been avoiding me?"

"Of course not," he said huskily. "Dancing bores me."

She giggled prettily. "Kat and I are bored too. Why don't we join you? I'm sure you can think of something to amuse us, Patrick." She took both his hands in hers, and he raised first one and then the other to his lips and suggestively traced his tongue across her palms. He heard the quick intake of her breath that told him he had aroused her. He was most familiar with Nan Howard's sensuality and imagined her naked, her soft pink flesh and blond curls spread invitingly for him.

He cleared his throat and wondered how they could rid themselves of Kat. He said low, "The game I have in mind is best played by two."

"Patrick, any game that two can play can be even more fun with three players, unless of course you are monkish by nature."

Hamilton's eyes widened in surprise. Christ, he knew the Howard daughters were exceeding sportive, but if he wasn't mistaken, they were both asking for a taste of his prick, and in the state Tina Kennedy had left him, he was ready for them. "I just happen tae have a small cask of aqua vitae in my chamber that cries out to be tasted," he invited with a wink.

The rooms in Edinburgh Castle were cheerless to say the least, but this night, in Patrick Hamilton's bed, the trio couldn't have been more cozy. The three of them rolled about as the girls playfully disrobed their willing victim. Patrick's lust was such that he took Nan almost immediately, without preliminaries. When Kat saw how willing and able he was to perform, she pressed her nakedness to his humping back, crying, "Don't be greedy, Nan! Save some for me."

As Patrick lay sprawled between them to catch his breath, they plied him with drink. He assessed Kat with heavy-lidded eyes. Her hair was a darker gold than her sister's, and her belly wasn't nearly so rounded. He decided he hadn't had such a fine piece in months.

Kat dipped her finger into the alcohol flavored with caraway and painted the head of Patrick's cock. As it started to rise again, she dipped her head between his legs and licked him, giggling, "Now I know why they call it liquor."

He groaned. Christ, was he dreaming, or had he died and gone to Heaven? "My angels." He sighed softly, closing his eyes.

The two sisters exchanged meaningful looks across the bared body of the Earl of Arran's heir.

The moment Tina returned to the hall she was claimed by Lord Howard. She gave a little sigh of relief knowing she would be perfectly safe in his hands and allowed him to lead her off for a dance. At first she thought she was imagining it, but as his hands became more and more playful, she knew it was not her imagination.

He held her much too close as his hand caressed her bottom. Tina was loath to make another scene, so she said pointedly, "There is Lady Howard. You must have the next dance with your wife."

He chuckled. "My wife gives all her attention to the younger men, hoping to lure husbands for our six daughters. Younger men, however, do not have the skill and experience of a mature man." He bent toward her ear. "We make much better lovers."

Howard was hot for the beautiful young redhead. He thought to follow the king and take a Kennedy lass for his mistress.

Tina's steps faltered. "My Lord Howard, I promised to look after Meggie Campbell. I really must go."

He looked down at her with a most understanding and indulgent smile. "What a fool I am. You are reluctant because you are still a little virgin, aren't you?"

Tina was shocked enough to blurt, "Yes, I am!"

He gave her a quick kiss upon the lips and whispered, "I'll let you go this time. But when you have lost your little cherry, come back to your uncle Howard and let him teach you all the refinements."

This time Tina ran from the hall. There wasn't a man who lived and breathed who wasn't ruled by his prick! Apparently Englishmen were as lecherous as Scots.

* * *

The next morning, Valentina, thinking there was safety in numbers, joined a merry group who ·decided to ride abroad. They wouldn't have much of a gallop in the grounds atop Castle Rock, but fresh air and exercise would be welcome after the dark chambers inside the ancient fortalice.

The king joined Tina and Janet Kennedy inside the long stables and insisted upon saddling the ladies' horses himself. He ran an appreciative hand over Tina's damson-colored Barbary. "She's a rare beauty," he enthused. James had as keen an eye for a filly as he had for a woman.

"Thank you, sire." Tina beamed.

He lifted her into the sidesaddle with his own hands, and Tina was quite breathless to be shown such gallantry by the king himself. He brought Janet's mare from its box-stall, and Tina, eyeing her cousin's fashionable riding clothes with envy, said, "My habit is sadly out of style."

Janet lifted the hem of Tina's cream riding skirt and tore open the small slit all the way up the seam so that Tina's lacy black stockings and garters showed daringly. "Voilà! Now you are up-to-the-minute."

Tina laughed down at her, knowing they were sisters under the skin. She raised her eyes as a tall figure approached. "There you are, Patrick. I feared you would stay abed all morning. His Highness had to saddle my mare for me."

Patrick flushed and murmured a profuse apology. Tina walked her Barbary out into the pale sunshine of the castle courtyard to give the men space to saddle up the other horses. She had not ridden thirty yards when she came face to face with Ramsay Douglas.

He stared in disbelief when he saw the mare upon which he had set his heart being ridden by the spoiled Kennedy bitch. A red mist of rage almost blinded him. He knew exactly how she had come to be in possession of his property. The fucking Gypsy had gone directly from the knife contest with him to steal his prize mare and bestow it upon his fancy piece. He snatched the bridle with a firm hand and ordered, "Dismount!"

The exotic filly's tail stood straight up, and she danced nervously sideways. Tina looked down into the murderous pewter eyes and raised her riding crop.

Ram's lips curved downward as he saw her intent, and he wrenched the crop from her fingers—but not before it had reopened the gash upon his cheekbone.

"Take your filthy hands off my Indigo, Hotspur!" she ordered icily.

"Your Indigo?" he repeated incredulously, his eyes raking her shamefully displayed legs and garters. "This horse is mine, stolen from me by your Gypsy lover!" He flung the riding crop from his hand and reached up to drag her from the saddle.

The riding crop hit Archibald Kennedy, Earl of Cassillis, across the chest, and he confronted Douglas with exploding rage. "Ye reiving borderer! I knew it was ye lifted ma horses, ye thievin' whoreson! I suspected ye from the first, and now here's the proof the king needed."

James Stewart, Janet Kennedy, and Patrick Hamilton emerged from the stables to overhear the quarrel. Valentina stood between the two men, who were ready to murder each other. When Ram Douglas pushed her aside, Patrick Hamilton sprang forward, drawing his rapier. Douglas swung around, instantly unsheathing his sword before he saw the king.

The Earl of Cassillis snatched up the bridle of the excited filly, which was now rolling her large eyes in a frenzied panic. "Yer Grace, here is the very special mare I intended as a gift before the thieving Douglas lifted her from under my nose."

James Stewart was furious at his brawling, uncivilized nobles. He glared at the savage Douglas and Hamilton until they sheathed their weapons. He refused to bandy words with them before the ladies—in fact, he did not trust himself to even speak with them at the moment. But deal with them he would. He took the lovely animal and gentled it with a firm hand and a soft voice. Then he stepped forward and placed the reins into Tina's hand. "Lady Valentina, please accept my gift to you. None other could grace the lovely creature as well as you, my dear." He turned to Janet. "Ladies, please take your ride. I have some pressing business."

The ladies hastily departed, and the king turned upon his heel and walked briskly back to the castle. The three remaining males stood in the courtyard, their blood high, screaming for release, yet impotent to do anything about it.

Within the hour Douglas and Hamilton were curtly told to gather their moss-troopers and depart for the Border Wardens' Court. Both knew they had earned their monarch's wrath and would need to do a creditable job when they met up with their English counterparts. They had not yet been punished for their raiding and knew it would hang over their heads until they returned from the Wardens' Court in a week or two.

That night Rob Kennedy sat up in bed enjoying the view. Ada removed the modest gray gown of a tiring woman to reveal her daring scarlet petticoat and corset. Rob's eyes kindled. "Come here, lass," he begged thickly. Ada came to the bedside, allowing him to unfasten her laces so that her voluptuous breasts spilled into his big hands. He groaned with pleasure as her dark brown hair fell across his barrel-chest, and she bent forward to give him a generous kiss.

Ada felt no guilt at the adultery. Elizabeth would have been devastated if she'd suspected, but Ada knew the sex act was a duty for her mistress, a duty that she avoided altogether these days.

Rob marveled at the differences of women. Ada was the same age as his wife, had never been pampered or indulged in her life as a servant, yet she was more exciting to a man in her plain gray gown than any courtesan. At his age he was no longer driven by lust, and his arousals happened only occasionally in a month's time, but Ada made him as horny as a rutting stag.

He couldn't get her out of her scarlet underclothes fast enough, but she playfully slapped his clumsy hands away, lest he tear the fabric in his haste, and finished undressing herself. She did it slowly, sensually, exposing a shoulder, a thigh, the curve of her back, so that by the time her breasts and bum cheeks were bared, he knew only that he had to have her beneath him while he plunged. He labored and groaned, his breath heaving, his face reddening alarmingly.

"Rob, are you all right, love?" she asked softly.

He grunted his delight, sweat breaking out across his brow and chest.

Her fingers brushed his temples, and she said softly, "Let me on top—you're going at it too hard."

He plunged a few more times, realized she was probably right, and rolled over onto his back. Ada clung to his great body so that she rolled with him, then lay still to allow him to catch his breath. Then she knelt above him and continued the plunging motion he'd begun. Ada built to orgasm quickly and allowed him to see and hear how much pleasure he was giving her. She was wise enough to realize how it thrilled the male to know he could give an aroused female deep satisfaction. Within a minute of her own writhing vocal climax, Rob Kennedy spilled himself profusely.

She rested in the curve of his arm, both of them grateful for what they had shared.

"Lass," he said hoarsely, "I wish we could stay fer a month, but it's no' to be."

"This is our last night?"

"Aye. I did ma duty by informin' James about the English attackin' ma ship, so there's no need tae tarry." He paused, then confided, "Cassillis practically ordered me home. The king's enraged over these clan feuds, and our

chief seems tae think our Tina inflames the men tae vio-
ence."

"I think it's best we go. The king has a weakness for
redheads, and in truth it does her reputation no good to be
in the company of Janet."

"Dear God, her mother would run mad if she knew,"
Rob said helplessly.

"Well, she won't know, so stop your worrying. Tina has
more good sense than to breathe the name Janet Kennedy
to her mother."

Rob pushed away thoughts of Elizabeth as he filled his
hands and his eyes with Ada's generous globes.

In the royal bed James Stewart breathed the name over
and over. He adored women in general and worshipped
this one in particular. "Janet, Janet," he crooned, en-
twining his fingers in the luxuriant red hair spread across
the satin embroidered pillows. Though he was forty, he
had the body of an athlete. He rode every day, as often as
he could—both horses and women. He had a preference
for red hair that was almost a fetish, an obsession. He
gazed at the burning bush at the apex of her thighs and
lowered his mouth to it reverently.

"James," she whispered, "I think I'm carrying your
child."

He lifted his head and gazed at her with joy. "Jan, that's
marvelous!" He loved all his children. "He'll be a little
redhead like the two of us." He kissed the round curve of
her belly reverently.

"Your hair is auburn, a far more beautiful shade than
mine," she protested.

"Not to me, sweet," he murmured against her flaming
mons, lost in her woman's scent.

She too was delighted at the prospect of the child. He
would keep her in luxury for the rest of her life, as he did
all the women who had borne him children. His council
didn't object to his mistresses and bastards—each new one

reconfirmed that he was not tainted by his father's depraved and degenerate homosexuality. Sodomy could not be stomached by the rough, masculine Scots.

Later, as they lay on the floor before the fire, where their last bout of coupling had landed them, James absently stroked her hair.

"What's troubling you?" she questioned as she fingered his roughened skin made by his chain of remorse. No body hair grew in a wide circle about his middle.

"The English," he replied. "Nay, if I'm truthful, it's my Scots . . . Clan feuds . . . only if we are united and stand together can we keep England at bay. The clans have been at their favorite pastime, cattle raiding, again."

"The Campbells and the Hamiltons?" she asked.

He nodded and bit her ear playfully, "And you damned Kennedys are as bad as any, if not worse."

"Ha! What about Douglas?" she demanded.

The king shook his head. "Young Hotspur would raid just for the pleasure of harassing the bloody Hamiltons. Not bad enough we have a running feud between Hamilton and Douglas—feuds have almost erupted between Campbell, Kennedy, and Douglas. I told Campbell tae get his daughter wed tae Donal Kennedy as soon as may be and ordered him tae sign a bond of friendship. I agreed tae have the wedding at Stirling."

"Why not a marriage bond between my cousin Rob's daughter and Douglas?" Janet asked.

"It wouldn't be the first marriage between Clan Kennedy and Clan Douglas," he said, remembering.

"It shouldn't have gone wrong. It was a good match," Janet said.

"It was a perfect match," James agreed. "Both their great-grandfathers married daughters of King Robert III. Damn, I'd love tae see an alliance between Kennedy and Douglas. I'd also like a bond between Hamilton and Douglas, but both houses have only sons."

"I have the solution! Rob Kennedy has two daughters.

Marry one to Hamilton, the other to Douglas, then they'll all be united. Order them to do it, and order them all to sign a bond of friendship."

The king smiled. "Ah Jan, ye make it sound so simple. Order this and order that. Black Ram Douglas wouldn't be best pleased tae be ordered tae take a wife."

"He's past thirty, it's time he had an heir!" she pointed out.

"Over time," chuckled James. "He's one of my finest young warriors, Jan. I'm counting on him tae use his vessels tae harry the English if their ships keep up their piracy. I dinna want him pissed off at me for ordering him tae wed."

She moved sensuously against him and lifted her mouth to his. "Sire, you are not nearly devious enough." His shaft raised its head and stretched itself like an animal awakening from a nap. "Call in your earls and tell them to put an end to the feuds, or you'll be forced to hang a few of your lords. Cassillis will soon give Rob Kennedy his orders. I admit you might have to bang your fist on the table to make Angus know you mean business, but I don't think even Ramsay Douglas would dare defy his chief."

She was right, James admitted. To say Archibald Douglas was frighteningly arrogant was an understatement—he was insufferable. As the king covered Janet's silken body, he wondered once again why Angus had allowed this delectable woman to slip through his fingers.

Chapter 13

James Stewart decided this time that there was safety in numbers. He summoned three of his earls —Cassillis, Arran, and Angus—to a private meeting and assumed a cold, implacable attitude.

Though the Hamilton and Douglas clans were sworn enemies, Arran and Angus never let it interfere with their civility toward each other. As chiefs, they were above petty feuds and left the quarreling to their clans.

The king looked at each in turn and finally said with a note of contempt, "Are ye growing too old tae control yer clans?"

They were on the defensive immediately—exactly where he wanted them. He proceeded with a blistering denunciation upon their abilities to put an end to the raids. "I want ye, nay I *demand* that ye eradicate these raids! They are an evil to which you turn a blind eye, but I'm warning ye for the last time, I will no longer tolerate fighting, burning, and taking booty among ourselves."

James Hamilton, Earl of Arran, tried to point out that there would be feuds as long as two Scots remained alive in the realm, but the king crashed his fist down upon the oak table. "Silence! Must I need spell out chapter and verse the various means at yer disposal?" His voice was raised in anger, which was unusual for the even-tempered monarch. "Bonds must be signed. Then if the bonds are broken, hanging is justified!"

Cassillis swallowed hard, for he knew damned well his Kennedys had been raiding. Arran too felt his neck—not only had his Hamiltons likely been lifting cattle, the king knew they'd been brawling with the Douglas up and down the Cannongate. On top of that, as admiral, he had to take the censure for allowing English ships to harry Scots vessels.

Only Archibald Douglas, Earl of Angus, remained undaunted. He was a borderer, and a good borderer believed that the goods of all men in time of necessity were by the law of nature common. The king had a goal in mind, but he had yet to reveal what he wished to accomplish with this passionate harangue. Angus veiled his shrewd eyes and waited.

The king turned to Archibald Kennedy. "Cassillis, you are the pivotal means tae an end of these hostilities. Blood bonds are the best means of forging together rebellious clans tae preserve the peace. I've already spoken tae Argyll. I want ye tae see that Donal Kennedy weds the Campbell girl immediately. Now Cassillis, ye've two nieces. I want one tae go tae Arran and one tae Douglas."

The Earl of Arran knew his son Patrick was ready to declare for Lady Valentina Kennedy, so he bowed his head in acquiescence. Angus, however, knew Hotspur Douglas would welcome marriage as heartily as the hangman's noose. He opened his mouth to protest, but James said smoothly, "Angus, you know how a bond of marriage cements good relations. Since yer son married Bothwell's lass, there's been peace between yer clans where once there was nothing but hostility."

Archibald Douglas's mouth turned down at the corners. The Hepburn wench enjoyed indifferent health and had yet to produce an heir. He almost told the king to forget wedding plans for Ram Douglas, then bethought how the clan was in need of heirs to carry on the bloodline. "We'd no' do well tae keep the best blood in Scotland bottled up when there's so many could do wi' a drop," Douglas said with a contemptuous look at the others.

The king stood up, and they knew the audience was over. "See to it," he added in conclusion.

As Cassillis and Arran departed, James said, "Angus, a word."

Archibald paused, wondering shrewdly what else James was after.

The king possessed great shrewdness too, however. "I assume all yer vessels are armed with cannon?"

Douglas nodded in a guarded fashion.

The king continued, "If it becomes necessary, I want ye tae put them at Ramsay's disposal. I know he's not above a bit of pirating."

"Sire, Arran's yer bloody admiral," Douglas pointed out.

James rolled his eyes. "I know, man. Is it any wonder I need the help of Douglas?" James let out an inaudible sigh. At last he had won him over.

Ramsay Douglas and his hardened moss-troopers usually wore scuffed leathers and rode about the wild borders armed to the teeth. Other years he had attended the Border Warden's Court attired this way and eyed with contempt the English penchant for pageantry. This time, however, his instincts told him to arrive with all pomp and ceremony.

He arrived at the meeting in Berwick-on-Tweed in black, half armor, inlaid with gold. His helmet sported a tossing black plume. His men's breastplates gleamed in the sun. Four trumpeters with their horns at the ready led the cavalcade, followed by two standard-bearers in colored tabards carrying the Red Lion on Gold of Scotland. Next came a piper in Douglas dress tartan, and directly behind him a flag bearing the Bleeding Heart of Douglas.

Ramsay dismounted from his massive black stallion and tossed back his crimson-lined cloak. His black head was erect with pride, and he smiled inwardly, thinking, top this, Dacre!

Lord Dacre, the English chief warden of the marches, had been given new orders by his spoiled megalomaniac of a monarch, Henry VIII. He was to raid into and devastate

Scotland as far as he could. Henry had an overpowering
ambition to gain control of Scotland, and he would use any
means to attain his goal—conquest, assassination, bribery,
or even intrigue with his sister Margaret, Scotland's queen.

James Stewart knew Henry had his pig-greedy eyes focused upon his realm, but he had no idea to what lengths
Henry would go to attain anything or anyone he desired.

Most of the small border clans posed no threat to Dacre,
even the ones who were wardens like Ferguson, Elliot, and
Lindsay, whom he discounted as without much power or
influence. It was the larger, more powerful clans like Hamilton who would pose trouble since the chief was so high in
the Scots king's favor, he had been named admiral. And of
course he feared Douglas. Henry knew the voracious ambition and power hunger of Clan Douglas. They were probably the most powerful family in Scotland—at least, they
had the greatest armed might—and they were easily the
richest.

Dacre came to the wardens' meeting with his own her-
alds and flags, but for once the English were outdone at
their own game. Lord Dacre had a long nose, and whenever he addressed a Scot, he looked down it as if he
smelled something rancid.

Lord Ramsay Douglas was the highest-ranking Scots
border lord, and he presided over the court with Dacre.
There was a panel of judges made up of the wardens from
both sides of the border; then there was a jury chosen from
English and Scots families who lived on either side.

Ram reviewed the usual list of cases that were to be
heard, which dealt with thieving, raiding, and the lifting of
sheep, cattle, and other goods. Some were charged with
poaching, and there were a couple of rapes, but nowhere
could Ram Douglas see the case uppermost in his mind:
Kerr versus Heron. Douglas pointed the omission out to
Dacre.

"Ridiculous. Heron killed no Scot!" Dacre said firmly.

"Perhaps not," said Douglas, holding on to his famous

temper, "but he is charged with the murder of Kerr, and we will try him in this court."

"Dare you challenge my word?" demanded Dacre in his most supercilious manner.

"I challenge *ye* if ye've guts enough tae step outside."

"You would love to reduce this court session to a free-booter's brawl, I have no doubt. Your temper and lack of self-control are perhaps why you are called Hotspur!"

Douglas froze him with a dark look. "No, the name was given tae me because of our motto, 'Never Behind.' I am a leader—always the first in battle or any other fight. The first tae right a wrong, the first tae punish injustice." He continued without pause, "You will summon Heron tae present himself within twenty-four hours."

Dacre thought discretion the better part of valor and nodded his agreement.

The next day, when Heron was conspicuous by his absence and Ram again challenged Dacre, the latter spread his hands. "Heron was nowhere to be found."

Ramsay looked at him incredulously. There were very direct means of making an invisible man appear, by simply threatening to torture one of his offspring. Ram realized this was a farce. His first instinct was to take Heron himself and hang him from one of his own trees, but the king had been adamant about doing the thing legally.

Late in the afternoon, Ramsay was informed that people had been gathering across the River Tweed. They had grievances but would not set foot in England. He rode across the bridge to speak with them, canny enough to take the other Scots wardens with him as witnesses. The savage tales he heard of pillaging angered him, the tales of butchery sickened him. One man claimed, "The bastards put the torches tae our village. The women and children took refuge in the stable, but they fired that too!"

Ram questioned them closely to see if they could identify the raiders. There had been no identifying banners or badges, yet some of the people swore that uniformed soldiers had slaughtered their animals and stolen their fodder. Douglas pledged his help to these border families, whose clan names were so familiar to him—Bruce, Scott, Hay, Armstrong; they were his people.

Once more Douglas challenged Dacre in a hard, cold manner. He knew if he allowed his temper to heat, blood would be spilled. Again came the supercilious excuses: "A warden cannot control every last moss-trooper who serves on border patrol."

Douglas was almost speechless. "I have no trouble controlling my men. I pity a man who lacks leadership qualities." They almost drew steel until he saw Patrick Hamilton's eyes upon him. Hamilton would love to carry the tale back to the king, of Hotspur losing control of his infamous temper.

In bed that night Ramsay reflected upon Dacre's words. It was true that men, especially hardened moss-troopers, were difficult to control, but surely that was what made a leader—he had to be stronger than the men under his command. He searched his mind for a man who was almost impossible to control and came up with himself. With a grimace he assured himself that even he obeyed Angus and the king. He had no idea this obedience would shortly be put to the test.

The Wardens' Court concluded a week later, with all the cases before it tried and justice dispensed, but to say that it had been an unsatisfactory meeting was a gross understatement. Douglas prepared a strongly worded report for James Stewart, recommending he make immediate, formal protest to the English Crown demanding redress and compensation and immediate cessation of hostilities. The alternative he suggested was simple. The king could look the other way while Douglas used his own methods to keep law and order.

When they left Edinburgh, the Campbells and Kennedys rode together as far as Glasgow. When Argyll had sold his cattle at the stockyards, they would make their way to Stirling to await the bridegroom and his clan.

Argyll grudgingly told Donal, his son-in-law to be, that since he'd driven the prize Campbell longhorns from Glasgow to Doon, he might as well carry on with the cattle drive and take them to Castle Kennedy at Wigtown.

Donal wanted to reassert that he had not stolen the longhorns, but he swallowed the protest that rose to his lips and thanked Agryll wholeheartedly. No sense starting out on the wrong foot with the irascible old devil.

Meggan rode beside Valentina and Ada. She was weak with relief that the wedding had not been called off. She would have much preferred not being on display at Stirling, but she knew better than to make the slightest protest. She had confided to Tina that Donal's seed was growing inside her, and she lived in daily terror that her father would find out she had a bairn in her belly.

Tina kept a sisterly eye upon her, and when the men set too hard a pace, she spoke up without hesitation to her father and Argyll, secretly amused at the hot glances the old earl cast in her direction.

When the Kennedys arrived back at Doon and Rob told Elizabeth that the king had graciously offered to hold Donal's wedding at Stirling, she was inordinately pleased. When Rob mentioned a date less than two weeks hence, she flatly refused. "That is impossible! Half Scotland will be there. Tina and Beth will need bridesmaidens' gowns—in fact, Beth will need a whole new wardrobe. Two months might just suffice, not two weeks."

Rob closed his eyes in an effort to summon patience and murmured to Ada, "Make her listen tae reason. We canna keep Argyll waiting, tae say naught of King Jamie."

Elizabeth looked askance at Ada. "The gossips would have a heyday if we rushed the marriage in such an undignified way."

Tina looked at her mother and said softly, "The gossips will have a heyday if we do not rush the wedding."

When her mother took Tina's meaning, her mouth fell open, and then she took her humiliation out on Tina. "You are a disgraceful girl, knowing of such things! 'Tis most unseemly for an unwed maiden to stand there so knowingly and discuss such a shameful subject unblushingly in front of her mother. Ada, you have made the girl brazen and immodest with your modern ideas!"

Ada conceded dryly, "Perhaps, but she won't make the mistake of getting a bairn in her belly."

Elizabeth's lips disappeared in disapproval, but she knew there was no time to lose lecturing. In less than a week and a half they would have to set out for Stirling.

Riders were dispatched with invitations that day—no mean feat to ensure none were offended by being over-looked. Elizabeth had to rely upon Rob to provide the guest list. The Gordons were high on the list, insufferable as they were with the Earl of Huntly calling himself the Cock o' the North. Then there were about eight other earls —Erroll, Montrose and their clans, and so on, and so on.

Their own clan was so widespread that over twenty invitations were dispatched, and when Elizabeth listed the Douglases, she was quite vexed that there were so many of the disreputable devils, stretching from Tantallon and Dunbar through Galloway, Mearns, and up to Kilspendie and Longniddy.

Invitations must not be extended to any of the clans who were out of favor with the king or with Argyll, namely MacDonald, McLean, and Cameron.

Every female at Doon was expert with a needle, and Ada designed, cut, and supervised Beth's new wardrobe, a new gown for Elizabeth, and the sisters' bridesmaidens' dresses. On the ride to Glasgow with Meggie Campbell, Ada and Tina had learned that the shy girl favored blue. So even though Tina thought there was nothing so insipid as blondes in powder blue, she shrugged a shapely shoulder and agreed, knowing her copper hair looked ravishing against blue of any shade.

Although Valentina hated to ply a needle, she did so now because Ada had no time to spare. She would have to take clothes that were not new, but at least no one at court had seen them before, and she lowered the necklines on the ones she decided to take. She would need enough clothes for a few days' stay and her most stunning riding dress in which to arrive.

As she surveyed the contents of her wardrobe, selecting and discarding various gowns, her hand fell upon an unusual creation she had never worn. She loved the varied colors of the sheer material, which were a mixture of orange, amber, and tawny, all over an underskirt of black, which showed through the paler colors, making it resemble the skin of a wild animal. On impulse she packed it with her other gowns.

In the kitchen Mr. Burque was busy mixing currants, raisins, and candied fruit with just the correct amount of liquor for the wedding cakes. He was to travel to Stirling with the family to assemble and decorate the cakes and to create other confections for the banquet.

Rob Kennedy had made a special trip to get the rare spices and nuts Mr. Burque had demanded from one of his ships that had just anchored at Ayr. Rob had been able to get sacks of almonds for the almond paste, or marzipan as the Frenchie called it, and he had obtained cinnamon and nutmeg for the custards, but he could not remember for the life of him the other spices the chef had requested. Rob found Tina perched upon Mr. Burque's worktable, one of her favorite spots whenever his kitchens were filled with heavenly aromas that would tempt the devil himself.

As Rob set down the supplies he named them. "Almonds."

Mr. Burque nodded, "Marzipan, *oui, oui.*"

"Cinnamon."

"Merci. Oui, oui."

"Nutmegs."

"Oui, oui, très bien!"

"I could no' get the other stuff—what was it?" Rob muttered.

"Merde!"

"That's it—the ships didna fetch merde," lied Rob.

Tina covered her mouth quickly before she laughed in her father's face. Shit-flavored wedding confections would be quite a novelty!

"Non, non—how you say ginger?"

"Ginger!" Rob said, remembering now.

"Oui, oui!" cried Mr. Burque.

"Wee wee? A real mon calls it piss," Rob said in disgust.

Valentina and Mr. Burque caught each other's eye and went off into peals of laughter. Rob Kennedy escaped, knowing he was out of his depth in the domestic environment. "Prancin' ninny!" he muttered.

Lady Valentina elected to ride with her brothers the forty-odd miles to Stirling. She felt a pang of pity for Ada, who had to ride with her mother, Beth, and Kirsty in the monstrous, uncomfortable carriage. All Rob Kennedy's retainers kept the slower pace with their lord and his wife and suffered the hard edge of his tongue with every mile.

Tina had refused point-blank to take two days and convinced her father she would be perfectly safe with Donal's men at their back. Duncan and Davie ragged Donal mercilessly about the shackles and fetters of marriage, but he took it all philosophically, knowing in his very bones that marriage, especially with his sweet lass, was right for him.

Tina tended to agree with her younger brothers on the subject of marriage but refrained from teasing, knowing it would be her turn only too soon. On the ride they passed lonely peel towers, ideal places where reivers could dwell, but the law stated that lairds were to construct these towers for defense purposes every few miles. Tina caught her breath at the vistas. They passed a burn that had come down for thousands of years, slashing open a fearsome wooded ravine. The fiercely rushing waters had battered and gouged their way, forging pinnacles and jagged rock facings. The hills were covered by pine and larch and fir. They rode through glens, past fan-shaped waterfalls and quiet ponds, where the fish lurked beneath hazel bushes before they darted upstream to feed.

They scattered hen and cock chaffinches and blackbirds and small furry creatures that disappeared down their burrows before they could even be identified. A loch's surface rippled like watered silk, and inside Tina a slow, delicious excitement stirred because she was engaged in an adventure that might afford her opportunities of disobedience and misbehavior.

The town of Stirling was on the River Forth with the purple ramparts of the Highlands just beyond the steeply winding, narrow streets. The sun was setting as they reached Stirling Castle, a hilltop citadel on various levels with towers, bartizans, and parapet walks. Grassy ledges and terraces with steps cut for access were utilized for gardens. Halfway down the northeastern flank was a plain consisting of a few acres where cows grazed peacefully.

They rode around the back of the fortress, past the bowling green and the quoiting pitch, to the barracks and stables. Valentina spoke to a royal groom explaining that her mare, Indigo, was valuable and must be kept safe from stud stallions. She laughed to herself later as she realized how shocked her mother would have been if she'd overheard.

The queen and her court were already in residence and planning festivities for every evening they would spend at the Highland castle, which was far more conducive to pleasure than the brooding castle at Edinburgh. There would be a couple of days for fun and games, then on the third day the marriage would be solemnized, and before everyone departed at week's end, the queen had planned a lavish costume ball.

It was highly entertaining just watching the guests arrive. Tina was surprised that a wedding was such a potent draw.

She had never seen so many tartans, mottos, and badges displayed in her life. She knew the Scots were wickedly proud, but she began to wonder if Ada wasn't right when she said that although they had a dour facade, they were romantics and sentimentalists to a man.

Before the rest of her family arrived, Tina had acquired some brown-gray Lazarus beads to conjure the Devil. The queen and her ladies thought it amusing and fashionable to practice magic. When her sister and her female Kennedy cousins arrived, Lady Valentina held her own court, which also included the bride and the many Campbell females who were quite countrified and thought Tina the height of fashion and sophistication. She was thoroughly enjoying herself among the vast company, showing off her rustling taffetas, pointed stomachers, and ruffs rimmed with pearls.

She got more than her share of electric glances from the lusty men. She adored the temptation to recklessness, but she had more good sense than to return their intimate glances of silent invitation. Yet she saw many a coy look from ambitious girls. She laughed with her cousins and said clever things about men: "He has neither rank nor virility, two necessary qualities in a man." But when she saw Colin Douglas limp into the hall with Black Ram Douglas's brothers at his side, her soft heart went out to him. On impulse, she crossed the large chamber and sketched him a curtsy. "Colin, welcome to our wedding."

His eyes were friendly and amused. "It is my pleasure, Lady Kennedy."

"I cannot call you Colin unless you call me Tina," she pointed out.

Gavin and Cameron Douglas grinned cheekily and elbowed Colin aside. Gavin kissed her hand gallantly and murmured, "Ye are even more beautiful than last time we met, Tina."

She arched her brows coolly at his use of her name. "Colin Douglas was kind to me in a trying situation, but that doesn't mean I embrace any other Douglas!" She swept off with an aloof shrug of her shoulder.

"Yer no' but dirt beneath her feet," Cameron needled.

"Christ, I'd like tae be beneath her skirt," Gavin said. "I'll never know why Ram hates the sight o' her—she has enough allure tae stiffen a corpse."

Ramsay Douglas did not think he would be bothered to ride to Stirling to the Campbell-Kennedy wedding. After he made his full reports to the king, he thought it expedient to return to the borders since they were in sore need of patrolling. But when the king and Angus took it for granted he and his men would escort them to Stirling, he capitulated without demur.

James Stewart and Archibald Douglas each waited for the other to bring up the subject of marriage to Ramsay. When Angus realized the king expected him to do the dirty work, he put it off until he had enjoyed the festivities at Stirling. He was damned if he was going to light the fuse of Hotspur's explosive temper quite yet.

The day was bright with sunshine, a rarity for the Highlands, which so often had a somber, brooding quality. Everyone young and not-so-young was outdoors crowding around the archery butts, quoiting pitch, bowling green, or the menagerie of bears. But all the youngest guests who were daring enough were gathered atop the northeastern flank, where a long, grassy slope led down to the plain. A raucous game of hurly-hackit was in full spate, a grass-sledging activity on the skulls of oxen, using the upcurled horns to steer.

Naturally Tina was the first female to challenge the hill. She raced both of her brothers, easily beating Duncan because her light weight made her sledge fly over the grass. Davie was too sly and cunning, however. He deliberately cut in front of her, causing her to swerve off and lose the race. This only spurred her on, of course, and by stooping to his tactics, she beat him at his own game. She thought she'd never laughed so much in her entire life.

Gavin Douglas joined in the fun, giving the other men a run for their money. There was a streak of recklessness in Douglas men. Gavin shot down the slope so heedlessly that he came a cropper before he reached the bottom. His great body flew over the oxen horns, and he lay sprawled directly in Tina's path. She screamed as her skull collided with Gavin's and she was flung directly on top of him. They stared into each other's faces for one horrified moment, then went off into peals of laughter at the undignified spectacle they were creating with their arms and legs entangled.

Ramsay Douglas had been watching the silly game for some time through jaded eyes that were drawn again and again to the streaming copper tresses of the Kennedy wench. She was truly a wanton, heedless of her grass-stained skirts flying in the air, making herself the center of attention. His jaw tightened as he watched her collide into Gavin, the pair of them laughing like lunatics.

As Tina and Gavin helped each other to their feet, she caught sight of his oxen skull and went off on another trill of laughter. "You ugly brute! Your great weight has crushed your damned skull!"

He felt his head in mock alarm, and Tina laughed up at him. "I suspect your brains are in a much lower place."

He grinned and rubbed his buttocks. Suddenly they sobered as they looked into the dark face of Black Ram Douglas, who was in no way amused. They were able to keep straight faces for a count of perhaps five or six seconds, then they both went off again into paroxysms of laughter, far too giddy to maintain a semblance of decorum.

"Ye've not the smallest shred of sobriety." His hard voice relegated her to the ranks of foolish, shallow women who cannot be held responsible for their stupidity. He was so tall and broad-shouldered, he blocked most of the sun.

"You are so old and dried up, you've forgotten what

innocent fun is. Have a care your face doesn't freeze with pious disapproval."

Violent, angry energy flamed between them like sheet lightning. In that instant it was apparent why he was called Hotspur and she Firebrand.

Chapter 14

Even though the chapel royal at Stirling was massive by church standards, there certainly was not enough room for all the members of all the clans who had gathered. Bishop Kennedy had come down from St. Andrews to officiate at this wedding, and the front of the church overflowed with the red-haired clan.

Archibald Cassillis, the Kennedy earl, looked about the church at all his people. He knew it would not be long before Rob Kennedy's lasses exchanged their vows. Ram Douglas and Arran's heir were spectacular matches for his nieces, yet he hadn't broached the subject to Rob because instinctively he knew Elizabeth would object to allowing her baby to go to Douglas. He agreed the poisoning years ago had been a bad business, but the damned woman must learn to forgive and forget. He'd had his orders from the king, and the Kennedys of Doon would have their orders from him, but he'd wait until they were back home before he issued them.

A pale Meggan Campbell walked down the aisle overshadowed by her powerful father, trying to swallow the lump in her throat as she wished her mother, long dead, could have been with her, or at least her elder sister Elizabeth. She shuddered. That was impossible, of course, for Elizabeth was wed to the traitor Lachlan MacLean and she would likely never see her again. Meggan's eyes caught sight of the back of Donal Kennedy standing so stiffly by the altar, and suddenly she was no longer afraid. Unlike the savagely cruel MacLean, Donal really loved her. In a world where women never got to choose their own fate, Meggie Campbell felt truly blessed.

The nuptials were being solemnized just before the hour of noon so the couple could receive the Holy Sacrament. Megan had the requisite six bridesmaids, all Campbell cousins except for Tina and Beth. Their dresses were a much paler shade of blue than those of the Kennedy sisters, but all blended together well enough.

The small bride had the lovely Blackwatch tartan of the Campbells draped across one shoulder, and she listened solemnly to the words of Bishop Kennedy. He exhorted the young couple and the congregation in general in a resounding sermon denouncing sinful pride.

Tina glanced down the chapel royal at the sea of high-held heads and thought irreverently that if he preached from now till doomsday, he would never rid the Scots of sinful pride. The bishop then gave a blistering declamation of women's lewdness and men's filthy lust. He had just touched upon adultery and fornication when the king cleared his throat and gave him a black look. Without missing a beat, the bishop demanded, "Who giveth this woman tae this mon?"

Argyll's burly figure stepped forward garbed in a silver wolf pelt. His scarred hands with missing top finger joint placed Meggie's hand in Donal's, then he planted his feet, declining to step back until he'd witnessed the marriage legalized.

Elizabeth Kennedy was crying openly, and Tina saw that Beth was shaking like a leaf to be exhibited before such a great throng. Silly child, thought Tina—doesn't she realize no one is looking at her?

The wedding banquet began at two o'clock and would go on for the next twelve hours. The food was plentiful because the clans' wealth was in sheep, cattle, and oxen and the rivers and forests surrounding Stirling teemed with fish and game.

The pièce de résistance, however, was Mr. Burque's towering wedding cake, the likes of which none had ever seen before. The top layer was an imitation of the deep blue sea, and rising from the waves was a great dolphin, the Kennedy device, cleverly wired so that it rose up from the water in a magnificent leap.

During the first hours of the banquet, decorum reigned, but by dusk most of the men were well on their way to being drunk. The king and queen, who had sat down together, were now absorbed in other partners. James Stewart danced tirelessly with Janet Kennedy, a natural-born wanton, wholehearted, generous, and unashamed of their affair.

Queen Margaret had hot eyes and hands for the Master of Douglas, that ambitious young man who had been taught by his father, the Earl of Angus, that power was the only thing that mattered.

The rest of the Douglases had spurned the wedding in favor of hunting. Colin showed to advantage in the saddle, while the dance floor was a nightmare for him. Ram hated the very atmosphere of weddings. They gave him a trapped, caged feeling he found difficult to dispel. Gavin and Cameron vied with their cousins Ian, Drummond, and Jamie to bag the most game. The stags were only just losing their velvet and coming into season. All knew that at day's end when they returned from their sport, there would still be plenty of roast bullock and ale to wash it down with, a bedding for their entertainment, and a castle filled with amenable young wives whose husbands would be unconscious or at least incapable with drink.

Valentina had so many men clamoring to partner her that she quite neglected Patrick Hamilton. She did it on purpose, to punish him for not showing up earlier in the week. He found that in order to dance with her at all, he had to cut in on an arrogant Gordon or a wild Stewart, most of whom were jumped-up whelps or by-blows in spite of their royal blood.

For miles outside Stirling, the crowds surrounded crackling bonfires and indulged in fighting, screaming, singing, and finally mass lovemaking, all to the accompaniment of skirling bagpipes.

Inside, the behavior of the celebrants was in danger of degenerating from bawdy to profligate. The matrons retired in disgust at the men's inherent coarseness, removing their youngest daughters from the danger. At this point the banquet turned into a bacchanalia. The lewd songs became grossly indecent and were accompanied by graphic gestures. Serving wenches now sat upon men's knees with their skirts pulled above plump thighs. The racket was deafening as silver goblets and sword-hilts were banged upon the tables to a rhythmic demand that the bride and groom "kiss, kiss, kiss, kiss!"

Donal obliged the crowd, while his little bride grew visibly more nervous. Archibald Campbell drained a silver drinking cup, hurled it down the table, then picked up another. Archibald Douglas, drunk as a lord, bellowed intimate appraisal of every female in sight.

Valentina stayed for only one reason: She feared for her little sister-in-law, Meggie Campbell, now Meggie Kennedy, as the crowd banged their goblets and chanted, "Disrobe, disrobe, disrobe, disrobe!" She knew she must rescue the bride and spirit her away to the nuptial chamber. Tina managed to reach Meggie and take her hand, but that seemed to be the signal the revelers had been awaiting.

The women, led by the queen and the Howard sisters, descended upon Donal and began to strip him, while a mob of drunken males tore Meggie from Tina's grasp and lifted her on high, tearing at her gown and veiled coif. Meggan screamed, her face a pale blur above the heads of the men as they began their exodus to the nuptial chamber, their progress impeded by the bodies of those who had lost consciousness and lay among the vomit-fouled rushes.

Tina followed helplessly, unable to aid Meggan. It was all she could do to protect her own person as she heard her gown tear, and to slap hands away from her breasts and bottom.

The bride and groom were stripped quite naked by the time they were carried into the bedchamber, and Tina could do no more than shrink into a corner in horror as the mob pushed the groom on top of the weeping bride and chorused, "Fuck, fuck, fuck, fuck!"

Ramsay Douglas glanced into the room with jaded eyes. They flickered over Tina Kennedy with disgust. She was in the thick of things, as usual. She was making for the door before they could strip her too. She looked up into his face with dismay. His pewter gray eyes reflected her image, but the depths were filled with contempt. He cast one last look at the women in the chamber. He had laid most of them, and there was not one he would have been bothered to lay again.

The bride was distraught. Through a bleary haze Donal saw that the fun and games had gone too far. He glanced about looking for help. His brother Duncan and Patrick Hamilton were enjoying the spectacle far too much to desist. Davie was hateful enough sober; drunk, he was almost demonic. Donal looked in vain for Meggie's father, but Argyll had been too far gone in drink to even climb the stairs to the nuptial chamber. The women with their hands at his groin and all over his body were even worse than the men. In desperation Donal appealed to the king: "Sire, I need yer help!"

The good-natured James elbowed his way to the bedside. "Ye want me tae bairn her for ye, laddie?" Then he saw that the little bride was past hysterics and going into shock. In a brisk deep voice that brooked no refusal, he took command of the situation. The revelers staggered from the room holding each other upright. The ones who were still bent on lewd and lascivious conduct suggested other bedchambers they could invade as the king herded them safely away from the newlyweds.

Meggie lay sobbing, her pale face pressed into the pillows. Donal in his clumsy way tried to comfort her. She shrank from his rough hands, never wanting to see or hear or smell another man as long as she lived. Gradually she became aware of a tender hand stroking her hair over and over and a voice pleading, "Dinna cry, lass."

She realized that from this day forward Donal Kennedy would be her only source of strength or tenderness or love. With a sob she turned blindly toward him. Donal's arm encircled Meggie's waist, her hand stole into his and held it tightly, and her head folded into his shoulder. Each fulfilled a need in the other's life.

Since Ram Douglas had enjoyed the hunting more than anything else at Stirling, he decided to go again the next day. His brothers and indeed most of the males were nursing massive hangovers this morning, so he went alone. In the royal stables he noticed that the lovely damson-colored mare he thought of as his was gone. He was mildly surprised that others besides himself were in the saddle this early.

In no time at all he was swallowed by the dense forest that surrounded Stirling. His senses were alert for any sound or movement that signaled game. His ears easily picked up a bellowing roar, and as he rode toward a clearing and a steep, grassy hillside, he knew what he would find. It was a wild bull, a relic of an ancient breed that had roamed all the uplands at one time. The bull had stolen two domestic cows that grazed the lower slopes to breed wild, misbegotten offspring.

A bull hunt was a far more exhilarating and taxing sport than hunting hart or boar. Bulls were totally unpredictable when maddened and would charge and gore anything in sight with their long, viciously curving horns.

Ram tried to drive the bull further into the trees, where he would be hard pressed to turn and charge, but the creature was far too wily to fall into such a trap. Ram watched the bull cautiously, wishing his brothers were there to aid him. His wolfhound, Boozer, would have been an invaluable help too.

The wild creature was a dirty white with a massive, thick-maned neck and a wicked six-foot spread of horn. For one split-second he questioned the wisdom of hunting it solo, but the challenge was far too tempting for Ram Douglas to ignore. The shaggy-coated creature with massive shoulders was obviously cunning as well as savage, for it ran out into the clearing, where it would have room to maneuver and charge.

Ram's eyes scanned the perimeter of the grassy slope, noting a long outcropping of stone that formed a ledge with a steep drop beyond. His horse must avoid that danger, but the rest of the ground didn't appear too rough a terrain.

The bull saw her before Ram did. Its red eyes rolled in its head, it pawed the ground, it let out a snort and charged downhill. Valentina Kennedy had seen Ram Douglas mounted on his great black stallion long before he emerged at the clearing's edge. She watched in disbelief as he waved at her and shouted, "Get the hell away!"

It was almost too late when she saw the maddened bull tearing up great clods of earth in its efforts to charge her. She spurred her damson mare cruelly, knowing if she did not, the bull would tear into her mare broadside.

Ram knew there was not a split-second to lose as he rode out into its line of vision and tried to divert it from its chosen goal. It was roaring now, savagely intent upon the girl and horse. Ram's knife was more a short-bladed sword. He screamed a Douglas war cry and headed toward the bull's rear quarters, hoping to crash into it and roll it over while at the same time avoiding its vicious horns.

His vivid imagination saw the Barbary's exposed underbelly being ripped like a punctured bladder if he could not divert the bull's attention from its intended disemboweling. Indigo was screaming, eyes rolling wildly, as she shuddered with terror. Ram glimpsed Tina, her face as white as her riding habit, her hat gone, her fiery hair licking across her face and neck like flames. Then he had no time for anything but his prey as the bull dug in its forelegs and pivoted about, thinking to expel its great fury upon its attacker rather than upon a creature intent upon fleeing.

Ram was now face to face with a head-on charge. He could save himself by leaping from the saddle, but his stallion would be sacrificed upon the vicious, upthrusting horns. He made his decision instantly, hurling himself with a vaulting spring upon the brute's back. He knew the reaction would be instantaneous.

The white bull thrust down its head, arched its back steeply, and convulsed its hindquarters into the air. Ram's powerful fingers dug into its shaggy mane to save himself from being tossed forward over the brute's head, then with thighs, calves, and ankles curved about its belly, he unsheathed his short broadsword and drove it into the brute's neck. The bull lashed its head to right and left, trying to hook its clinging burden with its great horns. It did manage to tear open his leather breeches and gash a shallow wound along his lower leg.

Ram was now as enraged as the bull, and he removed both hands from the thick mane to plunge his weapon deep behind the beast's shoulder blade. He felt the shudder convulse through the powerful body as it coughed but did not go down. He knew he had not found its heart. The enraged killer was going to toss and gore him any second if he bungled again. Desperately he drew his dagger and plunged it to its hilt a few inches farther back than his short sword. Finally he felt it stagger, but it did not drop.

Maddened by pain, it began to run. Desperately Ram struggled to pull out his weapons for another onslaught. The bull still had enough strength to roar as it hurled its massive body toward the trees where Tina had taken shelter.

Ram gazed upon her for one horrified moment before the bull faltered, tripped, its forelegs buckling, and he was thrown to the ground at her feet. The brute finally lay dead, its head twisted at a grotesque angle, scarlet blood flowing from its mouth. Her terrified mare shuddered uncontrollably as she tried to gentle her. "She's nearly mad with fear," she said huskily.

His eyes were murderous as they swept over the white velvet riding dress and the cool beauty of her face. No trace of fear could be detected in the golden eyes that viewed the carnage before her. Black fury was written in every line of his face. His leathers were slashed at chest and thigh, where the bull had tried to gore him, and he was drenched in blood. He was in the Devil's own temper. "Ye have a knack for attracting misfortune tae yourself, and ye don't give a damn if ye attract it tae others!" He seized her by her slim waist and shook her like a rag doll. "Have ye no brains? This forest is dangerous. Wild beasts and death lurk behind every tree. Yer a reckless little fool tae ride without even a groom." Ram Douglas seldom tasted real fear, but it had filled his throat when he saw the beautiful girl about to be gored before his eyes. He had expended a superhuman effort to save her, and now that he had done so, his fear was released by anger.

Her compelling eyes blazed like golden fire, fringed by black lashes above proudly slanting cheekbones. "Your bloody hands have damaged my velvet," she accused.

For a moment he stared at her in utter disbelief that all she cared for at this moment was her gown. Any other female would have fallen trembling in his arms. This one showed not the slightest gratitude. He tore his weapons from the bull's carcass and picked up the hem of her white velvet skirt. "Damage it? I'll ruin it," he threatened, intending to wipe his swordblade.

She shrank back from him, but still her eyes showed more defiance than fear. "So this is how a chivalrous knight aids a damsel in distress," she said with cool contempt.

He had the decency to flush. Christ, why did she always bring out the worst in him? He could charm any woman in Scotland save this one. He released her and wiped the dripping sword upon the grass. It gave him time to leash his blazing temper. He realized how easy it would be to physically dominate her—but where would be the satisfaction? He would cut her down to size with her own weapon: carefully chosen, cutting words. His eyes were the pewter of stormy seas. "I did it tae save the mare's life, not yours," he said bluntly, "so don't bother tae thank me."

"You apparently not only expect thanks, you'd like me to grovel. You think me a bitch who'll lick your hand and wag my tail. I'm more likely to relieve myself upon your leg!"

All women are bitches, he thought silently, but this one had managed to get under his skin. He was irked that he could not humble her; worse, he felt his loins blaze into a desire so intense, he caught his breath. Christ, she wasn't just under his skin—she was under his foreskin! With a lust he had seldom experienced, he wanted to take her on the forest floor. He wanted to arouse a response in her to match her suddenly savage beauty. His eyes licked over her, revealing his smoldering desire, and in a voice husky with sensuality, he stepped close and murmured, "I want tae tame ye."

She raised her riding crop and deliberately slashed open his cheek. Without hesitation he took hold of her whip hand and squeezed until she yielded it up to him. He turned upon his heel, ignoring the blood trickling down his leg from where the bull had gashed him, vaulted into the saddle, and cantered off without a backward glance.

* * *

By evening all traces of her morning's misadventure had faded in significance. More pressing matters were now upon the Kennedy ladies. On this last night at Stirling, there was the queen's fancy dress ball. Their mother, worn out from the emotions of the wedding, was not attending, and she argued with her daughters about their participation. When she saw the look of disappointment on Beth's face, she relented and agreed they could go, providing Kirsty and Ada went along to keep an eye on them. The four rushed to the sisters' bedchamber to solve the problem of costumes, and Kirsty immediately antagonized Valentina and Ada. "They can wear their blue bridesmaid's gowns again. So much work went intae them, 'tis a pity tae wear them only once."

"Absolutely not," said Tina impatiently.

"Well, the costumes must be appropriate fer modest young maidens. Perhaps simple shepherdesses. . . . I shall wear ma gray uniform, of course."

"You're simple," said Ada rudely.

Kirsty bridled. "Well, madam, what outlandish costume will ye opt fer?"

"I was thinking perhaps a nun's habit," Ada said dryly.

Kirsty compressed her lips. "Beth shall wear full dress Kennedy tartan," she said decisively, and took Beth back to her mother's chamber to gather the accessories they would need.

Ada said to Tina, "Well, I shan't presume to advise you. Whatever you wear will be a standout. I shall wear a gown with a neckline cut to the clavicle and a tiny mask to deceive them into thinking me a countess."

Tina's wicked juices had begun to bubble. Of course, to carry off her plan she would need a male accomplice. She immediately ruled out Patrick Hamilton. He would definitely frown upon his future betrothed making a spectacle of herself. She wished Heath were here—he would dare anything for her. By a process of elimination she was left with Davie. He'd do it if she turned it into a dare and perhaps sweetened it with some sort of bribe.

She took a gold-plated collar-necklace from her jewel casket and hurried along through Stirling's outbuildings until she came to the blacksmith's forge and with one brilliant smile pressed the muscular smithy into attaching a long chain to the collar.

Later she stood in front of a polished steel mirror to survey the effect. She was going as a wild jungle animal, whichever one was striped. Though she had never seen one, she thought perhaps it was a tigress. She wore the gown with the filmy orange and tawny markings with the black underskirt showing through.

She wore her flaming hair unbound in a wild mane and painted black stripes sweeping from her golden eyes, slanting across her temples to her hairline. Davie lounged on her bed in hunter's green, his bow and arrows lying negligently on the floor. As she fastened the collar about her neck, she admonished, "Now after you lead me in on the chain and present me to the queen, don't forget to detach the chain. You mustn't actually give me to her as a gift. It's supposed to be merely symbolic—the hunter presenting his spoils."

The great chamber at Stirling had what was called the "fire end" and the "throne end." Valentina had not dined in the banqueting hall, so that she could make her grand entrance in the great chamber. The costumes were amazingly inventive for people who had not been forewarned they would require such things. There were sailors and jugglers, Gypsies and shepherds, wizards and Vikings, Romans and goddesses—but there was only one tigress!

A small hush fell over the crowd as the young hunter led his prey down the entire length of the chamber to where the king and queen sat upon their thrones. The hush gave way to a murmur as more people stopped talking to stare

at the vivid creature. Flaming Tina Kennedy! The name
was on every lip.

Beth and Kirsty gasped, some whistled, others applauded. A man's voice said, "I'd like tae pierce her wi' ma
arrow!" The women's faces hardened, the men hardened
also. Davie, who never did anything without a little malice,
led her directly to the king. Tina tried to lead him toward
the queen, but he made a great show of yanking her chain,
so that she had to obey him. Tina looked as if she were
about to claw him. When Davie gave the chain into the
king's hand, some swore their monarch had selected a new
concubine.

James Stewart immediately released her from the chain
and led her out to start the dancing, gallantly exclaiming,
"The captor becomes the captive." Black Ram Douglas
stood at the far end beside the fireplace. As the couple
danced toward him, the fireshine played over Valentina's
molten hair and tawny gown, turning her into the most
breath-stopping creature he had ever seen. Desire flared in
him like banefire. He wanted something wild to tame.

When the dance ended, the queen asked her where she
could get such a gown for herself, and Tina was relieved
that she hadn't taken offense that James had partnered her
in the first dance.

Valentina looked up as a strong hand took possession of
her wrist. Her golden eyes widened so that the tiger stripes
slanted exotically as she realized who had taken hold of
her. "No, thank you, I don't wish to dance," she said in a
cool voice. Ram's eyes changed from pewter to midnight
black. "Ye *owe* me a dance." His voice cut like the crack of
a whip, and the pressure of his powerful fingers on her
wrist became painful. She set her will against his. "You are
hurting me," she retorted.

"I hope so," he replied with relish.

"You base-born dog!" she muttered low.

"Perhaps it is the dog in me that attracts the bitch."

"Oh!" she gasped as he swung her into the pavane. She

knew an overwhelming need to say something equally outrageous, and the scandalous words she had overheard at
court were off her tongue before she could stop them. "It
takes more than six stiff inches to attract me."

"More?" He raised an amused eyebrow. "I have more."

Her cheeks flamed. A witchy look flickered in her
golden eyes, telling him she was about to walk off the
dance floor again. He reached out a powerful hand to
clamp her to the spot. Tina found it intolerable to be overruled. She almost pretended to faint rather than dance
with him, but upon reflection she realized if she fainted,
rumors would fly about her being in a delicate condition.

She moved with fluid grace, dipping, revolving, her
breasts rising and falling in time to the pulsing music. She
saw that his brother Gavin would be her next partner, and
she sent him an inviting smile, knowing he would rescue
her. When the measure changed and Gavin approached,
Ramsay said, "Bugger off." Gavin Douglas, disconcerted
for only a moment, had no choice but to gallantly partner
the lady Ram had ignored.

Tina glanced about and saw she was surrounded by Kennedys, her own clan. Again his powerful hand reached out
to stop her from leaving. She smiled and said through her
teeth, "If you try to use your spurs on me again, I shall
create a scene you will never live down!" His lip curled,
and then he simply walked off the floor, exactly as she had
done to him, embarrassing her before the whole assembly.

He was a lout without scruples. It was a lady's privilege
to rebuff a man, but for him to openly scorn her in such a
public manner humiliated her to the core. If it was the last
thing she did, she would even the score. Douglas was certainly not indifferent to her, she knew. Was it her beauty
that attracted him, perhaps, or did he represent a challenge to the dominant male? Whatever it was, she would
use it to her advantage to best him and prove a Kennedy
was a match for a Douglas.

Chapter 15

The next morning, when Angus and his Douglas escort were ready to depart, he sent a message requesting Ramsay to ride with him. Now would be as good a time as any to lay down the law. He learned, however, that Hotspur had departed late last night, taking his borderers and leaving behind only his brothers and Colin.

Gavin dutifully attended the earl, whose escort was usually close to a hundred. Gavin didn't know why Angus should need Ram, but Archibald's lips disappeared in annoyance when he learned Ram had left. "Can Colin or Cameron or myself be of any service, my lord?"

"I'm tae ride with Arran and his bloody Hamiltons on the king's orders, tae repair some o' the havoc yer raiding has wreaked. Tell Ram I'll see him at Douglas tomorrow nicht!" Gavin stared hard at the ruthless earl. His words had an ominous ring.

Patrick Hamilton strode purposefully toward the stables. He would not keep his father, the admiral, waiting. On the king's orders they were to ride with the Douglas earl in a show of unity.

Nan Howard beckoned to him urgently, and he stepped into the herb garden to bid her good-bye. Her sister Kat, whom he hadn't seen bending over to pick a sprig of thyme, suddenly straightened, and he knew this was some sort of confrontation. He frowned as his instincts warned him to bolt.

Nan said, "Patrick, there's no way to wrap this up in pretty words. I'm afraid I'm going to have a child."

He swallowed as he felt the trap closing on him. "Christ, surely yer not accusing me of being the father!"

Her eyes narrowed against tears, and Kat spoke for her. "Deny it all you want. You have bedded her, and I am the witness."

"I bedded you both!" Suddenly he understood that Nan had baited the trap with the irresistible lure of two voluptuous bodies at one time. What a gullible fool he'd been! There was nothing so devious as a slut, unless it was two—two English sluts!

"I am betrothed to Lady Valentina Kennedy," he said stiffly.

"Not yet, you're not," Nan said.

"And you'd better not pledge yourself, if you know what's good for you," warned Kat. "The queen will be furious if you bring dishonor to one of her ladies-in-waiting."

He almost blurted, "Get rid of it!" before he realized this was her means to marriage with the heir to the Earldom of Arran.

Tina rode back to Doon in high spirits. The wedding at Stirling had proved to be an exciting diversion, and the party that now traveled south was quite large. The newlyweds were on their way to Castle Kennedy in Wigtown, and a large number of Campbell retainers were going with the bride. Donal had an equal number of Kennedy household servants, and it had been decided that some of the tenants from Doon would move with him permanently.

Archibald, Earl of Cassillis, traveled to Doon with the family, and Rob, ever suspicious, wondered if he had an ulterior motive. Tina was blissfully unaware of the undercurrents that would change her life forever once they were revealed.

When she parted company with Meggie, she promised to ride down for a visit with her new sister-in-law very soon; then she headed for home, vowing to be the first to clatter into the castle courtyard.

The first hint that something was in the wind came from Ada. When she came into Tina's chamber, she found that she had almost finished unpacking her own clothes. As Ada hung the remaining gowns in the wardrobe, she said, "Something's up. The minute we arrived, Archibald sequestered your father. When the door opened, I've never seen Rob so grim-faced. He whisked Elizabeth into the chamber, the door shut with a crash, and they are still in there."

"It must be something urgent. The very first thing my father does when he arrives back at Doon is enjoy one of Mr. Burque's sumptuous meals." She tapped her chin with a reflective finger. "The wedding went off without a hitch, and the newlyweds are on their way to Castle Kennedy, so it cannot concern them."

Ada agreed. "The earl had a queer look about him from the minute we left Stirling. He had something in his gullet, and I could see if he didn't disgorge it soon, he would choke to death."

There was a great clatter in the courtyard, and both women immediately went to the window. "It's Cassillis. He's leaving!" Tina said with disbelief. She experienced a prickling at the nape of her neck. The very air seemed ominous, and Tina knew the ripples from the whirlpool that had been stirred would reach her any minute.

A servant boy knocked on the chamber door and told them Lord Kennedy wanted both of them. Immediately. He led the way to the first-floor room Rob Kennedy used for business, and Tina's eyes went to her mother's face the moment she stepped over the threshold. Elizabeth looked as if she had been struck in the face. The door opened once again to admit Beth and Kirsty.

The moment Elizabeth saw Beth, she dissolved into tears. Ada took one step toward her, but Rob, his face a florid red, said, "Leave her. Ye'll have more than one hysterical woman on yer hands afore we're done here. Ye had better all sit doon." When his audience sat before him in a

semicircle, he gave each one such a fierce look, even Tina
knew he would stand for no interruptions.

"A pox on all my misbegotten offspring! I ha' nurtured a
nest of vipers here at Doon. The minute ma back was
turned, all hell broke loose! Dinna thank me for what ye
are about tae receive—thank yer brothers!"

Elizabeth sobbed. Rob glared at her fiercely, and the
sobs settled down to hopeless tears.

"The whoresons have been raidin', stirrin' up old ha-
treds and feuds atween Kennedys, Campbells, Hamiltons,
and Douglases, and the king won't stand fer it. He called
the heads of the clans on the carpet and told them if they
didna sign bonds of friendship and bonds of matrimony, he
was goin' tae start hangin' the culprits. Now, we've made a
start wi' the Kennedy-Campbell marriage, so that keeps
bloody Argyll frae ma throat. But that's just the start!
There's tae be two more weddin's without delay." He cast
a fierce look upon Tina. "Ye can expect a visit and a proposal frae Patrick Hamilton any hour now. Ye will accept
that proposal, and while yer at it, ye can get on yer knees
and thank God fer yer good fortune in landin' the heir to
the Earldom of Arran."

Tina flushed. If there was one thing she could not abide,
it was taking orders. She opened her mouth to speak, but
Ada laid a warning hand upon her sleeve, and when she
glanced at her father's face, she realized Ada had done
right to warn her. His face had gone from red to purple
and he looked as if his next words might kill him. "Our
youngest, sweet child, our baby girl, goes as a sacrificial
lamb tae none other than Black Ram Douglas."

Beth gasped, Kirsty choked, Elizabeth sobbed. Then
Beth went into hysterics, Kirsty looked ready to scratch out
Rob's eyes, and Elizabeth gabbled, "I'll take her to England, I'll hide her. She's only a baby, far too young to wed
any man, let alone a degenerate Douglas!"

"Enough, woman!" roared Rob. "We ha' no choice. The
head o' the clan has decided, and his word is law! This is

Scotland, woman. God's passion, ye've lived here donkey's years, and still yer ignorant of our customs."

Tina at last found the courage to speak up. "Black Ram Douglas won't come with cap in hand and a proposal of marriage on his arrogant lips. He's not the marrying kind."

Her father swung on her. "Ye forget—Archibald Douglas will be givin' him his orders. Can ye imagine any man breathin' not doing as the powerful Earl of Angus suggests?"

It took the combined ministrations of Elizabeth, Kirsty, and Ada to get the distraught and hysterical Beth to her bedchamber. Rob, his mouth grimmer than Tina had ever seen, said in an ominous tone, "Ye may tell Duncan an' David tae present their misbeggotten carcasses afore me."

Valentina was in a very subdued mood when she entered her own chamber. She sank down onto the bed to slowly digest her father's orders. She would make no protest about her marriage to Patrick Hamilton. She felt she was the luckiest girl alive when she compared herself with her young sister. It was unthinkable that innocent little Beth must become the mate of Black Ram Douglas. He would swallow the tiny morsel whole. She shuddered involuntarily as her mind conjured a picture of the dark, intimidating Scot.

The Prince of Darkness himself could not have been more compelling, yet more forbidding. She knew the horror her mother must feel at the mere suggestion of a match between her favorite child and the Douglas. My God, it was as if history were repeating itself. When a Kennedy daughter wed a Douglas, the result could only be tragic.

The next afternoon brought Patrick Hamilton, accompanied by his father, the Earl of Arran. Tina fidgeted while Ada pinned up her hair in a chignon. She was almost resigned to the inevitability of her marriage and was determined to act in a composed, mature manner when she was summoned before the men who were deciding her fate.

At last the knock came upon her chamber door, but the servant told her that young Lord Hamilton awaited her in the garden. She was glad that Patrick was thoughtful enough to propose to her in private, even though it was just a formality.

As she walked toward him she thought wryly, my God, he looks as if he's been handed a death sentence. He took her hands and searched her face. There were no words that would be kinder or less hurtful. "Tina, sweetheart, ye must know I want tae marry ye more than anything in the world."

"Yes, Patrick, I know how you feel," she replied, smiling to encourage him.

"I'm tae wed Nan Howard next week, by order of the queen."

Tina's eyes went wide. "But why? I thought the king had ordered a bond of matrimony between our clans."

Patrick looked ill. "I— she . . . Nan Howard is with child," he said miserably.

"Yours?" she asked softly.

"No . . . I don't know. Perhaps," he admitted. "The queen's ladies are such sluts, I don't suppose I'll ever know," he said bitterly.

Tina withdrew her hands. She looked up at the window of the chamber, where her father conducted his business. He and Arran must be having a similar conversation. Her pride was stung that Patrick had been having a liaison while courting her, but she bit back the cutting remarks that sprang to her lips as she realized it was much worse for Patrick than for herself. In a strange way she felt relief that she had been reprieved. She touched his hand again. "Patrick, I'm sorry."

"Dear God, how can ye be so understanding when I've been such a foolish swine?"

She could not explain her mood. Life had such unexpected twists and turns. The last thing in the world she had expected was rejection, for whatever reason. It was pointless to linger. What more could she say? "Next time we meet, we will still be friends." She turned and left him. She could not bear to witness the deep despair she saw clearly writ upon his face.

Tina did not recall climbing the stairs to her chamber, but before she could explain matters to Ada, they were both summoned to the first floor. When they entered the room, Elizabeth joined them and the Earl of Arran had apparently departed. Tina saw that her mother's face was still swollen from crying. Now she was to be upset again, and Tina felt wretched to bring her mother more unhappiness.

She took a seat and folded her hands in her lap. Her father's face was so grim, it took all her courage to meet his eyes. Tina felt guilty. Not only was Patrick devastated, her parents would be heartbroken, while she herself was almost unscathed.

"The clans o' Kennedy and Hamilton will no' be joined in matrimony," he said heavily. "Arran has informed me his son must wed the queen's lady, Nan Howard."

Elizabeth, in dismay, demanded, "Why?"

"Because he's put a bairn in her belly," Rob said baldly. Elizabeth was in shock.

Tina said low, "I'm so sorry, Mother. I only wish for your sake it was the other wedding that had been called off."

Elizabeth's face lit with a ray of hope. "Oh Rob, don't you see? Perhaps this is the answer to my prayers! Valentina will be free to marry. Perhaps the Douglas will settle for her instead of Beth."

Tina looked at her mother in disbelief as the words *"settle for her . . . settle for . . . settle for her"* repeated themselves in her brain. Tina felt as if she had received a blow to her solar plexus. It was unthinkable that she marry Black Ram Douglas, but even worse was the knowledge that her mother loved Beth so much more, she was willing to sacrifice Tina to save Beth.

With tart sarcasm Tina said, " 'Twould be a match made in Heaven."

Elizabeth agreed. "Yes, yes, Rob, don't you see that Valentina is much more suited to a brute like Douglas?"

When Tina felt Ada's comforting hand upon her shoulder, tears gathered in her throat, almost choking her.

"Rob, promise me you will see about it immediately, before it is too late," Elizabeth pressed.

As Rob Kennedy looked at his daughter, his heart was filled with pity for his beautiful little Firebrand. He wished Elizabeth had spoken to him in private—the woman had no sensitivity at all. "Well, it will be up tae the earls tae decide," he said.

Elizabeth was already on her feet. She couldn't wait to take the news to Beth. Hope wasn't dead after all. Ada followed Elizabeth from the room.

Tina hadn't moved. Her father said hoarsely, "Lassie, I'm sorry. She's right, ye know. If any can stand up tae Douglas, it's ye."

"Don't pity me, it's insulting," she said in a brittle voice.

His heart was heavy as he saw her shrug her shoulder before departing the room.

She paced up and down her chamber, giving vent to her outrage.

"It might not be so bad," Ada placated. "Marriage might alter him. People change, you know."

"No they don't—they just get more like themselves," Tina said with conviction. "Bloody men!" she swore. "Foul fall the lot of them!"

"Men can be managed," Ada said, "if a woman is clever enough." Ada had made a decision to stop trying to placate her. What Tina needed was help, advice, the truth. She would aid her any way she could, and she would begin by laying it all out on the table for her.

Tina stopped pacing. "What do you mean by clever?"

"A woman, a real woman, has weapons that can defeat

any man breathing, whether he's a lord, an earl, or even a king."

Tina sat down and gave Ada her full attention. "Do you mean my beauty?"

Ada shook her head. "Beauty is only a small part of it. It's not even necessary, though I cannot deny it is helpful. I'm speaking of a woman's sexuality. Most women never utilize it, never even achieve it. Like your mother."

Tina thought about that for a minute. "My mother gets her way with tears."

"Yes—and oh how much her man resents her for it."

"So just because you marry and give your husband children doesn't guarantee this sexuality?"

"No. It is in the way you dress, to lure a man, to please a man, to stir his imagination and inflame his desire. It is in a woman's eyes when she looks at a man, promising him Paradise. The eyes are very important, but not nearly as important as the mouth. The mouth is for making love and for speaking the words a man longs to hear. Soft words, seductive words, kind, sweet, understanding, and sympathetic words. The mouth is also for eating, and believe it or not, food and the way you eat it can be sensual. Never, ever forget the mouth is for laughing. Men love to laugh. A clever wit, like yours, is a gift from God."

"But Ada, I have no sexual experience," Tina explained, in case her woman suspected she had lain with men.

"I know that, but very shortly you will have. Remember that the most important sexual organ is your brain, not what's between your legs."

Tina's cheeks were quite pink now, but she was thankful that Ada was willing and able to discuss these things in such a forthright manner. "What's between my legs isn't important?" she questioned.

"Oh darling, it's very important. Only think! There are two places where a man and woman are different: your breasts and your mons, and men can never get enough of them. Your entire body is a weapon. Your skin like velvet, your hair like silk. A real man wants everything from a real woman. He wants to smell her and taste her."

Tina's eyes widened, which told Ada these ideas were all new to her.

"At the moment, you have an innocent sexuality that attracts men like a lodestone. When you gain experience, it will give you confidence over men in general and one man in particular. With men other than your husband, your sexuality must be subtle. When you are alone with your mate, however, it must be blatant. The single most important thing you must learn—that many women never, ever learn —is to *love* sex. You cannot fake it, it is impossible. You must be able to abandon yourself to him and truly enjoy anything and everything he does to you. Learn to be a sensual woman, ripe, endlessly yielding, and you will hold him in the palm of your hand. You will own him body and soul. Ramsay Douglas is a most powerful man, and if you gain power over him, it will be the most magnificent feeling you will ever experience."

Suddenly Tina began to laugh. She remembered their past encounters, knowing when they rolled in the grass he had wanted to rub dirt in her face. She remembered exactly the pewter eyes turning to a murderous black when she struck him with her riding crop and he had forced open her hand to disarm her of the weapon. But their last encounter was still most vivid in her mind: Black Ram Douglas had walked off the dance floor, dismissing her from his life. "God's passion, I'd like to see his face when they tell him he must wed Flaming Tina Kennedy."

"Our fate is written in the stars. We can't alter it," Ada said before she departed.

Alone, Tina's laughter subsided into a sob, and she threw herself upon the bed to soak her pillow with tears of pure misery. She cursed Old Meg, the Gypsy, who had foretold all this. She heard the words again, exactly. *"You *will be involved with a dark man whose symbol is the ram. He will rule you.*" In that moment Tina made her vow. "I will rule him!"

Chapter 16

The Earl of Angus was not best pleased in spite of the whisky Ramsay was pouring generously for him.

Ram downed his whisky in one gulp, letting its rawness eat at his innards. "The answer is no."

"Christ's holy wounds, I've swallowed ma pride an' signed a bond o' friendship wi' the bloody Hamiltons. I'm man enough tae do what's best fer the clan, an' so will ye, an' there's an end tae the matter!"

Ram protested, "Marry a Kennedy bitch, just because Jamie has decided?"

"It's no' just the king. *I've* decided it's time ye had an heir."

"Marriage is no guarantee of an heir. Has the Hepburn lass produced an heir fer yer son? Margaret has miscarried three times since the king wed her. She's finally produced an heir, but none know how long it'll live!"

"Ye can argue until yer black in the bloody face, but ye'll still form an alliance wi' the Kennedy lass." He drained his cup and threw it into the fireplace.

Colin tapped on the door. He was the only one in the whole castle who had enough courage to interrupt the two Black Douglases.

"Can ye no' see we're busy?" Angus glared.

"Aye, but Lord Rob Kennedy is below, and despite the

thickness of the walls, he can hear the two o' ye are havin' a slight altercation," he said dryly.

"Show him up," directed Angus. "This concerns him."

Colin looked to Ram.

"I'm still master in my own castle, though Angus here seems to have forgotten. Show him up," Ram directed.

Damaris sensed her brother's presence the moment Rob Kennedy stepped inside the castle. She left her old chamber and saw him ascending the stairs. "Robert, oh Robert, I haven't seen you for so long!" She bit her lip as she saw how the years had aged and thickened him. "Oh Robert, you can't see me or hear me, can you?" she cried softly. She touched his plaid sleeve lovingly. "Why are you here?" she wondered. She knew he could not answer her, but there was a very easy way to find out. As Colin opened the door to Ramsay's private living quarters, Damaris glided inside and sat down upon a cushion in the wide window-seat.

Kennedy had come in his full dress tartan, his face redder than his hair now that it was mixed with gray. Rob nodded his respect to the most powerful earl in Scotland— "Angus"—then his eyes swung to the earl's favorite nephew. "Douglas."

"Sit doon, mon," invited Angus. "We've never been enemies in spite o' the bad blood that happened over fifteen years back."

Rob jumped right in. "Ye rode back wi' Arran, so perhaps ye already have the news about the Hamilton-Kennedy wedding bein' off."

Angus waved his hand dismissively. "It canna be called off—the chiefs of the clans have agreed."

Rob Kennedy said bluntly, "I've just had a visit from the Hamiltons. Patrick's knocked up one of the Howard lasses, and the queen insists they wed."

Ramsay experienced a surge of triumph that his enemy's deepest desire had been thwarted. With contempt he said, "Patrick Hamilton's brains are in his prick."

Angus, irascible as always, said, "That stinkin' piece of English vermin! Howard likely told the lass tae spread her legs, so there'd be a bond o' matrimony wi' Scotland's admiral."

Ram at one time or another had bedded all the Howard daughters, and suddenly he was damned thankful they hadn't played this trick on him.

Rob cleared his throat and wished Douglas would pour him a dram to give him courage for his next words. He looked at the dark, closed face of the younger man and blurted, "Since ma elder daughter Valentina is now unpledged, I'm askin' ye tae take her instead of ma wee Beth."

Ram Douglas stared at him incredulously. "Ye have a hell of a crust, Kennedy, tae ever imagine I'd take either."

It was at this point that Angus went over to the other side. "Have a whisky, mon," he said, clapping Kennedy on the back. Rob swallowed the fiery liquor as if it was water, and he felt hope for the first time. "Naturally, I'd be prepared tae compensate ye generously fer takin' Valentina."

"How generously?" asked Angus.

Ram folded his arms across his chest and leaned back in his chair while the two men thought to arrange his life.

"I'll give her a dowry o' five thousand."

Angus was impressed, though his face remained passive.

An unbidden picture of Flaming Tina Kennedy rose fullblown in Ram's mind. He saw her mounted on the Barbary, the slit in her riding habit displaying too much leg, her glorious copper hair cascading like the mane of a tawny tigress. The memory of her blazing golden eyes and full underlip gave him an immediate erection. He could not deny that she was a splendid bitch!

He wondered how many erections in how many men she had been responsible for. Patrick Hamilton, the Gypsy, his own brothers—even Angus had said the sight of her made him scorch. All had courted the honeypot, the Campbells, the Gordons, the royal Stewarts, until she had finally landed the biggest fish of all, the Admiral of Scotland's heir and his own hated enemy.

Suddenly he realized the blow he could give to that enemy if he took the woman Patrick Hamilton was now denied. The delicious thought brought a rare smile to his lips. He'd be damned if he'd marry her, but have her he would. He looked across at the two men who were haggling over the female in question and drawled, "Double the dowry."

Rob smelled victory. "Done!" he agreed quickly.

Ram held up a lazy hand to show him he was not nearly finished. "Property?"

As Kennedy mentally sifted through all his holdings, Angus relaxed and allowed Ramsay to conduct his own affairs. His nephew was less a fool than any man he had ever known.

Rob first thought of Dunure, then got a better idea. If he offered Ram land closer to his beloved Castle Douglas in the borders, he'd be too covetous to refuse. "I have lands in Kirkcudbright, just across the River Dee from Castle Douglas. I'll deed them to Valentina and her heirs."

Ram admired his canny opponent. He'd not offered to put the lands in Douglas's name. "Nothing tempts me so far," Ram said bluntly.

Angus opened his mouth to protest vigorously, but he shut it again when Ram spoke. "I need more ships," he said in an offhand manner.

"Christ, ye drive a hard bargain," flared Rob, more possessive of his fleet of trading vessels than anything else he owned. Reluctantly he offered his smallest ship, the *Scotia.*

Ram nodded thoughtfully. "Ye've a vessel ye anchor in the Solway. I have a fancy for it every time I patrol the border down that way."

Kennedy compressed his lips in vexation. She was one of his finest vessels. The silence stretched between them. Douglas looked as if he didn't give a damn one way or the other. Tension mounted in the chamber until Kennedy almost felt suffocated. At last he capitulated. "Ye win, blast ye—I'll throw in the *Valentina.*"

Ram's lips twitched at the aptness of the ship's name. "I'll think on it," he replied casually.

"When will ye let me know?" Rob asked angrily.

"When I've made my decision," Ram said enigmatically.

Rob Kennedy clapped his bonnet on his head and turned on his heel in impotent rage. Damaris followed him out. She was appalled. She could not communicate with her brother, yet she knew she must do something—anything!

"Yer more devious than myself," Angus said with admiration.

"I doubt that," Ram said dryly.

Angus shook his head, "Yer a shrewd young bastard tae wring ships from him on top o' money an' land, especially when ye have no option whatsoever but tae wed."

"No say in my own fate?" he shouted furiously.

"The decision's been taken. Ye'll wed a Kennedy, whether ye like it or no," Archibald said flatly.

"We'll see about that," Ram said low, suppressing his anger by sheer dint of will.

Damaris watched with dismay as her brother rode away from the castle. He must be mad to sacrifice Valentina to a hated Douglas! Knowing what had happened to his sister in this castle, how could he allow his daughter to become a bride of Douglas? Damaris felt utterly frustrated that she could communicate with no one. She felt distraught that she could do nothing to intervene. Yet there was one other soul who could see and hear her. Alexander was her only chance. Perhaps together they could devise a plan of action. Though it compromised her principles, Damaris searched until she found him. "A marriage is being arranged between my niece Valentina and Ram Douglas. My brother was here, but I couldn't make contact with him.

Damn it, Alex, we must find a way to put a stop to this!"
she said desperately.

"Valentina Kennedy is exactly the right woman for Ramsay. I know all about it."

"Damn you, Alex! I listened to them. He doesn't even
want her. My brother offered him money and land and
even his beloved ships, and Ram was hardly even tempted.
Help me to find a way to stop this marriage?"

Alexander grinned at her. "He wants her, all right, almost as much as I wanted you. Nothing stopped me,
Damaris, and nothing will stop Ram. You know Douglas
blood."

"Yes, much to my sorrow, you ruthless, cold-blooded
bastard!"

Alexander's eyes were alight with pleasure. He threw
back his head and laughed with pure joy.

"Why are you laughing like a bloody heathen?" she demanded indignantly.

"Because yer talkin' tae me, sweetheart!"

She raised her hand to strike him, and he caught her
wrist and pulled her into his arms. "Never mind that we
are fightin' like cat and dog. After fifteen years of silence, I
love it. I love ye." His arms tightened about her, and his
mouth came down to crush hers. Damaris faded, but not
before she had been thoroughly kissed.

When Rob Kennedy returned to Doon, the entire
household was avid to learn what had transpired at Douglas. Elizabeth was the first to corner him. "My lord, put me
out of my misery. Did he insist on having Beth?"

"He did not," Rob answered truthfully.

Elizabeth sagged to the bed. Tears blurred her vision as
her husband removed his dress tartan. "I can tell ye no
more, except that Black Ram Douglas will ha' it his way or
no way. I hope yer satisfied, woman. I've sacrificed Tina tae
save yer precious Beth. He's a hard mon, she'll ha' none o'
her ain way anymore."

"Perhaps it's a good thing. Valentina has always needed a curb. The things Kirsty tells me about her are enough to make my hair stand on end."

"Wizened-up auld spinster! She's jealous because ma lass is so vibrant and filled wi' life. Even in a roomful o' beautiful women, Valentina is extraordinary."

Elizabeth wasted no time announcing to Beth the reprieve from her death sentence. Some color crept back into her face, and Ada excused herself so that she could take the news to Tina. She had just come in from a ride, and as Ada helped her change from her habit, she offered advice.

"When the Douglas comes to declare himself, you must be wearing your most becoming gown. You must make him aware of the value of the prize he is getting. Keep your sharp tongue folded behind your teeth and be all sweet, womanly submission. A man feels most masculine when he's in the presence of a soft, feminine woman. It will avail you nothing to rail and shout and set yourself against him. It will avail you everything to begin his enslavement the moment he proposes."

"You are wise in the way of men, Ada. I shall behave as you advise. Butter won't melt in my mouth."

Her woman picked up the fragile garment she was making. It was a transparent wisp of shell-pink gossamer she was fashioning into a nightgown for the bride-to-be.

Suddenly Tina felt weak at the knees. "Ada, I cannot do this thing without you. Would you be willing to leave Doon and come with me to Douglas?"

"Gladly, if you can persuade your mother to let me come."

"I'll go to her immediately. I shan't ask her, I'll inform her, and while I'm at it, I may as well tell her I'm taking Mr. Burque. She was the one who said we all have to make sacrifices," Tina said in a brittle voice.

* * *

For three days the apricot silk gown lay in readiness so it could be donned quickly when Douglas came a-calling. And though he took his own sweet time about it, come he did.

Ada slipped the gown over Tina's head, fastened the tiny pearl buttons on the square bodice, then sat her down before the mirror to thread creamy pearls through the loops of piled-up copper curls. Valentina felt confident. She knew she had never looked lovelier. When the summons came, she was ready.

As she approached the chamber, she heard his deep voice say clearly, "Fetch her in, and I'll have a look at her."

The arrogant son of a bitch sounded as if he'd come to buy a mare! Tina counted to ten, remembered Ada's instructions, and swallowed her anger. She took a deep breath, lowered her lashes, and stepped into the room.

Her beauty took him unawares. His features hardened so she could see no response in him. His pewter eyes held hers so long, her confidence faltered. His face was hard, his mouth sensual, his jaw stubborn. She saw clearly the arrogant pride in every line of his powerful body. He was garbed in black from head to foot, relieved only by his crimson badge, the Bleeding Heart of Douglas.

Valentina knew she was confronting her destiny. She resisted the narcotic of his presence and glanced away from him. Remember your eyes, remember your mouth, she told herself.

"Ye fly a high hawk, lady," Douglas accused tersely.

Her eyes widened. Did the swine mean she was reaching above herself? She bit down upon her tongue.

"How old are ye?" he demanded coldly.

"Seventeen, and I have all my teeth." She could not prevent the words. "I see that in courtship, as in war, chivalry must yield to expediency," she said with cutting sweetness.

"Courtship?" He laughed. "There will be no lack of candor. I am a blunt man. We are two totally incompatible personalities. Ye are bold and forward in temper. Ye are vain and spoiled and not much use tae a man. As well, all Kennedy women are rumored tae be honeypots.''

"Mon, yer blunt as a cudgel," protested her father.

With a disarming smile she gave as good as she got. "The Douglases are renowned for their ambition, pride, greed, and treachery."

"And valor," he added with a wolfish grin.

"You have a monstrous conceit of yourself," she accused.

"Aye, the Scots are like that," he agreed.

"This is the strangest proposal of marriage I've ever heard," she said, her eyes narrowing to golden slits.

He turned away from her and spoke directly to Rob Kennedy. "I'm not proposing marriage. Not for the present. A hand-fasting only. Both parties free tae withdraw if the union doesn't suit."

Valentina felt she had been struck by a thunderbolt.

Rob Kennedy's face purpled as he opened his mouth to protest.

Ram Douglas forestalled him. "Naturally, I'll sign a bond pledging tae wed her if she becomes pregnant wi' my heir."

The very air in the room crackled with outrage. "Let me speak with her alone," Ram said to Kennedy. "We'll let her decide."

Rob had to be satisfied with this. Reluctantly, he left the room.

"Ye are a lass not distinguished for yer chastity. It takes a great deal of sugar on the pill when other men have licked it. Fortunately for ye, yer parents are prepared to pay me a great deal to take you off their hands."

Hatred for this man almost blinded her. He thought her a whore! It was not possible that her parents were paying him! Through a violet mist of hate she saw the Douglas device upon his breast. She swore an oath in that moment that her heart would never bleed, but his assuredly would.

He was the challenge of a lifetime. She sent up a prayer to aid her to bring just one Scot low. "A hand-fasting suits me far better than marriage. It was clever of you to think of it. It satisfies the demands of the king and the earls, yet allows us to be free of each other in a few months' time."

"Then it's settled." It was not a question. His next words, however, were. His eyes dropped to her breasts. "Are they real?"

"What?"

"Yer tits. Is that ye, or is that padding?" In two long strides he was before her. He unfastened the pearl buttons and slipped his hand inside her bodice to cup the lovely round globe.

Her mouth opened in astonishment, and her heavy black lashes lifted to reveal the golden outrage blazing in her eyes.

Instantly the dull ache in his groin was replaced by the pleasurable feel of his shaft thickening and lengthening and hardening. He made no effort to conceal the enormous bulge.

Her eyes slid down deliberately. "Is that you, or is that padding?" Her daring hand reached out to cup his swollen manhood.

Ram felt his gut melt. His dark eyes bored into hers, and she knew a need to tear his rakehell face to pieces. Then his mouth was on hers savagely in a strong, male desire to overpower her. His need for her was naked in his face. She knew her boldness had placed her in jeopardy. Lord God, why did she say and do such impulsive, outrageous things without a thought to the consequences? He was a man who took what he wanted, whenever and wherever he wanted it, and he made no secret of what he wanted this moment. She knew she must do something to disentangle herself with her innocence intact. As his mouth descended upon hers again, she sank her teeth into his lip. Ram cursed, and Tina fled to the door, quickly fastening her gown. She turned the knob, saying, "Father, I believe we have reached an understanding."

The older man came back into the room feeling relief. Douglas departed without a backward glance. Suddenly she felt triumphant. Ada was right! She did have weapons. If she learned to wield them well, she would defeat him.

"Lass, are ye sure?" her father asked worriedly. "I'll go tae the king, I'll tell him it's an impossible match."

"No, no. It suits me well, Father. Only think of the pitying glances I would have received once it was bruited abroad that I'd been jilted by Patrick Hamilton. I don't pretend I won't receive glances as Ramsay Douglas's woman, but they won't be pitying." She shrugged her shoulder. "We are better acquainted than you realize. While you were at sea, I was a guest at his castle. There is unfinished business between us."

Lord Kennedy was surprised, yet not surprised. He'd seen them together in Stirling and knew they were a combustible combination, like setting a flame to a keg of gunpowder. At the moment they seemed to have a loathing for each other that held them in thrall. If that loathing ever turned to passion, their obsession with each other would bring rapture or madness. "If he should ever give ye hurt, promise me ye'll repudiate him and come home?"

She nodded, biting back a question about his paying the Douglas to wed her.

"Do ye need more time? Saturday will be upon us before ye can turn round."

"Saturday is as good as any other day. The die is cast. Think of the relief you will all feel when I'm raising merry hell at Douglas rather than Doon."

By Friday night, everything was in readiness. Her clothes alone filled ten trunks—then, of course, there were her linens, her silver, and her heirlooms collected over the years from her mother's family as well as the Kennedys.

Mr. Burque's kitchen equipment, utensils, and supplies filled two wagons. Tina had decided she would take as hers the bedchamber that had belonged to Damaris. She would not need to take her own bed, but her personal bedhangings had been cleaned and folded lovingly with woodruff. The damask woven in the east was a shimmering aqua with silver dolphins. Her silken carpet was patterned in dark gold and burnt amber. Her bathtub was handpainted with exquisite seashells and was fashioned in the shape of a great scallop shell.

She was taking her sorrel mare as well as her Barbary, Indigo. To spite Ram Douglas, she had almost decided not to take Indigo to be part of his stable, but then she realized that every time he saw her ride the mare he coveted, it would be a thorn in his flesh. She had said her good-byes to her mother, who had taken to her bed with yet another feigned illness so she would not have to travel to Douglas for the celebration.

Beth had tried to thank her for saving her from a fate worse than death, but Tina had brushed it off lightly and advised her to set about capturing Lord Andrew Kennedy before a mate was chosen for her. Now, however, as she sat pensively before the fire with Ada, all her mercurial energy had been sapped.

At last she heaved a great sigh and admitted, "Ada, I behaved outrageously when Douglas came with his insulting offer."

"Tina, a hand-fasting is not an insult. It is a time-honored Scottish custom. For all intents and purposes it is a marriage. You have a year in which to decide if the union will be permanent. After a year it becomes a legal and binding marriage for life. In your case he has pledged marriage earlier if there is a child. You will be accorded the place of honor in all his castles. You will be husband and wife. You will be Lady Douglas."

"I'll not take his damned name! I hate Ram Douglas!

He is a swaggering bastard. I want to bring him low—nay, more than that, I want to break him."

"There is only one way to gain power over him, Tina."

"Yes, I know. I'm going to try to make him fall in love with me. If I ever bring him to the point where he cannot live without me, I shall laugh in his face and end it," she said with intensity.

"Well, you'll never bring Hotspur Douglas to that point unless you can seduce him and make him a slave to your sexuality."

"I know he feels desire for me." She blushed. "He couldn't keep his hands off me. He undid my gown and fondled my breasts on the pretext of seeing if I was padded."

Ada's eyebrows rose. "With your father just outside the door? What did you do?"

"I—I touched his sex and demanded to know if he was padded."

"Omigod, Tina, you are the limit! Now I know what you mean when you say you behaved outrageously!"

"I have a slight problem. He assumes I have had a lot of sexual experience."

"I wonder why?" Ada asked dryly.

"In actuality I am abysmally ignorant about sexual matters. How on earth am I to make him a slave to my sexuality?"

"Darling, Ram Douglas will soon teach you all you'll ever need to know. Learn what he likes, cater to his needs. His reputation as a lover is legendary. Surely you realize the name Hotspur carries a wealth of sexual connotation?"

"No, I didn't realize. . . . Ada, I'm afraid. He's enormous, like a stallion. I've seen how mares scream when they are mounted for the first time."

"Oh love, you have to get beyond that first time. There will be pain and blood, but don't become repressed by it, as so many women do. Allow him to give you pleasure. There is nothing on earth to compare with total fulfillment. It starts with a spark of desire and builds to an unbearable pitch, and if you can simply abandon your body to his at that moment, you will experience bliss, rapture, paradise."

"It sounds mystical."

"It is! And the more he sees you enjoy it, the more he will enjoy it, and he will strive to bring you more pleasure with each encounter. Don't think only a man can experience lust. It is a fallacy that while men do it for pleasure, women only do it for love. You must switch that about and enjoy it purely for the pleasure. Men think of sex as conquest until they realize the power they feel when they learn how much pleasure they can give a woman. Indulge your own lust. Bind him to you with his lust. Soon he will be bound forever with chains of lust and love."

"Ada, he really intimidates me, but I'll be damned if I'll let him see it."

Ada put her arms about Tina. "Get some sleep. I have every confidence in you. You are passionate about everything in life—you cannot fail to be passionate in bed."

Chapter 17

Lady Valentina rode between her father and Archibald Kennedy, Earl of Cassillis. Her brothers Duncan and David with a score of Kennedy clansmen rode at the head of the cavalcade, and the baggage wagons brought up the rear. In addition to Ada and Mr. Burque, her father insisted she take her own groom, and her mother had provided her with one of the Kennedy maids by the name of Nell.

Every male wore the green and red Kennedy tartan, and

even Tina wore a plaid sash draped across one shoulder of her fashionable green riding habit. She sat her horse with the pride of a queen, with Ada's words ringing in her head. Because Ada was English, she saw Scotland and its people more clearly than they saw themselves. "Scotland is a savage, brutal land, rugged and uncompromising. Its men reflect this perfectly, Tina. They are strong, arrogant, and only half civilized. Only by pledging total loyalty to a clan are they able to survive.

"Scotland has the bloodiest history of any land. Gaelic blood makes the Scot wilder and prouder than other nationalities. You and Ram Douglas are much alike. You are both ruled by passion and fury. Your short tempers and your recklessness have fostered a personal feud where you enjoy fighting each other. If you intend to gain the upper hand, you will never do it by force, for he is stronger than you. You can only win by guile. Put on a velvet glove when you spar with him, keep the guard on the end of your rapier. Tease him, make him laugh with you, and make him love you, then when he is most vulnerable, you must disarm him, thrust home, and pierce him to the heart."

When the castle at Douglas rose up before her, she relived the day she had faked the riding accident and lain in the rain until Ram had come upon her and carried her inside. She shivered remembering his dangerous strength. Now that the season was changing to summer, the cold, wet chill was no longer in the air, and she had no reason to shiver, she told herself sternly as she unfastened the high neck of her velvet habit and fingered the gray-brown Lazarus beads she had deliberately worn today to ward off evil.

The sound of their horses' hooves upon the drawbridge was hollow, she thought, almost ominous. The moment they reached the bailey, she saw that preparations for today's event were well under way. She saw vivid splashes of yellow, orange, and green as vegetables spilled from their baskets. Barrels of oysters and crabs lined a wall where two scullions sat shucking them.

Across the courtyard a pair of oxen turned slowly over firepits, their juices dripping and hissing upon the coals beneath, while the wolfhound named Boozer sat on his great haunches giving the roasting carcasses his rapt, undivided attention.

Douglas grooms rushed to attend the arriving Kennedys, their dark heads contrasting with the bright red of their guests'. The Earl of Angus came forward to greet the Earl of Cassillis, and Lord Ramsay Douglas greeted Lord Rob Kennedy with great formality, before he even glanced toward Valentina.

Mr. Burque, who had ridden Tina's sorrel mare, dismounted immediately and went to her side, deftly shouldering aside both the Douglas groom and her own Kennedy groom. Ram's eyes widened, then narrowed as he raked the elegant, tall, slim man with the beautiful face. He'd received part of his education in Paris, and he had never seen a male as attractive as this one outside of France. His suspicions were confirmed as he heard the gallant raise his arms and say, "Allow me, *chérie.*"

Ram left Rob Kennedy's side to observe the tableau before him. Tina gave the Frenchman a brilliant smile and leaned down to him. Douglas growled, "Ye relieve me of my obligations." Tina went down into Mr. Burque's arms with a flurry of petticoats, then looked up at the dour Scot and said sweetly, "Mr. Burque is indispensable to me, my lord."

"In what capacity?" Douglas asked coldly.

"Mr. Burque is my chef."

"Yer chef?" he asked incredulously. "Think you we have no such servants at Douglas?"

Her laughter trilled out at his ignorance. "Ah, sir, cooks you may have aplenty, scullery maids and potboys, but you have no one who can even begin to compare with Mr. Burque. He is the finest chef in Scotland, and he is mine."

While Douglas glared fiercely, Mr. Burque excused himself to supervise the unloading of the precious tools of his trade.

"He's too pretty to piss," said Douglas with disgust, and Tina laughed up at him to show that he had amused her. He reached out a bold finger to touch the Lazarus beads at her throat. "Are ye trying to conjure Auld Horny?" he asked with derision.

She cast a sideways glance at the forbidding Earl of Angus and said, "It must have worked, for there's Archibald himself!"

Ram gave a shout of laughter, and she gave him a bewitching look from beneath her lashes. "There. We have amused each other. What more can a man or woman ask? Aside from money, land, and ships, of course?" she added wickedly.

Smoothly he replied, "Knowing women as I do, I'm sure ye'll be asking my favors come dusk."

His repartee was more skillful than she had expected. All his words could be interpreted to have more than one meaning. She found the witty repartee infectious and tried her hand at it, fastening wide eyes upon his mouth and breathing, "Ah, milord, I find I cannot wait until dusk for your favors. Will you not come upstairs with me now?"

"Yer *desire* is my command," he emphasized.

"Good—then you won't mind if I claim the chamber that belonged to my aunt Damaris." She turned and beckoned Ada and at the same time saw Ram's brother Gavin approach. "Ada, have my trunks taken up to my chamber. I am to have Damaris's room." She turned back to Ram, her wicked juices bubbling deliciously. "Here comes another to relieve you of your obligations. I'm sure Gavin will be happy to take me upstairs—so I can familiarize myself with things." She gave Gavin a saucy look as she took his arm. "What would I do without your aid, sir? I must get out of this riding dress and into my bath at the first opportunity." Gavin grinned like a heathen; Ram's ill-concealed fury added to his amusement.

* * *

The earls were impatient to get on with the business pertaining to this union, and the four men retired to the ancient Douglas weapons room where the business of the clan had been conducted for centuries.

Ram offered his guests purled ale, which Rob took thankfully to wash the dust of the journey from his parched throat, but the two earls turned up their noses, and he knew only whisky would satisfy their jaded palates. He splashed two measures of the dark amber liquor from a large Venetian decanter, and they all drew up chairs about the large map table.

First came the deed for the land in Kirkcudbright, which Kennedy signed over, and then came the ownership and captain's papers for the two vessels, the *Scotia* and the *Valentina*. It was understood by all that the ships would now be crewed by Douglas men.

In return, Ram Douglas signed the pledge to wed Lady Valentina Kennedy in the event that she quickened with child. The hand-fasting required no signed documents— just a verbal pledge, with both families as witness—and this would take place later in the day. Now came the all-important document the king had demanded from the chiefs of these two ancient clans. The bond of friendship between Clan Kennedy and Clan Douglas was signed by the two earls and witnessed by the other two men. The sealing wax was melted, and all four stamped their gold seal rings onto the crackling parchments. Finally, Rob Kennedy gave into Ramsay Douglas's hands a bank draft for ten thousand pounds Scots. Angus insisted they drink a toast to the occasion in pure, raw Scotch whisky, and Ram took perverse pleasure as he felt the hot liquor blossom inside his chest.

As Tina ascended the main staircase with Ada on one side and Gavin upon the other, they were met by Colin, who had been awaiting them. He held out his hand. "Welcome tae Douglas, Lady Kennedy. Ye will be in grave need o' a friend in this castle. I would be honored to fulfill the role."

"Colin," she said low, her eyes looking deeply into his with gratitude. "The honor is mine, sir."

He drew her closer to place a chaste kiss upon her brow, and Ada saw that their hands touched in a silent pledge. "I am to have Damaris's chamber."

His eyes took on a strange light. "I knew that ye would," he said simply, leading the way down the hall and opening the chamber door.

Tina entered and lifted her hand to the beautiful portrait above the fireplace. As Ada gazed up, she said, "The artist has captured her exactly. The man is a master."

"Thank ye," Colin said quietly.

Tina's eyes widened. "You painted this, Colin?"

"Guilty as charged. The lady's beauty is what ye admire, not ma poor talent."

In the far corner of the room Damaris blushed. She recalled sitting for the portrait as if it had been yesterday, and she knew in her heart that Colin had had more than a brotherly affection for her.

"I shall leave ye in the hands o' the servants. If there is a Douglas who does not do yer bidding instantly an' tae yer satisfaction, I shall deal wi' him."

Damaris stared as a dozen servants carted in the ten trunks, carpet, bedhangings, and fantastic bathtub. After more than fifteen years of relative solitude, here was change indeed.

A young squire came in carrying oat cakes and wine, but Tina could not be tempted. Ada took the tray from him and sent him for hot water for the bath. "Have you eaten anything at all today?" asked Ada, eyeing Tina's pale cheeks.

Tina shook her head and wrinkled her nose. "Oat cakes would be like sawdust in my mouth."

"Well, I dare not let you have wine until you put something on your stomach. You are outrageous even without wine." Ada set Nell to work unpacking and hanging Tina's clothes in the massive wardrobe. "While you have your bath, I'll lay out your gown. Now, where in God's name did I put that small cream ruff that matches this dress?"

It was a full two hours before Lady Valentina was bathed and gowned in the heavy cream satin with its bodice embroidered with delicate seed pearls. Its modest square neckline allowed only the merest swell of breast to peep above it, and her chin was held high by the small pearl-rimmed ruff. Her fiery hair fell about her in a loose silken torrent as befitted a maiden. Her shapely head was so proud and high, it almost looked too small to carry the luxurious weight of her tresses.

Her father escorted her down the staircase, but Ram was not there to receive her. Instead, the Earl of Angus slipped a proprietary arm about her and said, "She belongs tae Douglas now, Rob. Let me look ma fill afore Ram has at her." He bent his dark head toward her, and the whisky fumes almost overpowered her. "Come intae the hall, lass, while I show ye off. Every Douglas within a hundred miles has ridden in tae ogle ye an' steal a kiss."

As Ram's brother approached them, Angus said, "Nay, Gavin, ye randy young swine, let an auld man's flesh enjoy rising tae the occasion."

Inside the vast hall was an impossible crush of dark-visaged Douglases, all shouting and shoving, cursing and laughing, drinking and arguing. The smell of scores of bodies, mixed with acrid smoke from the vast fireplace and the cooking smells of the great platters of food that were now being carried in, caused Tina's empty stomach to do a flip-flop. When she felt herself sway, she clung to Archibald Douglas's arm tightly and gave him a disarming smile. He licked dry lips and tried to peer down the front of her exquisite gown. "Ye ha' delicious titties, lass—aye, an' a delicious mouth. God's passion, ye'll suck each other dry afore mornin'!"

Tina's face was no longer pale but blushing delicately at

Archibald's coarse appraisal of her charms. It was almost with relief that she saw Ram detach himself from a group of men and make his way across the hall toward her. Archibald turned her about with his powerful arm. "By Christ, the Douglas cooks have done us proud. Only look at this, lass."

A sow with her twelve baby piglets had been roasted whole, and her young had been placed artistically at her teats as if they were still suckling. Valentina, used to Mr. Burque's tasteful dishes, had never seen anything so obscene in her life. The blood drained from her lips, and she went down in a faint.

Ram Douglas stepped back from her, his eyes narrowing. Angus jostled everyone aside. "Christ, ye rough bunch o' uncivilized beasts! Let the lassie breathe."

The moment Tina's head was lowered, her faintness left her, and she allowed Angus to aid her to her feet. "The lass is faint wi' hunger. Christ, I could eat a well-salted saddle myself, my belly is fair rumblin'! Ramsay, where the hellfire are ye? Let's get the mumbo-jumbo out o' the way so ye can get some food intae this lass."

A cruel hand closed over hers as Ram Douglas plucked her away from Angus. He dragged her up on the dais that had been set up in front of the massive fireplace. A loud cheer went up and rolled about the hall in a great wave. As Tina looked into the dark, closed face of Ram Douglas, she knew only that he was furious. His anger, barely repressed, was there for all to witness. He had been forced to this union against his will, and as she stood beside him, she felt his rage wash over her. She wanted to cry out that she too had been forced against her will. Surely he could not lay all the blame upon her. She felt what could only be his hatred.

Ramsay was blackened by hatred. His hair and eyes were midnight black, his doublet also black, relieved only by the cream ruffle of his silk shirt at neck and wrist. A devil consumed him at this moment. He had seen her faint. Did she dare come to him with another man's bairn in her belly? If she was carrying Hamilton's by-blow, he would kill him—aye, and then he'd kill her. He'd snap that beautiful, fragile neck with his bare hands.

A curl of fear spiraled in Tina's belly. If he ever unleashed that savage temper upon her, there would be none to save her from the dark Scot.

He knew she was far too beautiful to be good, but if she had come to him pregnant, he would destroy her and take pleasure in the act. He tore his dark eyes from her and looked out at the sea of Douglas faces. Admiration and desire were writ plain in every male face. The vixen had seduced the lot of them with the shrug of a shapely shoulder. Her allure was devastating. He was too proud and stiff-necked to let them see that she might have tricked him. Suddenly he clasped her wrist and held her hand on high. He picked up the crystal wine goblet filled with ruby liquid and said the words that would bind them in the hand-fasting.

The traditional period was for one year. At that time they would wed, or they would part if either of them wished to end the union.

Valentina picked up her goblet and repeated the pledge. They drained the glasses, then hurled them into the fireplace, shattering the crystal into a million fragments. The crowd went wild. Ram's hands were ungentle upon her as he bent her back forcefully to submit to his kiss.

She knew the kiss was not for her but for the clan gathered before them, to show his mastery of her. It took every last ounce of Tina's determination, but she started out as she meant to carry on. She yielded to him, submitting her soft mouth, her body, and her will to his. He stared down at the warm creature in his arms, all soft womanly submission, and raged inside.

At table, none of the food seemed to appeal to Tina. With a bellyful of wine on her empty stomach, her blood was up and she was almost ready for him, but she noticed that he himself ate little and drank much, and she feared that drunk neither he nor she would have any control whatsoever.

When half a dozen dark-visaged Douglases started to banter with Ram, he arose and went down the long hall with them, laughing for the first time that day. Tina felt abandoned and glanced about her for support, but everyone seemed to take their cue from Ramsay to stretch their legs. She spied Duncan, but the moment she spoke to him, she could see that he had drunk so much, he was unsteady on his feet. "Where's Davie?" she asked hopefully.

"Fuckin' his way through the Douglas maids," Duncan said, grinning like a heathen.

She recoiled from him. What made men so coarse? They were like animals, every last one of them!

"Come, lass—the villagers outside ha' been linin' up fer hours fer just a glimpse o' ye." To her amazement, it was Archibald Douglas who was offering her his arm. No man in Scotland had a worse reputation than the Earl of Angus. He was known to be ruthless and power-mad. It was rumored that every man in Scotland feared him, even the king.

Tina reckoned that he must have a hard head for liquor since he had consumed whisky steadily for most of the day but seemed to have himself well in hand. She was secretly amused to discover that Archibald had allied himself to her. She knew that Janet Kennedy had been his mistress, and she thought perhaps the family resemblance had taken his fancy. Whatever it was, she would seize this opportunity to parade on his arm. If the Douglas Clan saw that she had their chief's approbation, they would accord her respect, perhaps even fawn upon her. His influence was *all-powerful,* and Tina had decided that power was no bad thing to have.

They walked together for an hour, during which time Tina charmed him with her prettiest behavior. She was gracious to all, be they prince or peasant, and Angus approved of the way she acknowledged the adulation she received. She hung on his every word, realizing she would never find a better tutor, for he knew more about the affairs of the country in general and of the Douglases in particular than any man alive.

After he had introduced her to yet another Lord Douglas, she laughingly protested, "My lord, enough, I cannot tell one from another. I was always told Scotland had more sheep than any other commodity, but I'm beginning to suspect there are more Douglases than sheep."

He grimaced. She suspected that was how he smiled. "Come wi' me, lass. There's summat I want tae show ye." She stood at the entrance to the weapons room and wondered if she dared trust him alone. She went in with him realizing she could never trust any Douglas.

A huge map adorned one wall, and he drew her toward it with pride. A good deal of it, from the border up to the Highlands, was shaded in dark green, which she assumed indicated forests. Angus soon corrected her ignorance. Her eyes widened as she saw that the dark green represented Douglas land. "This will give ye an idea o' our strength an' our power. The border counties of Teviotdale and Hawick are ours, as are the county of Angus and the bracs of Angus in the Highlands. This castle is here in Lanark County, and our lands stretch from here to the coast, clear across Midlothian and East Lothian."

"You own everything around Edinburgh for hundreds of miles," she said, trying to keep awe from her voice.

Archibald grimaced. "Why do ye think the capital was moved frae Stirling tae Edinburgh?" Though the question was rhetorical, she gave an answer. "Because some of the land about Stirling was not controlled by Douglas."

He winked at her quick grasp of things. "Those two laddies ye just met were Douglas of Kilspendie and Douglas of Longniddy." His callused fingers traced another line across the map. "Douglas lands stretch from Galloway in the southwest to Mearns in the northeast. We've more castles than ye've fingers tae count them on—Tantallon, Dunbar, and the castle of Aldbar at Brechin are all garrisoned. Here's Castle Douglas, our pride and joy, where Loch Dee and the River Dee come together. That's where the hearts of all Douglas lords are buried."

"Only their hearts?" she questioned curiously.

"Sometimes that's all that was left after a particularly bloody battle. The first earl directed his heart be placed in a casket an' buried beneath the altar in the chapel at Castle Douglas. Since then, our device has been the Bleedin' Heart o' Douglas. It is tradition that we shed our blood fer Scotland." He grimaced again. "We have a reputation fer livin' turbulent lives."

Valentina touched her finger to Castle Douglas on the map. Then her eyes narrowed. "This shouldn't be shaded green. Your map is wrong, my lord."

He drew closer and peered where she pointed. "The other side of the River Dee in Kirkcudbright is Kennedy land," she asserted.

"Nay, lass. That was part of the price yer father paid Ramsay."

"Blood of God, then it's true! My father paid him to take me!"

He responded to the anguish he heard in her voice. "Lassie, there's no shame in that. Have ye any notion the vast sum Henry Tudor paid King Jamie tae wed Margaret?"

Suddenly her heart filled with pity for the queen. Damn men to lowest hell. Women should not be bartered like chattels!

Archibald looked down at her, cleared his throat, and said, "Ram had tae be dragged kickin' an' screamin' tae this union. That's why he's bein' insolent an' neglectin' ye today. Lass, I'm countin' on ye tae bring him tae heel. Since he's derelict in his duties, I'm filling in fer yer husband."

"He's not my husband," she said quickly.

"That's soon remedied. He needs legitimate heirs, strong Douglas sons tae inherit all this." He waved his hand at the map. "I doubt ye'll ever tame him, but that's the measure o' his mettle. He has it in him tae be great. He has leadership qualities that are lacking in ma ain heir. Ram's sons, with a Firebrand like ye for their dam, will provide the strength Scotland needs for the future."

She wanted to protest, "I'm not a damned brood mare!" But she wisely held her tongue.

"He's sown enough wild oats. Oh, I've no objection tae him scatterin' a few bastards aboot. After all, we've the best blood in Scotland, an' most of the clans could do wi' a drop. Yer no' the sort o' woman who would cavil at that, are ye?"

Actually, she was stunned at the frank picture he painted. She shrugged an indifferent shoulder and said faintly, "No, let him scatter away."

"That's a wise lass. I've no doubt his neglect will end once yer inside the bedcurtains. When he's had a taste o' ye, I hope ye make it yer business to spoil his desire fer other women."

She opened her mouth and closed it again. God Almighty—did he too think her experienced?

"Well, lass, there's no hope o' savin' ye from his black temper, but I'm hopin' ye'll match him with a temper o' yer own."

It was her turn to grimace. "So I shall," she promised.

When he returned her to the hall, the shouting and arguing almost deafened her. It seemed all the Douglas men who were titled were wagering with Ramsay about how many alehouses were between here and Glasgow.

"Dungavel, Strathaven, Eaglesham, Coatbridge, Hamilton, and Kilbride," Cameron said with great authority.

"Ye forgot the one here in the village of Douglas," Drummond argued. He was a Douglas cousin and a captain of one of their ships.

"That's only seven," Gavin grumbled. "Hardly worthy of a good crawl."

Ram's pewter eyes glittered with recklessness. "There's ten. Ye've forgot Stonehouse and Blackwood. Christ, I've done it often enough, I should know."

"Stonehouse and Blackwood are brothels, not alehouses," Greysteel Douglas pointed out.

"Are ye complaining, man?"

"No, no. I'm up tae it, if ye are."

"Now yer bragging." Ram laughed. "Come on, lads—let's drink our way tae Glasgow!"

When Lady Valentina withdrew from the hall to the sanctity of her own chamber, it caused no comment. All Douglas females with a shred of decency removed themselves from the men once darkness fell. The Boozer padded up the stairs after her and followed her down the hall. He paused at the door to Ramsay's chambers, and when Tina swept past, he protested with a deep bark. She said, "You might wish to sleep with him, but I do not."

The wolfhound heaved what sounded like a reluctant sigh and slowly followed her. She opened the chamber door to find Ada and Nell awaiting her. The Boozer raised his hackles and refused to enter. Tina recalled that he had done exactly the same thing before.

Nell shrieked with terror as she glimpsed the tall, shaggy creature, but Tina said calmly, "He won't come in. The chamber is haunted."

Nell's eyes rolled back in her head. Ada laughed. "Come on, lass. Off to bed with you." She opened the door to the small adjoining room and said, "You can sleep in my room tonight. Tomorrow will be soon enough to go to the servants' quarters."

When they were alone, Ada looked at Tina anxiously as she unfastened her pearl-rimmed ruff. As she moved toward her to help her with the cream satin gown she said, "Well, under the circumstances, I think you held up remarkably."

Tina's chin went up defiantly. "I shan't cry, if that's what you're expecting. The swine will never make me shed one tear."

"Good! The last Kennedy to occupy this chamber likely did enough crying for both of you, and it availed her nothing."

"Nay!" protested Damaris. "Alex Douglas and I loved and laughed. I shed no tears until that last fateful day." If her own husband had ever treated her as Ram had treated Valentina, she would have been distraught. Her wedding day—and night—had been the happiest of her life.

Ada picked up the white silk nightrail sewn especially for this night. "I'll put this away for now . . . perhaps tomorrow night."

"Perhaps not!" Tina said decisively.

Ada was in agreement with her. "Always make him wait for sex. I once made a man wait until we were both undressed!"

"Oh, Ada," Tina said, dissolving into laughter. "Whatever would I do without you?"

"That's better. Salt tears never grew a rose. Good night, love. Tomorrow, if I know you, you will take this damned castle by storm."

As Tina gazed from the high window with unseeing eyes, she whispered, "I refuse to cry." The tears however, that had gathered in her golden eyes slid down her cheeks and dropped upon her heart.

Chapter 18

Tina finally managed to fall into an exhausted sleep, but she awoke about four in the morning. She thought about her situation for a full hour, during which her resolve hardened to marble. So the Douglases thought they were blood-proud, did they? She'd show them pride of blood! If Black Ram Douglas thought to intimidate her, he was in for a rude awakening. She'd not only take him on—she'd take on the whole scurvy clan!

She chose an elegant black silk gown, swept her hair up into a chignon, and opened the door. The Boozer groaned before he turned over and went back to sleep. She stepped over him and descended to the kitchens.

She expected fireworks from that quarter when Mr. Burque began to stake out his territory. She decided to enter the fray and assert her authority from day one. But instead of the chaos and curses she had expected, she found that Mr. Burque was in supreme control. All the Douglas cooks were female, and the Frenchman's facile flattery had them in the palm of his hand.

He pointed out to them that the kitchens should be kept immaculate. The place crawled with lazy scullery maids and potboys who should be set to scouring immediately. Only when the floors, the tables, and the last utensil were spotless should they exercise their profession—which, as any good chef knew, was more an art than a craft.

Tina took him aside. "Well done, Mr. Burque. We may as well start out as we mean to carry on. Yesterday I not only found the food inedible, the sight of it and the greasy smell of it would have made a goat retch. The castle's inhabitants may eat pig-swill for all I care, but Lord Douglas and I will eat nothing that is not prepared by you."

"Y a rien là," he said, assuring her there would be no problems.

She glanced at the women, who couldn't take their eyes off him and laughed, *"Chanteur de pomme!"*

At this early hour Colin was the only one about. He cast her such a sympathetic look, she laughed.

"My lady, I must apologize fer Ram's behavior yesterday."

"I'm afraid he'll have to do that himself," she said wryly. "However, I'm happy to see I have one ally in the Douglas camp. I shall need your help."

He bowed. "How may I serve ye?"

"Tell whoever is in charge of the moss-troopers that I shall see him in the hall in quarter of an hour." Before he could ask the reason for such an odd request, she had swept past him on her way to the servants' quarters. She informed the bleary-eyed steward, one William Douglas, that she would have a list of jobs for his underlings if he would attend her in the hall in quarter of an hour. In the meantime he could start by opening all the windows.

Tina was relieved when she saw Ram's second-in-command walk into the hall. Men-at-arms, when off duty, were idle, uncouth, loud-mouthed louts, and she had wondered if he would attend her. She took a deep breath. He was another damned Douglas, judging by his tall, dark visage, but he was still a man, and she would engage him by fair means or foul.

She gave him her most brilliant smile, noting that he was a little on the pale side this morning. She deliberately allowed her eyes to travel across the great breadth of his shoulders and said, "Please sit. If you tower above me, I shall strain my neck."

"My lady," he said warily. Christ—she was the sort of woman who made a man aware he was male.

"Most men-at-arms are uncouth louts, but I am told

Douglas moss-troopers are a breed apart. They are reputed to have more pride and self-discipline than those of other clans. Tell me, are any of your men able to even stand this morning?"

His mouth quirked a little. "Half a dozen hard-bitten veterans, and a couple of the younger men."

"Choose three or four of your best—men like yourself, with ramrod straight backs. I want them bathed and shaved and in the saddle in half an hour. I want you to escort Lord Douglas home."

"Where is he, lady?" he asked blankly.

"You'll find him in an alehouse or a brothel somewhere between here and Glasgow," she said matter-of-factly. "I'm sure he'll appreciate the aid and support of his best men this morning." She gave him a conspiratorial wink and left him so she could speak with the steward. Christ, if she'd been his woman, he'd still have her abed between his thighs this morning!

It was now the steward's turn to bask in the warmth of her smile. "This castle has such lovely furnishings, it seems a pity the servants have neglected them so shamefully. I don't blame you, of course, William. Any castle with a predominance of men is bound to take on a rakish, unkempt look. With you directing the servants for me, we'll soon rectify the matter." Another shameless smile was followed by lashes sweeping her cheeks. When she raised them, her golden eyes took away his very breath.

"I want all the rushes removed from the lower floors and the flagstones scrubbed. My woman will give you woodruff to mix with the new rushes. I want all the furniture polished with beeswax and lavender. If you don't have any, you had better get someone on his way to Doon immediately. While he's there, he can bring some decent candles until Douglas learns to make its own. We can't have these disgusting smelly tallow things dripping their grease on everything. I want all the windows washed, and you can send a couple of maids out to gather flowers. We'll leave the carpet beating and tapestry cleaning for another day."

He stole a glance at the sand in the hourglass. Hell's teeth, it wasn't much past six. The Douglas servants were still snoring their heads off after yesterday's debauch.

When Hotspur's moss-troopers discovered him under an alehouse table and roused him, he thought a battle-ax had been embedded in his skull. He opened one eye. "Where am I, Jock?"

"Ye made it as far as Hamilton," Jock replied with admiration.

Ram groaned. "Oh, Christ. I remember now," he said, feeling the swollen duck egg on his pate where a belligerent Hamilton had crowned him with a stool. The taproom was littered with the wounded, lying amidst smashed furnishings. Ram stood up slowly and said, "Look tae Gavin and Drummond." The landlord hovered in a dilemma. His alehouse was in Hamilton territory, yet he had a healthy fear of alienating Douglas. He nodded with relief when Ram said, "I'll pay all damages if ye forget ye ever saw us last night."

Ram went outside and submerged his head in the horse trough. Drummond was on his feet, but Gavin was still out cold and the moss-troopers slung him over his saddle.

Ram swiped his arm across his brow to push his dripping hair from his eyes. "Where's Cameron and the others?"

"They only made it as far as Shirley Blackwoods," said Jock, glancing at the Hamilton lying in the pub yard. "What about the signed truce?"

"To lowest hell wi' the truce," growled Ram. Hotspur did not vault into the saddle this morning. He eyed Jock and his three moss-troopers who were smartly turned out and had the decency to flush at his own sorry state. "Thanks," he muttered between his teeth.

"Thank yer lady. She sent me," said Jock gravely.

"So," he said through eyes narrowed against the bright

noon light. "Flaming Tina is ready for a fight. Well, I'm just the bastard to accommodate her."

When he arrived back at the castle, bellowing her name, however, he was informed that Lady Kennedy had gone riding. "These woods are dangerous!" he shouted at the stableman, needing to vent his spleen.

"She had a Kennedy and a Douglas groom glaring daggers at each other, and the Boozer went loping off ahead of her."

When he entered the castle, everything was shining clean, and it had never smelled so fresh. Flowers were everywhere. "Bloody meddling women!" he swore, going up to his rooms. As he bathed and changed his clothes, however, he was glad that she hadn't seen his dissolute state.

Shaving, and sporting a cream linen shirt, greatly improved his appearance, though his mouth tasted like he'd been sucking on a shepherd's stocking, and he knew his stomach would revolt at the sight or even smell of food.

The spirit of Alexander paced back and forth across the chamber restlessly. "Yer a bloody fool! Yer wastin' the chance I never had! A union between Kennedy and Douglas will be the best thing that ever happened tae Scotland, and it's certainly the best damned thing that ever happened tae ye. Christ, yer so much like me, I could kick your arse! Think yer the great bloody whoremaster! Think yer such a perilous character! The truth is, yer terrified of one small woman. Her beauty an' her wild free spirit scare the shit out o' ye, because yer afraid ye might fall in love wi' her. Where would yer reputation be then, Hotspur? I swear, if harm comes tae another lovely Kennedy lass through the bloody black house of Douglas, I'll hang ye by yer balls!"

As Ram ran his silver brushes through his thick black hair, his reflection reminded him of Alexander. God, how he resembled him—and if he didn't keep a tight rein on his temper, he'd end up murdering his woman too.

Before he opened his door, his mask of studied indifference and carelessness was in place. He went in search of his steward to learn how many guests were still here. He was glad that most of them had left and was especially relieved that Angus had departed—no doubt to report to King Jamie. He saw Drummond coming downstairs, still unshaven. "How's Gavin?"

"He'll live," came Drummond's terse reply.

"Good, there's work tae be done around here. When ye return tae Edinburgh tomorrow, he can go wi' ye. There's a cargo of tanned hides as well as the wool this time. He thinks he knows his way about a ship, but there's still a lot ye can teach him. I've acquired two more vessels, so we'll need more captains in the family."

They spent an hour going over the cargoes for Flanders, then Drummond reminded him it was time to sup.

"Ye must have a cast-iron gut," Ram remarked. "Before ye go, I want tae warn ye tae keep an eye out for unfriendly English vessels. Don't take chances—if they get close enough ye can smell them, blow the bastards out of the water!"

Though Ram's belly was empty, he avoided the hall knowing the smells would undo him. As he made for the front door he came face to face with Valentina, who had picked up the skirts of her sapphire riding skirt, exposing tall, black, high-heeled boots, so that she could more easily run.

Though he looked very forbidding and his wide shoulders almost loomed over her, she gave him a pretty smile. His eyes were hooded as he looked down at her, his face unreadable.

"Oh, do please forgive me, my lord," she said breathlessly, gifting him with another dazzling smile. "It is unforgivable of me to be late. I hope you dined without me."

"No," he said tersely. She was smaller than he remembered, and twice as beautiful. He forced his eyes away from her heaving breasts and tiny waist.

"Oh, my lord, it was so kind of you to await me, but—"

"I seldom indulge in kindness," he cut in bluntly. Where were her angry words, her questions regarding his whereabouts? He should have been the one apologizing, but here she was begging his pardon. He weighed the sincerity of her words, suspecting hidden insolence, but found none.

Her hand went to her disheveled hair, her eyes beseeching him to overlook both her appearance and her behavior. Her gestures were so feminine and pretty, he experienced a searing desire, followed immediately by anger. He had to find fault with her. He looked pointedly at the flowers. "It didn't take long before ye decided tae make changes."

"Oh, I'm so glad you like them, my lord. I apologize that your chambers were not cleaned, but I didn't dare to presume. After all, I've never even seen your rooms."

"I'm relieved that ye understand that at Douglas, my word is law." The statement was intended to goad her. Now she'd fly at him and unsheath her claws. But she just gave him another disarming smile. "If you will be patient with me, my lord, I will learn to do things your way. I give you my word I shall try to please you."

"If ye have a curiosity about my rooms, ye'd better come and see them," he said. The cream shirt against his dark face and throat gave him a feral look. The soft material emphasized his strong, hard features.

"Give me time to change, and I will join you," she said gaily, lifting her skirts above her knees as she ran up the staircase.

She had thrown him slightly off balance. He had expected either blistering anger or cool hostility and received neither. She had been almost amenable. It was an act, of course. The devious little bitch must be up to something. Since she couldn't rule him, she'd taken over and decided to rule the roost at Douglas. But she'd wasted her efforts, he decided with satisfaction. They were leaving for the borders and Castle Douglas day after tomorrow at the latest.

When she had insisted upon moving into the chamber that had once belonged to Damaris, he had assumed she'd resist his bed like a wildcat. Now it seemed she couldn't wait to get inside his bedchamber. Perhaps she was trying to seduce him. Well, if she had designs to spend the night with him, she was in for a letdown.

He went upstairs to await her, and as he glanced about the familiar rooms, he tried to see them through a woman's eyes. The furniture was massive, carved from black walnut. The velvet bedhangings were deep claret, and the floor covering was woven from the natural, un-bleached wool of Douglas sheep. His table and chairs were covered by Spanish leather, his walls decorated with his favorite swords, knives, daggers, and dirks. The stone fire-place in the outer room blazed cheerfully to keep out the damp. His chamber opened to the parapet walk, from which you could see the River Ayr to the west and the Pentland Hills to the east.

Where the hell was she? He grabbed up a poker and stabbed impatiently at the logs in the fireplace until they sparked and blazed. He was unused to being kept waiting by a woman. Was she taking all this time to adorn herself with some seductive chamber robe, thinking to entice him to ravish her? The elastic of his patience stretched and snapped. He flung open his door and went to fetch her.

As he raised his fist to pummel her chamber door, he heard laughter from within. He changed his mind about knocking as he realized she was talking with a man. He flung open the door upon a very domestic scene. She was sipping from a spoon that her bloody exquisite Frenchman was holding to her lips. "Forgive the intrusion," he said sarcastically.

She pretended she heard no sarcasm. "Not at all," she said sweetly. "You are just in time to enjoy Mr. Burque's delicious cuisine."

The chef bowed and departed, and she confided, "He spoils me outrageously. Of course, that's the reason I brought him."

"Don't remind me how spoiled ye are, madam. I've been

cooling my heels while ye have been entertaining yon fop."
She wore a high-necked black silk gown, not the seductive
garment he'd expected, and her hair was twisted into a
severe bun. As well, the aroma coming from the tray was
making his mouth water. Perversely, he was annoyed that
the smell of the food did not sicken him. "What is that?"
he asked, indicating the spoon she had been tasting.

The corners of her mouth lifted. "Ambrosia . . . no,
not really. It's merely soup—a few mushrooms, a little
cream, a little wine." Her eyes moved from his, down to his
mouth, then back up to his eyes. "I don't suppose I could
tempt you?" Her words hung in the air.

He stared at her full underlip. He was tempted, all right.

"No, of course not." She laughed. "You prefer great
lashings of mutton or oxen. I'll tell you what—I'll just put
the silver cover on to keep it warm until I return—that is,
of course, if the invitation to see your rooms is still open."
She was toying with him, and he didn't trust himself to
speak. He led the way, and she followed. He didn't turn,
yet he knew she had entered the chamber behind him and
closed the door silently.

"I know your secret. You are a devout coward."

He whirled upon her with an angry retort upon his lips
and saw that she was speaking to the Boozer. "Coward?
I've seen him tear the throat from a man."

She shrugged a pretty shoulder. "Anything that eats
meat is capable of killing," she replied. Was it a veiled
threat? "Nevertheless, he is a coward. He is rendered into
a quivering mass by a spirit."

"A spirit?" he echoed. Was she mocking him?

"The spirit of Damaris lingers in my chamber. You told
me of it yourself, remember?"

Ramsay knew there were such things. He'd lived with
them for over fifteen years. Other people however did not
believe in ghosts. Was she humoring him, or did she have
an open enough mind to believe? Suddenly he didn't want
her to leave. If only she'd had the food sent here, they

could dine privately and talk. He always ranged alone, but sometimes he longed for a companion, a soul mate. He watched her eyes as they traveled about the chamber, missing nothing.

"Do you like it?"

"Good heavens, Douglas, I wouldn't go that far," she said lightly. "It suits you, of course. For my taste, it's too dark, too large, too harsh." She could have been describing him. "Its saving grace is the parapet walk."

His male vanity was piqued. He grasped her wrists with his hard hands, imprisoning her. "Do *I* have a saving grace?" he demanded, lust and anger suddenly blazing in his gut like banefire.

She searched his dark face and whispered, "I hope so, my lord. I pray for both our sakes that you have a sense of humor."

He released her wrists. "We go to Castle Douglas day after tomorrow. Perhaps my bedchamber there will be more to yer taste."

"Perhaps," she murmured, allowing her lashes to sweep to her cheeks. God, they were like two scorpions circling each other, looking for the most vulnerable spot to leave their sting. "Perhaps I'll stay here."

"You, madam, will do as ye are told." His words had a hard, challenging ring.

She laughed up into his face. "You do have a sense of humor!"

It was outright insolence. By Heaven and Hell, if he didn't make her obey him, he knew he'd lose the whip hand! He took her chin between his strong fingers in a vicious grip. Her lashes flew up in time to see his head descend to take her mouth savagely. He slowed her very pulses. Once again she was determined to turn the tables on him. Her mouth softened and opened under his, allowing him to take what he wanted. When he finally lifted his mouth, she whispered, "Perhaps I'll come after all, Douglas."

She had an annoying habit of addressing him by his surname. He swore a vow he'd make her say Ram softly, pleadingly. He knew he would know no peace until he had had her.

She was aware of his excitement. She was also aware of her own. She felt an unbelievable physical attraction for the brute.

Damn her to hellfire! She held him off with the simple device of luring him on. The minute she behaved like a wanton, he was repelled. "Yer food will be cold. Ye may return tae yer chamber," he dismissed.

She dropped him a curtsy, as if to thank him for his consideration. Then she cast him a wicked glance from beneath her lashes that promised him the earth if he was man enough to take it. Then she was gone.

He swore foully. He knew exactly what he needed. He picked up his leather jack and made his way to the stables. The ride cooled his temper and his blood. When he arrived in the Valley of Galloway, however, he saw that the Gypsies were gone. He cursed again and went over the long list of women who would welcome him this starlit summer night. Unfortunately, none appealed. The woman he really wanted to bury himself in was back at his own castle.

Tina sat abed, her knees drawn up beneath her chin. "He actually said, 'At Douglas, my word is law,'" she said laughing as Ada perched on the end of her bed. "At any moment I expected him to demand that I remove his boots!"

"Men think they like women to be subservient to them, but if you were, he'd be bored in a week," Ada said.

"He wants to dominate me so badly, he can taste it. I think he'll only play if he can be in control. Just when he thinks he's controlling me, I knock him off balance."

"Women make the fatal mistake of loving a controlling man. The minute they fall in love, they are discarded like a bit of rubbish," Ada told her.

"Those are exactly the rules I shall play by," Tina said, laughing.

Damaris too sat upon the end of the bed, mesmerized by the conversation. She was so relieved that Tina had no intention of becoming a lamb to the slaughter. She seemed so wise to the ways of men, and what knowledge she lacked, Ada made up for.

"I've already discovered a secret. When I try to drive him away, he cannot resist me—but when I try to seduce him, it drives him away!"

"Once you are sexually intimate, that could easily change. Men, even aggressive ones, love it when the woman initiates sex occasionally. Probably the one single thing men hate most in bed is a woman who is unresponsive. Every man I've ever slept with has complained bitterly that his wife is like a corpse in bed. A lot of women are so passive, they might as well be asleep. A man always knows when a woman endures it and can't wait for it to be over."

Silently Tina wondered just exactly what "it" would be like. From what she had observed and overheard, it seemed men could not get enough. Sex was the one lodestone that drew every single one of them between the age of fourteen and death. Women, on the other hand, all seemed to be different. Some loved it and some hated it, and her own common sense told her there must be an infinite range of emotions between. By all indications, this deflowering was an earth-shattering, cataclysmic act that she both anticipated and dreaded.

"Ada, when he kissed me tonight, I had a decidedly physical response that I had no control over. My mind hated him, yet my body reacted with pleasure."

"Ah, that's the essence of the thing exactly. His physical response to you is something he cannot control, either. It's a power each of you has. If you are clever, you will be able to gain control over him in all sorts of subtle ways. You must make the power of love greater than his love of power."

* * *

The hour was late when Ram rode back to Douglas, so he was surprised to see a light in her chamber. He'd watched it while he'd ridden the last two miles. It winked at him, teased him, beckoned him, lured him. It drew his eyes from the bailey, and it drew his eyes again when he came out of the stables. Should he go and demand his rights? The ache in his groin was almost unbearable. As he looked up at her window, the light went out. He bit his lip. She was so bloody vain, she thought herself irresistible. Well, he'd show her she wasn't irresistible to him!

He made his way to the kitchens, which were deserted at this time of night, and was amazed to find everything spotless. He went into the pantry, then the larder, searching until he found some of the delicious soup Mr. Burque had concocted. The kitchen fires were banked low for the night so he decided to use the fire in his own chamber. He tucked a long French loaf under his arm, picked up the soup kettle, and stealthily made his way upstairs.

Chapter 19

"Nell, I do apologize for telling you to unpack when now you have to ready everything for Castle Douglas."

"Och, my lady, dinna worry aboot me. It's poor Mr. Burque I feel sorry fer," her maid said with feeling.

Good heavens, was Nell yet another of his conquests? "I'll wear the turquoise green gown today, and tomorrow I'll ride to Douglas in the pale gray riding outfit trimmed with black braid. Pack everything else."

Ada held the exquisitely embroidered white nightgown, as yet unused. "I'll leave this on your pillow for one more night, just in case."

Tina laid down her brush and put in the last hairpin. "I haven't seen half of *this* castle yet. But as soon as I've had something to eat, I shall rectify that."

At breakfast she learned that the Douglas had been up since dawn readying the wild horses for their journey to the border stronghold. Though not broken enough to be ridden, each horse had to become accustomed to a bridle.

The steward showed her the room he had assigned to Nell in the servants' wing, then smirked, "An' this is the chamber yer fairy godmother chose."

Tina knew he meant Mr. Burque. She didn't dignify his remark with an answer. The Douglas steward would eat his words if Mr. Burque stole his woman. "Thank you, that will be all," she said as she picked up her rustling skirts to ascend a stone staircase.

"Where are ye goin'?" he asked shortly.

She turned, the corners of her mouth lifted, and she said, "Wherever I wish."

"I'm sorry, my lady. I didna intend tae be rude. Mad Malcolm lives up there, and I would no' trust him."

Her smile widened into a laugh. "I wouldn't be foolish enough to trust any Douglas." She had heard oblique references to Mad Malcolm and had decided to see him for herself.

The old man in the high four-poster indeed looked demented, with his silver hair standing on end and a face as fierce as a hawk. He had been scribbling in a book and immediately pushed it beneath his pillows as if to guard it with his life. They stared at each other a full minute before she said, "You must be Malcolm."

"Ye mean Mad Malcolm, dinna ye?"

She smiled. "If you insist." She saw the jug of whisky beside him, smelled the fumes that emanated from the old

laird, and wondered if he was mad or just constantly intoxicated.

"So yer the lass Ram hand-fasted."

"I'm Lady Valentina Kennedy," she replied.

He nodded. "The Kennedy lass. . . . Have a care," he
warned.

She suspected he was mixing her up with Damaris.

"Yer tae be poisoned," he warned, "but it's no' yer husband Alex who'll do the deed—'tis the other young swine."

She knew he meant Ram. "How do you know?" Tina
asked, to humor him.

"I'm writin' a history o' the House o' Douglas. It's all
there!"

Colin arrived on the scene carrying a breakfast tray. He
looked alarmed to find Valentina alone with the demented
laird. "I was just leaving," she explained. "Good-bye, Malcolm. I'll see you when I return from Castle Douglas."

Colin followed her out. "Tina, he's capable of violence."

"I'll have a care," she reassured him. "Perhaps if he
didn't consume so much whisky, he'd be easier to handle."

"Poor old sod has few pleasures left in life," said a soft-
hearted Colin.

"You're right, of course. It's very kind of you to bring his
meals rather than have a servant do it."

Colin shrugged. "He gets few visitors, and after we leave
tomorrow, the servants are the only ones he'll see until we
return."

"Oh, I'm so glad you are coming Colin. Perhaps I can
persuade you to paint me, if you have time and inclina-
tion."

He blushed, and Tina told herself sternly not to toy with
this man's affections. It would be most unkind. She visited
the kitchens to apologize to Mr. Burque and tell him he
must spend the day repacking his kitchen equipment, utensils, and supplies for the journey to Castle Douglas.

"*Alors!* How am I to prepare the very special dishes for

you and his lordship if I am to repack my cooking equipment? *Sacre bleu!"*

"You mustn't even think about cooking today. Save your special dinner for when we're in residence in the border. The Douglas cooks managed to feed this castle long before you arrived."

Valentina made sure she was not late for the evening meal. She was amused to see that Cameron and his cousin had decided to sit with Ada and Nell—there didn't actually seem to be a servants' table. The Douglases mingled freely with the men-at-arms and servants, and everyone sat wherever he or she wished. There was little formality in this castle of men, and even Lord Douglas came to the board in his leathers.

Ram's eyes stroked over her like tongues of flame. Her turquoise green gown was as elegant as if she were dining with the king and queen, and he wondered if she was putting on fine airs to point up the contrast of his rough garb. She gave him one of her warmest smiles and felt disappointment when it was not returned. His face was set in harsh lines, his eyes unreadable. As he took the seat beside her, she saw his dark face was shadowed by the day's growth of beard. Her eyes also flickered over his cheekbone, where the skin had been broken open so many times from fighting and from her riding crop. It was a nasty gash that was going to leave a scar.

He threw her a challenging look, reminding her of an archangel whose dark beauty had been ruined. He carved the joint of mutton that was set before him and served her with a portion as large as his own. He took some turnips and parsnips and offered her the dish, then broke open a flour cake and spread it with butter. He took a mouthful of meat and chewed methodically. Then he grimaced and said, "I thought yer chef was supposed tae be a genius."

"Oh, he is, my lord," Tina said blithely.

He washed his meat down with ale and said belligerently, "Whoever cooked this needs a few lessons in the culinary arts."

She opened her mouth to agree, then closed it because she knew he did not want her to agree with him—he wanted an argument. So to oblige him she replied, "It's not too bad. The parsnips are tasty."

"Not bad? The damned stuff is hardly edible. He should be shot at dawn for ruining good food!" He was ready to sink his teeth into a good argument, if not the meat, so Tina took a perverse pleasure in thwarting him. "I'm sorry to disappoint you, Douglas, but your own chefs cooked this meal. Mr. Burque has spent the day loading his cooking equipment, utensils, and supplies for the journey to Castle Douglas."

Ram's eyes narrowed, and he chewed his lip for a minute. "Who the hell gave him permission tae come with us?"

"Don't cut off your nose to spite your face, Douglas. You said yourself this stuff was inedible. Once you've tasted Mr. Burque's cuisine, you'll think you've died and gone to Heaven after this muck."

She thought she was so damned clever, he wanted to slap her. When she moved, her gown rustled invitingly, and its blue-green color did glorious things to her flaming hair. She knew how beautiful she was, how alluring to a man. Well, madam, I won't slaver after ye like a bloody hound, he assured himself. She bestowed a radiant look upon Colin, farther down the hall, and it wrenched Ram's gut that the look was not meant for him.

The next time she looked at Ramsay, she caught the raw hungry look on his face and lowered her lashes to her cheeks in shy invitation. He radiated sexual hunger, and she knew if he touched her, it would feel as if she had been struck by lightning.

Ram, however, did not touch her. He did not dare. She turned his blood to wine. He had tried to build a wall against her, but suddenly he felt the edge crumbling. He stood up and moved away from her. He would maintain an air of indifference at any cost.

Ada watched silently. She knew Ramsay Douglas wouldn't be able to resist Valentina much longer. He had rights, and he would exercise those rights. When he looked at Tina, he was like a predator giving his prey a very wide circle, but Ada knew the signs of a raptor, knew he had marked her as his and would soon close in for the kill.

Ada wondered if Tina realized what a potent lure she was. Ada's eyes traveled down the room again to Ramsay, and she sighed. He was a magnificent male, like a beautiful, wily panther. What must he be like in bed?

For all his indifference Douglas prowled the hall as warily as a wolf who has scented a doe. He moved back down the hall toward Tina. Though she did not look at him, she was completely aware of him. "We leave at dawn. I'd better have a word with yer women so they understand I won't be kept waiting."

"I give my women their orders," she stated firmly.

"Why?" he demanded.

She shrugged a shapely shoulder. "For my own self-esteem."

"Ye already have far too much of that," he accused.

She looked pleased at his remark, and his mouth hardened. He turned on his heel and quit the hall. Tina joined Ada. "What a relief to be free of his high and mighty at last!"

Ada gave her a speaking look. "If I know aught of men, you are not free of him. He is not finished with you yet."

Valentina shuddered involuntarily. She went up to the chamber she imagined she shared with Damaris, and as soon as she opened the door, she glimpsed the cat before it jumped down from the bed and disappeared. She must remember to ask who fed it and who let it in and out of her room. "Come, puss. . . . Come to me," she coaxed, but she knew the nature of felines and accepted that it would come to her only when it was good and ready.

Nell had done a wonderful job of repacking her ten trunks, and Tina summoned a Douglas servant to carry them down to the front entrance since his lordship did not wish to be kept waiting in the morning. She saw the cat slip out the door between the servant's legs and sighed. She would have liked company tonight.

She bathed and readied herself for bed. The only night-gown she could find was the exquisite white silk that Ada had embroidered so painstakingly for her first night with Ram Douglas. She shrugged and slipped it on, enjoying the feel of it against her skin. She opened the wardrobe to hang up her turquoise gown and saw the gray and black riding dress hanging by itself except for a shell-pink night-robe that Nell had left unpacked. She closed the wardrobe door and fell into a reverie, wondering what the border country around Castle Douglas would be like.

Ram paced his chamber feeling caged. Everything was in readiness for the transition to Castle Douglas, and he knew his moss-troopers would welcome the ride and the wild borders as much as he would. He knew his temper had been short these last few days. His men had obeyed his curt orders immediately, not daring to glance at each other with raised eyebrows until after he had departed. He and Cameron had exchanged sharp words, and even Colin was avoiding him.

The lines about Ram's mouth had become finely drawn, and his eyes were red-rimmed from lack of sleep. He hadn't had a woman in weeks, and his body screamed its need. He spoke with such ferociousness to the maidservant who brought him fresh body linen that she was terrified, and she was almost incoherent when Cameron later asked her what was amiss. Cameron set his mouth in grim lines and tackled his brother. "Since Gavin isn't here tae challenge ye, I'll do it myself. Christ Almighty, ye are so evil-tempered, all who can, avoid ye like the plague. Yer face looks like a death-head. I know what ails ye, if ye don't!"

"Oh?" Ram said silkily. "And what is that?"

"Ye need tae lie abed wi' yer new wife 'til she drains ye o' yer lust and the evil humors of yer hot blood."

Ramsay's look was so black, Cameron stepped back in fear; then, so he couldn't accuse himself of cowardice, Cameron attacked further: "We know ye didn't want tae be shackled—Christ, the whole bloody world knows that, but did ye stop tae consider she was forced tae it as well?"

"Get out!" Cameron was glad to leave with a whole skin.

Ramsay swore a foul oath. No woman was of that much import to him and never would be, praise God. He threw off his doublet and sat down on his bed to remove his boots. It was true, he admitted, that he would like to master her. He licked dry lips. It would be good sport to tame her. His sex began to harden, and he flung his boots across the room and knocked a dirk from his wall. The Boozer, in his wisdom, moved to the door, hoping to escape.

Ram decided that what he needed was sleep. Without removing more clothes, he swung his legs up on the bed and stretched out full length with his arms behind his head. His blood pounded. He knew he would never sleep until he had eased himself with a woman. He allowed his imagination to conjure her vision, and what he pictured fueled his temper. He saw himself enter her chamber, saw her look of triumph that he could not resist the temptation of her incomparable beauty. She was quite obviously doing her utmost to tempt him, and tempted he was, sorely tempted, he finally admitted. Christ, hadn't that been Adam's excuse in the Garden of Eden? *The woman tempted me!* Well, his willpower was easily strong enough to resist her temptation. He thumped his pillow savagely and felt his blood surge higher. The more he tried to resist her, the more he wanted her. If he went to her, she would be triumphant. If he gave in to her temptation, it would feed her vanity.

She was vain enough. No, he'd never pander to her beauty. He stood up, restless as a panther and every bit as dangerous. He'd go to her. He'd pull the proud vixen from her pedestal. It was time she learned that her place in the

Douglas hierarchy was not as elevated as she imagined. He would take her without love words, praise, or flattery. Up till now, she'd likely had besotted poetry from her lovers and promises of undying love and devotion. He'd not worship at the altar of her beauty. He'd never fuel her vanity. He'd take her in the dark, where she would be exactly like every other female. Then he would leave her. He'd not lie beside her all night, so she could tempt him to make love to her again and again.

He flung open his chamber door, and the Boozer stalked through it with a look of reproach and disappeared down the dim passageway. Ram made his way to Damaris's old chamber with such resolution, the large, square quarions flickered alarmingly in their iron brackets upon the wall. His knuckles smote the wooden door only once before he threw it wide.

Tina's look was anything but triumphant as she half-gasped and swallowed her fear. She stood frozen to the spot, clad only in the white silk nightgown with its exquisite diamond-eyed butterflies. The candle she held dripped hot wax upon her hand, and it spurred her to action. She set the candlestick beside the bed and asked faintly, "What are you doing here?"

"That should be obvious," he said.

Her wide eyes took in the bare chest covered with its sable-black pelt, and she whispered, "You intend to sleep here?"

"Hardly sleep," he said with a laugh that contained no hint of mirth.

"You have come to claim your privileges," she whispered, as full realization of his intent dawned upon her.

"Privileges?" he ground out with contempt. "I think ye mean my rights and my duty. The king and the chiefs of our clans desire a blood bond between us. That can only be accomplished if I get ye with child."

Damaris was appalled, but she knew she could not stay and witness this consummation.

Tina flinched visibly at being told she was to be nothing but a brood mare. She could have sworn he had lusted for her, but perhaps lust brought out the most unpleasant characteristics men had.

Ram felt his blood stir with excitement as his shaft filled and his balls tightened. She was such a challenge, the anticipation stirred him deeply in spite of his resolve. Damn her to hellfire, he wanted to lie with her, and he suspected she was well aware of his too-eager response. "Get in the bed," he ordered, his pewter eyes flaming with what looked like ruthless, pitiless violence.

If she disobeyed him, would he flog her? He might. His temper was hot enough to do anything when roused.

He snuffed the candles before she could read the naked need in his eyes. Tina groped for the bed in the darkness and slipped beneath the cover. Ram was drawn into the bed by the magnet of her body.

Conflicting emotions washed over her; fear, curiosity, disgust. She was about to experience the unleashed sexuality and violent danger that every man suppressed just below the surface. The beautiful virginity that she had saved for her husband was there to be taken. She was a gift, a divine sacrifice to the gods of passion and love.

Ram lay rigid in the bed, forbidding himself to lust for her. She was just another woman. But nothing is more tempting than the forbidden. The white nightgown whispered its invitation. Her subtle scent stole to him, inspiring his imagination to vivid imagery. Her skin was like ivory velvet, her hair a cascading glory. He knew an overwhelming desire to dominate her.

She gasped as she felt him reach out two strong hands to take her. The Douglases owned half of Scotland. Tonight she would become just another possession.

Ram now regretted snuffing the candle. It denied him the visual pleasure of her beauty. He wanted to see her eyes widen with admiration as she gazed at his powerfully muscled torso and the size of his erect sex. He wanted to see them darken with desire as he washed away her resistance to him. He wanted to watch her lashes become heavy with sensuality as he made love to her. He knew a craving to watch her mouth soften before she yielded it up to him, to watch it curve with delight as he pleasured her. He longed to watch her remove the exquisite nightrail for him so he could watch the tips of her creamy globes rouch and harden as he aroused her. He ached to see the bright color of her flaming triangle between her legs. He'd imagined it a thousand times, and now he cursed himself for a fool for taking her in the dark.

As he pulled her hard against him so she felt all of him, the powerful legs, the muscular arms, and the wide chest, she went rigid for a moment. Ram felt her stiffen and took it as a sign of rejection. He was offended. No female had ever rejected him in his life. Till now, all his bed partners had been willing—nay, more than willing, they had been eager for his lovemaking. He closed his mind to the men who may have gone before him. He would show her he excelled and surpassed any other lover she had known.

He brought his mouth down upon hers in a demanding kiss. He fully expected the usual eager female response. He waited for her to open her lips, her mouth, and take him inside where they would duel, then his tongue would master her. He waited in vain.

Tina was rigid with fear. She could not think coherently, wrapped in the powerful arms of Douglas. What was it she was supposed to do? Yield to him—aye, that was it! She must become all soft and womanly. The last time he had kissed her, she had allowed her mouth to soften beneath his and had felt the tip of his insistent tongue tasting her, but now his tongue wanted to rape her mouth. She did not return his kiss, so taking it as an insult, he left off the kissing.

His beard was harsh and abrasive against her sensitive skin, and yet it was so masculine, she went weak. He was annoyed that she made no move to take off her nightgown for him, so with impatient hands he pulled it up to give him access to her woman's center. Her skin against the swollen head of his shaft felt like velvet. He buried his face in her flaming hair, and its fragrance dizzied him and stole away his senses. Touching her intoxicated him. He knew he must act quickly before love words tumbled from his lips. He pulled her beneath him, tearing the delicate silk as he positioned her with rough hands.

Tina braced herself to endure the pain that she knew was inevitable. Ada had told her she must get past this first time. She gasped as he mounted her, then bit down upon her lips to prevent further protests. She must yield without protests.

The intensity of his need for this woman tumbled him into the abyss. She excited him so much, he was going to spill himself if he did not soon achieve penetration. Then she would laugh at his lack of finesse. He gripped her with iron-hard thighs, then plunged into her with savage need. She cried out, and he knew it was clumsily done—he was nowhere near seated to the hilt.

"Tina, open for me," he urged.

"I cannot," she gasped.

"Will not, you mean!" he cried raggedly, then thrust home. He closed his eyes with deepest pleasure. She was so exquisitely small and tight and hot, he had never before known such a fierce response. He knew a need to arouse a matching response in her, so he plunged until his white-hot seed flooded up inside her.

He had spent so quickly, he was ashamed of his body's response to her. Not once had she touched him, caressed him, arched her body to fit his. Her arms had not stolen about his neck to cling to him, nor had her mouth kissed or tasted him, yet she had brought him to fulfillment. No sigh, or murmur, or cry of pleasure had passed her lips. She had deliberately held herself aloof from him. He withdrew and took his hands from her, leaving her sprawled and mute with shock. He flung from the bed, more angry now than before he'd taken her. "We leave at dawn—be ready!" he commanded.

The chamber door banged shut behind him, the crash of wood releasing her tears. In the next room Ada heard her weeping. She knew Ramsay had visited Valentina. He had stayed an impossibly short time, then left in a rage. She sighed. Would Tina never learn to curb her sharp tongue?

Ada opened the adjoining door cautiously, saw the room was in darkness and hastened to light the candles. The scene before her made her gasp. "Good God, I never dreamed he'd had time to consummate your vows. Are you badly hurt, child?"

The spirit of Damaris drew close to Tina, longing to take away her hurt.

Tina glanced down at the bloodied, torn nightrail and hastily covered herself with the sheet before she struggled to sit up. A feeling of betrayal curled inside her that included Ada. She had told her she must learn to love the sex act but that was an impossibility. Ada had told her there would be desire, then pleasure, then fulfillment, but she had clearly lied.

"I warned you that you must get beyond this first time. That there would be pain and blood, but I had no idea he would be so brutal, love."

Tina recalled her warning and transferred the animosity she felt toward Ada to the man she hated. She recalled, too, the rest of what Ada had said. "If you intend to gain the upper hand, you can only win by guile."

"You were right, Tina. He believed you were experienced in these matters. What was his reaction when he saw he had deflowered you?"

Tina gulped back her tears. "He saw nothing. The candles were snuffed."

"My love, if you want my advice . . ."

"I don't, Ada. I want you to go back to bed," she said firmly. "I shall see you tomorrow. Remember, we leave at dawn."

Ada knew she had been dismissed. Like a wounded animal, Tina wished to nurse her hurt alone. But Tina knew exactly what she must do, exactly what she would say. No force on earth would stop her from taking her revenge. Revenge would be her raison d'être, her reason to exist!

She threw back the sheet and took the bedgown from her empty wardrobe with shaking hands. She forced herself to breathe deeply and slowly to calm herself. She wanted to fly at him and scratch out his eyes—or better still, to take her knife and disembowel him. She schooled herself to patience. His physical strength would overpower her in seconds if she attacked him. She intended to be the victor in this battle of the sexes and so must mask her intent from her enemy and glove her weapons with velvet. She knew her victory would not be immediate, but it would be total and complete.

She tapped softly upon his chamber door and opened it quietly. She saw the look of surprise upon his dark face before he masked it. She came as a supplicant. Before he could question her, she spoke softly but firmly. "My Lord Douglas, I understand that I am free to withdraw from this union. I wish to do so. Tomorrow I shall return to Doon."

"Ye'll do no such thing. A hand-fasting is a trial marriage. We'll try it for at least six months," he stated flatly.

"My Lord Douglas," she said softly, "I cannot endure it for six days."

He stared at her in disbelief. The delicate hue of her pink robe was like a blush. She could have no notion of her breathstopping beauty at this moment, with her eyelashes spiked with tears.

"Neither of us can withdraw yet. 'Tis ridiculous!" he growled.

Her legs had no strength. She sank onto the edge of his bed and lifted her eyes to his so she might impart something confidential. "My lord, I was told that when a man makes love to a woman, it is heavenly. With us, it is hellish.

You spoke true when you said we were two totally incompatible personalities," she whispered.

"Ye liked it not?" he asked, stung.

Her golden eyes widened. "It was the disappointment of a lifetime," she said solemnly.

She was criticizing his expertise as a lover! He, who was called Hotspur and whoremaster because of his finesse in fucking!

Tina left him with his mouth open. By the time she reached her chamber he was only two steps behind her. She backed away from him toward the bed, where the bloodied sheets screamed their accusation.

Damaris said, "Thank God you had the presence of mind to make him return to the scene of his crime!"

His black eyes swept from the sheets to Tina's face, wondering what trick she played. A feeling of horror began to wash over him, and his hands tore open the pale pink bedgown to reveal his suspicions.

Her white silk nightgown lay in shreds about her mons. Her thighs were smeared with blood.

"Why didn't ye tell me ye were a maiden?" he thundered.

"You were so sure I was unchaste, you would have it no other way."

Splendor of God, he had honestly thought her sexually experienced. She was a virgin! His brain tried to adjust to this revelation about Valentina Kennedy. His conscience smote him deeply. He had ravished her! What he had done in the dark to this lovely creature was akin to rape. No wonder she wished to flee from him. There were not many young women in this day and age who came to their marriage beds with their hymens intact. Valentina was a rare exception. She had too much pride, too much self-respect to be a trollop. He cursed himself for a vile lecher. He wanted above all to undo what he had done, but he knew that was impossible. He would try to heal her hurt. The first thing he must do was beg her forgiveness.

His eyes softened as he saw the anguish on her lovely face. "Tina, I humbly apologize for hurting ye."

One small shoulder lifted in a half-shrug. "It wasn't the first time you hurt me," she said softly.

He remembered finding her lying in the rain and throwing her over his saddle like a sack of grain. He recalled vividly the blazing anger he'd felt the night he'd ridden to Doon, when he'd rolled her in the grass and longed to rub dirt in her face. At every meeting since, he'd done his utmost to humiliate her, and he had finally offered the ultimate humiliation to a nobly born lady—a hand-fasting instead of marriage! If he proposed now she would fling it in his face—and who could blame her? "I'm shamed of my insensitive behavior. I'm quite capable of showing tenderness toward a lass."

She actually had him on the defensive, a position he was totally unused to, she thought with satisfaction. "Tenderness?" she echoed wistfully, compelling him to elaborate.

"Let me hold ye, let me take away the hurt," he said gently, still struggling with his conscience.

Her head lifted pridefully. "That is completely unnecessary, my lord. I will survive in spite of you."

He was filled with admiration for her courage.

His mood was lifting. He was more than pleased that she had known no other men. Christ, he'd even suspected she might be carrying his enemy's child, which had been the reason for his inexcusable behavior toward her after the ceremony. He had a foul and filthy mind, and his temper was no better. "We will begin anew."

She drew the delicate bedrobe about her and shook her head sadly. "Everything is ruined between us. Our personalities clash, and even our bodies are unsuited," she said with a blush.

Her words, though said gently enough, challenged his very manhood. "That is untrue! Give me another chance, and I swear to use ye gently, my lady. Even kissing has its own foreplay."

Her cheeks were rosy although not by intent. When he

saw her almost imperceptible hesitation, he pressed his advantage. "In good faith, neither of us can dissolve the union at this early stage. We would both be accused of not even trying."

They heard a loud scuffle outside the door, and Ram threw it open to see who dared disturb them. Tina watched the Boozer tear into the room after the cat. "Oh, he'll kill it!" she cried.

"What?" he asked blankly.

"The cat—oh, where did it go?"

Ram looked into her eyes to observe her reaction to his words. "He cannot kill the cat. It is a ghost."

She gave him a startled look, then something seemed to dawn upon her. He knew she did not reject his explanation out of hand and think him a madman. "The cat belongs to Damaris. . . . Its name is Folly."

The lady they spoke of stood in the corner with Folly in her arms. She was delighted that their minds were open enough to accept the possibility of her existence, yet she felt totally frustrated that she could not communicate with Valentina and protect her against Ram Douglas.

The Boozer, now realizing where he was, slunk to the door and whined pitifully to be let out.

"Please go," Tina asked. "I must bathe."

"I'll send a maid with hot water immediately," he said gently, knowing he had received no answer from her but hoping against hope that she would not go running back to Doon.

Damaris went looking for Alexander. She found him in Ram's chamber. "Alex, he raped her!"

"The son of a whore!" Alex swore angrily. "If I were alive, I'd beat him senseless!" He crashed his fist into his cousin's skull. "Bloody Black Ram!"

"Oh Alex, it's happening all over again. One of them will kill the other."

"Damn it, woman—once and for all time: I didn't kill ye!"

"Don't start with me. Oh, how I wish they weren't off to Castle Douglas! If she were here, where I could watch over her, I just might be able to keep her safe. I think she is aware that I'm here."

"We may be able to go to Castle Douglas with them. I think it's possible to move to another place. All ye have tae do is bond with a living entity, and they will take ye with them. Ye try tae bond wi' Valentina, and I'll bond wi' Ramsay, just for the journey."

"You really believe I'd ever trust you again? And I would never leave Folly," Damaris said to cover her nervousness at moving from the castle where she'd spent fifteen years.

"Take yer cat wi' ye."

"No—I'd be afraid she might get lost. She'll be safer here, I think, and so will I."

"Sweetheart . . ."

"Don't sweetheart me. You're a bloody Douglas, and nothing can ever change that." She faded from the chamber instantly.

Chapter 20

Tina lay in her pretty bathtub a long time. The warm water soothed her battered body but not her thoughts. Ram Douglas was a force to be reckoned with, not unlike a violent thunderstorm. She would need to be extremely clever and resourceful to keep abreast of him, let alone one step ahead of him. No wonder the name Douglas inspired fear; she had more reason than the rest of the population to know why.

She finally climbed into bed, but sleep was as far away as the man in the moon. If she lay perfectly still, she didn't hurt, but she was so restless she tossed and turned the night away. Black Ram Douglas was so . . . what? Not coarse exactly, like Angus. So male, so masculine, it made her shudder involuntarily.

She tried not to think of his naked body touching her, covering her, entering her, but it was such an unseen mystery to her, she could not free her mind of it. She had seen his naked chest, so wide, so darkly furred, but the rest of him, the male core of him, remained a frightening unknown.

As the lavender dawn spread its fingers up the sky, Tina had not slept at all through the long night. She felt drained, exhausted before the day had even begun. Ada cast her a worried look as she helped her fasten the gray riding dress and handed her her gloves and riding crop.

Nell staggered in with a tray holding enough breakfast for the three of them, but Tina could not face the food. Ada gave her a warmed cup of ale, and Tina flashed a grateful look and sipped it slowly. When she emerged into the bailey and saw her groom holding Indigo, she knew a moment of panic. My god, she was too sore to ride any distance. But Ram Douglas and his hard-bitten moss-troopers were already in the saddle waiting for her.

He felt an overwhelming relief that she intended to accompany him to Castle Douglas, yet his hooded eyes gave no hint of it. He missed nothing. He saw her wince as she mounted, saw her head lift and her back straighten with pride. The gray riding habit made her glorious hair blaze in contrast, but it emphasized the delicate pallor of her skin and the blue marks of fatigue beneath her eyes.

His conscience pricked him, but he vowed he'd make it up to her. He couldn't believe his good fortune. Valentina could never be described as innocent—she was far too beautiful and had received the randy attentions of a score of men—but she was inexperienced, thank God, and if he

taught her skillfully all the mysteries of sex, she would be a
ravishing woman indeed. Granted, he had made a bad
start, but if he put all his efforts into pleasing her, he knew
there wasn't a woman alive who could resist his Douglas
charm.

One thing was certain: He had hurt her, and she could
not ride all the way to the borders. Fifty miles was no great
distance to his men, but with the wild horses and the supply wagons, they would be in the saddle hours longer than
usual. She was almost as stubborn and blood-proud as himself, and he knew that if he offered to take her up before
him, she would reject that offer. He must think of something subtler.

Ramsay seemingly ignored her while they rode through
the Southern Uplands and the Leadhills, but when they
passed from Lanark County into Dumfries, he rode up
beside her. His shrewd eyes saw her drawn face and her
weariness. "Perhaps I'm mistaken, but yer mare seems tae
have a slight limp."

She had not noticed but felt too tired to argue.

"I'll take a look," he decided. They drew rein, and he
dismounted and lifted Indigo's hoof. "Mm, just as I
thought. Her shoe is loose."

Tina felt resentful that he cared more for the horse's
discomfort than her own, but she also felt guilt that she
had ridden Indigo in such condition. Ram remounted,
came alongside her mare, and lifted her before him. She
protested, "I have my other mount," and stared up at him
defiantly.

He grinned down at her. "Yer precious Mr. Burque rides
yer other animal. Do ye want me tae take him up in my
arms before all these rough men?"

She couldn't suppress her laughter at the picture he
painted, and she had to admit to herself it was a relief not
to have to ride astride any longer.

At first she held herself stiffly aloof, but once they
stopped to water the horses at the River Nith, Ramsay

settled his mount into an even, rhythmic, slow gallop. Her body started to relax, then her eyelids began to droop.

He was acutely aware of her. The delicate scent from her warm body made him become instantly aroused. He shifted in the saddle to ease the pressure of his swollen manhood as it bulged the leather of his breeches, and his movements made Tina open her eyes and sit up straighter. Before long, however, she was again lulled to sway back against him, and he slipped an ironlike arm about her to prevent her from falling.

As she slumped against his body he became aware of how small she was. Desire pulsed at his groin with a sweet, almost unendurable ache. She was full asleep now, and he half-turned her so that she almost faced him. She lay heavily between his thighs, the heat from her body mingling with his. He was marble hard now in an agony of need, and he doubted he'd ever grow soft again in her presence.

Her breasts swelled against him, filling his arms and his lap with her loveliness. God, he wanted her in the bed like this, both of them naked. He'd never take her in the dark again!

Valentina missed all the beauty of the wild, rugged, often inaccessible land through which they rode. As they cut through the range of mountains bordering Kirkcudbright, there were precipices of rock, caverns, and morasses full of deep ruts. Then they passed one of Ramsay's favorite spots on earth. It was a waterfall that cascaded in three tiers. He had seldom passed it in his life without stripping and bathing there, diving from the second tier into the deep pool at the bottom. Today, however, he realized he would rather be right here in the saddle with his woman asleep between his thighs.

As Ram's eyes surveyed his beloved borders, he knew them to be a perfect hiding place where thousands of men could remain in safe concealment. The men and the horses picked up speed as they neared Castle Douglas. Ram would have known he was near home even if he'd been blindfolded, for the tang of the sea swept up the River Dee almost up to the very foundations of the ancient fortalice.

As Ruffian came to an abrupt halt in the bailey, Tina opened her eyes and gazed upward at the forbidding gray stones of Castle Douglas. Realization dawned that they had arrived and that she must have slept most of the way. She gave Ram a look of disbelief that he had held her between his thighs all the way. As he slowly grinned down at her, her cheeks flamed at the intimacy. He made no effort to hide that he was pleased with himself, and she learned a valuable lesson. If she let him play the dominant, masterful male and she fulfilled the role of helpless female, his mood was almost pleasant.

Ram was amazed that on the ride his young brother and cousins had looked to the horses and his men had smoothed the way for the supply wagons, mending wheels and pushing the carts out of endless ruts and foxholes so that he could get on with the serious business of wooing his woman. Now that they had arrived at their destination, all was taken care of, so that he was free to show her his favorite castle and tend to her needs.

Ram dismounted and held up his arms. Tina looked down at him with hesitation in her eyes. Then she made a decision: She would take the first tentative steps to bind him to her irrevocably. She went down into his arms softly, sweetly, in a flurry of petticoats, and he lifted her to the ground. They stood with their bodies almost touching, and she made no effort to draw away from him.

Then he swung her into his arms again and carried her into Castle Douglas. Her face was warmed by the hard flesh beneath his leather jack. He set her on her feet and offered her his cast-iron arm—but not before he caught her with an intimate look. He found her golden eyes intrigued him. They invited him to wickedness, yet at the same time they held him at a distance. He captured her hand, and she allowed him to keep it. "This time ye won't be able to accuse me of not showing ye my chamber—our chamber," he amended boldly, gauging her reaction.

She remained silent at his invitation, yet did not say him no. A protective hand went to the small of her back as he guided her up the winding staircase designed in the ancient style to free the sword arm against invaders.

Tina expected a replica of his other rooms, but she was most pleasantly surprised. The chamber was magnificent. One whole wall consisted of a huge fireplace. From floor to ceiling was polished-pink granite, almost as beautiful as pink marble. The floor was carpeted with black sheepskins, and the massive bed was covered by a luxurious lynx fur that was so large, it spilled to the floor.

He bestowed his first compliment upon her. "This pink and black chamber enhances yer own lovely coloring."

"You silver-tongued devil," she bantered. "Have you been taking lessons from Angus?" His laughter rolled about the chamber, and they said in unison, "At least you have a sense of humor." Because they said the same thing at the same moment, they both went off into peals of laughter.

He took her through a door that led out onto the ramparts of Castle Douglas, where they stood together looking out toward the mouth of the River Dee and the sea beyond. As black and white terns glided and screamed above their heads, he said low, "Will ye share this chamber wi' me if I promise not tae ravish ye again?"

She did not ignore him, but she made him wait a few minutes before she answered: "Are you truly promising to be civilized?"

He grinned. "Never that, but next time I'll try tae seduce ye."

"Seduction sounds most wicked and inviting, yet I've never succumbed to it before."

"That's because ye weren't seduced by Black Ram Douglas," he promised arrogantly.

She turned to him and said quite frankly, "This first night I want only to sleep, my lord."

He looked into her eyes. "So be it," he said solemnly, then his pewter eyes crinkled in amusement. "That will give ye a fighting chance against me tomorrow night."

She sank down before him in an acquiescent curtsy, and he raised her and took her hands to his lips before he departed. She gazed after him. After a good night's rest, she'd be more than a match for him. She was learning how to handle him. Tomorrow night, with Mr. Burque's tempting dishes laid before him, she would see who would do the seducing.

Down in the great entrance hall she found Ada talking with the castle steward, while Nell sat atop one of her ten trunks. "To which chamber shall I tell the servants to take your trunks?" Ada asked.

"Why, the master bedchamber, of course." She glanced at the Douglas steward and said, "I *am* the mistress here."

Ada rolled her eyes heavenward, knowing she'd get scant help from that direction.

Tina asked the steward to show her about the castle, and she complimented him on its general upkeep, since she could see that a firmer hand was on the tiller here than at the castle they had just left.

In the kitchens the male chef was having an altercation with Mr. Burque, and it had unfortunately degenerated into personal insults. The thick-tongued Scot had already hurled *degenerate, queer,* and *prancin' pansy* at the Frenchman, who had a much more subtle revenge in mind. The chef's first assistant was his wife, a dark, plump little woman with rosy cheeks. She couldn't keep her eyes from Mr. Burque. Admittedly he was bonnier than any lass, but the way his eyes had caressed her curves and winked at her over her husband's head indicated clearly he had a taste for the opposite sex. The next time the Frenchman lowered his eyelid, she winked back. A feeling of excitement was bubbling inside of her. When Mr. Burque kissed her hand, she went all wobbly inside. Her husband would never suspect her of knocking it off with the pretty laddie.

The steward told Tina the chef's name was Burns, and she hoped it wasn't too apt. "Mr. Burns," she said firmly, "name-calling will not keep your position secure. Only the quality of the dishes you prepare can do that. The superior chef will naturally hold the position of superiority in the castle kitchens. Instead of frittering your time away hurling epithets, I suggest you channel your energy into the evening meal. If my palate is pleased, who knows? I may even keep you on in the kitchens."

When she walked off, Mr. Burns looked baffled and needed Mrs. Burns to interpret. "If she dinna like what ye cook, she'll stick it up yer kilt," she told him graphically.

Tina asked the steward to select especially nice rooms for Ada and Nell, then took herself off to the stables. She reprimanded her groom for not checking Indigo's shoes before their journey to the borders, but he insisted the mare's horseshoes were all firmly intact and showed Tina that it was so. Mildly surprised, she wondered if Ram Douglas had taken her up before him for her sake or for his own, and she smiled her secret smile.

She wandered around the outbuildings, saw the vast dairy-still room, the forge, the men-at-arms' quarters built into the thick curtain wall, and the washhouse, where all the castle linens were washed. There were storage sheds for the sheared wool from the thousands of Douglas sheep, and a tannery where cowhides and deerhides were cured before they were shipped away across the Channel.

The afternoon shadows lengthened on what had been a glorious summer day, and she wandered toward the banks of the River Dee which lay to the west of Castle Douglas. She was startled by a man, naked to the waist, standing in the river where a great pool had formed. He turned when he heard her approach, and she saw that it was Ramsay Douglas and that he was fishing. She hoped he didn't think she had followed him or that she had been looking for him. "I didn't mean to disturb you, Douglas."

He thought, Ye disturb me whether ye are near or far, and even when I sleep—I've begun tae dream of ye. He said, "Come, I'll teach ye how tae fish. 'Tis the most pleasant, soothing thing a man can do."

"I'm a woman," she said, coming to the very edge of the river.

"I've noticed," he said. "Ye likely wouldn't be good at it. Women don't care for hooking worms and such."

Tina enjoyed doing men's things. It gave her a perverse pleasure. "I'll try anything once," she called.

He waded to the bank. "More than once, I hope," he said low, and she took his meaning and blushed. "Ye can take my rod and sit on the bank. I'll fashion myself another," he said, wading from the water and reaching for his knife. He had soon selected and cut a straight branch, then attached a fine piece of black cord.

"Where's your worm?" she asked.

He shook his head. "They prefer flies. They come tae the surface of this still pool, where the insects hover over the water's surface, then *snap*—they jump right out to catch the fly."

He held out the end of the black cord, and she was amazed that his deft fingers had fashioned what looked exactly like a dragonfly. "I'll teach ye how to fish."

She shook her head. "No, I'll watch you, and once I learn the secret, I'll be as good at it as you."

His dark eyes held hers for a long time. "There's a secret to everything. . . . I've always known that, but most people don't. Yer a perceptive lass. Perhaps we have more in common than we know."

Her cheeks warmed again. Bugger the brute, she thought—he enjoys keeping me in a perpetual blush.

He waded out to the middle of the pool and cast his line so that the dragonfly flitted across the surface of the water, then quietly and patiently he did it over and over again.

Tina turned her back upon him while she removed her shoes and stockings. If he thought she would sit on the riverbank like a ninny, he could think again. She hesitated, but only for a split-second, before she removed her gown entirely. Then she kilted up her petticoat and waded into the river.

Ram glanced up in astonishment when he heard the splash of water. He opened his mouth to comment, but she quickly placed her finger to her lips, demanding silence. She was taking this business of fishing most seriously. He had thought her excessively vain in her elegant gowns, but now he saw Tina Kennedy had another side to her. She was a hoyden, a tomboy, ready for any dare. He could clearly see she'd be off and running at any madcap suggestion, and that explained her unearned reputation. He found it difficult to withdraw his eyes from her exquisite undergarments. The smart gray riding habit had hidden the sauciest scarlet petticoat and corselette, from which the swell of her breasts now rose temptingly.

With difficulty he concentrated upon casting his lure. The pool's dark surface was rippled by the rings of a rising fish; then suddenly a streak of silver flashed from the water, then took off until all his line was used up. "I have to play him and try tae get him upstream where the rocks make the water shallow before he slips the hook!" he shouted. Ramsay succeeded in getting the fish to swim up among the stones, but suddenly it was off the line, and he was after it in a flash.

"I'll help you," Tina cried, lunging after the silvery creature with gusto. She fell full-length into the water, but the slippery thing slid out of her hands with mercurial magic.

Ramsay at last captured it, swooped it from the water, and held it aloft triumphantly.

"It's a salmon!" she cried happily.

"Of course it's a bloody salmon—did ye imagine I was after sticklebacks?" When he realized how bedraggled and

muddied she was, he apologized. "We'd better get ye back
tae the castle before ye catch cold."

"Like hell!" she cried mutinously. "Not until I've bagged
my salmon."

"Well, we'd better wade down tae that quiet pool beneath the larch trees. Ye'll catch nothing here after floun-
dering about like a demented mermaid."

"Me? What about you, Douglas?" she demanded.

"I blend into the shadows, while yer hair and deshabille
scream so loudly, the only way you'll catch anything is by
fright!"

She smiled a secret smile. She was almost certain she
had Black Ram Douglas hooked. All she needed to do now
was land him, then before she was finished, she'd bone and
fillet him.

As the pair of them entered the castle with the two large
salmon, both were sober in dress and countenance. Only
the water streaming from sodden garments beneath her
severe gray riding dress, leaving puddles wherever she
trod, hinted at any impropriety.

The great hall at Castle Douglas bulged at the seams.
Every man, woman, and child crowded in to get a glimpse
of Lady Valentina Kennedy, who was hand-fasted to their
lord. Even the high windowsills were filled with squires and
scullions. The women's eyes went from her face to her
belly to see if he'd gotten her with child. The men's eyes
went from her face to her breasts, then undressed her with
their eyes.

Tina, in elegant yellow silk, made quite an entrance, and
with head high she walked a direct path to Lord Douglas,
who sat on the raised dais, his dark, shoulder-length hair
contrasting vividly with the Bleeding Heart of Douglas on
the banner behind him.

Ah, my fine lord, your device is an omen, if you but knew
it, she told herself.

He arose the moment he saw her and came to meet her

with all courtesy. As he helped her mount the step and held her carved chair, he murmured, "I would apologize that ye must be on display tonight if it weren't fer the fact that I know ye relish being center stage."

She smiled sweetly. "You enjoy the spot so much, it must gall you to be knocked from your pedestal."

"Ye have a fine conceit o' yerself," he parried.

She gave him back his own words. "Aye, the Scots are like that. Perhaps we have more in common than we know."

When the flagons were filled, he again stood and raised his arms for quiet. He did not use her title, nor even her Kennedy name, but there was not one soul there who did not know exactly who she was. "A toast. This is Valentina, my new lady. If she proves as fertile as she is beautiful, I may just keep her."

Angry sparks flew from her golden eyes. She said low, "You swine, Douglas! I'll propose my own toast and tell them that if you prove impotent, I may not keep *you*!"

"If ye dare stand and say that, I shall strike ye." His words came at her like steel-tipped arrows, and his black eyes blazed their fury.

She stood and lifted her goblet. "A toast."

Ramsay's jaw clenched like a lump of iron.

"This is Douglas, my new lord. If he proves as chivalrous as he is valiant, I may just keep him."

As cheers rolled around the hall, she glanced at him and saw his eyes were narrowed against laughter. He had said she was his new lady. She wondered just how many women had sat here beside him in the past and felt a stab of— surely not jealousy—contempt for his womanizing. Well, one thing was certain: These arrogant Douglases may not like her, but by God, they would never forget her, and that went double for Hotspur!

When the meat was served, a whole rack of lamb was set before Ramsay for him to carve. It was cooked to a turn, crisp on the outside and pink on the inside, and Tina knew

Mr. Burns had outdone himself. While she ate, Ram never took his dark eyes from her. They lingered on her face, staring boldly into her golden eyes when she raised them to his, then they would drop to her mouth to gaze at her full underlip. She felt warm under his close scrutiny. His eyes lingered upon her mouth as if he were making love to it, and suddenly she knew what he had meant when he said even kissing had its foreplay.

She knew the roses bloomed and faded in her cheeks. He radiated sexual hunger with every glance. His eyes dropped still lower, and he indulged in imagining her naked. That was a mistake. He had been semihard yet comfortable, but now he was hard and throbbing, and he felt his blood beat in his throat and the palms of his hands. He picked up his tankard of ale to cool his hands.

"Are you quite finished staring?" she demanded.

He shook his head. "I'll never have enough. The light from the torches makes ye all gold and shadow. Yer hair is burnished flame."

So the wooing has begun, she mused, not a little apprehensive that she had agreed to share his chamber. His eyes touched her everywhere intimately, and slowly she realized that a feeling of excitement was growing inside her. His dark glances promised forbidden delights and tempted her to recklessness. His blood grew ever warmer from the sight of her, and she knew it. She could feel his raw desire reach out to touch her. Golden devils danced beneath her dark lashes. "Why do you look at me so . . . intimately?" she asked, innocent as an angel.

"I'm trying to picture what undergarments ye chose to wear beneath the yellow silk."

"You are the most infuriating man I've ever known."

"I certainly hope so," he said with relish, and a feeling of exultation surged within him that he had taken the prize from beneath Patrick Hamilton's nose. In fact, if Hamilton ever dared touch her, they wouldn't be able to identify him.

He had promised to leave her in peace so she might sleep this first night, yet not for a moment did she believe he would keep that promise.

Ram had made up his mind to take her upstairs as soon as his erection was not quite so evident. Suddenly two men rushed into the hall and raised the alarm. "The signal fires are blazing!"

Ram Douglas was on his feet instantly, running for his mail shirt and broadsword. He never glanced back.

Chapter 21

The village of New Abbey, a dozen miles to the east, had been attacked by English borderers, but by the time Douglas and his men arrived, the free-booters had departed. They had stripped every building of anything of value, including the church. They had driven off the animals and even stolen food supplies. They had killed men, raped women, and set the thatched homes ablaze before moving on.

Another signal beacon glowed on a hill, and Ram knew the English swine were ravaging the village of Kirkbean, four miles away. His anger blazed hotter than any fire. He left half his men to aid the victims of New Abbey and headed for Kirkbean.

Ram intended to capture some of the raiders alive to learn whence they had come and on whose orders, but he found he was outnumbered three to one after leaving half his men behind. They knew they must slaughter or be slaughtered, and a fierce and bloody battle ensued.

The animals had already been driven off, and Ram knew

the number of looters had been even greater. A dozen English lay dead while Douglas men had received only wounds. Ram's thigh suffered a long sword gash that was bleeding profusely, but he was almost certain it had not gone deep enough to sever tendon or bone.

The inhabitants of Kirkbean told the border lord that three of their women had been carried off with the cattle. Ram vowed to return them, and he rode hell for leather toward the rocky coast. Again they were too late. A ship had weighed anchor, and another was fast disappearing into the darkness of Solway Firth toward the shores of England.

Because they had been so hotly pursued, they abandoned the women but not before they had slit their throats. Ramsay, Jock, and Cameron drew rein and dismounted when they came across the bodies of the women. Cameron turned away and vomited into the gorse. Ram pressed a fist to grim lips and closed his eyes. If he hadn't given his promise to return the women, he would have buried them where they lay. It would have been kinder to let them think the women had only been stolen.

"Since when do borderers raid by ship?" Jock asked Ram.

"The whoresons have received their orders from a high authority. Dacre—or mayhap King Henry himself." He gazed out to sea in that early hour before dawn and made a decision, then he spoke to his moss-troopers: "Tomorrow we man our own ships. Most of ye know how tae crew a vessel, and those who don't will learn in a hell of a hurry."

Jock, Ram's first lieutenant, said, "I'll round up our wounded back at Kirkbean. Get ye tae Douglas and get that leg cauterized."

Ram shook his head. "I'll ride tae Kirkbean first. I promised tae return the women. Are ye all right, Cameron?" he asked, wishing he'd left his young brother to stay and help the people of New Abbey.

* * *

Ada and Tina had sat talking for two hours in the luxurious master bedchamber at Castle Douglas. Ada sewed upon a shift as finespun as a dream. It was the palest seafoam green, and she told Tina she was going to make her some very saucy garters with red hearts on them. "You don't think his lordship will think we are mocking the Bleeding Heart of Douglas, do you?"

Tina laughed and shook her head. "It matters not—Ram Douglas has a sense of humor." She embroidered a cream linen shirt with his initial. She had debated whether to use the R or the D and finally settled on the D because she refused to call him by his first name.

Soon Tina began to yawn, and they set aside their embroidery silks. "It seems I shall have this fine chamber to myself tonight after all," she mused. Ada gave her a swift glance from beneath her lashes. Did she detect a note of disappointment?

Tina laid a deep purple bedgown across the foot of the bed in case Douglas returned in the middle of the night. She would cover herself as a defense against those dark, hungry eyes. She slept soundly until a couple of hours past midnight, then she awoke, and when she saw he had not returned, she became restless and dozed only fitfully. A vague feeling nagged at her.

Certainly it was not worry over his safety—it was a nameless feeling of unease. It was dawn before she heard horses and men clatter into the bailey, and she knew she could stay abed no longer. She put the bedgown over her lavender nightrail and slid her feet into her slippers.

She took the torch from its bracket in the passageway and ran down the winding staircase to await his entrance through the massive studded door. When no one entered, she became impatient. She preferred to be in the thick of things, not to stand waiting patiently in the shadows.

She went out into the bailey and began to make her way

to the stables, but incredibly, she saw they were all at the forge. Ram had lost enough blood to make him light-headed. When he dismounted, he swayed on his feet, his weight bringing a throbbing pain up the entire length of his leg. He leaned heavily on Jock's shoulder until he reached the forge, and Valentina arrived just in time to see two of his men-at-arms lift him onto a workbench. He caught sight of that flaming head in the torchlight and ground out harshly, "Get her out of here!"

"Hold!" she cried in alarm. "What are you doing to him?"

Cameron put a hand to her shoulder. "Cauterizing a wound he took. Go back to bed."

"Nay, I'll do no such ridiculous thing."

"Please," Cameron murmured low, "he won't be able tae scream in front of ye when they put the hot iron tae him."

"Stop what you do instantly! Bloody barbarians, the lot of you! You there, Jock—carry him up to our chamber."

"The bleeding must be stopped," Ram said harshly. "Don't interfere in men's affairs."

"I will stop the bleeding by stitching the leg," she declared firmly.

"You?" Ram asked incredulously.

"Certes, me!"

The corner of his mouth quirked. "Ye willna faint at the sight of my blood?"

"Ha! Celebrate, more like. Fetch him up," she repeated. She thought it uncivilized that the Douglas had no woman to tend his wounds. She would take perverse pleasure in having him at her needle's mercy.

To Ramsay, this was a novelty indeed. That his woman came down in her bedgown to see how he fared and that she offered to tend his wound herself was unbelievable. That she cared about whether that wound and its cauter-izing left him scarred was nothing short of a miracle.

Jock and Cameron carried him upstairs, and she swept

the lynx cover from the bed and told them to lay him upon the linen sheet. She picked up her scissors and began to cut away his leather breeks. "Don't stand there like a clod!" she told Cameron. "Fetch hot water." He ran to do her bidding, and Jock grinned, "Would ye like me tae hold him still for ye, lady?"

Ram ground out, "I won't be the one tae flinch. Are ye sure ye've guts enough fer this, lass?"

"A wager," she proposed, "that my hand will be steadier than your leg."

Ram's eyes narrowed, and he jerked his head toward the door, ordering Jock to depart. Cameron came back with hot water, and Ram said, "Go and gloat over some other's wound. We wish tae be alone."

His chausses were saturated with blood, and she cut them away along with the leather of his breeks. When she exposed the jagged wound, she blushed that it reached from inside his knee up to his groin. As she washed and cleansed it, he held his leg steady as a rock, and she thought, wait until I stick my needle through your flesh.

A deep frown came between his black brows as he eyed her needle. When she saw at what he scowled, the corners of her mouth lifted. "I shall sew you up with cream silk and embroider it with French knots," she teased. She took a deep breath and deftly plunged in her needle.

"There's no need for such dainty stitches," he told her.

"Don't teach you grandmother how to suck eggs. You are ugly enough—I don't want you scarred into the bargain."

He grimaced. "Too late, when ye see me naked, ye'll faint."

"Ha! I'll not faint over a man's scars."

" 'Tis not my scars that'll make ye faint," he promised, grinning.

"Oh!" she said, and dropped a stitch. "You have a swollen head."

"Aye, among other things," he said wickedly.

She was working very close to his genitals, and remembering how they had hurt her, she jabbed him with the needle. "Sorry."

"Yer not, Vixen. Yer in yer element having me at a disadvantage."

She compressed her lips and concentrated upon knotting the silk after the final stitch. "There. Anything else?" she half-asked herself.

"I have a tremendous thirst, lass," he said low.

"Forgive me. How thoughtless I am. It's because you lost so much blood." She summoned a page and sent him running for a jug of ale. "Perhaps you'd prefer whisky for the pain?" she asked anxiously.

He shook his head. "Ale is fine."

When it came, he quaffed the whole jug, then lay back. It was the first time Tina had ever seen him look tired. When she drew the lynx fur cover over him, he took hold of her hand and lifted it to his lips. "Thank ye. I promise we won't always sleep in shifts," he said with a humorous gleam in his eye.

In the early afternoon when Tina went up to check on him, she was surprised to find him up and dressed, writing missives. "You shouldn't be on that leg."

He looked at her, weighing her words to see if her concern was genuine or assumed. He cared naught for the wound, but he found he cared deeply about her solicitude. "There are matters that need my attention. The English raided by ship. Every coastal town, village, and farm will be vulnerable."

"But Donal and Meggie are at Castle Kennedy on the coast! We must warn them."

"I'll send a message, if it will make ye feel better, but they won't raid the castle if they know the Kennedys are in residence."

"Donal's men-at-arms are not like your hard-bitten soldiers, Douglas," she pointed out.

"Few are," he replied. "They only dared come within a

dozen miles of Castle Douglas because they thought we were still north, and one day earlier we would have been." He frowned. Someone must be leaking information, or else it was outright spying. He was jaded enough to suspect everyone, even the people within his own castle.

Ram did not wish to alarm her, and he kept his mouth shut about the women who had been carried off. "I'm sending to Angus for another fifty Douglases. Ye'll be quite safe here."

She shrugged a pretty shoulder. " 'Tis not the English I fear."

"Surely it's not me—I'm wounded and harmless."

"Harmless as a scorpion!"

He arose from the desk. "I was hoping ye were woman enough tae draw my sting." As their eyes met and held, the very air was charged with sexual tension. He drew close and lifted a flaming tendril. It curled wildly about his fingers. He lifted it to his nose to inhale its fragrance. "Honeysuckle," he murmured, and she was surprised that he was knowledgeable about such feminine things.

He traced the tendril down his throat, and his look became so intense, she lowered her lashes. She was acutely aware of the dark shadow of his unshaven jaw and remembered the shockingly masuline feel of it against her skin.

"I'll shave for ye," he whispered, and her lashes flew up, wondering if he could read her every thought. He slid his hands about her neck and thumbed her velvet skin. Her golden eyes went liquid with apprehension. How simple a thing it would be for him to snap her neck if he wanted to rid himself of her. Instinctively, she moved her hand toward his wounded thigh, ready to claw at it if his hands tightened.

"My red vixen," he whispered, covering her hand with his, rendering it useless as a weapon. He wanted that hand at his groin, feeling him swell to bursting when he kissed her, yet he longed for her to touch him of her own volition. He dipped his dark head, and his lips brushed her soft mouth. "Take supper here wi' me tonight?" It was an invitation rather than an order, yet no less compelling. He whispered, "Early to bed, early to rise . . ."

For a moment Tina thought he would fill her hand with his "rising," but he resisted the temptation to force her. His pewter eyes held a silent invitation that she intended to accept, despite her apprehension. She gathered her courage. "Devil-eyed Douglas, how am I to resist you?" she purred.

His face was unreadable, but she could have sworn her words pleased him. When he departed, she sank to the bed on knees weak as water. "I shall always hate you." She sighed, as softly and gently as a kiss.

Tina summoned Nell to strip the bed and freshen the chamber, then hurried off to the kitchens. "Mr. Burns, the lamb was exemplary last evening. I hope it was the rule rather than the exception, and I hope your culinary experience lends itself to other than mutton. If not, Mr. Burque will soon tutor you."

Valentina drew the Frenchman aside for a private word, and Mr. Burns turned to his wife for a translation. "She's no' ready tae hoof ye in the sporran just yet," then added silently, But she's right about learning a few tricks from Mr. Burque!

"Mr. Burque, Lord Douglas and I will be dining privately tonight. I'd like something special."

"How about the salmon you caught?"

"Oh yes, that should really please him, and don't forget dessert."

Mr. Burque nodded. "Most men have the—how you say?—sweet tooth."

"If he has, it's the only sweet thing about him," Tina said, laughing.

Colin came into the kitchen looking quite drawn. "Was Ram wounded badly?"

"No, not really. It was an ugly enough gash that bled a lot, but it will heal quickly," she assured him.

He asked a scullion for alkanet and inquired if there was any syrup of poppy.

"Were others wounded?" Tina asked him.

He nodded. "None fatally," he assured her. When he was told there was no syrup of poppy, he cursed. "There was plenty last time I was here. Things are forever going missing."

"Perhaps it's the ghosts," Tina said lightly.

"Ghosts!" he scoffed. "Grown men don't believe in such."

"Ramsay does," she assured him. "He believes the spirit of Damaris lingers."

"Wishful thinking," Colin muttered. "He fancied himself in love with Damaris. He and Alex came tae blows more than once." Colin's mouth snapped shut as if he had said too much, and he immediately changed the subject. "Perhaps yer gifted Mr. Burque can concoct somethin' fer pain."

"He is a miracle man. He once cured an agonizing toothache for me." As she made her way back upstairs, her mind was busy. What was it Mad Malcolm had said when he insisted Alex hadn't poisoned Damaris? " *'Tis the other young swine,*" he had said. How old had Ram been when the tragedy occurred? Seventeen or eighteen would certainly fit the description of *young swine,* she thought as a seed of suspicious horror took root.

Ada brought the sea-foam green negligée she had finished embroidering. "I think you should wear this tonight —with a velvet bedgown covering all, of course."

Tina shook her head. "He'd have it off me in less than a minute and probably in shreds. I intend to be fully dressed from head to toe." She chose a gown of palest pink, and every last one of her undergarments matched down to her stockings, slippers, and garters. She even chose to wear a ruff and selected a pink and silver-tissue creation. The effect was quite dramatic in the pink and black room.

Tina could hear him moving about in the adjoining

chamber he used as a dressing and bathing room. She told Ada, "Leave me—he'll be here any moment."

She barely had time to touch her pulse with perfume, before he entered without knocking. Tina had not expected him to knock upon his own chamber door, however. Ram wore black, and she thought they must look like actors in a play, costumed for dramatic effect as they delivered their lines in the intimate setting. "How is the bleeding leg of Douglas?" She was ready to match wits with him, and he recognized it as a defensive strategy against him. He regretted that his actions had made her defensive. He had his work cut out for him tonight if he was to make her respond to him physically. "I'll show ye mine, if ye'll show me yours." He hoped his banter would put her at ease.

"Ah, then I take it we are not to have a blackout tonight?"

Her words were provocative, and he was aroused immediately. She knew he had only taken a few hours of sleep, yet all his weariness had vanished. She could clearly see he burned with life. He moved purposefully to the fireplace, threw on a log, and settled it into place with his soft leather boot. Just so would he ruthlessly put his boot to an enemy's ribs or temple, she thought. He would remove any obstacle in his path without pity. Perhaps he had removed Alexander? She banished the thought instantly. There was no way she could allow this man to make love to her if she dwelled upon him committing murder.

He turned from the fire and bent a look upon her that made her shudder. Tonight his eyes were the pewter of stormy seas. She reminded him of a forest creature. She looked ready to flee the hunter, yet he had no desire to hurt, only to capture and half-tame. "I had hoped ye would wear yer hair down for me." His voice had a deep, husky quality about it that made her want to shiver, or was it his words?

So her hair held a fascination for him. She would use it

to render him mindless. "I put it up so you could have the pleasure of taking it down," she said softly.

It was his turn to shudder. She was fully clothed so he'd also have the pleasure of undressing her. The thought of her delicate undergarments went straight to his groin. He could not take his eyes from her. He drank her in like dry ground in a thunderstorm. "I should get Colin tae paint ye."

She wondered if he had asked Colin to paint Damaris, then pushed the disturbing thought away. As they looked at each other, they knew they were about to step off a precipice together. Her blood slowed, and she felt an absolute languor.

Ram was the complete opposite. He almost burned and crackled with life and lust. She was the object of his desire, and he concentrated his total and complete attention upon her. She was compelling. He was obsessed. She was incandescent. He was consumed. Gently, he took her into his arms, stared down at her mouth until all her composure fled, then lowered his mouth to hers. The kiss was a prelude to what would come after. He touched and tasted her softly in a suggestive caress. He was closer than she had dreamed possible. Their dark eyelashes brushed together, and their breaths caught and mingled.

A low knock upon the door effectively separated them. Tina was vastly relieved. He had evoked an odd sensation inside her, and she felt almost dizzy. He opened the chamber door somewhat impatiently, and there stood Mr. Burque with their dinner. Ramsay bade the Frenchman enter in his own language, and Mr. Burque replied in French.

"Un moment," said Ram, picking up the table he used as a desk and setting it before the fire.

"Merci, seigneur," murmured the chef, setting down the heavy tray with a bow. *"Bon appétit."*

"Grâce à vous," replied Ram, nodding.

As he bent to bow, Mr. Burque's eyelid closed in a definite wink to Tina, and she rewarded him with a ravishing smile.

When Ram closed the door, she said, "I didn't know you could speak French."

"Can ye?" he asked.

She shook her head regretfully. "I have learned a few odd words . . . *derrière, lingerie, déshabillé.*"

He quirked an eyebrow. "Odd words indeed." He drew two chairs to the table and reached his hand toward a silver cover. "What do we have?"

Tina's hand slipped beneath his to lift the cover. "Allow me, Lord Douglas." She presented the dish as a magician presents a rabbit. The aroma was so subtly tantalizing, he could not resist taking a deep breath as she said, "Salmon poached in samphire with white butter sauce."

His eyes showed his pleasure. He was a man who appreciated fine food, though in his native land he seldom enjoyed anything but plain cooking. There were candied chestnuts and crudités. There was also a game bird stuffed with apples and raisins and garnished with chervil. Mr. Burque had chosen a light chablis for them, and though Ram preferred ale or whisky to wine, he knew the chablis had been chosen to complement the dinner and would be delicious upon the palate.

He held her chair and dropped a kiss upon her silken head, murmuring, "I thought my hunger was for other than food, but I must admit the Frenchman has tempted me."

"Isn't that what Eve said to Adam?"

He threw back his head and laughed. She gave him a sidelong glance from beneath her lashes. "You don't laugh often enough."

"That isn't because I'm not amused. It's from having learned tae mask my emotions."

"You have great control," she said.

"Over some things, yes; others, no."

"Such as?" she asked, as he had hoped.

"Arousal," he admitted frankly. "I think I have it under

control, then the whisper of yer silk gown, or the careless shrug of yer shoulder, or the fireshine on yer hair makes me ache with lust."

She wondered if these things were really true, or if they were the things a man always said to a woman when he wanted to bed her.

He put the last morsel of salmon smothered in its white butter sauce into his mouth and closed his eyes. "This food is absolutely decadent."

"Mmmmm," she sighed in ecstasy.

"A woman who enjoys food usually takes deep satisfaction from all life's sensual pleasures."

She smiled at him. "Since you insist upon educating me, tell me more."

"The lessons would be better learned if I showed ye rather than told ye. Actions speak louder than words."

"Give me the words as well, or I shall feel deprived."

"Did ye say depraved, my sweet?"

"No—that's you, Douglas!"

He was around the table in a flash, lifting her into his lap, unable to keep his hands from her one moment longer. "Ye always call me Douglas, never Ram," he complained.

"I care not for the name; I'll not say it."

"You shall!" he vowed, lifting the silken waterfall of her hair to kiss the nape of her neck.

"Douglas, we still have dessert!"

"I know," he said wickedly, slanting a black brow at her.

"But only look," she said lifting a silver cover. "He has made us a *gâteau d'amour.*" It was a work of art. The almond-flavored cake was designed in the shape of a shield, its crimson heart was crushed raspberries and its sauce was incomparable burnt caramel crème fraîche. She dipped in her finger and held it to his lips. He licked it and murmured, "It is tae die for." She picked up two spoons and presented one to him. He took it, and together they tasted the heavenly creation. It was so rich that two or three tastes satisfied them, and Ram soon forgot the food as another hunger needed satisfying.

Suddenly there were no words to spoil the magic of this moment they shared. His lips had found her face and begun their slow seduction. He kissed her temple and brushed his lips along her eyebrow, then when she lowered her lashes, he very gently kissed her eyelid.

His lips burned her skin as they drifted across her cheekbone, then nibbled at her ear, biting the pink lobe with his sharp white teeth. The tip of his tongue came out, and she drew in her breath as he traced the outline of her lips with it.

His hands lifted her hair, and she thought he would again kiss her nape. He did—but not before his deft fingers unfastened and removed the pink and silver ruff. His midnight black eyes stared at her mouth a long time before he kissed it, and Tina was almost undone. He made love to her with his eyes as skillfully as he did with his lips. When the kiss finally came, it centered upon her full underlip that had tantalized him and almost driven him crazy whenever he had gazed at it. He took it between his lips to taste and suck and lick as if it were a ripe and succulent cherry.

His experienced fingers soon opened her gown to allow his strong hand to roam at will. Ram was wise enough not to go directly for her sensitive nipple. Instead, he curved his warm fingers about the delicious swell of her breast and cupped it in his palm. Tenderly, he allowed his thumb to stroke the velvet skin, evoking sensations she had never known before.

Slowly, like the rising sun at dawn, she realized what was happening to her. Curled in his lap before the fire with his hand inside her gown and his lips stealing kisses, she was becoming aroused. He took such deep pleasure from doing these things to her that she felt the power of her own femininity. Ada was right—it was possible to enjoy sensuality for its own sake. It was not lessened by the fact that you hated the man who aroused you; perhaps it was even heightened!

He was a bold and dominant man who would learn all the secrets of her body, but he could never learn the secrets of her mind. With firm yet tender hands, he pushed the gown from her shoulders, then shifted her slightly in his lap to pull it from her entirely.

She was quite breathless, and her breasts rose and fell temptingly from the delicate pink shift. As his insistent hands removed the shift, she was aware of his sex, hard and throbbing against her bottom cheek. His hands did not stop until she sat nude upon his knee, save for her pink stockings and garters.

Ram stopped himself from thinking of the bed. He put an iron control upon the lust that demanded the drive and force of the dance of death. His urges were deeply sexual. He wanted no handkerchief to tuck into his doublet, he wanted everything. He wanted her body and soul. He knew how to stoke the fires of desire by whispering wanton words into her ear as his hand stroked down across her hip and belly, seeking the scented, secret place that shielded her woman's center.

She made a murmur of protest and closed her legs, denying him.

"Hush love, 'tis easier tae get used tae my hand first." Gently, he coaxed her legs apart long enough for him to slip his hand between. "Are yer curls as fiery down here?" he whispered, and suddenly she knew that between his legs would be blacker than soot. "Have ye any idea how often I've pictured it nestled beneath yer fancy laces?"

She hid her face against the hollow of his throat and knew her continual blushes secretly amused him. He slipped a finger inside her, and she gasped at the intrusion.

She hesitated, thinking such a thing was shameless, then gave way, knowing Black Ram Douglas would always take exactly what he wanted. The damnable part of it was he made her want it too! He stroked and circled, feather-light, until her core was afire. "You must stop," she whispered.

"Nay, if I stopped it would leave ye yearning and unsatisfied. Your body as well as mine has needs. This is just a little foreplay tae heighten our desire for each other. If we play out the game of love tae its natural conclusion, ye'll experience fulfillment. Give yerself up tae me, and I'll guide ye along the path tae paradise."

She lifted her face from his throat and looked deeply into his eyes. She saw herself there and thought, I am already a part of him. He needs me now and forever. I must become like a narcotic to him so that when I withdraw, he will die of it.

As their eyes locked together, an innate knowledge came to her. She would not give in too soon or too easily, but when she did she would hold back nothing. She would not met him halfway, she would go all the way. It would be unconditional surrender; it would be cataclysmic!

He lifted her against his heart and carried her to the bed. He laid her upon the golden lynx fur and stood at the foot of the bed gazing enraptured at the velvety texture of her skin against the fur. She lifted her feet playfully and rested them against the great slabs of hard muscle on his wide chest.

With teasing hands he peeled one stocking and garter from her leg, then in no hurry at all to remove the other, erotically threaded his fingers through her fiery red triangle until she arched into his hand. Naked, beneath his hot gaze, she was provocative. She could not help herself! She slid over onto her stomach and rubbed her tingling mons into the soft fur. Her uninhibited behavior was making him wild. Her hair spilled across the golden lynx in a shimmering torrent, and he tore at his clothes to rid himself of the impediment.

He ached with the need to cover her naked body with his, to feel the soft silken curves along the whole, hard length of him. He straddled her, his iron-hard thighs, enfolding her softness. He lifted her hair and trailed kisses all the way down her spine. His hands slipped beneath her to cup her breasts. "Turn to face me," he demanded.

"No," she teased, and rubbed her cheek into the luxurious fur. "Your pelt is not so soft."

"By God, it's not soft ye want!" he said hoarsely.

She moved her bum evocatively against his groin and experienced a thrill of pleasure when he moaned. Her power over him was growing. He bent to her ear. "Are ye afraid tae see me?"

She was, a little, but this only heightened her excitement. She decided to admit it. "I think I am afraid. I'm not ready to let you go further."

"I only want tae kiss ye," he promised, and the magic words did the trick. She turned over, and her golden eyes devoured him. His skin was smooth, tanned a dark, swarthy copper. A heavy black pelt covered his powerful chest. He reminded her of a satyr. She dared not glance at the upright evidence of his manhood and slipped her arms about his neck to bring his mouth down to hers.

He could deny his hunger no longer. His kisses were not leisurely now—they were hot and demanding, taking not giving. They were ravenous, smoldering, and savage. Her own kisses grew in intensity. They were wicked and scandalous, erotic, yearning, yielding.

His tongue plunged in to take all her sweetness, and she opened to him, allowing him to plunder her mouth, ravishing her as surely as he had before, only this time he had her consent. They were both lost to reason. She lay trembling in the furs, sensual and ripe.

He did as his dark, sensual nature compelled him to do. He despised caution, thought it showed a miserly attitude to life. The head of his shaft glistened with the sheer drops of his body's lubrication. He opened the tiny folds between her legs, took hold of his manroot and rubbed her cleft to moisten it, then he plunged in and saw her eyes dilate with pleasure-pain. When one jumps across a deep chasm, it is better to do it in one bold leap than two.

For one agonizing moment she thought he had done it to her again, but by sheer force of will she gave herself up to him. He branded her insides so erotically, she screamed from excitement. Together they were like fire and ice, love and hate, life and death. Deep spiraling sensations blotted out all words, all thoughts for both of them. He made love like a whirlwind, like a storm raging in the Atlantic.

Their senses reeled, built then shattered, over and over, like waves tossing high, before they pounded the shore. Their coming together was too intense, too consuming to be drawn out. Their cries and their mouths and their fulfillment mingled together in a feral explosion. His look was so fierce, she wondered if he hated her. The Douglas passion unleashed was devastating. Suddenly she burst into tears.

Instantly he was contrite, cradling her. "Honeylamb, did I hurt ye?"

"Yes . . . no," she whispered.

He stroked her hair and her back tenderly. "I'm sorry. Was it still life's greatest disappointment for ye?"

She lifted her face and sought his eyes. Her eyelashes were spiked with tears, and her hair tumbled in wild disarray. "No, it was like a revelation."

He hugged her to him and began to laugh with relief. It was contagious. Suddenly Tina was laughing through her tears. She didn't know why exactly, except perhaps in the game of war in which men and women engaged, she was no longer the victim, but the victor.

He was reluctant to part with her, so they lay curled together beneath the furs. She had a great curiosity about his body and its workings, but she would save her explorations for next time, when some of her shyness had vanished.

He dipped his head to kiss her good night and murmured, "Honeypot."

She stiffened, for he had hurled the promiscuous name

at her with contempt in the past. His arms tightened. "*My honeypot*," he emphasized. God help him, he already wanted to take her again. But he curbed his lust. She was in wonder over what had happened between them, and he would not spoil it for her for anything on earth. "Tomorrow we'll ride tae Solway Firth, and I'll make a sailor of ye."

Chapter 22

When she awoke in the big bed, she was alone. She sat up and blinked in disbelief that it was morning. How could she have slept so soundly in the same bed with a strange man? And that man her enemy!

She was relieved that Ram Douglas was not there with his dark, intense eyes to watch her rise, yet at the same time she experienced a sense of loss. When she threw back the fur and swung her legs from the bed, she blushed to see that all she wore was one stocking. It felt even more scandalous than sleeping nude.

Ada was ready with her bath. She cast her an anxious glance. "Are you all right, Tina? I heard you screaming in the night, but I didn't dare to come in."

"Scream?" Tina repeated blankly, then her cheeks suffused with pink as she recalled how vocal both of them had been. The corners of her mouth lifted. "It must have been Douglas when I gave him the *coup d'éclat.*"

Ada knew it was when Ram had given her the *coup d'épée,* or swordthrust, but she decided the moment called for a little discretion.

As she stepped from the water, Tina said, "He said

something about riding to the Solway. Probably wants to get a good look at the Kennedy land I've brought him along the River Dee and gloat over it."

Gavin and Drummond Douglas had returned in the night. They had anchored in the Dee, not seven miles away. Tina breakfasted alone and hoped she kept Hotspur waiting, but when she finally emerged into the bailey, she saw that no sign of impatience marred his dark brow. When his eyes swept over her, she felt beautiful.

A man-at-arms held Indigo for her, and as she mounted and rode forward, she was amazed that her mare touched noses with Ruffian, who though beautiful was a vicious creature, untamed except to one man's hand.

Ram felt the warmth of the radiant smile Valentina gave his brother Gavin like a twist in his gut. She steeled herself against Ram's teasing, fully expecting him to banter and make her blush about what had taken place between them.

"Ye were right about yer French chef. I never tasted anything like that salmon before."

She gave him a bewitching look from beneath her lashes and said, "I thought the dessert was spectacular."

The look he gave her was so intense and forbidding, she realized that whatever had happened between them was absolutely inviolate. Whatever happened in the privacy of their bedchamber would never be referred to in public. Against her volition, her opinion of him rose a notch.

She cleared her throat and changed the subject. "My mare Indigo is suddenly accepting Ruffian."

"When I had her in my possession, I hope he served her as stud. She could be in foal," he speculated.

Suddenly she was blazing mad. His bloody stallion had spoiled her lovely Barbary, and he sounded damned pleased about it! Why did he think he could take whatever he fancied? He'd gotten possession of Indigo again through her, and now he'd own the colt too! She rode in angry silence then raised her eyes to look across the River Dee and saw the land he'd snatched from her. "Your

Douglas land on the far side of the river is far superior to
the *Douglas* land on this side."

He cocked an eyebrow and corrected her. "Yonder is
still Kennedy land. I hold it in yer name until we are wed."

We'll never be wed, she vowed silently.

The Douglas ship that Drummond captained, the *Antigone,* lay at anchor in Kirkcudbright Bay. The posse of men
drew rein, and Ramsay invited, "Come aboard, my lady,
and choose a gift brought back from Flanders."

Although Tina was mollified, she chalked up two more
black marks against him for the time when she would even
the score. She loved ships and all things nautical but had
never been allowed to indulge her passion, even though
her father owned a fleet of merchant vessels.

Though Ram handed her aboard, he summoned Colin
to look after her needs while he went to the forecastle with
Drummond and Gavin. Tina was enchanted with the cargo.
There were bolts of cloth, everything from fine wool to
shimmering brocade. A shipment of tapestries caught her
fancy. One in particular, depicting a tawny-coated lynx
with its short tail, long legs, and silky ruff on each side of
its face, appealed to her most. It would look spectacular
hung above their bed at Castle Douglas.

Colin rolled it up for her. He was happy that Drummond
had remembered to bring him a fresh supply of oil paints,
pigments, and canvases from Holland. To get into the aft
holds required first going up on deck, and as she glimpsed
Ramsay, she saw he was grim-faced and having a most
serious discussion with his men. She did not question
Colin, though she was curious. The Douglases were clan-
nish, and she wanted no tales carried back to Ram about
her unseemly interest in their affairs.

Before she went down into the hold, her nose told her
the *Antigone* had brought back spices. Mr. Burque would
never forgive her if she did not acquire a little of each for
him. She knew the spices were not native to Flanders or
Holland—Colin explained they were from the Indy Islands,

owned by the Dutch. There was nutmeg with its distinct piquant aroma, and pepper, which tickled the nose and produced sneezing. Then there were cloves that she knew cured toothache and were so precious, they were doled out one at a time. Cinnamon had by far the nicest aroma and the sweetest taste, but ginger too was delicious.

After she had examined and smelled all the different spices she began all over again with the perfumes. The oils and musk had been distilled from exotic plants and barks, then in Flanders they had been mixed with poppy and freesia and lily that grew so abundantly in the fields. Tina chose a fragrance that was a mixture of spice and freesia, with only a hint of musk. Most of the perfumes were too heavy and cloying for her taste.

At last Ram was ready to disembark, but Drummond stayed aboard and some of Ram's moss-troopers stayed behind with him. Gavin, however, stayed at his brother's side, and as they remounted their horses, Tina heard Ram say, "Wait until ye see her. Sleekest lines I've ever seen. Nothing will be able to catch her."

The Douglas rode up beside Tina. "Did ye find something ye fancied, lass?"

"Everything! I chose a jewel-toned velvet from a place called Veere, and I begged spices for Mr. Burque. He'll be able to make gingerbread."

"Did he ever bake ye a gingerbread man?" Ram asked indulgently.

"Oh yes, they are the best kind of man to have. Always sweet and silent, and if they give you trouble, you can bite their heads off."

He laughed with her. He had begun to enjoy the little barbs she threw his way. There were a lot of things he was beginning to like about her that had once annoyed the very devil out of him, but that was before she belonged to him. Now he admired her wildness, and the way she rode rather than needing a carriage. The way she let the wind stream through her hair to show it off to the world. The way she wore fine jewels and gowns so elegantly, as vain as any French courtesan. But most of all he liked the reckless way she threw herself into lovemaking, holding nothing back, giving all. A small voice warned him, Don't let her think she has you on a string.

They rode west to Wigtown Bay, where several ships rode at anchor. The *Valentina,* however, stood out like a jewel. She had been built for speed, so her lines were sleek, and like her namesake she was most pleasing to the eye. She was all white and gold, glittering in the afternoon sun.

Tina had deeply conflicting emotions when she saw the ship. She was proud of the Kennedy vessel that had been named for her, yet a wave of resentment washed over her that her father had used it to bribe Douglas to take her. If she felt resentment toward her father, it was unadulterated black hatred she felt toward Hotspur Douglas at that moment.

As he admired the ship, she noticed, his eyes had the same possessive look as when he looked at her. Though it was not her ship, had never been her ship, in that moment she wanted to own it. She decided to try her power over him. "There is one more present I would have from you this day," she said prettily.

"Name it," he said low, his voice almost a caress.

"The *Valentina,*" she said, nodding toward the ship.

His face hardened. "For once yer sense of humor doesn't amuse me. Come, I'll take ye aboard."

"Hold!" she cried, raising her voice for all to hear. " 'Tis still Kennedy property until I formally turn it over to you. *I* shall take *you* aboard."

He cocked a black eyebrow but held his peace. They dismounted, and all crowded into a great longboat and took their seats at the oars. With a solemn countenance, he handed her an oar. "Proceed."

A look of dismay came into her face as she glanced down at her expensive sky-blue riding dress, but as she looked up, she saw him exchange a wink with his men. Her resolve hardened. "Be damned," she said, and pulling her riding gloves from her belt, she jerked them on and picked up the oar.

He had not expected this reaction. He laughed and said, "Give me the oar—I was teasing ye."

Her golden eyes narrowed. "I'll row this damned boat if it's the last thing I ever do!"

"Yer almost as stubborn as me," he mused.

She was so inept, she only hindered the men in their rowing, but when the boat pulled alongside the graceful ship and the Douglas men climbed the rope ladder to the deck, at least a dozen hands reached down to aid her aboard, and she felt warmed by the grins of approval the dark-visaged Douglases bestowed upon her.

The *Valentina* had only a skeleton crew of Kennedys, and Tina marched straight to the forecastle. She recognized the men aboard as her brother Donal's men and spoke up immediately. "Fetch me the logbook," she ordered, and the wind whipped her hair and lifted her blue skirt playfully to show her legs and undergarments. While a Kennedy seaman hurried below for the log, Tina stood facing Ramsay, her chin high and her eyes blazing. The long minutes stretched out, while all his moss-troopers stood enjoying their confrontation. When the log was handed to her, with great ceremony she held it out to him. "The lady is in your hands, Lord Douglas. Though she has beautiful lines, she isn't as easily handled as you presume." Her look was triumphant, and none present missed the double entendre.

"As her new master, I can assure ye she will never be in better hands."

She bit her lip. Damn the arrogant swine—must he always top her? "I hope you can read storm clouds," she warned.

"When it storms at sea, I am in my element. I only hope ye are aware of how violent it can be."

Should she heed his warning or accept his challenge? As she stared into those pewter eyes, she had a moment of misgiving and decided upon the former. With a shrug of her shoulder and a rueful little smile she said, "Your hospitality is shamefully lacking to keep me standing here, freezing to death."

"I'll take ye below and warm ye up," he murmured in her ear.

She could smell the resin of the white pine decking and the odor of the wet canvas sails. She turned to her brother's man. "Would you be good enough to carry a letter to Donal and his new wife Meggie for me?"

He nodded, and Ram said, "Ye had better be brief—I intend to weigh anchor and take her out to sea."

Tina was excited at the prospect. "I won't write after all. Donal isn't one for letters anyway. Just give them both my love, and tell them I shall drop in for a visit one day."

Ram led her below, noting with satisfaction the paneling and other fine appointments of his new vessel. He opened the door of the main cabin, and she stepped inside. The moment the door closed, he took her by storm. She was swept into his arms against the hard length of him as his mouth took fierce possession of hers. She was thoroughly kissed before he lifted his lips. "Blood of God, I've been wanting to taste ye all day tae see if ye still taste like last night."

"And do I?" she asked provocatively.

He tasted her lips again and licked her full underlip. "Mmm, not quite as sweet—a little more tart," he teased, referring to her temper. He perched on the edge of the table, spread his legs wide, and brought her between. His hands had her bodice unfastened to the waist before she knew what he was about. Her breasts were in his palms, and he lifted each one so he could taste and lick her nipples and aureoles. As they rouched, Tina gasped, "You have no shame."

"None whatsoever," he agreed, as strong hands went behind to her buttocks, and he pressed her secret part against his swollen sex. He glanced at the bunk. "It's wide enough for two if we lie touching."

"One would have to lie on top of the other," she protested.

He nodded enthusiastically. "We could take turns."

She tried to pull away from him. "Your men are awaiting your orders to weigh anchor."

"They won't expect me for some time. All heard ye invite me down here tae warm ye up. Ye deliberately stoke the fires of my passion in public."

"That's so you can't fall upon me and tear off all my clothes, you madman!"

"Aye, mad!" he said, taking her mouth again and breathing in her woman's fragrance. His lips trailed up her throat to her ear, then he whispered, "After being at sea all afternoon, yer skin will taste salty when I lick it tonight." A queer little shiver made her spine tingle. "If ye behave yerself, I might let ye lick me," he whispered outrageously, and chuckled deep in his throat when he saw her blushes. He became serious and buttoned up her riding dress. "I'd like nothing better than tae make love tae ye, sweet, but I know how embarrassed ye are in front of all these rough men. I'll behave myself until bedtime." He brushed her lovely hair back from her brow and tenderly kissed her temple. "Come on, let's go fer a run into the Irish Sea."

Tina moved forward to the prow while Ram shouted his orders. He stood between Jock and Gavin at the wheel. Jock said, "She'll need cannon."

"Where do we buy cannon?" asked Gavin.

Ram's eyebrows went up. "Buy? Are we not reivers? We lift cannon the same way we lift cattle. Tomorrow the first order of business is tae capture an English vessel. We'll pick our mark today. Keep yer eyes open."

Tina watched as the topsails broke from the yards, tumbled loose, and were sheeted home. How she would love to have been a man! To shout orders from the quarterdeck, to own a fine sailing ship such as the *Valentina* and every man

jack aboard! She leaned against the rail and watched the
sea and the sky and listened to the shrill screams of the
seabirds that seemed so fierce and so free. When she tired
of watching the sea, her eyes sought out Ram Douglas.

She watched him as he spoke with every single one of his
men. She noticed that when he spoke with a man he gave
him his full attention and listened intently to what that
man said back to him. Before he moved on to the next
man, he always put a hand on the shoulder or a slap on the
back. Women didn't have that one-for-all and all-for-one
camaraderie that men shared. Two women could be close
friends like Ada and herself, but a large group would be
more like enemies than friends.

Thinking of Ada reminded her of her advice. She had
made a tactical mistake today to allow her anger and hatred to show through, making her tongue sharp and her
behavior outrageous. She should have waited until they
were abed to ask Ram Douglas for the *Valentina*. She shivered. He was a dangerous man—she must never let him
know that what she did now was so that she could wreak
revenge later.

In the late afternoon he joined her at the rail and
slipped a possessive arm about her as the red balloon of
the sun dropped down the sky to be swallowed by the black
sea. "I hope all this fresh air has worked up an appetite."

"I'm starving," she said, leaning against him, all soft
compliance.

"Good! A couple of the lads have prepared a veritable
feast. Mind ye, they aren't quite on the same level as yer
Mr. Burque, but there's oysters, scallops, and big prawns.
We're all going to eat it here on deck, if yer game?"

It suited her to a tee. She loved nothing more than being
treated like one of the lads, and she and Ram sat cross-
legged with the men on the deck, held the platters of shell-
fish on their knees, and washed it down with tankards of
ale.

The wind dropped as they sailed into the mouth of the

River Dee. The *Valentina*'s sails were furled, and she went up river on the evening tide. Ram wanted to know just how close he could get the midsize vessel to Castle Douglas. "Let's stay aboard tonight?" he implored her. "Tomorrow I'm back patrolling that damned border, and God knows how often I'll get tae spend the night with ye, since most raids take place at night."

Since he wanted it so much, she fulfilled his desire. She would deny him nothing. In the small cabin she allowed him to undress her, making sure both her stockings were removed. Then his hands were on his own clothes, flinging them off with all possible speed.

As she stood in the golden glow of the ship's lantern, he beckoned her to the berth. "There is something between my legs that needs yer ministrations," he told her, unable to mask the laughter in his dark eyes. He handed her his sharp dirk and opened his thighs.

She looked at him blankly for a moment, not comprehending the savage game he wanted to play. "Take out yer stitches," he explained, "Lord, woman, what did ye think I wanted ye tae do?"

"Foolish Douglas to trust a Kennedy with a knife," she taunted him, touching the point to the taut skin of his belly. I could ruin the arrogant bastard, she thought. Of course she'd be dead, but he'd be castrated. But then she thought of the pleasure he gave her and knew she'd never do it.

She moved the lantern closer, and its light spilled across his groin, making deep shadows in the dark pelt and highlighting his phallus, which rose up like a tree trunk from a forest. His eyes licked over her like a candle flame, scorching her mouth, the tips of her breasts, and her mons. All the while the ship rocked gently, lulling them with its rhythmic undulations.

She forced her eyes away from his man's center and examined the long gash she had stitched. He had healed amazingly well in such a short time, and she felt a pang of

regret that he had not suffered more. Carefully she began
to cut the silken threads and pick out the stitches, proud
that her handiwork would leave no permanent scar.

With her hands upon him, his shaft began to buck. "Be
still," she murmured.

"I'm not making it do that—ye are," he explained.

"That is a lie, Douglas. 'Tis your own impure thoughts
make you like a ram in rutting season."

"My god, vixen, you kneel before me naked, tormenting
my flesh until I know not if ye are angel or devil then
accuse me of impure thoughts. They're not impure, they're
profligate!"

"Degenerate Douglas," she purred, the tip of her tongue
between her teeth as she almost reached the end of the
stitches.

He grabbed for her, dragging her between his thighs, his
mouth taking hers prisoner, capturing the delicious tip of
her tongue. The point of the dirk went in and spurt blood,
but he was oblivious to anything save the fiery temptress
who aroused him to madness. His hot mouth moved down
her throat, kissing, sucking, licking. He lifted her body
higher so that his mouth was on her delicate breasts, tasting, biting, stroking her silken curves with his tongue, curling it about the hard little fruits that thrust so impudently
into the hot wetness of his mouth.

He tongued her dimpled navel and ran his lips down the
gentle curve of her belly, making her cry out with the intensity of his mouth on her golden flesh. He turned with
her and laid her back upon the berth, spreading her copper
tresses across the pillows, then when he had gazed his fill,
he knew he must taste her honeypot or go mad.

He threaded his fingers through the curls on her triangle
of fire, and she arched into his hand, longing to be filled.
He dipped his dark head and kissed the soft flesh on the
inside of her knees, then ran his tongue along the silken
insides of her thighs.

Tina's hands could not resist his midnight black hair and

the long tendrils curled about her fingers in thick spirals. His kisses lingered on her upper thighs, then suddenly she knew where his lips would go next. She cried her shocked protest, her cheeks aflame, her blushes reaching all the way to her breasts. Her cries changed to low moans as he opened the delicate folds between her legs with his thumbs and ran the tip of his tongue around her tiny bud. It became erect and swollen as he toyed with it, licking and tasting and caressing the very center of her womanhood.

Her fingers clutched his hair as the feelings and sensations intensified. The intimate thing he did to her was so exquisite, she could not tell him to stop. When she thought she could bear no more, when she felt her bud must surely explode into a dark blossom, he thrust his tongue inside her like a searing spear. She screamed his name, "Ram!"

It was the first time she'd said it, and it brought his mouth up to hers to taste it upon her lips. Tina tasted herself upon his lips, and it was the most intimate, private thing she had ever experienced. He braced himself above her, and she held her breath as she saw the stark, compelling, obsessive look upon his face. One second before he boldly plunged down, she saw his blood spurt onto her.

With the stormy urgency that was becoming familiar to her, he began to move his powerful body into hers. At first his blood ran onto her thigh, but as his thrusts became more powerful, it spurt upon her belly. To her great surprise it aroused her unbearably, and she knew the meaning of bloodlust. She arched her neck and reached her mouth up to his, kissing him deeply, all her body clinging to him, moving with him. Together they stepped off the precipice into infinite space. They knew not if it was the chant of life or the dance of death, and they cared not at all.

After a long time, when they could again think coherently, Tina said, "You are bleeding again—the sheets will look like a battlefield."

"And so they are," he murmured, drawing her close. "Ye only nicked me, it will heal by morning."

"What if it infects?" she asked seriously.

"It won't. Wounds heal well at sea and never infect." He searched her face with wondering eyes. "Ye are concerned over my least scratch. It is most novel for me tae have someone who cares."

Her conscience pricked her sorely. She pretended to care about his minor wounds so that he would leave himself vulnerable enough for her to inflict a mortal wound.

He gestured toward a decanter. "Fetch me the whisky."

As she turned back to the bed with the decanter in her hand, she caught his look of unguarded vulnerability. He masked it immediately and reached for the liquor. She shook her head playfully. "Allow me—I enjoy inflicting pain upon you."

She splashed the whisky into the open cut and he yelped in mock agony. She surveyed the bunk in dismay. The well-used sheets were covered in blood and whisky. "My God, we'll have to burn the sheets before anyone sees them. They look and smell like we had a drunken orgy."

"And what do ye know of orgies, my honeypot?" he asked, stretching out full length with his arms behind his head.

"Not half as much as you, I warrant," she challenged, reaching out a finger to touch his male flesh. His shaft began to grow. She experienced the delicious feeling of her power over him. " 'Tis a most curious weapon. I'm abysmally ignorant, Douglas."

"Call me Ram as ye did before," he commanded.

"I never, ever called you that."

"You did," he insisted, "in the throes of passion."

"Rubbish! I don't recall saying it," she lied.

He had her on her back in a flash, spreading her legs. "I recall exactly what it takes tae make ye cry Ram," and he proceded to show her most graphically.

"Ram, Ram," she cried, "not again!"

"Yes, again," he insisted, and she was lost.

When she opened her eyes in the gray dawn to find

herself sprawled on top of his magnificent body in the far too narrow berth, she told herself that she had done it all for revenge.

When they were dressed and had broken their fast, he took her up on deck. "We are only three or four miles from Castle Douglas," he said. "Colin will take ye home. He's gone tae fetch the horses. I'll be back tonight or tomorrow at the latest. Angus will likely come with the fifty Douglases I requested."

His face was closed this morning, and she had the distinct impression that he had already withdrawn from her. When Colin arrived she left Ram standing on the deck. Before she mounted, she spoke softly to Indigo and stroked her velvet nose. She told herself she wouldn't look back. She did, of course, when she had ridden about a hundred yards, and she received quite a shock. The ship was no longer glistening white and gold. It had been repainted a shadowy gray in the night. It no longer bore the name *Valentina,* either. In place of her name was the word *Revenge.*

She stared in horror. Did he guess she was out for revenge? Or was he too playing a deadly game? Perhaps he would never forgive her being forced upon him and he would have his revenge in his own time and his own way. She thought of her Aunt Damaris and felt chilled to the bone.

Chapter 23

"Now that I have a supply o' oil paints, I can capture ye on canvas," Colin said to break the silence as they rode to Castle Douglas with a packhorse holding the things they had brought from the *Antigone*.

"Yes," she replied absently, her mind on other things.

"Tina, watch for badger holes," he warned.

"I'm sorry," she replied. "I was a million miles away. Forgive my rudeness. How do you go about painting a portrait?"

"We'll ride out one afternoon. I'll take my sketchbook. I try tae capture many different poses wi' charcoal, then I select the best sketch an' paint it from that."

"That eliminates the necessity of having to pose for hours on end, I suppose?"

He nodded. "I have a retentive mind an' an eye fer detail, which helps."

She promised, "We'll ride out soon before autumn sets in. Already the purple heather on the hills is turning to russet, and the ferns are turning to bracken."

"The borders are beautiful at this time of year. Castle Douglas is just over the next rise."

Before they got to the castle gates, Valentina's quick eye saw a red paper flower upon a bush, and she recognized the sign instantly. They were made by the Gypsies, and she knew it had been put there by Heath. She dropped her riding glove, and when she dismounted to retrieve it, she snatched up the flower. The message read, "Haugh of Urr."

In the bailey she instructed a young squire to carry

the bolt of cloth and the tapestry to Ada, and she took the spices herself to Mr. Burque. By the time she reached the master bedchamber, Ada had ordered her a bath and was just unwinding the bolt of cloth. Tucked inside was the perfume, and Tina put a few drops in the hot water.

"This emerald velvet is the finest I've ever seen," said Ada. "It must be from Veere."

"Ada, you know everything. I hope there's enough for a cloak as well as a gown."

Ada eyed her as she stepped into the water. "I don't know everything, but one thing I do know—you look like a sleek cat."

"That's because I'm filled with cream," she said wickedly, sinking down with a sigh of appreciation.

Ada smiled. "When a woman becomes aware of her sensuality, even bathwater feels erotic."

"Mmm, you are wise in the ways of woman, my prophetess!"

As a tingling sensation grew between her legs, Tina said shyly, "Ada, there's something I'd like to ask you about, but—I . . . you may think it somewhat indecent."

"If it's something Black Ram Douglas did to you, I don't doubt it," she teased.

"Ada . . . he—put his mouth . . . down there."

"I envy you," said Ada bluntly.

Tina's cheeks flooded with color. "I—I enjoyed it, but my God, how could he?"

"Some men do. The rare ones. You mustn't worry that you don't taste nice down there—you are young and tender and sweet. If you are worried, slip in the tip of your finger and taste yourself, just to be sure."

"My God, Ada, I couldn't do that!" she protested.

"A sensual woman can do anything. You usually taste of whatever you've been eating. Drink a lot of fruit juice, then taste yourself."

Tina climbed from the scallop shell and rubbed herself vigorously with a towel.

Ada gave her a sidelong glance. "Have you never wanted to put your mouth on him?"

For a moment, Tina didn't take her meaning, but when she did, the idea shocked her to the soul. She immediately changed the subject. "Did you get around to dividing one of my riding skirts?"

"Yes, I did a couple of them so you can ride astride. Are you going out again?"

"Yes, the Gypsies are camped a couple of miles east on the flat ground by the River Urr."

Tina took only her Kennedy groom as she rode off to visit Heath—she wanted no tales carried back to Ram Douglas. Her eyes soon picked out the tall figure she adored as she rode pell-mell into the Gypsy camp. "Heath! Heath!," she cried happily as he picked her up, swung her around, and kissed her. He set her feet back to earth and searched her face for long minutes. "I've been worried about you, love. Are the Douglases treating you well?"

Heath had been furious when he learned she'd been forced to a hand-fasting with Black Ram Douglas. He wanted to hear from her own lips that she wasn't being mistreated, or he knew he would have to commit murder.

"You can see for yourself that I do very well, thank you."

"I can see the outside. What I want to know is how you feel on the inside," he said low. They sat on the steps of his caravan and shared a coney he had roasted on a spit over a fire.

"Are you sure this isn't a hedgehog?" she teased.

He looked at her with open tenderness, and she knew she must share her inner feelings with him as she always had. She shook her head. "I thought I had everything so well planned. I was almost at the altar with Patrick Hamilton, until Fate took a hand."

"The marriage with Nan Howard didn't take place. We were in Edinburgh. Old Meg provided her with an abortifacient."

Tina looked at him oddly. She did not question his

knowledge of court affairs. "So . . . Patrick is still free to marry?"

Heath nodded. "But you are not."

"I *am* free!" she said passionately. "I *will be* free," she amended. "I'll never marry Douglas!"

"What if there's a child? He has pledged to marry you."

"That's my revenge—my revenge for everything. They took Davie prisoner and burned him terribly. Then when I freed him, Black Ram Douglas came to Doon and wrought vengeance upon all of us. It was the most humiliating, humbling experience for the Kennedys, but that wasn't the end of it. When the king ordered a blood bond between our clans, my father had to *pay* Hotspur to take me. Even then he wouldn't wed me. Humiliation is a burn that never comes out."

"Valentina, the game you play is too dangerous. Old Meg told me she provided the poison that was used on Damaris all those years ago. She also told me in whose hands she placed that poison."

Tina stopped breathing. She wanted to scream a denial of the knowledge he was about to impart. Finally she whispered, "Ramsay?"

Heath nodded.

She flung the bone away and ran down to the river. Mad Malcolm's words echoed in her brain: *"It was the other young swine."*

Heath slowly followed her. "Tina, there's something else I must warn you about. The borders are unsafe. We traveled from Edinburgh to Berwick following the route we've always taken, then along the border through the Cheviot Hills. The English have been mounting raids in the east and middle marches."

She shrugged a shapely shoulder. "Border raids and cattle lifting are a way of life."

"Nay, these are no cattle raids. The English are committing the most heinous crimes. They are pillaging and burning, raping and murdering. Promise me you'll not ride out alone again like this?"

She remembered the raid shortly after they arrived at Castle Douglas. Ram had told her very little, but he had certainly been in a vicious swordfight. "Promise me that you too will take care," she begged him.

"We usually winter in England, but this year we may not. We'll stay around Dumfries at least through the autumn."

"I suppose I must get back before dusk," she said wistfully.

"Come on, I'll ride back with you."

"Wherever did my groom get to?"

"I'll find him," Heath offered, knowing the young Kennedy would be paying Zara for her favors.

That evening, Tina ate dinner with Ada and told her the gossip about Nan Howard. She also repeated what Heath had told her about the English raids. She did not, however, repeat the things he had said about Ram Douglas. After dinner, Ada helped her hang the tapestry depicting the tawny lynx above the wide bed. It complemented superbly the luxurious fur that spilled to the floor.

When she retired, Tina stretched out in the big bed, recalling how impossibly narrow the berth had been last night. She was restless, her mind like quicksilver running over the events since that fateful night when her brothers had gone to Douglas on a raid. She tossed and turned, refusing to acknowledge to herself that the empty bed felt lonely.

At first she was too cold, then too hot, until finally she threw off her nightgown, sighed deeply, and settled into a light sleep. Somewhere between the hour of three and four, when the human spirit is at its lowest ebb, Ram Douglas undressed in the pitch dark and slipped quietly into bed. He was shaking with fatigue. He had driven himself to the limit of his endurance that day, capturing an English vessel with an unarmed ship, literally carrying the heavy cannons from one deck to the other. He had put the

captured crew ashore on the Isle of Man, then towed the
English ship with the *Revenge*. A storm had blown up in the
Irish Sea that he had fought for over three hours. It had
been no easy task to bring the two ships safely into the
Solway Firth. As soon as darkness fell, he had seen the
beacon fires signaling a raid as they sailed past Gretna. It
was in the territory Douglas patrolled, and he knew he had
been derelict in his duty. They had to disembark, take the
horses from the hold, and beat back a sizable raid that had
been launched from Liddlesdale, England, up into Niths-
dale, Scotland.

Once again, they were far outnumbered, but the fury
with which Ram and his moss-troopers had attacked the
enemy eventually made the raiders turn tail and flee back
across the border. He had slaughtered many, perhaps a
score, but two of his own men lay dead and one was mortally wounded. What they had found at Eaglesfield was too
much for even the hardest-bitten of his men. The women
and children had taken refuge in the church, but the English had committed the atrocity of putting it to the torch.
The little charred corpses lay piled behind the stone altar.

Back at Castle Douglas, in the bathhouse close by the
knights' quarters, the water had run red with blood. By the
time all the wounds had been tended, Ram staggered on
his feet, but he still found the strength to climb the stairs to
his chamber—to his woman. Though he was physically and
emotionally drained, his mind was overactive, alive with
scenes he could not blot out. Death's skull grinned at him.
He had provided the gravediggers with employment this
night. His eternal soul was damned, anyway. He'd done an
obscene amount of killing in the king's Highland cam-
paigns, and then there had been the part he'd played in the
death of Damaris.

Tina stirred in her sleep, and Ram's mind mercifully became centered upon her. He turned on his side, reached
out his arms, and drew her against him. She too was naked,
and the feel of her was so comforting, it gave him solace.

She awoke with the feel of his lips feathering kisses on her brow into her hair. She could hardly believe this was the same Ram Douglas who made love like a storm.

His kisses were so sweet, so gentle, so breathtakingly tender, her heart skipped a beat, then quickened its pace. As her arms went about him, she was shocked to feel him shaking. "Hold me," he said huskily. The need in his voice was palpable. In this vulnerable moment, she knew he would allow her to draw closer to him than he had ever allowed before. She slid against the hard length of him and tightened her arms. He sighed, and she felt the great slabs of muscle in his back relax. "Hold me," he repeated low, and incredibly she knew what he wanted.

She arched her mons and lifted herself upon his marble manroot. He eased up inside her until she sheathed the entire length of him, then he buried his lips in the warm hollow of her throat and drifted in and out of blissful repose. It was as if he had found sanctuary.

It was early morning when Tina awoke. They still embraced each other, but Ram was now in a heavy sleep. As she eased her body from his, he mumbled an unintelligible protest, but did not awaken. She noted that his jet black hair had blood caked in it and he had a two-day heavy growth of beard, yet in his sleep he looked younger than his thirty-two years. If he hadn't been born a Douglas, if part of him hadn't been blackened by hatred and killing since boyhood, who knows what might have been?

She sighed and slipped a bedgown over her nakedness, then went next door to Ada's room. "Have the servants heat water for a bath, and then would you be an angel and ask Mr. Burque to prepare a special breakfast for two? He knows I cannot eat oatmeal without a jug of syrup and another of cream. I want some sort of fruit and a fillet of tenderloin beef—no mutton, I pray you."

The best part of an hour elapsed before Tina carried the breakfast tray to the bed. The irresistible aroma of the food caused Ram to open his eyes and sit up. Tina climbed onto the bed and perched cross-legged with the tray before them. He looked amused. It was a novelty for him to eat in bed. "What are ye doing?" he asked curiously.

"You were exhausted last night. I am restoring you to your normal state of vigor. I'm going to feed you."

He picked up the jug of syrup, stuck in his finger, then licked it. She slapped his hand, took the jug away from him, and poured a thick layer of it onto the steaming porridge. Then she drenched it with cream and lifted a spoonful to his mouth. "Open up!" she commanded.

Miraculously, he obeyed. They devoured the pears filled with red currant jelly, and the beefsteak was so tender, she was able to cut it with the edge of the fork.

"Jesu, that's almost as good as sex," Ram said.

"Better!" she teased, and he grabbed her with mock ferocity. A knock upon the chamber door sent her scrambling from the bed. She admitted the servants with the bathwater, and Ram lay back against the pillows, intending to enjoy watching her bathe. When they were again alone, she smiled at him and announced, "Now I'm going to bathe you."

He hooted, thoroughly bemused by all the lavish attention she paid him. Then his eyes narrowed. What did she want? Some devious purpose lay behind this most pleasurable interlude. If he kept a wise silence, she would soon make her point.

Ram got out of bed and put the empty tray upon the table, then stepped into Tina's pretty tub and sat down in the scented water. She laughed at the sight he made. She could sink down up to her chin, but he was so large, the water came only to his hips. She slipped to her knees beside the scallop shell and plunged her hand beneath the water for the sponge. "I will be your handmaiden, my lord."

"Ye have a fantasy tae be a houri in a harem?" he teased.

"Ah, I will never reveal my fantasies—all my mystery

would vanish." She lathered his broad back and then the crisp black mat upon his wide chest. The hair in his armpits wasn't wiry—it was like black silk and at least three inches long. "There are things about you I am only just discovering," she murmured.

"I am a man of many parts, some of them more prominent than others," he punned and her eyes flew to his groin. It reared its head above the water like a sea serpent and she studied its shape and contour with curious eyes. She reached out a finger and delicately ran it along the ridge beneath the head. He shuddered erotically.

"Why is it made so?" she asked.

Huskily he explained. "The purpose of the ridge is tae draw the delicate skin of yer sheath out and in tae create friction."

Her throat went dry, and she hastily arose. He glimpsed her naked limbs when her bedgown parted, and his eyes followed her every movement as she gathered a towel and his shaving razor. His eyes went from her to the tawny lynx tapestry, and he saw the resemblance immediately. The golden eyes were almost identical, and all her movements were decidedly feline. She had a wild, elusive, and untamed quality that held him in thrall, and he knew he wanted her no other way.

She saw the smoldering intense look of desire and held up her hand to keep him in the water. "Your hair is caked with blood." She brought the water jug. "You soap, I'll rinse."

He scrubbed his head impatiently, and she drenched him with the cold water. It had no effect on his raging desire, nor hers. She handed him the large, thirsty towel and purred, "Don't shave until after you've made love to me." She opened the bedrobe and let it slither to the rug.

He lifted her against him onto his engorged phallus. She wrapped her slim legs about him and he carried her before the polished silver mirror. "See—ye look exactly like a cat." In the mirror's depth she saw the reflection of the tapestry behind them, and indeed she felt like a wild little animal. She could already feel the sensuous lynx fur beneath her back. Her nails clawed his back, and she bit him on the neck. He growled, and she felt him lengthen. Her tight gloving lured him deeper, and unable to stand up a moment longer, they sprawled across the bed.

They both made fierce demands upon each other. Tina did not love him, but before God, she loved the things he did to her, loved the way he made her feel. She was aware of her whole body, from her tingling scalp to the soles of her feet, from her fingertips to the tips of her breasts. His beard was so masculine and abrasive, she felt a bone-softening passion. She asked herself how he could have this effect upon her, but she knew the answer. It was his danger, his violence that attracted her. This thing between them was as dangerous and as hot as fire.

His long, rampant maleness was buried deeply within her. Her sheath possessed him convulsively. They were so hot, they scalded each other, and she imagined she could actually feel the ridge beneath the head of his shaft drawing the honey-drenched walls of her sheath in and out until it quivered with exquisite pulsations.

They exploded together, and he spilled his delicious, white-hot seed into her, making her writhe and shudder convulsively. She savored his heaviness upon her before he withdrew. He certainly had the right name—he was as masculine as a battering ram.

This morning he felt alive again. He was filled with vigorous energy, and he knew it was all due to this incredible woman. Valentina had restored and replenished him. As he kissed the softening peaks of her breasts, his keen ears picked up the reverberation of hoofbeats. He stepped out upon the parapet walk, then came back in to fling on his clothes.

"Angus is already here—I've dallied overlong. I'll take all the men he's brought." He cast her an apologetic look. "Sorry, ye'll have tae entertain Archibald. I'll have tae leave immediately." He looked at her wistfully, realizing she hadn't wanted anything from him after all. "I'll come tonight if I can manage it, but it will be very late again."

"Would you like me to wait up for you?" she asked.

He shook his head and murmured huskily, "No, I want ye lying down."

Only when he had departed did she allow thoughts of Damaris to intrude. Old Meg's word could never be trusted—she would say whatever suited her purpose at any given moment. But Heath had told her Ram had procured the poison, and Heath would never lie to her. Malcolm had hinted the same thing, and she wasn't convinced of his madness—he seemed more drunk than mad. She did not doubt for a moment that Douglas was capable of killing a woman. Women had little enough value in a man's world, and if one stood in Ram's path, he would remove her without pity. With poison? she asked herself shuddering. Though she did not want to acknowledge it, she knew he would use any instrument that offered itself.

She decided to find out what Angus knew of the past. Of course, he was far too loyal to Ramsay to betray him, even if Ram were guilty as sin. She'd have to be subtle about it. If she learned nothing from Archibald, she would set to work on Colin.

Chapter 24

She stood in her bedrobe on the castle parapet to watch Black Ram Douglas and his clansmen depart. It was a thrilling spectacle of dark, powerful men. They were not mounted on stallions but rode sturdy garrons, strengthened by wintering in the harsh Highlands. Almost seventy men, bound by blood, laughed, shouted, and cursed as they turned their weatherbeaten faces into the wind and rode into the borders. She saw that not one man wore a badge or a plaid that identified him as a Douglas, and she knew it was deliberate. This somehow lent them a sinister air.

She chose a pretty gown for the Earl of Angus, in sky blue. It was ruffled at the wrist and about the hem, but its neckline was deceptively plain, allowing her breasts to swell above it. Ada rolled her eyes when Tina threaded a girlish ribbon through her fiery curls. "Have a carc, or he'll be dangling you from his knee," she mocked.

Archibald's face lit at the sight of her. She stretched out her hands to welcome him. "Has the steward been looking after you, Angus? I'm sorry to be so late abed."

He leered at her. "Like a stag in ruttin' season, is he? Let's hope the laddie has planted his seed deep enough. Ye look a right fecund female tae me."

She blushed at his frank coarseness but laughed prettily. "You Douglas men are the very devil. I haven't had a chance to see aught of Castle Douglas yet save the bedchamber."

"Come, lass—I'll give ye the grand tour," he said, glad of the excuse to draw her to his side and place a proprietary arm about her. Of course, Tina already had an intimate knowledge of the kitchens and the outbuildings, but there was one place she hadn't been. As Angus proudly led her into the chapel he pointed to the crypts that contained caskets bearing the hearts of all the Douglas forebears. The place was dimly lit and had a shadowed, eerie feel to it. As she watched Archibald, she wondered if that could possibly be a tear in his agate eye. Softly, she asked, "Is Alexander's heart buried here?"

He compressed his lips and shook his head. "Bloody priests wouldn't allow it." His look was so grim, Tina was sorry she had brought up the subject. "A suicide must be buried in unconsecrated ground—but I'm no' so sure it was a suicide."

"What do you mean?" she asked innocently.

"Come, lass—'tis no fit place fer a bride, especially one who might be breeding."

They emerged from the chapel, and Tina did not tell him she was not a bride and that she was not breeding. If it pleased Angus to think these things, she wasn't about to contradict him. Angus thought the sun shone out of Ram's arse, so who in the world did he suspect of murdering Alex?

They went into the dining hall and walked toward one of the great fireplaces. Tina bade a page, "Fetch my lord whisky, and I'll have red wine."

Angus was well pleased with a woman who didn't pull her face over a man having a dram before the hour of noon. She pressed lightly, "I always wondered why the title went to Ram instead of Alexander's brother, Colin."

"Colin's a by-blow," he said without hesitation. "Ramsay was the legitimate heir."

Tina realized she should have guessed the reason, and it struck her forcefully that Ram would have had a most compelling motivation for eliminating Alex fifteen years ago.

Angus said, "A damn good thing, as it turned out— Colin gettin' himself crippled an' all."

Blood of God, had Angus and Ram conspired to make Hotspur the Lord of Douglas? Archibald's reputation was such that there was no deed too foul for him to commit.

Colin came into the hall and limped toward them. Tina flushed uncontrollably, her heart going out to him. "I'm sorry I wasn't here tae greet ye, my lord earl, but I've been tendin' wounds since the middle o' the night."

"Successfully, I hope," Angus growled.

Colin hesitated. "Fer the most part. One man succumbed tae a fatal wound a short time ago."

"Whoreson bastards!" spat Angus. "When I patrolled that border, my favorite pastime was hangin' the English. The trees in upper Teviotdale and Hawick bore a grim crop o' fruit. Jamie is too bloody lenient! Foul fall the House o' Tudor! Do ye know when I was about tae put Jamie on the throne, that dirty little dog turd, Henry VII, offered me a fortune in gold tae kidnap the laddie? Me do anything so dishonorable tae the rightful King o' Scots?"

Tina hung upon his every word, wondering why his righteousness didn't choke him, for he was rumored to be the man who had assassinated the previous King of Scotland for being a homosexual.

Ada came into the hall, and Angus cleared his throat and lifted his head like a wolf scenting prey. Tina could read him like an open book. Her golden eyes filled with amusement. "Could I persuade you to stay for dinner, my lord earl? I think we are having stuffed pheasant."

"Mmm, I'm galled by this steel armor against my body. Do ye suppose yer woman could help me take it off while I have a good soak?"

She beckoned Ada and whispered to Angus, "You'll have to do your own persuading, my lord, but I wager she won't be able to resist you."

When Angus and his dozen attendants rode north, Castle Douglas heaved a collective sigh of relief. When Tina's eyes met Ada's, they sparkled with amusement. She couldn't begin to imagine what Angus was like in bed.

"He has the constitution of an ox!" Ada said, her voice tinged with grudging admiration. "I think I injured a groin muscle—it wasn't mine, however," she said with a twinkle.

The Black Ram did not return to Castle Douglas that night, nor the next seven nights, as it turned out. Wherever they patrolled along the border, they heard tales of atrocities, of men hunted like deer, and they saw the evidence of sacked farmsteads and villages with their own eyes. They even had to put out fires where forests had been set ablaze. In one day they discovered the Elliots, Fergusons, and Lindsays had been burned out, and Hotspur had seen enough. He decided to take the law into his own hands, and as night fell, he led his men across the border into England.

They killed only when necessary, and Ram forbade the taking of women. Their main objective was to carry off as much loot as they could get their hands on. They lifted grain, fodder, sheep, cattle, horses, and household goods. They burned crops, barns, and hayricks. Ram knew flames were more terrifying in the dark hours past midnight.

Once back across the border, they began a systematic distribution of goods among the Scottish families who had lost everything. The Douglas men then seemingly disappeared. In actuality they boarded the *Revenge* and raided along the English coast from Kingstown to Whitehaven. At the end of a week's time, when they slipped back up the River Dee, Douglas had two more English vessels in tow.

Ram exercised a fierce control over his men when they patrolled and even when they raided, but once back at Castle Douglas, he knew they were in a mood for revelry and put no curb on them whatsoever. Every spit and cooking utensil was utilized to prepare a feast, and pandemonium reigned. The racket they made was enough to raise the rafters, and inside and out men wrestled, gambled, drank, and wenched.

Ram watched Tina's reaction with tolerant amusement.

She had been used to a household of men at Castle Doon, but Kennedy men were worlds apart from Douglas men, a law unto themselves. Before dusk had completely fallen, the Gypsies arrived and the bailey rang with wild music and dancing.

Zara walked a direct path to Ram and laid a possessive hand upon his arm as they conversed. As Valentina watched them she knew they had been intimate. She shrugged a shoulder—his reputation with women was legendary. This was only one of his conquests—he'd probably lain with every female from the border to the capital who was over the age of fourteen. And yet something inside her wanted to assert her power over him. She needed to know that he desired her above all other women.

Ram had been aware of Tina's presence since she had stepped outside. He left Zara with Jock and strolled around the courtyard until he stood beside her. "Decent women retire to their chambers when the Gypsies come on the scene."

She gazed up at him. The flare of the torches sent the light and shadow flickering in his dark face, emphasizing his saber-sharp cheekbones. She tossed her glorious hair about her shoulders. "Not a chance!" she told him.

"Don't bother tae look for him—he isn't here."

She didn't ask who he meant. She knew damned well who he meant. Jealousy flared in him as the corners of her mouth lifted in a secret smile. "The Gypsies think they are a breed apart. Their men all horse thieves, their women all whores. And yet . . . and yet—I bet you and I could beat them hands down."

His jealousy was now mixed with hot desire. "I know I'm a good horse thief, but what makes ye think ye'd make a whore?" he asked huskily.

"That's exactly what I am—your whore."

He pulled her hard against him, and his mouth ravaged hers. She did not pull away but slid her body against his sensually as the wild beat of the music entered their blood, pulsing in wine-dark waves that were almost too intense to bear. He reached into his doublet and pulled out a handful of gold coins. "I expect my money's worth," he taunted.

Insolently she picked up one of the coins and bit down upon it to see if it was real gold, then tossed it to Zara as she walked past clinging to Jock. "Where do you want it? In the hay of the stables, or under a hedge?"

Ram was shocked. He gave her a sharp slap across the bottom. "Seek yer room, Firebrand. I'll join ye there in a few minutes."

Her hand slid playfully across his power bulge. "That's to keep you primed," she said outrageously. Tina did not seek her chamber immediately—she wanted a word with Old Meg.

The Gypsy had set up business in a corner of the hall, and there was a lineup of females waiting, ostensibly to have their fortunes read, but some were there for less legitimate reasons. Meg saw her immediately, but took perverse pleasure in making her wait a few minutes. Finally she gestured the other women away and beckoned Tina.

The old woman fixed her with a malevolent black stare. "So what I prophesied came to pass. You belong to the man on the throne with the symbolic ram's heads who fulfills all your erotic needs."

Tina willed herself not to blush. "I want to know about the poison," she whispered.

Meg held up her fingers and made a cabalistic sign. "Speak not the word, think not the word. Do you not realize we can conjure these things for ourselves?" she demanded, her eyes blazing.

Tina opened her mouth to speak and closed it again. What was the use? The old witch would never implicate herself. Tina could feel the woman's animosity toward her. She shrugged a careless shoulder and laughed aloud. Tina enjoyed flirting with her own danger—it made life exciting.

At the entrance to the hall a young Gypsy male had an array of dirks and knives set out on a brightly woven rug.

Tina examined some and bought a small knife with a very sharp, pointed blade. Its sheath had leather thongs that could be tied about the leg.

She glanced up and saw that Ramsay had tired of waiting and had come to get her. His face masked the emotions beneath the surface. Though annoyed, he was not yet smoldering with anger, so she did her best to inflame him. "Ah, the Master of the Universe demands my presence!"

"Not so," he denied. "The Master of the Universe awaits yer pleasure." He grinned. Her eyes danced. "I once bathed naked in Black Loch at midnight and offered to sell myself to the Devil. I see you've come to claim me—but I think I've changed my mind," she said stubbornly.

His eyes narrowed. "Ye are bought and paid for with gold, Vixen! I expect ye tae perform for me."

She dug her hands into her hips and tossed her hair back over her shoulders. "As a matter of fact, *you* are the one who is bought and paid for with land and ships. I expect you to perform for me!"

His powerful hands closed painfully over her shoulders. "Never speak tae me in that insolent manner again," he said harshly.

She licked her lips over him. "Anger and lust are a potent combination," she teased.

"I'll show ye potent," he growled, sweeping her into his arms and carrying her upstairs. He set her feet to the carpet, and she whirled away from him to fling open the parapet door. The throbbing music and laughter floated up from the courtyard and insinuated itself about the chamber.

For the first time he noticed she was wearing the gown with the tawny markings of an exotic animal—the one she had worn with the chain about her neck when she had been given as a prize to the king. Possessive jealousy now mingled with his lust and anger.

Tina kicked off her shoes, raised her arms above her head, and began to undulate with the music. Her movements were hypnotic, holding him mesmerized. At first her motions were subtle, teasing, tempting, but gradually her gestures became more overtly sexual. She lifted her skirt to peel off her stockings, then fastened the knife about her thigh.

Slowly, sensuously she lifted off her dress and threw it at Ram. He caught it deftly and buried his face in it to inhale her fragrance. Then she removed her undergarments and threw them at him. He lifted them to his nostrils to savor her woman's scent. She was naked now, save the knife, and he wondered where in the name of hellfire she'd learned this erotic dance. The answer came back immediately: She'd spent too much goddamn time in Gypsy camps! He had been leaning his wide shoulders against the mantel of the fireplace, but he straightened and took a threatening step toward her.

"Hold!" she ordered, withdrawing her knife from its sheath and aiming it directly at his heart. His eyes widened in horror as he saw her draw back her arm and fling it toward him. The gold pieces he'd given her hit him in the chest and rolled merrily across the carpet, while miraculously the deadly blade never left her fingers. She sheathed it and threw back her head with laughter. "I'll fuck you for free, Hotspur!" She stepped before the mirror to admire herself.

He was inflamed to madness and knew that was her intent. He grasped her about the waist and lifted her ceilingward until she screamed. "Ye look at yer tits the way I look at my cock," he said huskily, tossing her upon the bed while he tore off his clothes. "Ye enjoy playing the wild little bitch," he said, biting her neck, then running his tongue around her ear.

"I enjoy matching you in sensuality," she admitted. His eyes were black with passion as he straddled her.

"Match this," he challenged, then proceeded to lick and suck and tongue her throat, her breasts, and her belly with a mouth ravenous with hunger for her. Ram lifted his head to watch her lips part and moan with breathless pleasure. Her eyes grew languid with the loving, and he was thrilled with her physical and vocal response.

Golden devils danced in her eyes as she crooked a finger and beckoned him closer. How could he come closer to her? Unless, praise God, she wanted him to bring his sex closer. With his knees still on either side of her body, he slowly moved up until the tip of his phallus almost touched her chin. Very delicately, like a cat licking its paw, the tip of her tongue touched the velvet head, and it turned carmine as it engorged with blood. She found the ridge and placed her lips just beneath it, then swirled her tongue around, tantalizing, teasing, tempting, tasting.

Ram arched his neck and back and cried out at the exquisite sensations her tongue provoked. "Stop love—I'll spill," he warned.

She lifted her mouth, but murmured against his tip with her lips, "I don't mind."

Black Ram Douglas had to take the aggressive role in sex. He was simply made that way. He put all his weight upon his hands and levered his body downward so that he covered her completely. Her thighs opened of their own volition, welcoming his savage thrusts, while her lips parted beneath his hot mouth to welcome his tongue as it delved deeply.

She could not wait for him, she lost control as he carried her over the edge, and her body pulsed to the rhythm of the wild Gypsy music. Ram ignored her cries. A serpent had coiled in his brain, its fangs pumping the poison of doubt. Who had taught her these things? The king? The Gypsy? Patrick Hamilton? He knew he had taken her virginity, but she could have been experienced in other ways. His imagination nearly sent him berserk.

He took complete control of her body, arousing her again, this time to a frenzy. It was as if he wanted to brand her as his, to mark her forever as his woman, to make every other man pale by comparison. Whenever she thought of lovemaking for the rest of her life, this was the time she was going to remember. It went on forever. She yielded to his every demand as he endlessly took.

In that moment she would have given him everything—her body, her mind, her soul, her life. Everything except her love. She shuddered with the bliss of it all, yet unbelievably his shudder was ten times more violent than hers. Finally he withdrew and rolled his weight from her, and as she gazed down in wonder at where their bodies had been joined, she saw her thighs were covered with drops of what looked like melted pearls gleaming in the fireshine.

His voice was ragged as he demanded fiercely, "Who taught ye tae love a man with yer mouth?"

"Ada," she whispered.

"Ada?" he roared.

"I—I told her you tasted me, and she asked if I didn't want to do the same to you. Tonight I did want to."

He laughed with pure relief and pulled her to him. "Lord God, how ye make me quiver. Ye are my torment and my delight." He kissed her long and hard. "I love the way you smell. I love the way *we* smell." It was the most intimate, private thing he'd ever said to her.

Castle Douglas was so quiet and subdued after Ram and his borderers left that Tina felt almost bereft. It was as if the sun had disappeared. She was as restless as a tigress, and after two days she felt cooped up, almost smothered by the stone walls of the massive fortalice.

Mr. Burque packed her a sumptuous picnic lunch, and she and Colin rode out upon the moors. He was more cognizant of the dangers than Valentina, since he'd seen the wounds the men had sustained, and so he insisted they have castle guards ride out with them. The men could hunt in the vicinity while Colin made his sketches, and that way Tina would not feel hemmed in and watched over. She wore a vivid jade-green riding dress and long, dangling jade earrings. Her magnificent hair fell to her waist, and

Colin seemed amused that she had such definite ideas about how she wished to be painted. She shrugged a delicate shoulder, knowing better than any other how she looked her best. What was the point of false modesty?

Colin asked her to hold the pose while he captured it. She had ridden Indigo, and the dark purple coat against her jade-green velvet made such a rich contrast that Colin made some sketches of her leaning her copper head against the Barbary's satin neck.

They sat down among the wildflowers to eat the food they had brought, and Colin wafted away the wasps that gathered. They had crusty bread and goose pâté spiced with herbs. There was a jar of pickled mushrooms and pine nuts. There was also smoked salmon with capers and savory pasties filled with minced lamb and scallions. To wash it all down, there was blackberry wine, and tucked in the corners of the basket were russet apples and damson plums.

"Let me capture ye sitting among the clover and the Queen's Lace. . . . Ram will be delighted."

"Colin," she said bluntly, "you appear to harbor no animosity toward Ram."

"Why should I?" he asked.

"Because of the unfairness of his inheriting the title of Lord Douglas when your brother Alex died."

He shrugged. "I was illegitimate, though I never knew it. Ramsay had known for years, but out of kindness he protected me from the knowledge." He sketched in silence for a few minutes, then said, "I was away from home when the tragedy happened, and before the week was out, I sustained these crippling injuries in a border skirmish. I came so close to death, I had more pressing problems than the succession to worry about."

Tina frowned. So Ram had known that if anything befell Alex, he, not Colin, would become Lord Douglas. "You hinted once that Ram was in love with Damaris," she said lightly.

"She was so lovely, we were all in love wi' her." He smiled wistfully.

"So it was no more than a boy's infatuation?"

"I hope not," Colin said quietly.

Tina knew she would get no more out of him. What a closed-mouthed, tight-lipped clan these Douglases were.

At the end of the day Tina expected to be shown the sketches, but Colin was adamant—the sketches were his. Not all of them were good enough to display. He would select the best, and she was most welcome to see her portrait when he had painted it, and not before.

She tried to tease him into a more generous mood, but try as she might, her feminine wiles were useless against the stubborn determination of Colin Douglas.

Drummond Douglas, on orders from Ram, took his crew to Scotland's east coast where the *Caprice* was anchored. They painted the merchant vessel gray and renamed it *Revenge,* exactly as Ram had done with the *Valentina.* They began systematic raids down England's eastern coast, from Berwick to Tynemouth.

Ram himself alternated between land raids and sea raids. Word soon flew to Henry Tudor's Court that a scourge by the name of Lord Vengeance was playing merry hell with England's ships, and rumors abounded that he had been seen on both coasts, which was a virtual impossibility. At the same time, wherever Lord Dacre had mounted a raid into Scotland, borderers had swept down into England taking not only revenge but everything of value they could lay their hands upon.

Writs of protest were immediately sent from the young King of England to the King of Scotland, and a warrant for the arrest of "Lord Vengeance" was dispatched by a royal courier.

James Stewart ignored the writs and warrants. He was delighted that one of his nobles had the reckless courage to hit back at the English, and hit back hard. He speculated upon who it could be but he did not really want to know, for then he would be honor-bound to deal with the renegade who was breaking Scotland's solemn treaties with England. James had many wild clansmen to choose from. It could be a Hamilton under his admiral, the Earl of Arran, or it could be a hard-bitten borderer like Lord Home, Lord Douglas, or the Earl of Bothwell. It may even be his own cousin, Matthew Stewart, Earl of Lennox, or that uncivilized, fierce Highlander Archibald Campbell, Earl of Argyll.

Whenever time or distance permitted, Hotspur rode home to Castle Douglas, usually arriving in the middle of the night. Valentina had become his lodestone, drawing him as irresistibly as a lunar tide. He would arrive depleted and depart again shortly, fully restored.

Sometimes his mood would be so black, Tina had to drain all his savage violence. Yet sometimes, like tonight, his infinite tenderness almost melted her heart toward him. He had started his lovemaking very slowly, gently taking off her nightgown, spreading her hair across the pillows, then caressing every curve, every warm hollow of her body with reverent hands. Then he had spread her legs apart to examine every detail. He took each delicate layer of pink flesh, touched, stroked, separated, and kissed. His touch was as light as a butterfly's wings. Hours later, she lay in his arms limp and surfeited as he traced a pattern of ecstasy upon her face with his lips. He half lifted her against him. "Honeypot . . . my honeypot!" He only ever used this term in the privacy of their bed. "Tina, when I make love tae ye, it feels so right. I've never felt this way before. Ye make me feel warm, quiet, still. Ye make me feel whole—complete. I think I am in love wi' ye."

Her heart missed a beat, and she tried for a light note. "Where's your hard evidence?" she demanded bawdily.

He ignored her taunt. "I've decided tae marry ye."

The words hung in the darkness, and she was aghast.

"Nay, we have an agreement of one year! We'll decide then."

"Tae lowest hell wi' the agreement. I've decided now," he said firmly.

"I'm not with child," she pointed out.

"How do ye know? Ye might be," he said firmly.

Blood of God, that could be true enough, the way he made love to her. Tina pulled out of his arms. "You arrogant swine, Douglas! You think you just have to snap your fingers, and I'll do your bidding."

"Dammit, Firebrand, listen tae me! If I waited until ye were pregnant, ye'd think I was marrying ye because of my heir. I want tae marry ye because I love ye!"

She put her hands over her ears to block out his voice and the sound of the raindrops pelting against the windows. She decided to take the guard from her rapier and hissed, "I don't want to wed you. Douglas men poison their wives!"

"Only when they're unfaithful," he jested cruelly, but Tina was not joking—she was deadly serious. "My answer is no, and that's final," she declared.

He threw back the furs and quit the bed. He lit the candles and began to throw on his clothes. She could see and feel his anger. He meant to leave, even though it was the middle of the night and he'd been home less than three hours.

In the candle glow her hair was an aureole of flame. Her hands brought the fur up to her throat as if she could protect herself with it. He dragged her from the bed with one powerful hand. "I'm not asking, I'm telling ye." He towered above her, then suddenly his magnificent, weatherbeaten face, so brutally handsome, laughed down at her. He bent her backward in his arms. "I am your destiny. When I come next, I'll fetch the priest."

Chapter 25

Oh what care I for my goose-feather bed,
with the sheets turned down so bravely-o?
Tonight I will sleep in a wide open field,
Along with the raggle-taggle Gypsies-o.

The chamber was suddenly very cold after he had left, as if he had taken all the warmth with him. Tina climbed back into bed and huddled beneath the fur. The wind and rain made her shiver, although he was the one riding out into it. It would take more than inclement weather to stop Black Ram Douglas. Curse him! Curse him!

Was it possible that he loved her? Perhaps she could take her revenge sooner than she had thought. Nay, he hated her, and she him, yet somewhere at some point love and hate must meet, just as Heaven and Hell were but two sides of the same coin.

Her mind dashed about like quicksilver going over her alternatives. She would leave. She would go home to her father. The thought of her mother and Beth made her search elsewhere. Donal and Meggie were at Castle Kennedy, not much more than thirty miles off, on the coast. Then she thought better of it. She had seen Black Ram Douglas in a temper and didn't envy the man who stood in his way. Poor Donal had been no match for him before.

Suddenly she stopped shivering. She knew exactly where she would go: the Haugh of Urr. She would do it with panache!

As Ram rode deep into the borders with his men, he ignored their curses and grumbling at being routed out of bed hours before dawn. He never noticed the sheep huddled together for comfort against the drenching rain. He was too deep in his own thoughts. Bloody females! To a woman, kindness meant weakness, and they despise you for it and put a knife in your back. A clout round the ear wouldn't be amiss. Nay, an inner voice rose up. 'Tis you who are at fault. Do ye ever bring her a bauble, a jewel? Do ye ever pay her a compliment, or thank her for the shirts she embroiders? Do ye ever praise her for the meals she has her Mr. Burque prepare special? Do ye ever play a game of chess or dice with her, or talk with her? Do ye ever share yer fears or yer victories with her? Do ye ever tell her how much she means tae ye, except in the throes of passion?

He treasured the memories of the afternoon they'd spent fishing. He wanted someone to share his life with, and he knew he had found her. He longed to share everything—the laughter, the tears, the wild moments, and the quiet ones. Blood of God, did she really fear him? Fear he'd poison her? It was untenable. The mere thought of aught happening to her knotted his gut.

He'd turn back now and beg her to wed him, not issue his orders. He sighed. He knew he was far too blood-proud ever to beg for anything in this world. He wanted her to be the mother of his children. What splendid sons and beautiful daughters they'd make together! A fear rose up. He'd never had a child. Other men scattered their bastards to the wind, but no lass had ever come to him in tears because she was in trouble. He mastered the fear. Valentina would bear him children—he knew it as well as he knew the sun would rise and set.

Once they reached the sea, Ramsay was kept too busy for introspection. They took the horses aboard the *Revenge,* then slowly patrolled the coast of the counties of Kirkcudbright and Dumfries all the way up the Solway Firth to the point where Scotland joined England. They ate aboardship, then disembarked to patrol the borders of Roxburgh.

They found the lairdship of Armstrong burned out and most of them fled north. There was little they could do, so they pressed on, hoping to catch the English raiders red-handed. At Rowanburn they got their wish—only some of the animals had been rustled, and a dozen men, drunk with bloodlust, were raping women and girls upon the ground beside the bodies of their dead fathers and husbands. Not one of them escaped the wrath of Douglas!

The thing that infuriated Ram was the fact that they were soldiers in uniform. Once his men had dispatched the raiders, they wasted no time. Without hesitation Ram Douglas led the way across the border deep into Liddlesdale. When four men herding a large flock of sheep saw the Scots borderers in pursuit, they abandoned the animals and rode hell for leather over valley and dale. The terrain was treacherous with rock and bog. English army horses were no match for the sturdy, sure-footed garrons.

The borderers herded the four men together as if they were sheep, totally surrounding them so there was no chance for escape. The look of sheer panic on their faces showed clearly they feared they would get their necks stretched, which was the penalty for rustling.

If they had known what was in store for them, they would have begged to be hanged. The dark eyes of the Scots sought those of their leader as every moss-trooper reached for his dirk. Lord Vengeance nodded imperceptibly, and they closed in on their prey, pulling them to the ground for what was known as a "prinking." It was an age-old Scots tradition for a detested enemy. Each borderer took his turn, stabbing with his dirk. Each wound was superficial though cruelly painful. However, by the time seventy such wounds had been inflicted upon every part of the body, the unfortunate victim had usually bled to death, screaming in agony and begging to be dispatched. The fourth and last man babbled everything Douglas wished to know before he received the merciful coup de grâce. The information confirmed Ram's suspicions: The English garrison was in Carlisle. The commanding officer Lord Dacre.

They rode back into Scotland, and Ram called a meeting of all Scots border wardens. They met at the Earl of Bothwell's impregnable Hermitage Castle. Any other than a borderer would never have found it, let alone gained entrance across the hazardous bogs. The Hermitage was a massive pile of gray, forbidding stone, its great hall so large, it took two walk-in fireplaces to heat the place. As the Homes of Wedderburn rubbed shoulders with the Hamiltons, Bruces, Kerrs, and Elliots, Bothwell filled their trenchers with roast oxen and their leather horns with October ale.

The wardens of the east marches, Lindsay and Hay, told sickening tales of the English crossing the Tweed, not merely to loot and pillage but to destroy Scottish shipping and impress their crews and to commit atrocities against women and children. They had discovered a large garrison of soldiers at Berwick. They all knew formal protests had been made by the King of Scotland to the King of England, who had paid lip-service to the treaties by promising to suppress border banditry or restore the prizes taken by pirates. But now the border lords had proof that it was not bandits or pirates but Henry Tudor's army and navy that harried their land and their people.

Bothwell spoke. "The fuckin' whoreson is nobbut a greedy bairn, no' yet twenty-one, but he's set his voracious sights on Scotland an' willna be satisfied until it's all-out war."

"The first thing James should do is send that bloody traitor Howard packing back tae England," said Patrick Hamilton.

Ram swept him with a look of contempt but kept his peace. Ram could afford to be generous—Tina was his.

Home of Wedderburn, however, quipped, "Politics makes strange bedfellows."

Kerr, who knew naught of Patrick's affair with the Howard girl, said, "Hamilton's right, and while James is ridding himself of vermin like Howard, he should pack his whore of a queen back tae her brother."

Before the meeting broke up, two things were decided. The English garrisons in Carlisle and Berwick would be raided to learn their strength and numbers, and one of them would have to inform the King in Edinburgh that the borders were already at war. They were unanimous in their choice: Douglas was the one who had James Stewart's ear.

On the voyage home an English vessel made the mistake of firing on the *Revenge*. Ramsay thought it a waste to sink the tall, unwieldy ship when he could easily outmaneuver and capture it. Why waste cannonballs when they could board her, claim the cargo, then sell the vessel? Some of the crew was still alive when Hotspur stood in command on the quarterdeck, and he leniently put them ashore at Silloth on condition they report that they owed their miserable hides to Lord Vengeance.

Ram was in high good humor when he sailed into the mouth of the Dee and stopped to pick up the priest from Kirkcudbright. He fancied taking his new wife to Edinburgh to show her off to the court. His mind was full of plans. They could sail up to Ayr, where he could sell the six vessels he'd taken as prizes. He'd take Valentina home to Doon so she could tell her family of their marriage, then they could sail up the Clyde to Glasgow and ride to Edinburgh. It would be a honeymoon trip, far more romantic than a hard ride overland of more than a hundred miles.

He put the priest in the capable hands of his steward, then went straight to the bathhouse in the barracks, whistling his head off. The castle servants looked at him askance, keeping a wise silence. News of Tina's departure two days since had swept Castle Douglas like banefire, and they dreaded the explosion they feared might be strong enough to blow them all to kingdom come.

Ram was starved for a glimpse of her and went upstairs

to seek her out. He was disappointed to find the large, master bedchamber empty and went out upon the high parapet walk to see if he could see her below. He had become so accustomed to returning home to her, it felt like a part of himself was missing when her golden eyes and flaming hair were nowhere to be seen.

He was about to go in search of her when his eye fell upon a note upon his pillow. A cold finger touched him, for suddenly, without reading it, he knew she was not there. As he unfolded the letter, he thought she'd probably gone off for a visit to Castle Kennedy with her new sister-in-law Meggie, and a wave of disappointment swept over him. When he began to read the letter, however, his feelings underwent a drastic change. He blinked in disbelief as his anger blurred the words upon the page, and he had to read it again to credit what she had written.

"Douglas, it's over, I've gone. Please see that Ada and Mr. Burque have safe return to Doon." She had signed the missive Flaming Tina Kennedy.

"The little bitch! Just like that—no explanation, no nothing." A filthy word dropped from his lips. " 'It's over,' " he quoted. "By Christ, it's over when *I* say it's over, and not before!" She had had the audacity to sign it Flaming Tina Kennedy. He'd drag her back by her flaming hair, then tan her arse till she couldn't sit fer a week! If she set her will against his, he'd show her who was master. She would learn to obey him if he had to put her under lock and key!

The logs were neatly stacked by the fireplace, and he aimed a vicious kick at them with the toe of his boot. One hit the beautiful pink granite so sharply, a large chip flew off. Curse her! Curse her!

He flung open the chamber door, bellowing for Ada at the top of his lungs. He entered her room without knocking, and the little maid, Nell, screamed and hid herself in a wardrobe. Ram brandished the letter in Ada's face.

"Where is she? When did she leave? I'll kill her!" he ground out.

Ada's face was pale, but her lips were firm and her voice steady as she confronted him. "My Lord Douglas, it will avail you naught to browbeat me."

"Browbeat ye? I'll flay ye alive!" he growled, grabbing her shoulders most ungently.

"I told her how angered you would be, but it was like waving a red flag at a bull—it only made her more determined to leave."

"Where is she? 'Tis obvious she didna go home tae Doon, or she wouldha taken ye with her. Has she gone to Donal?"

"I don't know where she is," lied Ada.

Ram's hands tightened painfully upon her.

"Lord Douglas, if you strike me dead upon the spot, it will not restore her to you."

Her cool reasoning penetrated his fury. He flung her from him. "How long has she been gone?" he demanded.

"Two days," she said quietly.

"Two days?" He cursed, his gut knotting. "The goddamned Frenchman will tell me where she is. I'll truss him on one of his bloody spits and roast him alive!"

"If she wouldn't tell me where she was going, you don't really believe she'd confide in her chef, do you?" she reasoned.

"Why in the name of Christ didn't Colin mount a search when she hadn't returned by nightfall?"

"Likely because he has more intelligence than to interfere between you and one of your women," she dared to reply.

"One of my women? Is that what ye think Tina is?" he asked incredulously. "I've dragged the bloody priest here from Kirkcudbright tae wed us!" he shouted.

"That's why she left," Ada explained.

The logic of it all eluded him. "I must be thick in the bloody head. I don't get it."

"She is Lady Valentina Kennedy. Have you no notion of the enormity of the insult when you offered her only a hand-fasting rather than marriage? Added to that was the fact that Rob Kennedy had to pay you to take her. A woman with her pride and spirit was bound to avenge such humiliation."

As her words hit home, he felt as if he'd received a blow to the crotch.

"This is her woman's revenge," Ada explained.

Ram Douglas was in turmoil. He was unused to explaining himself to a woman. He knew he could extract Tina's whereabouts from Ada, but at what cost? If he behaved brutally to her servant, it would not advance him in her eyes, nor his own.

He went back to his own chamber and slammed the door in frustration. He picked up a decanter of whisky and lifted it to his mouth, taking a long pull on the fiery liquor. The burning sensation in his gut gave him perverse pleasure, and he raised the decanter again. At least he was certain of one thing—she hadn't gone running to Patrick Hamilton. He'd been at Bothwell's Hermitage. A damned good thing too. If she had hung a pair of horns on him, Hamilton would be a dead man. Then he'd kill her! He'd choke the bloody life out of her!

He took another swallow, then heaved the decanter against the stone wall of the chamber. Christ! He'd never, ever told a woman he loved her before. Never even let his guard down in the presence of a female. Bitches every last one! It was possible she had gone to Court, but somehow he doubted it. There was only one place she could have gone and that was Castle Kennedy. She'd gone so that he would go chasing after her. Well, he'd be in no hurry. He'd get a good night's sleep. He'd stop for her on his voyage to Ayr with the ships he was taking to sell.

But he'd be damned if he'd marry her now. She was expecting him to run after her and beg her to wed him. Well, she could whistle! He'd let the hand-fasting run its course before he'd humble himself again by baring his heart to her. If the little vixen liked playing vindictive games, he'd oblige her. He was very good at games.

Ram was so restless he prowled about the chamber like a caged animal. He absently ran his hand over the thick fur of the lynx pelt and fingered the finespun material of her nightgown. He lifted it to his face and absently rubbed it against his freshly shaven cheek. The fragrance that stole to him aroused him. He flung the thing from him and picked up the objects from the nighttable, carefully weighing them in his hand, then setting them down before he was tempted to pitch them across the room.

His eye fell upon a red paper flower, and he picked it up and began to crush the petals when he noticed the writing upon it: *Haugh of Urr.* Suddenly he went ice cold. His heart froze within him. She had gone to the Gypsy. He knew a moment of madness—a blinding flash of fury that consumed him. In that instant his love turned to hate. With deliberate hands he removed his knife from its sheath, took a whetstone from the mantel, and honed its blade to a razor-sharp edge.

Heath and Valentina were fighting, something they had never done before. Their barbs flew hot and furious, deliberately wounding each other. " 'Tis sheer male arrogance! You have been wintering in England for as long as I can remember, but now that I demand you take me with you, suddenly you decide you'll winter in Edinburgh instead."

"Are you deaf as well as stupid?" he demanded. "England is unsafe! Why the hell have you suddenly got a maggot in your brain to go to England?"

"I never thought you, of all people, were a sniveling coward!" she taunted.

His eyes blazed. "Me a coward? 'Tis you who are running away like a scared rabbit!"

She let go of her anger and tried another tack. "Oh Heath, don't you see? If I'm in England, I'm safe from him. I'm even safe from the king who ordered this ridiculous blood-bond between Kennedy and Douglas."

"What exactly do you mean, 'safe from him'? You tell me he has never harmed you, and in fact his only crime is wanting to marry you. And he damned well ought to marry you after hand-fasting you! You're blind, lass—can't you see marriage to someone as strong as Douglas is the best thing that could happen to you?"

"You care nothing for me! You care only for your own damned neck."

He looked at her with exasperated tenderness. "Don't ever question my love, 'tis unworthy of you, Tina."

She flung herself in his arms and sobbed against his shoulder. "You don't know him, Heath. Somehow he'll find out where I am, and he'll stalk me relentlessly until his property is restored. He thinks he owns me! You must be able to understand the anathama of that. To a Gypsy, freedom is life itself! I must be free to decide my own fate. He'll come, he'll come," she insisted.

He stroked her hair to soothe her. "I'm not afraid of Black Ram Douglas." Before dark descended he had the chance to prove his words.

Ramsay Douglas rode onto the flatland of the River Urr, where the Gypsies were camped. He did not come at a wild gallop, as his nickname Hotspur suggested; rather his speed was slow, sure, deliberate; his expression grim and implacable.

Tina was nowhere in sight, but he knew she was living with the Gypsies because Indigo was corralled with the other horses. Heath saw him come, watched him dismount and tether his horse. Heath's long, firm strides carried him toward Douglas, away from his caravan, where Tina was safe.

The two swarthy men confronted each other like dogs with hackles raised. The savage expression on the face of Black Ram Douglas would have daunted a less courageous man. Heath spoke first. "Ye can depart in peace or depart in pieces—the choice is yours."

The challenge was too insulting for one as blood-proud as Douglas. With a snarl that bared his teeth, he palmed his knife and lunged toward his rival. Heath did not underestimate him—it wasn't their first encounter. Heath had drawn his knife by the time Ram launched himself through the air. The initial impact sent the two men sprawling in the dirt, locked in mortal combat. One look into Ramsay's eyes had told Heath this would be a fight to the finish.

Douglas courted death this night. They smashed and battered each other with their left fists and jabbed and tore with their knifehands. The two were well matched, both young and at their physical peak. Both could endure a great deal of punishment without impairing their ability to destroy an enemy. Douglas wore a leather jack, Heath a sleeveless leather vest. Both garments were slashed open across the heart; both men were bleeding from superficial wounds.

With powerful arms locked, they rolled about the ground, scattering sqawking chickens and barking dogs and frightened, excited children. They rolled into a cooking fire, setting their long hair ablaze, then rolled away from the embers back into the dust, which smothered the flames effectively.

The screams of the children brought Tina to the doorway of Heath's caravan. The excited cries of, "A fight! A fight!" sent her heart into her throat. She picked up her skirts and ran as fast as she could past the caravans and cooking fires to where the dark silhouettes of the combatants rolled over and over in the shadows. Fear for Heath at the hands of Douglas filled her heart until she thought it might burst. She screamed at them to stop, but it was as if neither of them could even hear her. Because of her, one was going to kill the other. She should never have come, never made Heath vulnerable to the black hatred of Douglas!

She could see how well matched the two were as each inflicted damage yet avoided receiving a fatal knife thrust. She was crying now, begging them to stop, but they would not. The men's concentration upon each other was so intense, nothing else in the world existed for either of them. The thing that tipped the scales was Ram's black, unadulterated hatred and jealousy for his rival. With one large boot clamped down upon Heath's thigh, his powerful hand clamped about Heath's throat, Ram raised his knife arm high in preparation for the death plunge.

Valentina, uncaring for the danger, recklessly threw herself between Heath and the knife. "Heath is my brother!" she sobbed hysterically. Ram's knife was deflected toward his own midsection. It jammed against his belt buckle, and the blade snapped in half. Ram sat back on his haunches staring down in horror at the girl he had almost impaled.

Her eyes had gone from golden to smoky amber in her distress, and he shook his head to clear his vision of the red mist of hatred that clung like cobwebs. Ram filled his lungs with air, and her words penetrated his brain. "Your brother?" he repeated blankly.

"Yes, yes, Heath is my brother, you uncivilized swine!"

Ram Douglas wiped the sweat from his eyes. "You're Rob Kennedy's bastard?" he asked the Gypsy.

Heath nodded. "Aye, Kennedy is my father. My mother died in childbirth. She was Old Meg's daughter."

As they all got to their feet, Tina was the only one who hadn't gained a measure of control over her emotions. She slapped Douglas across the face. "You are a bigger bastard than Heath will ever be! You are a savage, brutal animal!"

Ram lifted her by the waist and set her aside. "Is there somewhere private we can talk?" he asked Heath.

The two dark men walked away from her toward the caravans. She stared after them, dashing the tears from her face, trying to swallow the sobs that choked her.

Inside the wagon the two tall figures took each other's measure as they had done once before. Ram acknowledged the worth of the man who stood before him. He knew that if he himself had ever produced such a son, legitimate or no, he would have seen that he took his rightful place at his side. Heath's Gypsy blood was responsible for his handsome looks and his courage. His self-reliance was a result of the hardships he'd suffered at an early age. Why had Rob Kennedy not provided him with a castle and settled some land upon him? Ram said simply, "If we both love Tina, we are on the same side."

Heath said, "She's always been such a little vixen. I've kept an eye on her without smothering the spark of passion that is her essence. I know she's spoiled and vain and willful, but dammit, she's magnificent. She's funny and generous and as courageous as any man. She's the best one of the litter," he said with a grin. "We have a sister who is a sniveling little rabbit. Donal and Duncan are good men, but our brother Davie is a nasty little turd."

"I'm aware," acknowledged Ram. "I've had dealings with him."

Heath searched Ram's face. "She tells me this trouble between you cropped up because you want to marry her."

"I do," acknowledged Ram.

"The last Kennedy-Douglas union ended in tragedy. Old Meg claims she put the poison in your hands," said Heath.

"She tells the truth, but I swear tae ye that that poison was meant for wolves for our tenant farmers. That year we lost hundreds of lambs. Even so, I still bear the guilt of carrying the poison tae Douglas."

Heath nodded, satisfied. "Shed your guilt, man, it serves no useful purpose." His white teeth flashed in a smile. "Tina is fit for a king, or a Douglas," said Heath, giving his approval.

Their hands were covered with each other's blood as they clasped wrists in a pledge.

"I've use for a man wi' your qualities," Ram said.

"Aboard the *Revenge*?" asked Heath, revealing just how much he knew about Black Ram Douglas.

The corner of Ram's mouth lifted. "If that's what ye fancy, but I had something else in mind. It seems tae me yer nomadic lifestyle would be a perfect cover for a bit of spying. You usually winter in England?" Ram asked.

"We do, but I've seen the raiding, and I've been undecided about going this year."

"Gypsies are considered a breed apart, neither English nor Scot. I don't think ye'll run intae any trouble. I want tae know if Henry Tudor is amassing an army. It would be fairly simple for a man such as yerself, moving from town tae town, tae find out. Our king must know if he is tae muster the clans fer war."

The two men talked for so long, Tina feared murder had been committed inside the confining caravan. When at last they emerged, she ran toward them with her hand at her throat. Ram flicked a glance at her. "Get yer horse," he ordered, then strode to where his own horse was tethered.

"Dream on, Douglas!" she called insolently.

Heath gave her a sharp slap across her bottom. "Your husband gave you an order. I'd advise you not to keep him waiting."

She turned on him, eyes blazing, and flew at his face, intending to scratch it to ribbons. He caught her wrists firmly. "He indulges you too much. If you were my woman, I'd beat you."

Her mouth fell open. His dark face was forbidding and closed against her. What in the name of hellfire had Ram Douglas said to make Heath take his side against her? She ran toward Douglas. "You lying, conniving whoreson— what have you said to him?"

In a terse voice he said, "I would prefer it if my wife did not curse and swear every time she opens her mouth."

"I'll never be your wife!"

"Ye may just be right," he warned.

She turned to find Heath holding out Indigo's bridle for her.

Ram said coldly, "I suggest ye mount before yer arse is too sore tae sit yer saddle."

She set her jaw stubbornly, refusing to mount. Heath simply handed the reins to Ram, who shrugged his shoulders. "Ye can ride or walk, 'tis all the same tae me."

Even when defeat stared her in the face, she hated to admit it. Black Ram Douglas was five hundred yards away before her reluctant feet began to follow him.

Chapter 26

With each successive step she wished that Ram would turn around and come back for her. Then she wished he would slow his pace enough so that she could catch up with him. Finally, she took off her boots and wished only that her feet would stop hurting.

She knew full well he intended to make her walk the three miles to Castle Douglas. Ram took his time stabling the horses. He timed it so that they entered the hall together. Tina limped in barefoot, her face streaked with grime, her hair a windblown tangle. Though the hour was advanced, none at Douglas had retired for the night, and they all stared at the bedraggled creature who was usually so elegant.

Tina stiffened as she saw the priest. She intended to resist with her last breath. Hotspur could beat her to a jelly, but she'd never wed him willingly.

Ram said coolly, "I'm sorry tae have wasted yer time, Father. There will be no wedding."

All eyes were on Flaming Tina Kennedy, who had been brought home in disgrace. She flushed, drew herself up to her full five foot two inches, and quit the hall. Halfway up the stairs, Ram's voice followed her. "Pack yer things. We sail on the morning tide."

"For where, pray?" she asked haughtily.

"We make port at Ayr," he said coldly.

Ayr? My God, he was returning her to Doon! She was hurt, piqued, downright furious. She was the one who wished to repudiate him! How dare he make it seem that he was packing her off home because he'd had enough?

Ada stared at the disheveled picture Tina made. "Is Heath all right?"

Tina said, "He threw me out."

"Well, you couldn't look more wobegone if Douglas had made you walk all the way."

"He did!" Tina flared, and Ada could not stop herself from laughing.

Tina glared at her. "You may well have hysterics. We are being sent home to Doon."

Ada sobered immediately. The thought of being relegated to the ranks of Kirsty and being at the beck and call of Elizabeth and Beth was hard to swallow. "Men want a woman to be sweet, accommodating, pliant, and obedient," Ada said with regret.

"But that's begging for unhappiness. A woman must be able to have opinions and needs of her own. A real man would feel no threat," Tina insisted.

"If you think Ram Douglas no real man, you are deluding yourself, Valentina."

"I'm tired and filthy. I'll need a bath before . . ." Her voice faltered. She had almost said "before he comes," but she knew he would not come. Damnation—in bed she could make him do anything. Upon reflection she admitted that the opposite was also true: In bed he could make her do anything. She crushed down the empty feeling of loss that threatened to overwhelm her. "I'll need a bath before we tackle the packing," Tina said with dull resignation.

It was the *Antigone* that Tina and her ladies boarded in

the early light of dawn. The *Revenge* was nowhere in sight, but six other vessels, all English prizes, accompanied them. The weather was not promising—an early autumn gale threatened, and Ram knew he'd need eyes in the back of his head to assure that all the ships reached Ayr without damage.

Tina stood alone at the ship's rail, holding her emerald velvet cloak close about her. She had plaited her hair and fashioned it into a flaming coronet and looked as regal and remote as a queen this morning. The screaming herring gulls set her nerves on edge, but she'd be damned if she'd go down to the confining cabin with Ada and Nell and her mountain of baggage.

She felt utterly alone, as if no soul on earth gave a tinker's damn about her. Then she laughed at herself and lifted her face into the wind. There was nothing quite so pathetic as self-pity.

They were no sooner out into the Irish Sea than a squall blew up. Ram sent one of his men to order her below, but she sent him back to the bridge with a rude retort. Minutes later he was back. "Lord Douglas wants ye on the quarterdeck. If ye willna go, I've orders tae carry ye below and lock ye in yer cabin."

She could make her way on the tossing deck only by clinging to the ship's ropes. By the time she reached him, they were both soaked to the skin. Ram did not trust himself to speak to her but gripped her firmly and pushed her into a somewhat sheltered alcove behind him, where it would be impossible for her to be swept overboard.

She watched in fascination as the storm took possession of him. Incredibly he looked as if he were enjoying himself. His dark face was running with water, and his clothes were plastered to his powerful body, showing clearly the bulge of his sex. She saw that he was in his element, at one with the sea. Both were wild, savage, and untamed. Ever restless. She had been able to lull him to calmness, but she could see that without her, he would be lonelier and wilder than ever.

The squall was soon over. It had swept down the North Channel from the Atlantic, then moved on to batter the coast of England.

With one hand still on the wheel, he turned and dragged her up to stand beside him. "Ye little bitch—ye enjoy defying me."

"Aye," she said defiantly, and he threw back his head and laughed. Exhilaration still gripped him, but now it was heightened by desire. His arm went about her like a band of steel to anchor her to his side, and he dipped his head to take possession of her mouth. His tongue soon mastered her. "Ye've no desire tae be a decent wife, ye much prefer playing mistress."

"Not *your* mistress!" she spat.

His pewter eyes brimmed with amusement. "Do ye think I've never seen desire in a woman's eyes before? Yer as hot for me as I am for you." He spoke with the confidence of a man who is very sure of himself. "Since ye must remove yer wet clothes anyway, will ye hazard a toss wi' me?"

She was outraged. "Profligate swine! You'll slake your lust on me today, then pack me off to Doon tomorrow!"

"Doon?" he repeated. "I'll never let ye go." The amusement had left his eyes. He was deadly serious. He turned over the wheel to Jock and propelled her belowdecks.

Tina found herself in a tiny paneled cabin. The wardrobe was built in next to the narrow berth, and the only other thing there was room for was a table strewn with charts and instruments. He removed her soggy cloak and set to work on the fastenings of her gown.

" 'Tis ruined," she said with a shiver.

"Never mind, I'll keep ye in barbaric luxury," he promised. Her gown and wet undergarments followed her cloak. She felt the excitement building within her. It was overlong since he'd made love to her, and she acknowledged to herself that she was longing for it.

Ram stripped then trapped her against the paneled wall of the cabin with an arm braced on either side when he saw she would elude him. "I've no time for games, just a quick tumble tae show ye who's master." He taunted her for the sheer pleasure of seeing her golden eyes blaze and smolder. Her body was chilled from the cold wet garments, and though she wanted to scream a denial, she longed for the touch of his hands, mouth, and body, which always scalded her.

His shaft stood out from his body like a lance, and she was in a fever of need as it nudged her belly, then jerked and bucked as it came into contact with her female flesh. For a man with little time to waste, he was making her wait for the impaling while he watched her pupils dilate and her mouth open with sensuality.

She tongued his throat, then when he still did not give her what her body begged for, she bit his shoulders. Any moment she expected him to carry her to the berth, but he did not. His lips touched her ear. "I'm going to take ye standing up." Her knees went so weak, they almost buckled. The head of his pulsing shaft teased her belly, yet still he did not begin making love to her. His hot mouth again whispered into her ear: "Would ye like it right here?"

"Yes!" she cried.

"Yes, what?"

"Yes, pleeease!" she begged. Tina could wait no longer. She climbed up his body. He bent his knees slightly so that she could stand on his thighs, then she grasped his marble shaft firmly in the position and angle she desired and slid down onto it until it was seated to the hilt. She cried out from the sheer bliss of the penetration. It felt like a sizzling-hot branding iron. His hands cupped her buttocks to support her as he lifted and plunged her onto his upthrust phallus. His mouth fused over hers, and his tongue thrust with the same rhythm as his sex organ. As his hands cupped her bottom, he was able to touch their bodies where they joined with the tips of his fingers, and the sensations he aroused were so wickedly thrilling, she screamed with excitement. He slowed, thinking he had hurt her, but she wrapped her legs about his back and urged, "Take me! Take me!" She knew not if he was her damnation or salvation. She felt no shame; since he had aroused her to madness, she opened wide so that he could satisfy her body's needs.

As she rose and fell upon him, she exulted in his moans of helpless pleasure. They were like two savages. She sheathed and unsheathed him; he rammed her like a stallion. They both stiffened violently, their passion naked on their faces. She collapsed upon him as his silken seed filled her to overflowing. He covered her face with kisses before he set her feet to the floor. Then he opened the wardrobe and wrapped her in one of his shirts.

She leaned against the paneling for support, and as he dressed in dry clothes, he paused to kiss her lingeringly, his dark, triumphant, possessive eyes seeing everything, missing nothing. Inside, Tina felt her own triumph for the power she still had over him, that she feared she had lost.

When she joined Ada and Nell clad in only a shirt, she said simply, "We won't be going to Doon after all."

The flotilla of ships managed to reach the Port of Ayr before nightfall. The sunset stained the sky crimson and in the distance the mountains seemed to be dark purple shadows. Tina immediately recognized the *Thistle Doon,* and when she saw the burly figure of her father aboard, a lump came into her throat. When he had paid Douglas to take her instead of Beth, she thought she could never forgive him, but just the sight of him made her realize that she and her father shared a deep and abiding affection for each other. She heard the chain rattle through the hawsehole as the anchor was dropped, then Ram was at her shoulder. "I'll send a note tae yer father inviting him tae dine tonight."

"Oh, let me take it! I've a fancy to walk the deck of the *Thistle Doon*."

For one moment he wondered if she would return to him if he let her go to her father. Then he grinned at his own foolishness. He was her lodestone; she'd always return to him. "I'm inviting Admiral Arran and a lot of other captains also." He hesitated, "Why don't ye stay aboard the *Thistle Doon* tonight? I'd just as soon ye weren't here. Ye are far too distracting when I have tae do business."

"What business?" Tina asked.

"I have tae sell some ships."

She saw Scotland's flagship, the *Great Michael*, and wondered if Patrick Hamilton was aboard with his father. Probably not—he was more likely to be patrolling the borders.

Tina, accompanied by Ada and Nell, made their way along the wharf to where the *Thistle Doon* was anchored. They were accompanied by a forbidding-looking Douglas, which prevented the sailors and seafarers gathered in Ayr from touching, propositioning, or even whistling at the women but not from looking their fill.

Rob Kennedy enfolded his favorite daughter in his huge arms and winked at Ada. Then he set Valentina away from him so he could see for himself how she had fared in the hands of Douglas. He had to admit she looked radiant. "I've missed ye, lass. When ye left Doon, it was as if ye took all the sunshine an' fresh air wi' ye."

"How are Mother and Beth?" she asked dutifully.

"Naggin' and whinin' as per usual," he jested. "I've spent a lot of time at sea lately. Took Douglas's advice and installed cannon. Sank one o' the English bastards lyin' in wait fer a Scots vessel behind Holy Island." He flung out his arm toward the ships that had accompanied the *Antigone*. "Looks like Douglas has wasted no time. How the hell did he capture so many?"

Tina shrugged and handed him Ram's note. "Ask him yourself. He's inviting you aboard to dine tonight, but I warn you, Mr. Burque is back at Castle Douglas."

Rob shook his head. "I never thought I'd say this, but I miss yon prancin' chef almost as much as I miss ye. Ye dinna miss the water 'til the well runs dry." His eyes strayed to Ada, and he and Tina burst into laughter as he knew she had read his thoughts. "Davie's aboard. Ah, here he is. We're invited aboard the *Antigone*."

"Hello, Firebrand," David taunted. "Ye might have tae put up wi' Douglas's demands, but I sure as hell dinna." He swept Nell with a leer. "Hello, Nellie." The girl shrank from him, and Tina frowned. "Ada, take Nell belowdecks, we can all share a cabin tonight. Come, Davie—you can entertain me." She took his arm. "Been on any raids lately?" she murmured.

"This isn't the entertainment I had in mind," he grumbled. "I'll spare ye an hour, then I'm off tae the Spotted Dick."

"Ugh—why do taverns have such disgusting names?"

"It's no' a tavern, it's a brothel." He chuckled.

She accepted a tankard of ale, and they stood at the taffrail watching as darkness descended and the ship's lanterns were lit all across the harbor. "Where were you going when the English ship attacked you?" she asked.

"We were returning from France."

"Oh David, you're so lucky to go to all these places! I wish I'd been a son instead of a daughter! Show me the things you brought back."

He took her below to show her the rich furnishings they'd brought back to sell. There was a great demand for French mirrors, which were fast replacing the old keeking glasses. There were padded silk screens, display cabinets, graceful boudoir chairs, footstools, and writing desks.

"Oh, this little laptop desk is so cunning, I must have it. It's a perfect gift for an old gentleman I know."

Davie laughed. "If ye know any gentlemen, I'll swallow my sword without gaggin'. Take it—I don't suppose father will mind. Belonged to the mistress of a French *duc*. Wrote all her *billets-doux* in bed, and it's more cunnin' than ye realize. Here, feel the fancy fretwork around the edge of the drawer and press."

Tina placed her fingers where he showed her. "Oh, a secret drawer within a drawer. How fascinating!" When she tired of the furniture, she said, "You didn't go to France without bringing back perfume. Father will never miss one bottle."

David said dryly, "No, but he'll miss half a dozen. I've already pinched five."

"Oh, surely you don't need French perfume to impress the lassies! Tell them how you sank an English galleon, and you'll be the talk of every tavern along the quay."

"No fear of that. All the talk is o' the darin' and dangerous Lord Vengeance."

"Lord Vengeance?" Tina asked, intrigued by the sobriquet.

"Dinna tell me ye haven't heard o' the valiant Lord Vengeance. The raids he's mounted in retaliation ha' almost impoverished the English borders. He strikes by land an' by sea—both coasts on the same night wi' his phantom ships."

"That's impossible!" Tina declared.

"Nothing is impossible fer the valiant Lord Vengeance, it seems," said David enviously. "He's fast becomin' a legend. He dinna just sink English vessels, he boards them and gallantly spares the crew by leavin' them on some remote shore."

"Who is he?" Tina asked.

"Ah, therein lies the mystery. One day rumor has it that it's the admiral himself. Next day, it's the king's cousin, the Earl o' Lennox. The bettin' is rife, an' the odds-on favorite at the moment is Bothwell wreakin' revenge."

Tina's hand flew to her mouth. "Black Ram Douglas," she whispered.

"What about him?" Davie asked.

"Lord Vengeance is Black Ram Douglas! He changed the name of the *Valentina* to the *Revenge*!"

"Don't let yer imagination carry ye away, Firebrand."

"No, Davie, I'm serious. He's brought six English vessels he captured to sell here in Ayr."

David masked his thoughts. Then he began to gently ridicule her. "This Lord Vengeance risks his neck tae do good deeds. He's someone with a great sense of social justice who gives tae the poor an' rights the wrongs done them. It's someone valiant and kind and soft-hearted who puts others afore himself. Does that sound like Douglas?"

"No." She laughed. "Lord Vengeance would give his ships to the king for the protection of Scotland—he wouldn't sell them to line his pockets."

Rob Kennedy, in a smart new French-cut doublet, came up on deck. "Well, lass, I'm off. I'll join ye fer breakfast afore Douglas steals ye away again."

"Good night, Father."

"I'm off too," David said with a wink. "I've business of ma ain needs attention."

Valentina stood at the taffrail for a long time after the two Kennedys departed. The more she thought of Ram Douglas, the more she became convinced that he could be Lord Vengeance. She wished she'd kept her mouth shut in front of Davie. If it was true, it was incriminating information.

When Tina awoke, she was swept with a wave of nausea. She groaned. "I swear, rocking at anchor all night is ten times worse than riding out a storm." She struggled into her clothes and joined her father. She watched him eat a hearty breakfast, her face as pale as his porridge. She denied to herself that she might be with child, and yet an inner voice whispered, it had been ages since she's had her woman's courses.

"Ye know, lass, there are some people who are smart, an' some people who are smarter. Ram Douglas knows the secret of makin' gold. The king should give up his alchemy experiments of heatin' quicksilver tae produce gold, an' hire Ram Douglas tae do the job fer him."

Tina did not want her father to know she was suffering nausea, so she concentrated on the conversation. "In other words, he sold you a ship?"

"Two of 'em," he confirmed. "Arran bought two fer the navy, an' the others went tae O'Malley, an Irish shipping magnate who was in port frae Innisfana." He looked at her keenly as she sipped some watered wine. "Douglas seems right fond o' ye, lass. Says he's takin' ye tae Glasgow fer a new wardrobe afore he takes ye tae court in Edinburgh." He hesitated, then asked the question that had been plaguing him ever since the hand-fasting. "Is there any kindness at all in yer heart fer him?"

Her golden eyes sought her father's and held them as she said very distinctly, "I shall hate him forever." Her words gave him only a momentary pang of guilt. He felt he had done the right thing by giving her to a man as strong and powerful as Douglas. These were disquieting times for Scotland, and he felt in his bones there was worse to come.

When she went back aboard the *Antigone,* Tina went straight to her cabin, crawled into a bunk, and stayed there until they sailed into the Port of Glasgow. She awoke amazingly refreshed, and all signs of nausea had disappeared as if they had been figments of her imagination. By the time she dressed and went up on deck, the horses had been taken off the ship and her baggage was being loaded onto a wagon. Glasgow's quayside was on the River Clyde, which was broad and crystal clear.

Ramsay, who had been watching for her, escorted her from the ship. "Are ye rested? Ye looked a little pale when ye came aboard this morning."

"An empty wardrobe plays havoc with my constitution," she said innocently.

He raised an amused eyebrow in the direction of her mountain of luggage. "Little vixen! Yer father told ye how much money I made last night."

"He did, my Lord Douglas, and I seem to dimly recollect your promise to keep me in barbaric splendor."

He laughed, his face a startling contrast from the harsh, grim expression he usually wore. "Angus has a townhouse in Garrowhill. Tomorrow I'll take ye shopping along the Great Western Road."

"I may have anything I desire?" she pressed.

"Aye, anything," he promised.

Angus's townhouse turned out to be a magnificent fifteenth-century mansion. For the first time Valentina began to think of the vast wealth and power attached to the name of Douglas. The house boasted frescoed ceilings, an elegant oval staircase, and salons crammed with art treasures and paintings from around the world.

Ram bade Ada take one bag only from the baggage cart and take it to the master bedchamber. He summoned Angus's majordomo and told him to plenish two chambers in another wing for Tina's servingwomen. He wanted her to himself tonight.

When Tina entered the master bedchamber, she was pleasantly surprised. It was easily twice the size of any chamber she'd ever seen. Its walls were covered by the palest green watered silk, and its ceiling was painted with scenes from Greek mythology. Its windows were really doors made from small panes of glass. These doors opened onto a small stone balcony with steps that led down to a private walled garden. At the moment it was ablaze with chrysanthemums, Michaelmas daisies, tall hollyhocks, and late-blooming roses. There was a small fountain with a sundial, and a large lime tree that held a swing.

The chamber had the luxury of a carved mantel and fireplace, but they would need no fire on this warm autumn night. The townhouse was the antithesis of a drafty castle. It had a room just for bathing, with water brought in by pipes.

Tonight they had dinner in the formal dining room. Tina found it a unique experience to sit at the opposite end of the polished refectory table and be waited on by two footmen in livery who anticipated their every need. Ram was in a teasing mood, and he played an outrageous game of openly discussing what they would do after dinner. He used polite euphemisms and wicked allusions in front of the footmen, who kept perfectly straight faces, but Tina knew full well that only halfwits would not have guessed what Ram meant by "the tall gentleman belowstairs" who had an insatiable desire to visit the perfumed garden again and again until every flower and bud was plucked.

Ram threw down his napkin and arose from the table. "My compliments tae the chef," he said, nodding to one of the footmen. Then he took Tina's hand and led her from the room, whispering, "Christ, I didn't know what I was eating—all I could taste was ye."

Upstairs in the lovely master bedchamber, he did not fall upon her to undress her but held himself in check. He invited her to play a game of chess and regaled her with tales of his youth when he had visited some of the far-flung castles of the Highlands. He was describing Castle Huntly that belonged to the Gordons. "It stands seven stories tall, made from thick red sandstone. From the distance it's like a castle from a fairy tale, all turrets, gables, and parapets. It overlooks the green hills of Fife. Ye enter through a forecourt on the third level."

He watched her moves carefully. They were clever without being devious. He was quite impressed with her for the simple reason she was the first woman he'd known who didn't cheat.

Tina said, "Aren't the Gordons supposed to be quite eccentric?"

"Ye are being kind. Mad as hatters is more like it. A staggering number of them are illegitimate. Lady Gordon once had her eye on me for her daughter Louisa. She told me not to fret myself about the streak of insanity, for there wasn't a drop of Gordon blood in her!"

Tina laughed. "You're making it up to distract me! Check," she said, thinking she had him trapped.

He moved his bishop. "Checkmate," he murmured softly.

"Damnation!" she swore.

"Why don't ye put on one of those negligées Ada designed especially tae drive a man tae commit depravities?"

"Would it throw you off your game?"

"Not the game I have in mind."

When she opened the bag Ada had brought upstairs, she found the nightgown inside was black lace. As her hands closed over the sensual garment, she knew it would have the power to distract him. His eyes never left her as she slowly undressed, drawing it out to deliberately tease and tempt him. She was confident in the power of her beauty and her body, arching her back, tossing her hair, pouting her lips, and stroking her breasts. Before she donned the black lace, she touched perfume to her nipples, navel, and pubis, then let the peekaboo lace fall to her feet, covering her body, yet not covering it.

"Ye play the mistress very well, chérie. Have ye been at the game long?" he teased.

"*Oui.* All my lovers have been well endowed."

His lips twitched. "Ye like big cocks?"

"Big cocks are not enough. I need big brains too."

They played another game of chess that Tina won because he didn't even pretend to concentrate. She slipped his queen down inside the lace between her breasts and gloated over his defeat. "I'm going to keep your queen so that whenever you become insufferable, I'll pull it out and taunt you!" She pulled it from between her breasts and slipped it back again.

He moved toward her with deliberate intent. "I'll pull it out and taunt ye."

"Oh yes, please!" she giggled. The laughter left her face as he began to disrobe. Her golden eyes changed to smoky amber with the intensity of the passion he aroused in her. His strong hands slipped the straps of her nightrail from her shoulders, and it slid down her body to make a black pool at her feet. The queen rolled beneath the great bed, forgotten by both.

He kissed her for a full hour, then played with her hair and her body for another hour before he made love to her. He enjoyed the foreplay as much as she—more perhaps, for she was writhing in spread-eagled abandon before he completed penetration. He whispered, "Christ, yer so hot fer me, ye make a man feel like a man more than any woman I've ever known! When I see ye flushed wi' passion, excitement stabs through me like great shards of glass."

She gasped as the plunging heat of his blade made its relentless demands upon her to yield up everything to him. The throbbing fullness inside her set her whole body a-shiver. She loved his animal maleness. Everything about him was hard as iron. His arms, his chest, his legs, even his thighs were corded with rigid saddle muscles. When Ram's shudder came, it was so intense it entered her and she shuddered also, becoming one with him.

He loved the quiet time after he'd made love to her. He always felt so completely satisfied. He felt whole. She restored his vigor. He was filled with life and love. Finally he rolled from her but kept her bound to his side with one possessive arm. The ceiling above the bed depicted Aphrodite, Greek goddess of love and beauty, naked, rising from the sea, her golden-red hair falling to her hips, one hand cupped beneath a delicately voluptuous breast. "Ye are more beautiful than Aphrodite," he mused.

"Is that who she is?" murmured Tina.

He chuckled. "Ye are a decidedly uneducated wench. Aphrodite, goddess of love and beauty, is fabled tac have risen from the sea near the island of Cyprus. Her husband was Hephaestus, and she was always attended by the Graces and by Eros, sometimes called Cupid. The paintings always show doves."

"Mmm, who is that devil-eyed dark creature with the big you-know-what?"

"That is Mars. She had a notorious intrigue with him."

"How can she possibly look so much like me?" she puzzled.

Ram chuckled. "Angus had it painted. Janet Kennedy probably posed fer the artist. Ye don't think yer the first mistress tae lie in this bed wi' her lover, do ye?"

She rubbed her cheek against his chest. "Do you think the king loves her?"

"He loves all women. They are his weakness."

"No, I mean, does he truly love her?" she pressed.

"No, he doesn't," Ram said low. "The one and only true love of his life was Margaret Drummond. I believe they were secretly wed, then due tae pressure he agreed tae take Henry Tudor's daughter, Margaret, uniting England and Scotland by a bond of blood so there would be peace. James married Margaret Tudor by proxy in January 1502, but when November rolled around he was still sharing his bed with Margaret Drummond, who'd given him a child by then. He hadn't even signed the marriage treaty. Someone took it upon himself to remove Margaret Drummond, who was such an impediment tae the union between England and Scotland. Someone poisoned her. It broke James's heart, but within a month he signed the marriage treaty at St. Mungo's Abbey here in Glasgow, and preparations for Queen Margaret's journey to Scotland began. It is any wonder he hates her? Every time he looks at her, he knows his beloved was sacrificed for the Tudor bitch."

To dispel the darklings, Ram poured them wine and sat on the edge of the bed to share the loving cup with her. Tina sat up, her back against the padded silk headboard, the tendrils of her hair curled about her breasts like flames, and Ram could not help letting his fingers play among the curls until her nipples stood out like taut rosebuds. "This is indeed a luxurious chamber. Naked nymphs upon the ceiling are most conducive to lovemaking."

Ram teased, "I prefer a mirror above the bed."

Tina picked up a hand mirror from the bedside table

and said dreamily, "Just think of all the secrets a mirror's depths must hold, hidden away in its crystal cave."

"Ye are fanciful and fey tonight," he murmured against her temple.

She put the mirror down and picked up a small lacquered box. Inside upon a black velvet cushion sat five tiny ivory spheres. "Ivory marbles from afar."

Ram's mouth curved with amusement. "They're not marbles, sweetheart."

"Then what are they?" she puzzled.

"Sexual toys."

"Whatever do you mean?" she asked, her curiosity piqued.

"These are Chinese pleasure balls. Chinese culture is more civilized than ours. Their concubines are given these by their lords. When their lords are absent for many days and nights, these ivory spheres bring pleasure. They are designed to keep a woman from taking a lover. They keep her chaste."

"How?" asked Tina, completely baffled.

He put his lips to her ear and whispered, "The wee balls go up inside ye, then ye sit upon a swing and glide back and forth until ye come."

"Ram!" she cried, shocked. "You are making it up!"

He touched his lips to hers, then murmured wickedly, "I'll show ye." He picked up the black lace nightgown and put it on her, then he laid her back against the pillows, opened her thighs, and gently inserted the ivory spheres. Then he swept her into his arms and carried her down the steps that led to the walled garden. She clasped her arms about his neck and clung to his naked body, already aroused by the taboos they were breaking.

The night was all dark shades of lavender. A cuckoo called hauntingly. He sat her upon the swing and pushed her. The sensations happened at the apex of the swinging when she changed direction and glided back to Ram.

"Oh!" she cried with surprise. "Oh, oh, ohhhh."

Immediately Ram stopped the swing and lifted her in his arms. "I cannot bear ye tae become aroused by anything but me," he said fiercely. His mouth came down savagely upon hers, branding her as his woman, and his woman alone.

He sat down upon the swing and took her onto his lap. His hand went beneath the black lace and his finger slipped inside her to remove the ivory spheres. "Straddle me," he commanded.

She pulled up the black lace and straddled his lap. As his marble shaft penetrated her from this unique angle, she knew she had never experienced anything so deliciously intense before. As Ram pumped his legs to set the swing in motion, the friction against her taut woman's bud made her scream with excitement. Threads of molten, burning gold shot up through her belly into her breasts and all the way down her legs to her knees. All she could do was cling and gasp and ride upon the wind with him to paradise.

Chapter 27

The first stop Ram made along Glasgow's Great Western Road was at the fur merchant's shop. Valentina could not resist the lure of the soft, luxurious pelts on display. She touched dozens of different furs, each appealing more than the last. Womanlike, she twirled in front of the polished mirrors and stroked the deep pile.

Ram, however, knew exactly what he wanted. When the furrier settled the black sable cloak upon her shoulders, Tina knew she had never looked lovelier. The inside was lined with cream satin, and both the black and the cream contrasted with her hair, turning it to red flame.

The furrier, wise in the way of men and their beautiful mistresses, brought out an emerald velvet cape with a red fox hood. There was a red fox muff to match the cape. "Oh Ram, 'tis my favorite color!" Tina cried.

"Try it on," he said indulgently.

She surveyed her reflection in the mirrors, then turned to him for his reaction. His pewter eyes licked over her like candle flames. "Ye look exactly like a vixen." He nodded his assent to the furrier and told him to have the two furs sent to Garrowhill.

At the dressmaker's Ram left all the choices up to Tina. Her gowns, whether simple or ornate, always put other women in the shade. He knew she had impeccable taste and that she knew best what suited her vivid coloring. The *modiste* had two shop assistants who helped Tina remove her gown so that they could take her measurements. As she stood before them in white lace stockings and short embroidered white shift, the women oohed and ahed at her undergarments and asked where she had acquired such exquisite creations.

Tina's cheeks flushed. "My woman designs and sews them for me. I am lucky to have her. I need a couple of gowns for court."

The moment the women turned their backs, Ram slipped an arm about her and drew her close. "Ye are tempting as original sin," he murmured huskily. Tina pulled away from him, cheeks flaming, as the dressmaker returned with a gown over each arm. "I don't care for the red, but I'll try on the black and silver." The bodice was low-cut, with billowing, black velvet bishop sleeves and a pointed stomacher. The skirt was rustling silver taffeta. The ruff she chose to go with it was black rimmed with tiny silver beads.

The gown needed the waist taken in, and it also needed shortening. The dressmaker pinned it to fit, and her assistants helped Tina remove the gown. When they moved down the mirror-lined room, Ram again drew her close and caressed her bottom.

"Stop—they'll see us," she protested.

"Ye are the one who wants tae play mistress. I just want tae play." His fingers slipped beneath the short shift and glided between her legs. She pulled away from him, horrified that he would do such an intimate thing when they were not private.

The *modiste* brought two more gowns. One was apricot silk, its bodice made up of a hundred tiny pleats, its billowing skirt quilted for fullness. The other gown was white. Its cut was simple but very daring, following the natural contour of the body. Tina loved them both, and the dressmaker said, "The white is deceptively simple to show off your jewels. There is a goldsmith next door, if—"

Ramsay cut in firmly, "I have my own goldsmith, madam."

The white gown was removed and taken to the alterations room. Ram pulled Tina onto his lap. Furiously she said, "I didn't come here to be molested!"

"Where do ye go?" he teased.

She knew the women could see them in the mirrors and that they were aware of his feeling and touching her body. She brought her open palm up and slapped him across the face. As she struggled into her own gown, she said angrily, not caring that the women overheard, "I have changed my mind. I have no desire whatsoever to be your mistress, Lord Douglas!"

He caught up with her as she emerged onto the street. "Slow down, Vixen. I was only trying tae teach ye a lesson. I have no desire for ye tae be my mistress, either. Ye know I want ye for wife."

Tina burst into tears.

"Now what the hell have I done tae upset ye?"

Tina was angry with him, angry with herself, and angry with the whole world at the moment. She was afraid she was breeding. She had had morning sickness again, and now she was bursting into tears at the slightest provocation. "Leave me alone, you lecherous swine!" she hissed, and turned her back upon him.

His mood had turned black. Women! There was no bloody pleasing them, even when you spent a fortune spoiling them rotten. He summoned a Douglas moss-trooper who had been patiently waiting with their horses. "Escort her ladyship back tae Garrowhill, and be warned—her tongue has the sting of a scorpion today."

Tina kept her mouth shut about her suspicions, not daring to confide even in Ada yet. It was all very well in theory to bear Douglas his much-desired heir, then repudiate him for the sheer pleasure of ruining his happiness, but the cold reality of it was more than a little daunting. Now she realized she didn't want her child to be a bastard. She also realized she'd have little success in keeping Black Ram Douglas separated from his child, especially if it was a son. He'd simply come and take him. A woman who stood between a man and his goal could be so easily, so effectively, so permanently eliminated!

To lift his mood, Ram went into one of his favorite haunts in Glasgow. Inside the tavern he recognized members of the King's Guard and learned that James was inspecting his fleet and watching a new ship being built in the royal shipyard on the Clyde. Ram lost no time seeking out the king and found him with Admiral Arran, who had sailed to Glasgow on one of the ships he'd purchased from Ram in Ayr.

"Douglas, these are damned fine ships ye've just sold my navy. Why in God's name didn't ye let us have all six?" the king demanded.

"Some English ships are top-heavy. They wouldn't have been seaworthy in our fierce northern waters," explained Ram.

Arran concurred. "He's right, sire. The sea rocks of Scotland are treacherous."

"I asked Angus tae let ye have the use of his ships, and we'll need them all, I'm afraid," said the king. "The English are raiding our cities to the far north. The magnificent cathedral at Elgin has been totally destroyed. Argyll's Campbells are patrolling the north for me now. To add insult tae injury, England's new admiral is none other than the Earl of Surrey's son, Thomas. I packed Ambassador Howard off tae England, with a strongly worded warning for young Henry Tudor."

"Good riddance," said Ram. "He was privy tae all Scotland's business and has kept the English leopard informed of our every move."

"Margaret writes tae her brother every week, but unknown tae her, from now on I'll intercept the letters," James said grimly.

"The borders are being devastated, sire. The border lords held a meeting at Bothwell's Hermitage, and they sent me tae bring ye the facts. We have learned English soldiers are garrisoned at Berwick, and Lord Dacre commands the garrison at Carlisle. Henry Tudor has a naked ambition tae gain control of Scotland, and he'll use any method to achieve his goal. The English chief warden of the marches has been given orders tae raid and devastate as far into Scotland as he can, and the south is wide open tae his savagery. Towns, villages, abbeys, whole lairdships are going up in flames, and terrible atrocities are being done to the people."

"Dine with me while we discuss what's tae be done. I would tae God I had a dozen like the valiant Lord Vengeance." James looked from Arran to Douglas, feeling in his bones that one of them knew the identity of the elusive figure. "Did ye know King Henry has offered a thousand pounds annual pension tae any who can take him prisoner?"

"By Christ, I'd turn him in myself fer that kind o' reward," laughed Douglas.

Ramsay outwaited Arran before he made further disclosures to James. Once Arran had departed along with the king's chief adviser, Lord Elphinstone, Ram told James that Heath Kennedy had agreed to winter his Gypsies in England and scout information about troops.

"Thank ye. I too have spies out there. If it comes tae war, at least it is too late this year. The autumn gales have begun, and Henry won't march an army through our winter snows. Untrained and untried as he is, I doubt even Henry Tudor will make his decision before spring."

"Henry may be untried, sire, but the English Army and Navy are better equipped than any in the world, and their infantry and horsemen have one thing we Scots lack."

"Discipline," answered James regretfully. "Well, we still have the old alliance with France. If either country is attacked by the English, the other is bound by treaty to declare war against them."

"Treaties can be ignored or broken if it's expedient," reminded Douglas.

"If I muster the clans, I believe I could amass an army of at least twenty thousand. I don't think Henry Tudor has the slightest notion we can match him in numbers. Would ye be willing tae go tae London and apprise him of what twenty thousand wildmen could do tae his bloody diciplined soldiers?"

James was asking him to put his neck in a noose. "I believe I'm more effective in the borders or aboard ship than acting as ambassador," Ram said truthfully. "Will ye issue me letters of marque against the English, sire?"

James lowered heavy eyelids over his shrewd eyes and realization dawned. "Sooo, now I know. I'll draw them up myself and bypass the admiral, but I warn ye, they won't do ye a damn bit of good if yer captured. Henry Tudor will hang ye fer piracy!"

"England's new admiral, Thomas Howard, is nothing but a bloody pirate, so it will take a pirate tae outmatch him."

"I don't mean now, but later, before I declare war—would you consider going to Whitehall?" asked James.

Ram placed his hands between the king's and solemnly repledged his oath. "This man is yours. I'll winter at Douglas—but what of the borders?"

"I've already sent reinforcements. The Kerrs of Cessford, the Hepburns, and Logan of Restalrig are on their way."

Though the hour was advanced when Ram returned to the townhouse, he immediately dispatched a message to his stronghold, Castle Douglas, telling Colin to return to Douglas and to fetch Mr. Burque with him. Tina would be disappointed that they wouldn't be going to court, but her chef would certainly make life at Douglas more palatable. He hesitated to disturb her at this late hour, but the lure of her was irresistible. Inside his doublet lay the jewels he had purchased for her, and his fingers fairly itched to clasp the emeralds about her throat. His mouth went dry when he thought of lifting the silken mass of her hair from the nape of her neck to fasten the necklace. He turned the doorknob softly and cursed when he found that portal locked against him.

"Tina, unlock this door," he commanded.

"Go away," came her heartless reply.

"Tina, I'm warning you!" he growled.

The silence told him she heeded him not.

"I'll count to three," came an ominous ultimatum.

"You may count to three thousand, if your intelligence level enables you, but I shan't open the door."

Her challenge fanned the fires of his fury. "Little bitch! If ye think ye are safe behind a locked door, think again." He strode to the top of the stairs, where an Italian sculpture stood upon a pedestal. He snatched up the pedestal and proceeded to batter down the door.

Tina, now exceedingly apprehensive, cried, "If you break down the door, it will do you no good—so you'd better go and seek one of your other mistresses!"

The door caved in under Ram's insistent battering, and his eyes were dangerously black. "Where the hell do ye think I've been fer the last eight hours?" he taunted.

She gasped. "Lecherous swine! You'll have no more of me."

His eyes swept over her neatly braided hair and pristine white nightgown. "You need a disheveling," he said with relish. He fastened a strong, brown hand in the neckline of the gown and tore it to shreds. Her lovely full breasts rose and fell rapidly with her agitation. She reached up to rake his cheek with her nails, and he laughed at her. "Ye need a lesson in obedience, lady. Know this—I will have ye any time I please, any place I fancy, on the bed, on the floor, or on the bloody high street! Ye will yield tae me as many times as I desire ye. Never, ever deny me again!"

"You can beat me senseless!" she cried with bravado.

"I won't just beat ye, I'll ravish ye," he said with quiet intent.

Her chin went up, and sparks of fiery hatred flashed from her golden eyes. "You wouldn't dare!"

With deliberate hands he removed his belt and wrapped it about his knuckles. He sat on the bed and with an iron hand dragged her across his knee. He raised the belt with every intention of beating her.

"Douglas, no!" she cried, "I think I'm with child."

He dropped the belt and cupped her shoulders in his massive hands. "Is this another of yer tricks, like losing yer memory?"

"Nay, I have morning sickness," she said faintly.

Hope soared in his breast. "Ye little vixen, ye provoke me tae violence!" His arms enfolded her, "Honey love, did I hurt ye?"

"Yes! You hurt me this morning when you treated me like a strumpet, and you hurt me again when you stayed out carousing until midnight. Then you come home reeling drunk, smash down the door, and rape me."

"Reeling drunk? I haven't had a drop," he swore.

"Then your behavior is inexcusable!" she cried angrily, taking full advantage now she had him on the defensive.

"Christ, Firebrand, I can't win with ye!" She struggled from his arms and slipped on her bedgown. "Have you only just realized that, Douglas? When we get to court, I shall tell the king it is finished between you and me."

"Aren't ye forgetting the child?" he asked suspiciously.

"Not for a moment. There's no way I'll carry a brat of yours. I'll dose myself with smut of rye!"

He towered above her, not daring to raise his hand, for he knew if he did, he might strike her dead. With a murderous rage almost choking him, he went to the door and bellowed, "Ada!"

It was like a battle cry, and within a minute her women came running. In a deceptively quiet voice he said, "We do not go to court. We go to Douglas. Guard her well. If she aborts the child she carries, I won't be responsible for my actions."

Before he slammed the door, Nell lay in a swoon. "Tina, what in God's name are you playing at?" Ada demanded.

"I think I'm having a baby," said Tina.

"And you don't want it? Tina, I'm ashamed of you! No wonder Lord Douglas is furious."

"I told him I'd dose myself with smut of rye, but it was just to hurt him."

"Damn it all, you have a love of havoc! I think it's time you grew up. If you'd take a look about you, you'd see he keeps you in the lap of luxury."

Tina saw the silk-covered walls, saw the painted ceiling, and saw the boxes in the corner of the room that held new gowns and furs. "You have no idea what he's like!" cried Tina. "He rules with an iron fist. He's not satisfied with anything less than total domination!"

"Don't you realize he has to take a firm hand with you? You are so willful, you would ride roughshod over a man who was soft with you."

Tina was stricken that for once Ada was not her champion. She bit her lip and said quietly, "Let's get Nell on the bed, poor little mouse."

Chapter 28

Ram set such a careful pace on the ride to Douglas, it took five hours before Castle Dangerous came into view. Tina knew he could have made it in under two hours on a hard gallop. He had insisted she wear the sable cloak to keep out the chill autumn winds, and before they were halfway there, she was most thankful for the fur's warmth.

She had glanced at him only once and saw that his face had that dark, closed, forbidding look that told her a black devil rode upon his shoulder.

The spirit of Damaris hovering at a high window was elated to see Valentina ride in safe and sound. She had not ventured from her chamber in days, but now she glided down to the entrance hall, making sure she left Folly in the room because she could already hear the excited commotion the Boozer was making now Ramsay had returned. Tina was the first one through the door, and the Boozer stood with his paws on her shoulders to lick her face.

"Down!" The grim command that fell from Ram's lips immediately told Damaris things were not going well between this man and this woman. Damaris stiffened as she sensed Alexander at her shoulder. "Lovers' quarrel," he whispered into her ear. Why were men so insensitive? She glided away from him, pretending he wasn't there. Alexander took absolutely no notice of the snub. He followed her and pulled a tress of golden hair. Damaris snatched it from his fingers and turned her back upon him. "I dinna ken why ye are so worried for Valentina—she can certainly hold her own against Ram," he said.

"Even he won't resort to rape here in the hall. It's what he'll do in the privacy of their bedchamber that I'm waiting to see," she hissed.

"Voyeur," Alex teased. "Perhaps I'll watch also. Might give me a few ideas."

"You need no lewd lessons from Ram Douglas, you devil!"

"Ah, ye do remember, then?" He grinned.

"Why did I ever begin talking to you again?" she asked with exasperation.

"Because ye enjoy the intercourse!" he chortled.

Damaris departed.

Tina said to Ada, "Have the servants take my luggage to Damaris's chamber."

Ramsay did not countermand her words. He told the steward he had brought sixty Douglas men with him, then went into the dining hall to see which of his Douglas cousins was in residence.

Ada and Tina dined upstairs, then Tina's bath was prepared for her. As she stepped into the tub, she smoothed her hands down her belly. "The child doesn't show yet—perhaps I am mistaken."

"How long since your woman's time?" asked Ada.

Tina hesitated to put it into words, then she lifted a careless shoulder. "To tell you true, I haven't bled since the hand-fasting."

"Three months!" Ada counted.

Damaris couldn't contain her delight. "Oh how marvelous—you must be overjoyed!"

Tina said, "I'm certainly not overjoyed about this child, Ada. I wish to God I hadn't conceived so quickly."

Damaris was stunned. "Tina, how can you possibly feel this way? My tragedy wasn't just that I died, but that I died before I had time to have a child. If I had left behind a son or a daughter who I could watch grow up, my demise wouldn't even matter. The longing and yearning for a child that you know can never be almost devours your soul. For over fifteen years I've hungered, and now you will have the child I could not have."

Tina looked up and blinked back tears. "The damndest part is, I already love it."

Damaris closed her eyes and let out a long sigh.

Ada held out the towel she had warmed at the fire. "Of course you do, and one day you'll be damned thankful his father is so much man."

As Tina sank into the soft bed she said, "I'm weary. I wish Mr. Burque were here. I have a craving for hippocras, and he has a secret recipe for the stuff."

Dawn saw the return of Gavin Douglas deeply tanned from his sojourn aboard the *Caprice,* now renamed the *Revenge.*

"Ye didn't anchor at Leith, I trust?" asked Ram.

"Give me credit fer some brains! She's well hidden at Bo'Ness. We just had tae ride directly south."

"Henry Tudor has offered a reward of a thousand pounds per annum for the capture of Lord Vengeance."

"Christ, I'll turn him in myself!" laughed Gavin.

Ram said dryly, "My exact words tae the king. Joking aside, if yer captured, they'll hang ye for piracy. Yer every bit as much Lord Vengeance as I am."

"The English vessels stay well out in the North Sea, but we sank a couple skulking on the far side of the Isle of May."

"When ye raid, stay clear of Berwick," Ram warned. "The English have troops garrisoned there."

Gavin's mouth became hard. "Coldstream and Kelso have been devastated. All the fine autumn harvests are now just charred fields."

"Did ye replace their winter fodder?" Ram asked.

"Aye, we went clear down tae the Tyne and raided al along its fertile banks." He grinned.

"Did Drummond captain one of Angus's ships?"

Gavin nodded. "Ian also, an' Jamie's almost ready tae command a ship. It seems tae come naturally."

"Douglas blood is in reality salt water," Ram confided.

"What about our little brother Cameron? Dinna ye think it's time ye let him out of leadin' strings?"

"He's got all the responsibility he can handle at the mo ment. I left him in the borders in charge of a score of moss troopers."

Gavin whistled, feeling slightly envious. Ram guessed hi thoughts. "Be satisfied, man—ye can't do both."

"You seem to manage it," Gavin said dryly.

Tina found that if she lay quietly for half an hour afte she awoke, the nausea receded. When she surveyed hersel in the mirror, she realized that pregnancy had given he radiance. Her hair crackled with a life of its own, curling madly about a face that fairly glowed with good health Her breasts were definitely larger, giving her body a ripe sensual allure.

When her thoughts strayed to Ram Douglas, she knew she enjoyed their personality clashes, their shouting matches, and their blazing quarrels as much as she enjoyed their sexual jousts. He was a worthy enemy. She did no regret anything that had passed between them—not one word, not one look.

She dismissed Ram from her thoughts, eager to take the lap desk she had brought up to Mad Malcolm.

Jenna had just bathed him, and he was in a feisty mood but when Malcolm saw Valentina and the present she had brought him, his eyes lit with pleasure. He waited with a suppressed air of secrecy until Jenna departed, then pulled his writing sheets from beneath the mattress and laid them out on the desk top.

Tina was pleasantly surprised that the room was not lit

tered with wine and whisky decanters, and for once Malcolm was not reeling drunk. She showed him the clever mechanism that revealed the secret drawer, and he grasped its workings immediately. "Yer the answer tae a prayer, lass." He carefully placed some pages he had selected into the secret drawer, and when he pressed the ornate carving, they were concealed as if they had disappeared into thin air. "I'm almost finished the grisly history of Castle Dangerous," he confided. "Has *he* returned?"

"Who?" asked Tina.

"The poisoner?" he said low. "Alex! No, not Alex—I get them mixed up. The other dark one."

"Do ye mean me, Malcolm?" asked Gavin, coming in and hearing his last sentence.

"Ram?" asked Malcolm, peering up at him suspiciously.

"Now I am insulted," laughed Gavin. "Ram's the ugly one."

Tina bestowed a dazzling smile upon the handsome young Douglas. "How thoughtful of you to visit him."

"What rubbish! I was looking for you, lass. I'm only here for a day."

The old man chuckled. "Women ha' been the downfall o' every Douglas since the first earl's wife ran off wi' her groom. It's all in my history, ye ken," he said, tapping the desk.

Tina knew Gavin was most likely looking for Jenna if he was here for only a day. "You've just missed her. I think she went down to the hall." They left Malcolm to his writing, and as they descended the stairs, Gavin said, "I wager ye canna read Ramsay as easily as ye read me."

"No, I'm aware of only half his foibles," she said lightly. "I'd appreciate it if you'd ask Jenna to keep the wine and whisky away from Malcolm."

Ram overheard her. " 'Tis the only pleasure the poor old sod gets. Let him have his drink," he said, overruling her.

"Excuse me," Tina murmured to Gavin. Then she delib-

erately turned her back upon Ram and remounted the
stairs.

Gavin looked at Ram. "Brr—fire an' ice. I'd ha' though
ye'd ha' melted her by now. Why dinna ye give her a bairn'
There's naught mellows a woman like motherhood, they
say."

"Mind yer own damn business," snapped Ram. A hun
dred things needed his attention before he could return to
the decks of the *Revenge,* which he'd instructed Jock to
conceal at the mouth of the River Doon. Though Douglas
had close to a hundred stockmen and tenant farmers to
look after their herds of cattle and vast flocks of sheep
they took their orders from Ram Douglas regarding the
numbers to take to market or to slaughter. Carrying too
many animals through the winter could prove most unprof
itable when Douglas wealth was measured in land and live
stock. There were still many fields to harvest of their clover
and oat crops, and the sky threatened a downpour that
could last a week once it started.

In the bailey Ram glanced at the clouds and decided to
put his men-at-arms into the fields. There was nothing like
scything crops to tone the muscles. He saw Tina go into the
stables and decided to forbid her to go off on one of her
wild rides. He followed her inside and said to the groom
saddling Indigo, "The mare won't be leaving her stall to
day. She's with foal."

Tina swung about, eyes blazing. How dare he trumpet
her condition about the stables and allude to her as if she
were a broodmare?

As their eyes locked in combat, he thought her the love
liest woman breathing. He'd lay burning for her all night
and all she wanted was to be free of him. He almost pulled
her into his arms and lifted her against his heart, before his
resolve hardened. He'd made a monumental mistake with
this woman, baring his heart to her, allowing her to see
how vulnerable she made him.

Suddenly Tina realized he'd been referring to Indigo

and not to her at all. She bit back her insolent words. The atmosphere of the stables with its scent of hay and horse-flesh was arousing to their senses. The lovely mare had been impregnated by his stallion Ruffian, and they were both aware of the analogy. Desire raged in him to take her on the spot, and he battled with his emotions to regain iron control over himself.

Tina could feel his powerful arms about her, taste his hot mouth on hers. The corners of her lips lifted as she realized her power over him, and she swayed toward him.

He saw her look of triumph and stepped back from her. She hesitated, then murmured the double entendre, "I promise to ride with care."

"I'm not concerned with yer miserable carcass—'tis the mare I value."

His words cut her to the heart, and she ran from the stables before he saw the tears spring to her eyes.

In the early afternoon, Colin and Mr. Burque arrived. Tina was glad Colin was back at Castle Dangerous. His lack of temperament was soothing—he somehow acted as a buffer between his lordship and herself.

"Yer prettier than ever," he said softly. "My painting doesna do ye justice."

"Is it finished?" she asked hopefully.

"Not quite. I beg ye'll be patient a wee while longer."

Tina and Ada went down to the kitchens to welcome Mr. Burque's return. Tina was quite amused to see that all the kitchen and scullery maids had appeared on one pretext or another and blushed or giggled whenever the handsome Frenchman glanced in their direction.

"Darling Mr. Burque, I don't know how I survived with-out you," said Tina, perching on a high kitchen stool.

"Nor I," drawled Ada with a wink, and it was Mr. Burque's turn to blush.

"What do you fancy for dinner, chérie? It will be my pleasure to prepare anything you desire."

"Coq au vin," said Ada, rolling her eyes and licking her lips.

"Shameless hussy!" Tina said, trying to keep a straight face. "I have a craving for hippocras. Would you give Ada your secret recipe so she can make it for me when you are absent?"

"The recipe is simple; sweet red wine, cloves, lemon rind, ginger, and cinnamon. The secret is one of ritual. It must be heated in a caldron and served in a chalice. I shall make some for you tonight."

Ram and his men worked against the elements to harvest the fields. A cold wind blew in from the sea, numbing their limbs, but they worked on, knowing that when the wind dropped, the drenching rain would start. The deluge didn't come until eight o'clock, and by that time they had scythed and gathered in twenty fields. They stacked it in the sheds, managing to keep it dry, but they themselves were soaked to the skin and more than ready for the blazing fire and hot meal awaiting them in the hall.

Colin and Gavin sat with Tina before the fire, listening to her pluck out a hauntingly beautiful Scots lament upon her lute. The hall had been empty except for a handful of servers. It quickly filled with dripping-wet men who were frozen to the bone. They jostled and cursed each other heartily and called for whisky.

Ram came toward the fire just as a page handed Tina a steaming chalice. "My lady, here is the secret brew ye bade Mr. Burque prepare," he piped. A look of alarm crossed Ram's face, and he knocked the chalice from her hand into the fireplace. "Flaming vixen!"

She stared at him in disbelief, her cheeks suffused with embarrassment. Colin immediately retrieved her chalice while Gavin slipped a protective arm about her shoulders. "'Twas only hippocras!" she said with stiff lips. "I hate you," she breathed.

Ram felt the sympathetic looks the two men gave her like a twist in the gut. "Seek yer room," he ordered.

Like a prideful cat she threw him a look of utter contempt from her golden eyes, then walked from the hall like a queen.

Gavin clenched his fists, holding himself back from smashing his brother in the face. Finally he said, "I think I'd better be on ma way; the weather isn't likely tae clear even if I wait 'til mornin'."

Tina went straight to the kitchens, where Mr. Burque warmed more hippocras for her. She took it upstairs, but perversely the last place she wished to go was her room. As she passed Colin's chamber, she remembered all the sketches he'd made of her that he'd refused to show her, and her curiosity got the better of her. She was in a reckless mood, and invading Colin's sanctuary was a challenge she couldn't resist.

His chamber was exceedingly untidy, a thing she would never have imagined. There were easels, canvases, paints, and charcoal everywhere. There were stacks and stacks of sketches, some piled neatly and some scattered about until the floor was littered with his creations. As she bent to look at them, she saw they were all of naked women. Her eyes widened. Drawings of naked women did not exactly shock her—it was just that there were sketches of nothing else. She lifted a stack in the corner, yellow with age, and gasped as she recognized the unmistakable face of Damaris. "Omigod, if she posed for Colin—if she was unfaithful with Alexander's own brother, no wonder he killed her." She must show Ada. She slipped one of the drawings from the pile, blushed at the erotic pose, and quickly rolled it up. She was almost at the door when a painting sitting on an easel caught her eye. She drew closer, not quite believing that she stared herself in the face.

She lay stark naked in the purple heather, her arms stretched out to some imaginary lover, her face just as it must be when Ram was about to take her. The full, high creamy breasts were hers exactly, the flaming glory of her hair unmistakable, the fiery triangle of curls arched to lure her lover. Anyone who saw it would stake their life that she had posed for it. She fled from the room before the walls closed in on her. The smell of linseed in her nostrils made her want to retch.

Damaris's chamber had been fitted with a new door, but there was no lock on it, and Tina felt vulnerable. She sat down on shaky legs and spread the sketch of Damaris across the bed.

Damaris arose from the window seat to see what Tina examined. Shock at what she saw almost felled her. "Oh, no!" she gasped. "Alexander spoke the truth!" The quarrel she had had with her beloved husband over fifteen long years ago was as vivid as if it had happened yesterday. She remembered every accusation, every angry word, the ugliness, the betrayal, the hurt, the pain, the tears, the lingering death, the screams, the silence. Damaris returned to the window seat oblivious to her present surroundings. She was drifting back, lost in a reverie.

Tina went to the fireplace for another look at the portrait of her beautiful aunt. Her fingers traced the delicate features, the lovely blond tendrils of hair, the sweet vulnerable mouth. She somehow felt the young woman's innocence through the contact of her fingers upon the haunting face. Tina's mind flew back down the years. In her mind's eye she saw Damaris out upon the moors with Colin, just as she herself had been. She distantly heard their words, their laughter, and she knew the girl had posed innocently, unaware of the dark longings of the man who was sketching her. Tina jumped as Ada spoke to her: "Oh, Ada—I didn't hear you come in."

She saw Tina pale and trembling. "Are you all right?"

"Yes . . . no—oh Ada, whatever do you make of this sketch I found in Colin's chamber?"

A look of comprehension came into Ada's face as she

looked at the erotic drawing. "Damaris and Colin were lovers," she breathed.

"No! No, they were not!" Tina said sharply.

"Tina, don't be naive—the evidence speaks for itself," Ada said.

"You are wrong," Tina insisted. "He's done a nude painting of me that is far more erotic than this! His room is filled with drawings of naked women."

"Colin?" asked Ada with disbelief. "He must be as twisted as his body. What if Ram sees it?"

"If Ram sees it, he will be convinced I posed for it. He will think me whore. He once said all Kennedy women are whores."

"You must get the painting and destroy it. Come, we'll go to his chamber now." The two women hurried to the west wing of the castle, but Colin's door was locked fast. Ada lifted her fist to bang upon it, but Tina grabbed her arm and pulled her away. She whispered, "I don't want a confrontation with him, Ada. I'd die if anyone saw the painting. It must be done in secret. I'll get it tomorrow, when he leaves his chamber." Ada nodded, and they slipped quietly back to Damaris's room.

In the morning when Ada reported that Colin had gone down to the hall for breakfast, Tina hurried to his chamber. She was appalled to find the painting gone from the easel. In its place stood a half-finished painting of her in the gown she had worn that day, her hair blowing prettily in the breeze of the moors. Though she searched frantically, she could find no trace of the nude portrait. She was certain of only one thing: She had not imagined the erotic painting.

A finger of apprehension touched her. There was something indefinably sinister in the very air today. Castle Dangerous . . . *Castle Dangerous*. A shudder ran down her spine as the two ominous words repeated themselves in her brain. When she told Ada the painting had been replaced by a respectable one and that the nude had disappeared, Ada seemed to look at her oddly, as if she had been letting her imagination run away with her.

Tina could not throw off her mood of apprehension. It was as if the day had a foreshadowing of disaster. What if Ramsay had already seen the painting? He might deny the child she carried was even his. He had spoken to her so cruelly in the stables. What were his words? *"I'm not concerned with yer miserable carcass."* Nay, she told herself, if he'd seen the painting, he would have said more than that. He would have slapped her senseless. She hoped and prayed he would leave today. She needed time to locate the damning portrait and learn more about Colin. She decided to go down and talk to Gavin. Perhaps he knew something of Colin's dark side. When she learned that Gavin was long gone, however, she felt almost afraid.

Today the downpour had eased to a drizzle as fine as mist. Ram set the men to sharpening their weapons and repairing the harnesses. He knew he must leave on the morrow, yet he wondered how he could leave Tina when things were so bad between them. He had been a fool to knock the hippocras from her hand. If he loved her, he must trust her. It was as simple as that. In the borders at Castle Douglas, things had been so good between them. He remembered the night the Gypsies came and how they had made love. He wanted it to be that way again between them. How had the rift happened? They were like strangers, not even communicating anymore. It was ridiculous and could not be allowed to continue.

He should be the happiest man on earth now that he had filled her with his child. Tonight he would set things right between them. He would love her and give her the emeralds. He closed his eyes as his shaft filled. Just thinking of her aroused him. He allowed himself the indulgence of remembering how she felt when he was buried deep inside her, and he went weak at the knees. They had been so hot, they couldn't keep their hands off each other. He could taste her mouth and her other lips between her lovely legs, and she had tasted him, making his gut melt. He stood in the bailey gazing up at her window, oblivious to the soaking drizzle that penetrated every layer of his clothing.

Tina felt utterly forlorn. Perhaps she should go to Ram and tell him what Colin had done. Suddenly she didn't want him to think badly of her. She wanted to be special in his eyes. She wanted him to love her! Why, why did she want him to love her? They were sworn enemies. She had vowed to take revenge for the insults he'd offered the Kennedys. But that wasn't me, she told herself, that was a spoiled, willful girl. I'm a woman now, with a woman's maturity, a woman's needs. Soon I'll be a mother, responsible for a child, his child. Dear God, how had things come to such a pass? He had loved her, loved her enough to want to marry her, and she'd scorned him and run off. Even then he'd given her another chance, brought her back. She had killed any love he'd had for her when she had repudiated his child. Now he had a disgust of her and likely wanted to be rid of her.

She went to the window and gazed with unseeing eyes down into the courtyard. Gradually she became aware of him standing in the bailey. He was soaked to the bone. She was immersed in guilt. What sort of a woman was she, for God's sake? She would go down and order Mr. Burque to make him something special for supper—something spicy to ward off the chill. Then she'd lay out dry clothes for him and have the fire lit in his chamber.

Her hands went to her belly protectively. She carried the Douglas heir. It was his God-given right to inherit the title, the castles, the wealth that was Douglas. How could she throw it all away by refusing to wed her child's rightful father? Was she that selfish, that self-absorbed, that self-centered? Life wasn't a game. Life was infinitely precious!

Tina laid out Ram's black doublet with the crimson

Bleeding Heart of Douglas embroidered upon it. She held it to her lips for a moment and brushed a teardrop from her cheek. Suddenly her ears picked up the faint sound of someone raving and cursing. She sighed. It sounded like Mad Malcolm. She would go and visit him; perhaps if she listened to his ramblings it would quieten him.

As she climbed to the tower room, she couldn't believe the way he was carrying on. Someone must have restocked his chamber with drink.

"Och, lassie, help me!" he cried, his eyes rolling in his head. "He's goin' tae kill me!" Malcolm was reeling drunk, and the fumes coming from the bed were overpowering as he thrashed about.

"Hush, Malcolm. Who is going to kill you?"

"Alex!"

"No, Malcolm. Someone told you Alex haunts the castle, but there are no such things as ghosts."

"Nay, not Alex, the other. He put yon pillow ower ma face!"

"Hush, Malcolm. He's gone now. You're perfectly safe."

"Christ, I'm no' safe—yer no' safe!" he howled. "He saw ma pages! He knows I'm goin' tae expose his evil!"

"Damn it, Malcolm—who brought you all this whisky and wine?" Tina was angry. This would never have happened if Ram Douglas had not overruled her orders. She went to the bed and straightened the covers. As Malcolm clutched her arm, she reassured him. "He's gone now. I'll get Jenna to sit with you." She made a moue of distaste at the array of intoxicating drinks within his reach. Two jugs of whisky lay empty, but there were still half a dozen bottles and decanters of wine.

Tina explained matters to Jenna. "Don't let him have anything more to drink. He'll have to sleep it off."

Malcolm was cursing a blue streak now, but his voice had lowered somewhat. Tina picked up two decanters as she left the room. As she descended the stairs, she saw that Ramsay was in his chamber. Without hesitation she swept in and deposited the decanters of wine on his table. "Malcolm is raving. He's almost out of control with drink." She saw that he had changed into the dry clothes she had laid out for him. The firelight showed her that his black, curling hair was still wet.

He took a step toward her. "Tina, I want a word with ye." His swarthy face was like rough-hewn granite. The light from the fire cast his gigantic shadow up the wall and the foreboding feeling she'd had all day gripped her so fiercely, she felt faint.

Fear that Ram had seen the naked portrait swept over her, and she put her hand out to the back of a chair to steady herself.

Ram's eyes narrowed. Quickly, he poured a glass of wine and closed the distance between them. "Drink this," he commanded.

As she took the glass from his hand, her fingers brushed his, and a small shudder went through her. She lifted it to her lips and drained it. The moment she swallowed, she knew! He had just poisoned her!

Chapter 29

The glass fell and shattered. "No!" Tina cried, clutching her throat, her eyes filled with terror. Her throat burned and closed in a spasm. The poison peeled the skin from the back of her tongue and down her throat. Her mouth was filled with a bitter, acrid taste. The moment the wine touched her stomach, she doubled over, clutching her belly as pain tore through her midsection.

Ramsay knew immediately that she had just swallowed poison. Her cries were so anguished, they pierced his heart. He swept her up into his arms and began to run. "Hold on, hold on, no matter what, Tina!" he commanded. She was screaming and writhing with pain as Ramsay sped down the winding stone staircase to the kitchens. His own gut was knotted with fear. He had no idea what to do for her, but instinctively he knew that immediate action of some sort was imperative.

"Burque, Burque, where the hellfire are ye, man? Tina's been poisoned, help me!"

Mr. Burque's face registered shock, anguish, and fear. He had no clear idea what to do for her, yet because she was dear to him as a daughter, he knew he must do something. He had comforted her all her young life with bonbons and chocolate, had cured her toothaches and soothed her childhood cuts and burns with things from his kitchen. He shrugged helplessly. "Cream?" he asked Ram. "It might coat her stomach. Stop some of the poison being absorbed into her system while we purge her."

"Yes, cream," Ram agreed decisively.

She was sobbing and screaming, yet it did not sound like his Tina. Her throat was so raw, the sounds she made were husky, hoarse. Mr. Burque held the cream to her lips while Ram held her. She pushed Mr. Burque's hand away hysterically. To make her swallow would be torture. "No, no, no," she cried hoarsely.

"Force it down her," Ram ordered, and held her wrists in a vise grip. They got about a pint inside her before she began to retch. Now Ram held her tenderly, his hands feeling the convulsive spasms of her stomach as he bent her over his arm with her head down to aid her vomiting.

Tina retched, heaved, and spewed; retched, heaved, and spewed. She gasped and choked, retched and heaved, until Ram wanted to run mad from the kitchens. Inside he was in a total panic. She was going to die. She was going to die an agonizing death, and there was little or nothing he could do about it.

She was exhausted now, yet her eyes were liquid with fear and dread. He had little knowledge of poisons save that they resulted in death, but there was one thing he could give her of which he had an overabundance: He could give her his strength. "Ye'll be all right love. I'm here. Hang on to me."

She clutched him weakly. "More cream," he ordered Mr. Burque. The cream acted as a purge, and Mr. Burque was greatly relieved. He had been rapidly going over the noxious nostrums that would purge her, but now they would not be necessary. There was very little could be done to counteract poison other than try to purge it from the body.

The apparition that looked upon the scene was distraught. It was happening all over again. Lord Douglas had poisoned his wife! Damaris relived taking the goblet of wine her husband had placed in her hands. Watched herself as she lifted it to her lips and drained the cup. She could not go through it again. Damaris flew off searching out Alexander. She found him with Mad Malcolm and Colin. She flew at him with clenched fists and pounded them against his chest. "Tina is dying, damn you, Douglas! Damn you to everlasting hell!"

"Damaris, stop! It wasn't me! I told ye years ago who did it, and now the insane swine has done it again!"

Damaris threw a look of horror at the crazy old man in the bed. "Alex, come. We have to do something." The two spirits faded from the chamber and materialized in the kitchen. Alexander saw himself in Ram's place, reassuring the small female in his arms; the look of intense desperation in his dark eyes was almost too much to bear.

Half a dozen scullery maids were running about, cleansing the stone flags of the kitchen floor that Tina continually befouled. Tina was deathly pale now, with a blue color about her mouth. Her stomach spasmed with cramps every other minute. The excruciating pain had robbed her of all strength. She huddled in Ramsay's arms with her hands clutching her belly.

The last bout of retching had alarmed him terribly because she had begun to vomit blood. She felt cold and clammy, and Ram knew her body was losing its warmth as well as its strength. With a firm resolve that he was far from feeling, he said to Mr. Burque, "I'm taking her up tae bed. She needs something tae ease the pain." He thought of something they used after a battle to deaden mortal wounds. "Make a brew from rue and watered wine. She cannot go on like this."

Ram took the stairs two at a time up to his chamber. He laid her on his bed, then went to the fireplace to build up the fire. Her moans wrenched his heart. Quickly he went back to the bed. "Ram," she whispered, "help me!"

He went on his knees and gathered her to him. "Hush, darling, I won't let you die. Hold on to me. I won't leave ye for even a moment."

Ada came in, her face white as death, her throat closed with fear. She brought bathing water and towels. "Quick, Ada—spread a towel on the floor." Ram lifted Tina to the edge of the bed, his firm hands pressed into her stomach muscles to prevent them from rupturing while she retched. Ram's eyes met Ada's, and he shook his head in impotent frustration.

Tina drew her knees up to her chest and rolled across the bed, moaning like a wounded animal. Each moan ended in a whimper. "Help me undress her, Ada. Get a loose bedgown. Her clothes are far too constricting."

Tina was gray-lipped now, her body limp as a rag doll between the convulsive spasms of pain. Her breathing became labored, and she fought for breath. Ram broke out in a sweat of fear that any minute she would draw her last breath.

Ada set the bowl of water upon the bed, but Ram said softly, "I'll do it." His tenderness toward her was heartbreaking to watch. He slipped on the loose bedgown. She had stopped retching and vomiting, but he did not know if this was a good or bad sign. He did know one thing: If she needed further purging, he didn't have the heart for it.

She was crying softly, mewling like a baby or a young animal as she doubled her fists and thrust them into her belly. The eyes that met his were filled with anguish as the bone-softening fear of death overwhelmed her. "I'm dying," she whispered brokenly.

"No!" he said savagely. "No, yer not dying! Is the pain bad?" he demanded. She nodded weakly. "Good! So long as ye can feel the pain, ye are nowhere near death." He had no idea if his words were true, but he said them with such strong conviction, she had no choice but to believe him.

Mr. Burque brought the rue. Ram climbed onto the bed with her and lifted her so that her gray cheek rested against his shoulder. "Little love, I want ye tae try and sip this. Mr. Burque made it especially for ye." He held the decoction to her lips, and it broke his heart to see how trustingly she sipped from the cup. Dear God, the last thing she had taken from his hand was a cup of poison.

Silently, he began to pray. Oh Holy Saint Jude, apostle and martyr, great in virtue and rich in miracles—God in Heaven, she will need a miracle to survive this. After the rue, it seemed to Ram that her writhing was less painful. She cried and tossed and turned in agony, but she did not knot into the spasms that had made her scream.

The hours of the night dragged by slowly. Ram lay beside her, holding her when she would let him, encouraging her to hang on, to ride the waves of pain, but above all to stay with him. Their fingers were entwined, and sometimes he thought that was the only reason she did not slip away— he had too firm a grip upon her.

By morning, her fever started to rise. Her face became a dull red, and she dozed spasmodically. Ram tried to make her drink, but she vomited it back and looked at him with wild, accusing eyes. By midday, her fever raged so high, she began to shiver, then suddenly she went into a convulsion. "Quick, Ada, get the servants tae fill the bathtub. Tell them not tae heat the water, it just needs the chill off it."

He lifted Tina from the bed and clasped her firmly against his body. He walked back and forth with her, talking to her all the while the servants filled the tub.

Damaris, clutching Folly in her arms, had hovered by the bed through the long night and day. When the servants departed, Ram knelt and removed her loose bedgown, and with gentle hands he lowered the convulsing girl into the cool water. Ada brought more towels and a fresh bedgown.

Ram sponged Tina over and over. First her shoulders, then her breasts and belly. Finally in desperation he let her hair fall back into the tub and let the water from the sponge trickle over her face and neck.

Gradually her eyes stopped rolling back in her head, and her arms and legs stilled. He kept on sponging her for another half hour. When he was finally convinced the convulsion was over and her body temperature was lower, he lifted her into his lap and patted her dry.

As he carried her back to the bed, her eyes flickered open, then her lashes seemed too heavy and her eyes closed. "I'm still here, sweetheart," he murmured. "Don't fret, yer not going tae die, yer going tae live!"

Finally Tina fell into a deep sleep. Ada said, "I'll watch her while you go and eat and have a rest." He shook his head quietly. "I couldn't eat. Don't let anyone in the castle drink any wine. It might all be poisoned. My dagger awaits whoever is responsible fer this," he vowed.

While Tina slept, he never took his eyes from her. She made such a tiny mound in the great bed, it brought a lump to his throat. He'd never seen anyone suffer such misery so bravely in his life. Her breathing seemed so dangerously shallow, he took to watching a tiny pulse in her throat.

At last Tina awoke and tried to speak, but she choked on

her words and violent pains bent her double once more. He held her until it passed, wondering what he could give her to alleviate the agony and give her a little strength. He brushed back the damp tendrils from her forehead and murmured words of love. Midnight approached again. She opened her eyes and managed to croak, "Ram, I feel so ill."

"Yes, my darling, I know," he said in a strong voice. "Ye will feel ill for days, but all the danger is past now." He lied to give her strength to bear it; he lied to give himself strength to bear it.

Mr. Burque came every couple of hours with something different to try, but each time she sipped, violent cramps twisted her innards, telling them her body was not free of its toxin.

Ada came to him. "Colin has something he must tell you." Ram nodded, and Ada admitted Colin into the chamber.

"It was Mad Malcolm who poisoned the wine. I found rat poison beside his bed. God knows how long he's had it hidden."

Ram's mouth hardened. "Christ, I should have known he was dangerous. I can't leave her, Colin. Have him watched until I can deal with the mad bastard."

"He's dead," said Colin. "I found him an hour since."

Ram bit his lip. "Thank ye, Colin. It's my fault. I knew he was mad. I should have seen that he was locked up."

"Don't blame yerself, man. We are all of us tae blame."

Mr. Burque arrived as Colin departed. This time he brought honey. "Honey has magical properties," he told Ram. "It can heal a wound without a scar on the outside. Let's see if it soothes the inside."

Ram dipped the tiny spoon and held it to her lips. Tina licked it slowly, and miraculously it caused no pain to her throat when she swallowed it. The two men looked at each other with renewed hope. Mr. Burque warned, "Give it to her sparingly—too much will take her breath and choke her." Ram nodded his understanding. For the next three hours he patiently fed her one tiny spoon of honey every ten minutes. Finally she fell into an exhausted sleep, still clinging to his hand.

He had a lot more hope now that she would survive this nightmare, but as the immediacy of the situation receded, his mind had time to wander. Would she ever believe that he had not poisoned her? This would put an end to the hand-fasting. She'd never marry him now, never stay at Castle Dangerous after this. He tried to push the unwelcome thoughts away. All that mattered was that she survived. He ran a hand through his hair. Perhaps it had been Mad Malcolm who had poisoned Damaris and not Alex after all. Malcolm had had the freedom of the castle in those days, before the drinking bouts had condemned him to his bed. Perhaps he had even pushed Alexander from the parapets. Ram shuddered. If Alex had watched helplessly as Damaris died of poison, no wonder his spirit still roamed about the castle. Alex would stay until he was avenged.

He knew that he himself would have avenged Tina's suffering if it took all of eternity. Fate had stepped in and done the dirty work for him. Malcolm was dead. His mind roamed to the king. James must have suffered the tortures of Hell when his beloved Margaret Drummond was poisoned. Ram crossed himself and gave up thanks that Tina's life had been spared. He closed his eyes and drifted to the edge of sleep.

Something awakened him. He sat up with a jolt. "Tina!" he cried, springing from the bed to catch her in his arms as she collapsed. Her nightrobe was covered with blood. His worst fears had come to pass: She was miscarrying their babe!

Ada and Nell hovered in the background for the next twenty-four hours, fetching fresh linen, changing the bed, bringing food to Lord Douglas, which they took away untouched.

Ramsay did all the nursing, all the bathing, all the comforting within his power. Most of the time they were hand-clasped, and gradually it seemed he infused his strength into her. Her lifeblood stopped draining away, her fever abated, and the pain finally stopped racking her body. Tina's mental anguish, however, did not abate. When she saw the silvery trace of tears upon Ram's cheeks, her heart constricted. This was her punishment for threatening to abort his child. He would never again ask her to wed him—where was the need? She could not bear to see accusation in his eyes, and she turned to face the wall.

"Tina," he whispered.

"Leave me," she begged.

Damaris occupied the window seat in her own chamber. Slowly the spirit of Alexander manifested before her, surrounded by a strong, brilliant light. He would be denied no longer. "Damaris, we must talk. The things I told ye almost sixteen years ago were the truth and nothing but the truth, so help me God. Are ye ready tae believe me?" he demanded.

Damaris stood slowly and reached out a delicate hand to him. "Yes, Alex, I am ready to believe you."

He enfolded her in his arms. "Never for one instant have I stopped loving ye." He kissed her teardrops away, then sat down on the window seat and drew her into his lap.

They talked for hours. The years between seemed to fall away until they became as close as they had been on the day the pledged lovers had claimed each other. Damaris mourned the loss of Tina's babe as if it were her own. "I thought Ram and Tina would have the child that was denied us."

Alexander's arm tightened about her. "Things ha' gone so wrong between them. Let's pledge tae stay wi' them till they acknowledge that they love each other."

"We cannot leave her yet in any case—the danger is too strong."

"I feel so damned impotent. If only I could communicate wi' the living. I could set this mess tae rights an' justice would be done."

Damaris laid her hand upon his clenched fist and quoted from the Bible: " 'The mills of God grind slow, but they grind exceeding small.' "

Ram bathed and shaved for the first time in close to a week and joined the men in the hall to break his fast. Colin had quietly seen to the burial of Malcolm, and Ram was most grateful for his aid. Within the hour, Jock, his first lieutenant, rode in from where he had been awaiting Ram aboard the *Revenge*. "I scented trouble of some sort," he explained, "and just couldn't sit there at the mouth of the Doon."

"There was trouble, all right, but it was personal," Ram said. "We won't be able to leave here for a few more days." He gave no other explanation, and Jock, knowing him so well, expected none. Ram dispatched a message to Angus thanking him for the use of his ships and men and told him that he would not be in residence at Castle Douglas in the borders this winter. He did not commit to paper where he would be, leaving that up to Archibald's canny common sense.

Before the afternoon shadows had grown long, three separate messengers rode in with letters for Black Ram Douglas. He called his men-at-arms together to give them the grim news. "It seems the English are raiding deeper and deeper into Scotland. I have messages from three different lairds who were raided over the last two days. Fisherton on the coast, and Ochiltree and Cumnock, which are too far inland for my liking."

Jock's fears were confirmed. "We saw the beacon lights and suspected raiders, but I had yer orders tae stay hidden."

"Ye did right tae stay put. If the bastards are raiding this far into Scotland I'll have tae leave at least a score here tae defend Douglas. Who volunteers?"

Those who responded were mostly men who had women or wives at Douglas. Ram made a mental note to warn the Kennedys. He cursed the circumstances that chained him at the moment. Once he was aboard the *Revenge,* he'd soon put a stop to the bloody raids.

His heart was in his mouth as he climbed the stairs to his chamber. He hadn't seen her for hours and prayed that she was still on the mend. An obscene curse dropped from his lips when he entered his chamber and found all traces of Tina gone. She must indeed be feeling recovered if she had taken it upon herself to vacate the master bedchamber in favor of Damaris's room. He threw open the door to find her sitting in the window seat. His heart lifted that she no longer lay abed close to death, but his brows drew together with a hurt look. "So ye no longer need me," he flung at her.

Tina searched his face anxiously for the least telltale sign of condemnation for losing their baby. She saw none and thought he masked his hatred well.

Ram wasted no time arguing but placed one firm arm about her, the other beneath her knees, and carried her back to their chamber. He knew she had no strength to fight him. He turned back the covers of the freshly made bed and set her down. "We have tae talk." They said the words in unison.

His eyes softened as they looked at her. "I think that's the first time we have ever agreed about anything," he said with a catch in his throat.

"Me first?" she pleaded, her voice still husky from the damage done by the poison.

"Ye first," he conceded, sitting on the edge of the bed, yet not touching her.

She took a deep wavering breath. She was going to confess all, no matter the cost. "I plotted against you, long before I ever met you. When my youngest brother didn't return from the raid, I knew you had captured him. The very name Douglas was synonymous with fear and loathing to me. As you know, I faked a riding accident outside the castle, but you don't know what was in my heart that day as I lay out in the rain waiting to be discovered. I feared and hated you, and I swore an oath that I would free my brother from the degenerate Douglas or die in the attempt. So you see, from the first moment I laid eyes upon you, you were my sworn enemy." She closed her eyes for a moment, took another deep breath, and plunged on. "When I saw David's burns, I placed a curse upon you. It was months later before I admitted the burns were his own fault for setting the fires. The night you came to Doon and single-handedly knocked down my brothers and bested Patrick Hamilton, I conceived a deep loathing for you like nothing I had ever experienced. When you humiliated me, I was such a vain creature, I wanted to kill you for that act alone!"

Ram recalled how courageous she had been to stand up to him when he had just beaten four men. He admired courage more than any other quality. No wonder he'd fallen in love with her!

"My whole family hated the House of Douglas because of Damaris. When our clan chief ordered that my sister Beth must marry you, it almost killed my mother. When my own marriage plans with Patrick Hamilton were called off, my mother begged my father to ask you to take me instead of her favorite. The humiliation I felt at that moment was only surpassed by the humiliation I suffered when I learned my father had to bribe you to take me."

Ramsay had the decency to flush. His role had been disreputable, to say the least. Tina's voice was husky now. She was fatigued and reached for every breath. Ram poured her a goblet of honeyed mead and took the precaution of tasting it. Tina's heart skipped a beat at the gesture. "When you came to offer for me, I learned exactly how deeply you resented me. When you offered a hand-fasting instead of marriage, you were symbolically rubbing dirt in my face." She hesitated, then decided to hold nothing back. "I swore, vowed, and pledged I would have my revenge upon you. I knew that somehow I must get such a hold upon you, it would destroy your happiness when I repudiated you. Ada told me there was only one way a woman could gain that sort of hold upon a man. She explained that I did not need to love you, so long as I learned to love sex." Her lashes swept to her cheeks to hide the tears that started. "When you changed the name of the *Valentina* to *Revenge,* I thought I knew what was in your heart. Our whole relationship has been based upon revenge. Our hatred for each other obliterated any love we might have had. Our child didn't stand a chance. I shall bear the guilt forever."

As he covered her hand with his, he felt her tears drop upon it. "Don't cry, Tina. I cannot bear ye tae shed one more tear."

She whispered, "The Bleeding Heart of Douglas. I swore it would be your heart that bled, not mine. What a fitting pair we are . . . Lady Vengeance . . . Lord Vengeance."

Ram stiffened. "Ye know?"

She lay back against the pillows in utter exhaustion. Her hair flowed across the bed like a river of fire. Never had she looked so delicate, so vulnerable, so exquisitely beautiful. Ram felt empty, hollow, as if a great hole had been blown in his gut. If there were such a thing as a low point in one's life, he had just reached his. Without a shadow of a doubt he knew he loved this woman beyond reason, yet all he represented to her was revenge.

It all seemed as inevitable as a Greek tragedy. Like Pandora, the first woman, she had been sent to him as a punishment, and between them they had opened the box that let loose all human misfortunes. Only Hope remained in the box to comfort him in his misery. And if he were being truthful, hope did remain. Tina knew he was Lord Vengeance, yet she had not betrayed him. She claimed that all she wanted was revenge, yet she had not taken that revenge.

By the time he undressed and slipped in beside her, she was asleep. His lips touched her brow in a featherlight kiss. "I'm here if ye need me," he murmured.

Chapter 30

Tina awoke at first light and lay very still so that she would not disturb Ram. He had thrown off the covers in the night and lay upon his back with his arms stretched above his head. Her eyes roamed over his rugged, animalistic physique. His flat belly, taut rib cage, wide chest, darkly furred, massive shoulders and corded neck bespoke his splendid strength. There was something most attractive and seductive about a man with great strength. His magnificent body bore battle scars, but they only added to his dangerous attraction.

She pushed the covers down to her waist and held out her arm. The contrast in their coloring was marked and had aroused her from the first time he had made love to her in the light. Her fine skin, so smooth and pale, was almost luminescent, while his was like dark leather. Whenever he ran his swarthy hands over her body, she almost screamed with excitement. Her fiery tresses were trapped beneath his body, and she marveled that such opposites existed in the same race. His jaw was like granite, his cheekbones sculpted, his shoulder-length hair was blue-black. She blushed at her own thoughts, which turned her nipples into little spikes, her mons to molten fire. His physical attraction was like a magnet, luring her to touch, to taste. For the first time she admitted to herself that it was the man, Black Ram Douglas, for whom she cared. It was making love with him, not just making love, that she enjoyed so much.

If her body hungered for him, Tina knew she was well again. She knew she was still very weak, far too weak for the onslaught of Ram's lovemaking, but she longed to be held, ached to be kissed. Suddenly she realized his pewter eyes were watching her. She drew the covers up to her chin, shy as a virgin. "You never got your turn to talk last night," she said huskily.

"There was only one thing needed tae be said. Tina, I didn't poison ye," he said quietly.

She raised her lashes, her golden eyes seeking his, so that he would believe her words that came from the heart. "Ram, I know you did not." She licked dry lips, and her lashes swept to her cheeks. "I am so very sorry about the baby. I know the loss is as painful for you as it is for me."

"Look at me. Ye were in no way tae blame! The poison did it—the poison in the wine that I poured for ye!"

"Ah God, do not blame yourself. You saved my life! I would be dead now if you hadn't given me all your strength."

He took her hand and lifted it to his lips. "Can we start afresh? I know we cannot wipe out what has gone before, but I promise ye there is no revenge in my heart. I pray tae God there is none left in yours."

The lump in her throat almost choked her. She began to cough uncontrollably. Alarmed lest she do more damage to her throat, he jumped from the bed and poured her some mead. He automatically tasted it before lifting it to her lips. His eyes masked his inner feelings. Tina had not denied she still needed to avenge herself. "I have tae leave shortly, but I wouldn't have a minute's peace if I left ye here alone just now. I want ye tae rest and regain your strength so ye can travel wi' me tae the coast. The *Revenge* is hidden at the mouth of the River Doon. When I return tae the ship, it will give ye a chance tae visit wi' your family. If they hear rumors ye've been poisoned, it will cause more hatred between our clans. I want them to hear about it from yer own lips and see for themselves that ye are recovering."

"Thank you." A great relief washed over her. She knew he should have departed a week past and had only stayed to nurse her. She hadn't expected Ram to wait until she felt strong enough to go with him. "I'll write them a letter telling them I'm coming home for a visit, if you can spare a man to deliver it."

He dressed as quickly as he could. The desire to make love to her was ever present. With difficulty he curbed the desire, managing to suppress it just beneath the surface. She was like a fever in his blood, and he knew if he began to kiss her, he would keep her abed for hours.

It had been a blow to his masculinity to learn that she had set out deliberately to learn the secrets of passion and use them to make him obsessed with her. She had more than succeeded. He wondered wildly if he had become addicted to her and if it was possible for him to do without her. He had no intention of finding out. Though probably disreputable, his intention was to make her love him. The challenge was irresistible.

After he had departed the chamber, Tina lay resting, but her every thought was of Ram. She could feel his mouth upon her and longed for its tenderness and its fierceness. Whenever he made love to her, it was beyond discretion, beyond reason. His rampant maleness was like an electrical storm, shocking and violent, and she felt she would die if he did not soon make love to her again.

For Tina the day was endless. Alone in the vast bed where Ram's scent lingered, she recalled in minute detail everything he'd ever said, everything he'd ever done to her. She shivered as her skin remembered his touch. She wondered wildly if she loved him. He certainly made her feel secure when he was close by. She felt empty inside and ached with the need to have him fill her. She might never know his long, thick manroot again. She moaned softly as she remembered the feel of his shaft deep within her and the intense quickening of her breasts when his hot mouth was upon them. Finally she could stand the isolation no longer. Ada helped her bathe and dress, and she went down to the hall, determined to join him for dinner.

The violet shadows beneath her eyes smote him to the heart. He was polite, kind, oversolicitous for her health, but he did not look at her intimately. She longed to have his eyes lick over her curves like a candle flame, but his thoughts were unreadable tonight. Ram urged her to eat from his own plate and she did manage some of the delicious salmon Mr. Burque had baked and a syllabub custard he had prepared especially for her. When she yawned, Ram's eyes grew concerned. "Ye should be abed. We depart tomorrow."

"Don't be silly, Ram. I'll be able to ride with you tomorrow."

"Ride? I think not," he said firmly. "We'll be taking a dozen wagons. The towns of Ochiltree and Cumnock were raided. The people need everything we can give them." He patted her hand gently. "There'll be room in one of the wagons tae make ye a bed. We won't go tomorrow," he decided. "I want ye tae rest at least one more day."

Tina wanted to scream. She knew she couldn't lie abed again all day. Perhaps if they went fishing. She recalled how much fun they'd had that day long ago, then she realized how selfish she was being. Ram must find food and supplies and winter fodder for the people who were in need. She would pass the time somehow.

Tina spent the day with her ladies packing her trunks. Occasionally she stood at the high windows watching the men load the wagons in the bailey. Ram Douglas was easy to spot even in that company of black-headed Douglas men. He was the key figure in the powerful Douglas clan.

The Earl of Angus was aging and had passed the leadership on to Lord Douglas. Angus had chosen well. Ram was a lodestone to the men. He would be the central figure in any company. He was a rogue, a pirate, a freebooter, a borderer, but by God's holy grace, he was a man.

Dusk had fallen before Ram came into the hall. Jock and his moss-troopers had not yet returned, and he sensed they had encountered trouble with the English. He would leave in the morning whether they were back or not. He might run into them on his way to the coast, but if not, they knew where to find him.

He felt a pang of disappointment that Tina was not in the hall to greet him. Worry for her creased his brow. He went through to the kitchens to ask Mr. Burque to prepare something to tempt her, then ascended the stairs to the master bedchamber.

Tina stood gazing pensively into the fire. When she turned at his coming, he saw immediately that she had been crying. "Tina?" He was before her in two strides, his heart hammering with apprehension.

She brushed away her tears and tried to smile for him. "I —I just learned about Malcolm. Ada thought you had told me. Why didn't you?"

"Ye were upset enough, losing the child because the mad old bastard had poisoned the wine. 'Tis better he died by his own hand than by mine," he said firmly.

"There have been two deaths, there will be another." Her golden eyes were liquid with apprehension.

"Superstition," he said dismissively. "Ye shouldn't be alone up here brooding. I've asked Mr. Burque tae send up some food."

Ada, carrying a large tray, knocked on the door. Ram opened the door, thanked her, and relieved her of her burden. Alexander and Damaris hovered at the threshold. Alexander reached out a restraining hand to keep Damaris at his side. "We won't invade their bedchamber," he said firmly. "Tomorrow they leave again."

"I must know if they are at each other's throats," Damaris protested.

Alex shook his head. "I would never have countenanced the privacy of our bedchamber being invaded, and neither would ye, love."

Damaris sighed. "You are right of course."

"If they love each other, they will work through this bad time, as we did."

"Are you always right, my lord? 'Tis a wonder your smugness doesn't choke you," she teased.

"Sixteen years of tenacity proves my patience, wench, but that's it, ye've had the lot."

Damaris gave a little scream and flew off, knowing he would pursue.

Ramsay drew two chairs close to the fire. "Sit where ye'll be warm and comfortable. I'll serve ye."

There was a tureen of lobster bisque laced with cream and brandy. Tina thought she had never tasted anything so heavenly. Ram allowed her the pleasure of lifting the silver covers to discover the treasures Mr. Burque had placed there. She uncovered a hot brie cheese sprinkled with herbs and surrounded by crusty fingers of French bread. It was delicious, melting on the tongue like ambrosia. Tina sighed with replete pleasure as Ram dipped in the last piece and fed it to her with his fingers.

When she lifted the next cover, there sat two racks of small spareribs smoked with juniper berries and beech-wood. She had only a token taste and watched Ramsay enjoy the rest. When she uncovered the dessert, it looked too perfect to eat. "Mmm, *chocolat*," Tina said, pronouncing it exactly as her French chef did. The soft-centered truffles were identical, perfect works of art, each crowned by a gold-tipped cone of chocolate-coated butter cream. She closed her eyes as she bit into the luscious delicacy, then licked her lips with the tip of her tongue. She held one out to Ram, who shook his head. "I insist," she said playfully, and held it to his lips.

To please her he ate one, then reached for another. "Enticing, mouthwatering seduction. These are sinful—the man is a magician."

Tina was delighted that he appreciated Mr. Burque's wizardry with food. Her eyes were brimful of laughter as she watched him savor the exquisite truffles.

Ram's eyes never left her face. Her tears were all gone. "Are you happy, Tina?" he murmured.

"I'm happy now, this moment," she told him truthfully.

He knelt before her chair on his knees. "This moment is all we ever have." His hands went up inside her loose-sleeved bedgown to caress her arms. "There's one more dish," he reminded, his dark eyes watching her closely.

"I couldn't eat another thing," she protested; nevertheless, she lifted the silver cover from the small dish. She gasped as she saw the emerald and diamond necklace he had hidden there for her to discover. With trembling fingers she lifted the precious stones and the candles, and firelight scattered a thousand tiny rainbows dancing about them. "Oh, Ram, whenever did you buy these for me?"

"The same day I spent a fortune on ye. The day ye played mistress."

She threw back her head, and her laughter spilled over him. In unison they said, "At least you have a sense of humor." Suddenly, Tina had a catch in her throat. She lifted the jewels to her neck, but he took them from her, lifted her flaming hair, and clasped it about her throat, then he lifted her and set her down before the mirror. The glittering, dark green fire of the emeralds had surely been designed for a woman with hair of flame. His hands went to her bedgown to remove it, but he knew if he saw her naked loveliness, the fire she ignited in him would flash out of control. This night she needed his strength, not his lust.

In the mirror his dark figure towered above her, strong, all-powerful. In her imagination they made a fanciful tableau. He looked like some mythical avenging god sent to protect her. The tears spilled down her cheeks, and he swept her up and carried her to the bed. Fiercely he demanded, "Promise me ye will never shed another tear."

She swallowed hard, gaining control for his sake.

"Promise me!" he insisted.

She nodded and lifted her hand to touch his cheek. "I promise," she whispered.

He held her close all that night. Somehow he knew that what she needed from him was his strong arms. She clung to him, never loosening her hold even in slumber.

Valentina hated traveling in the wagon while everyone else, including Ada, was mounted. The only thing that prevented her from springing down from the warm nest of the featherbed was the fact that it eased Ram's mind about her comfort. Whenever he rode alongside her to verify that all was well with her, she forced herself to smile sweetly and curb her fiery temper.

Cumnock was less than twenty miles from Douglas, but nevertheless the wagon train did not arrive there until the afternoon, and Ram decided they would rest there all night.

For the first time Tina saw Black Ram Douglas through other eyes. The people of Cumnock, from the laird down to the lowliest tenant, treated him as if he were a deity. Lord Vengeance was their divine benefactor, come to bring food for their children and fodder for their beasts. He brought gold to pay for new trappings in the church. He brought manpower to help them rebuild their burned homes. He brought medicine, ointment, and bandages for their wounded and burned, but most of all he brought them new hope that the enemy who had descended and destroyed would be hunted down by Hotspur Douglas in retaliation for their suffering. He would wreak revenge for them.

The men shook his hand or touched his shoulder, the women kissed him, the children came up to him shyly to stare at the valiant Lord Vengeance. Tina saw him pick up one child after another. He tickled them, ruffled their hair, whispered in their ears, and succeeded in bringing smiles to their serious little faces. She had had no idea until this moment how much he loved children. And suddenly she knew she loved him. So this was love then, this passionate, wild, all-consuming emotion as powerful as hatred, nay, more powerful. *Love* was far too tame and pallid a word to describe this thing that was between them. It was closer to madness than sanity, closer to violence than peace. It was primitive, savage, wanton, untamed, reckless, and unquenchable.

She gazed at him with the eyes of a woman who is proud of her lover. She recalled the verbal exchange they'd had when he came to offer for her. "The Douglases are renowned for their ambition, pride, greed, and treachery," she had said.

"And valor," he had added with a wolfish grin. He had spoken the truth. Ram Douglas was innately valiant, and she adored him for it.

They ate sparingly, and after Ram saw her and Ada bedded down in comfort, he and his men worked far into the night restoring some of Cumnock's destruction.

When they departed in the morning he left behind ten of his men-at-arms with instructions to meet him at the ship when they had finished rebuilding. Lord Douglas was received at Ochiltree with the same adulation as at Cumnock. By now, Tina thought it amusing that they treated him as if he had just descended from Mount Olympus. They should see him when his Douglas temper was unleashed, or see his unsavory condition after a night of debauched drinking, she thought wryly. Then he cradled a burned child so tenderly, it touched her very soul.

Again, he left men to help rebuild the village. The River Doon lay only seven miles away, and they expected to reach it by dusk. Tina looked forward to spending the night with him aboard the *Revenge* before she went home to Castle Doon. He had been very careful not to make any demands upon her since her illness, but tonight Tina was afire to make demands of her own.

They rode along the banks of the Doon until the ship came into view. She was amazed at how camouflaged it was, tucked into a bend in the river. They only had three men with them, so Ram came himself to lift her down from the wagon. She was grateful for the strong hand at the small of her back as they ascended the gangplank of what had once been the *Valentina.* She looked up in surprise as her brother Davie came forward. She did not recognize the man with him.

Black Ram Douglas had no trouble recognizing him, however. As Lord Dacre stepped forward, a score of uniformed men surrounded them and held Lord Douglas at swordpoint. "In the name of the king, I arrest you for piracy on the high seas." Dacre turned to David Kennedy. "Do you identify this man as the infamous Lord Vengeance?"

"I do," said Davie Kennedy with relish.

"No!" gasped Tina, rooted to the spot by the enormity of what her brother had done.

Ram Douglas struggled fiercely and received a smashing blow to his temple from a heavy swordhilt. It drove him to his knees. Tina screamed, and as Douglas raised his pewter eyes to her, she saw hatred written there. She was the only one who knew he was Lord Vengeance. She had betrayed him! "No!" she cried again, her hand going out to him in supplication.

Hotspur saw her through a red mist of fury. Their entire relationship had been based upon revenge. She had emerged the victor in the battle between them. To this vixen, love had meant weakness, and she had put a knife in his back.

Tina's eyes never left his face, lingering on the hard, chiseled mouth and strong arrogant jaw. His prominent cheekbones reinforced the impression of power and ruth-

less vitality. His dark, harshly handsome features brought a
rush of love. As they dragged him past her, she threw out
both hands in supplication, the gesture begging him to believe she had not done this dishonorable thing.

Ram's eyes were murderous. They bored into hers,
promising her the thing she understood better than any
woman alive—they promised revenge.

Chapter 31

"Get the women off the ship," Dacre ordered
David Kennedy, and like a sleepwalker she allowed
her brother to lead her down the gangplank. In
shock she stood on the banks of the Doon and
watched her own ship being sailed away to England. Her
heart constricted as she realized there was only one way
they would keep Black Ram Douglas aboard, and that was
in heavy irons.

She turned to Davie with an incredulous look upon her
face, as if she could not quite believe that this was not
some nightmare from which she would soon awaken. "You
filthy little turd!" she screamed, and flew at him, her nails
raking his face.

David grabbed her wrists with cruel hands, and she almost vomited at his touch. "How could you betray him to
the bloody English?" she cried in anguish.

"Douglas is more my enemy than Dacre. I met him
many a time when I visited Carlisle with mother."

"God's passion, you've not seen the atrocities Dacre and
his English raiders have committed! They fired the entire
village of Ochiltree, burning women and children!"

"Don't speak tae me of burns!" he spat, holding up his scarred arm.

She looked at him in disbelief. "You think you'll get your thirty pieces of silver, but let me tell you, Davie Kennedy, you have just frittered away your life! The powerful Douglas clan will hunt you down like a dog. You are a dead man!"

He looked at Ada, standing with a protective arm about Nell, then his eyes narrowed and fastened upon Tina. "You are the only witness, and women are soon silenced." He raised his hand to strike her, but Tina was quicker. The moment he let go of her wrist, she slapped him full in the face. At the same time she brought her leg up and kneed him in the balls. He went to his knees, howling for his men to grab her.

Tina turned to face the four red-headed Kennedy men with a sweeping look of contempt. Not one of them made a move toward her. Her golden eyes blazed their challenge. "Is there any one of you man enough to drive my wagon to Castle Doon?"

The men looked at the three women who stood defenseless before them and felt hot shame. The oldest stepped forward. "I will take ye home, Lady Valentina," he said grimly.

When Tina arrived home, she learned that her father had taken her mother to Castle Kennedy to be with Donal and Meggie because Meggie's time was near. Tina's heart sank. She had counted upon her father to take her to the king. Ada cast her an anxious glance. Tina had only just begun to recover from the double ordeal of the poisoning and the miscarriage. She must be ready to collapse.

Tina kept on her feet by sheer willpower alone. There was no time to think of herself. There was not one moment to lose. She knew without a doubt that Henry Tudor would hang Lord Vengeance when he was delivered to London. Tina went out to the stables to speak with the Kennedy grooms. "Ada and I will be riding to Edinburgh at dawn. I want the two best mounts you have, and I'll need an escort of at least two men. I don't want young boys," she told the head groom.

"I'll attend ye myself, Lady Kennedy," he offered, thinking his young mistress looked ill.

Tina felt almost uncomfortable in her old home. Beth was distant with her, and she was at a loss for the reason. Kirsty, however, was her old hateful self. She looked down her long nose at Tina's slim waist and said snidely, "I see yer not breeding yet. 'Twould be a pity if ye proved barren when the Douglas only agreed tae take ye tae provide him with an heir."

Dear God, there would be no Douglas heir if they hanged Ramsay. "I'll say good night," said Tina stiffly. "I must be away at first light."

"Oh, I have your bedchamber now," said Beth ingenuously.

Tina pressed her lips together. "That's all right. I'll sleep in your old chamber."

Kirsty said smugly, "I now occupy Beth's old chamber."

Ada intervened. "Tina, come, I'll ready your parents' room for you."

Kirsty pressed her thin lips together in outrage. "Ye canna use the master bedchamber!"

Ada fixed her with a steely eye. "Watch me!" she challenged, and took a menacing step toward the woman. Kirsty fell back instantly. She was no match for Ada.

Valentina could not sleep, but at least she rested her body. They arose before dawn and dressed warmly for the long ride to Edinburgh. When they arrived at the stables, Tina felt weak with relief when she saw the burly, mail-clad figure of Bothwick armed to the teeth. "Oh, Bothwick, this is so good of you. But I'm honor-bound to tell you that Dacre and his soldiers were as close as the River Doon yesterday. What if they return and attack the castle?"

Bothwick clenched a meaty fist. "When I saw what the whoresons did tae Fisherton, I sent messages tae all the clan, including the Earl o' Cassillis. They should ha' men here by tonight," he assured her.

Tina wore the fox cape whose fur was identical to the color of her hair. She sent Ram a whispered thanks upon the wind for buying her such a luxurious garment to keep her warm. The head groom had done an efficient job of strapping her luggage and food for their journey to the backs of two packhorses. He had also chosen a sure-footed garron for her to ride, and another for Ada.

The journey of about thirty-seven miles would take five or six hours, depending upon the weather and the stamina of their mounts. Tina thought with pride that Hotspur could do it in just over two hours. The first part of the journey seemed to invigorate her. She was racing against time, and danger had ever been a spur to her. They did not stop to break their fast but ate bannocks and washed them down with ale as they rode.

After almost three hours they stopped to water the horses in the Clyde, very close to Patrick Hamilton's castle at the town of Hamilton. When Tina thought of the young man she had almost married, goosebumps stood out upon her skin. What a close call that had been. Only Fate, much wiser than she, thank God, had saved her from a disastrous marriage with the immature son of Scotland's admiral. Her mind could not help comparing him with Ram Douglas, and he suffered greatly by that comparison. Just thinking of Ram's capture made her lean against her horse, weak-kneed.

Bothwick said gruffly to Ada, "She's as pale as a corpse."

Ada bit her lip. "She shouldn't be riding this hard. She lost her bairn only last week."

"Christ, woman, do ye want tae kill her?" he growled.

Tina felt herself lifted in Bothwick's strong arms. It was exactly like being picked up by a bear. Thankfully, she slipped her arms about his neck and clung to his strength. He mounted and tucked her in the crook of one massive arm. "Rest child, auld Bothwick will get ye tae Edinburgh, though I canna promise the king will see ye."

"Angus," whispered Tina.

Bothwick was alarmed. Surely this child wasn't courageous enough to beard Archibald Douglas? Tina smiled up at him. The golden eyes slanting from the red fox hood reminded him exactly of a sleek vixen. "He has a soft spot for me." Bothwick's heart did a little dance inside his massive chest. Valentina Kennedy was indeed a man's woman.

They caused no little stir at Edinburgh Castle. The beefy giant with the fiery red head and beard swept along the stone passageways carrying the beautiful young woman wrapped in furs, her flaming tresses trailing to the floor. He hammered his beefy fist upon the Earl of Angus's apartment door and contemplated belting anyone who refused to admit her. Tina was tired, cold, and hungry, and in that moment he was her gentle *parfait* knight in armor, fulfilling the quest she had set him.

When Angus's servants saw who it was, they were admitted immediately, and a page was dispatched with a message to the earl. When he arrived and Bothwick saw with his own eyes that the full power of Clan Douglas was at Tina's beck and call, he departed for Doon with a much easier mind.

"When did they take him?" growled Angus.

"Yesterday, early in the morning," replied Tina, fiercely ashamed that David had tainted the Kennedy name.

"Ye did real good, lass, gettin' here so quick. But where in the name of Christ were his men?" he demanded.

"His first lieutenant, Jock, took a score of men from Douglas after three towns were raided. Ram was busy looking after me—I drank poisoned wine."

Granite-faced Archibald Douglas looked shocked.

"It wasn't Ramsay who poisoned me!" she protested hotly.

Angus looked relieved. "Nay, poison is a coward's weapon. In any case he had only tae send ye home tae rid himself of ye an' be free of the hand-fasting. What about his other men? He had sixty of mine."

"He left some at Cumnock and more at Ochiltree to help the villagers rebuild. Their plight was heartrending."

"Reckless young fool! I never ride out these days without a hundred Douglas at my back."

"How long will it take Dacre to get him to London?" Tina asked fearfully.

"What makes ye think they'll take him tae London?"

"Because he's Lord Vengeance, and there's a big price on his head. Before he hangs him for piracy, Henry Tudor will want to see what he got for his money."

Angus cursed and sat down immediately at a desk littered with papers to write out orders and seal them with his earl's signet ring. He could clearly see how agitated Tina was over Ram's capture, and he explained some of what he planned. "I've orders for Gavin, Ian, and Drummond Douglas tae raid all along the east coast of England tonight and tae make sure they leave Lord Vengeance's callin' card. I'll go tae the king, and we'll send Henry Tudor word he's got the wrong man. If Dacre took him yesterday, he'd take him tae Carlisle. Dacre couldna take him tae London and wouldna spare the men it would take tae ride tae the capital. Too much chance fer Ram to escape overland. He'd transport him in irons in the hold of a ship. That would take at least three, mayhap four days tae reach London. That's ample time tae get a courier there wi' messages. I'll offer a kingly ransom fer him, lass. Henry Tudor might take the money, especially if we convince him Lord Vengeance is still free and raiding every seaport from Berwick tae Yarmouth."

"I'm going to London," announced Tina.

"Ye'll do no such foolish thing!" he scowled, not really taking her words seriously. "I'd go myself, except they'd hold me fer ransom, an' Jamie would empty Scotland's coffers tae gain ma release."

Angus stood with his back to the fire, sipping whisky

he'd poured himself. Tina slipped to her knees before him
in supplication. "Don't you see, my lord? It is my fault he
was taken. My brother learned he was Lord Vengeance
through me and so betrayed him. If you do not help me get
to London, I will go without your aid. I am determined
upon it. I vow to save him or die trying!"

"Lassie, lassie, it took the party of women who accompanied the queen twelve days tae ride from London tae Edinburgh."

"Then give me a ship, my lord earl. We could sail there
in two—less if there is a fair wind!"

He gazed down into her lovely face. "Ye love him this
much?" he asked with awe.

"More!" she declared emphatically.

Angus began to pace. Like all active men who couldn't
be caged, he thought better on his feet. Ada folded her
tongue behind her teeth. She knew she could not dissuade
Flaming Tina when her mind was set. She sat quietly beside the pile of baggage waiting for Angus to decide their
fate. She knew better than to interrupt a man who carried
more authority than any save the king himself.

"A fast ship tae transport ye tae London is no problem.
Yer safety is the problem." He stopped pacing in front of
Ada, stared at her breasts for two or three appreciative
minutes, then said, "Ye can take diplomatic messages from
Queen Margaret to her brother Henry. The queen will inform her brother that Ram Douglas is not this Lord Vengeance they seek and demand his immediate release."

"But Angus, how in the name of Heaven do we persuade
the queen to write such things to the King of England? I
only met her once and have no influence with her whatsoever."

He laid a finger beside his nose and winked at her. "I
willna persuade her—ma son Archie will."

Tina stared at him blankly. They were speaking of Her
Majesty, Margaret Tudor, Royal Queen of Scotland, not
some kitchen wench who could be coerced.

Angus was nothing if not plainspoken. "He's fuckin' her
—she'll write the letters tonight, or she doesna get laid. Ye
dinna think he bangs her for pleasure, do ye? Christ, even
Margaret is not that naive!"

Tina blushed, and Ada laughed.

"My servants are at yer disposal, lass. Ye rest while I go
tae consult the king. He'll run mad when he learns Black
Ram Douglas has been taken."

After they bathed and dined, Tina and Ada fell asleep in
the earl's great bed. Their baggage stood ready at the door
with their cloaks. They knew they would be awakened before midnight for the short ride to Leith, where one of
Angus's ships would take them from the Firth of Forth into
the North Sea on the floodtide.

Angus had put his sleekest, fastest vessel at her disposal,
and miraculously the salty wind blew fiercely from the
north, taking her down the coast of England as if it were
aware that she was in a race against time. Angus had given
her gold, as well as a letter of credit drawn on a London
goldsmith. He had produced sealed personal letters from
Queen Margaret to Henry Tudor, and a document of safe
passage.

Tina did not recognize the weatherbeaten ship's master,
but she knew he was a Douglas even in the dark. He told
her they would arrive at their destination under cover of
night in less than twenty hours. He also informed her he
would go back out to sea the moment she and her servants,
along with their mounts, disembarked. For though he had
ship's papers signed by the King of Scotland and the Lord
High Admiral of the Fleet to satisfy London's port authority, he was keenly aware that the English were taking as
many ships as they could, impressing their crews and hanging their captains out of hand.

Angus had insisted the two females be accompanied by
two strapping male servants, and as they stood upon the
London docks with their mounts and a mountain of luggage, Lady Valentina Kennedy realized that without the

men's physical strength, she would never survive long enough to reach the royal court.

They learned that the court was now at the king's favorite residence of Greenwich, which sat on the River Thames before the City of London. Greenwich sat in its own vast parkland only a couple of miles from where they had disembarked. Although it was after midnight when the small party arrived, the lights of Greenwich, both within and without, still blazed brightly. Her male servants remained in the stables while Ada accompanied her to the palace.

With the pride of a cat, Tina spoke with a liveried footman who sent a message to the palace steward. "I am here as an emissary from Her Royal Highness, Queen Margaret of Scotland, with messages for her brother the king." The steward found her a tiny suite of two rooms and told her that her grooms would have to be housed over top the stables. "I will speak with the chamberlain on your behalf, and perhaps tomorrow he will be able to furnish you with chambers more fitting, my lady. As you may see for yourself, Greenwich is overflowing at the seams. Some are even sleeping in tents and pavilions set up in the great park for the celebrations."

"Celebrations?" Tina echoed.

"The Harvest Home, my lady. 'Tis celebrated every year at the end of autumn before winter sets in. I suppose it started in pagan times, but now it is most definitely the Christian holy day of All Hallows." The steward was a busy man, kept running from dawn till dark by the demanding courtiers of Henry Tudor. He departed much more quickly than he had arrived.

Tina threw open the leaded casement windows that let in the balmy night air and the laughter of people who were obviously enjoying themselves. She leaned against the casement wondering if she would ever laugh again. The merrymakers in the gardens and great park of Greenwich were oblivious to the fact that her heart was bleeding. Tina was superstitious and believed it was her destiny. It was the

Bleeding Heart of Douglas. She bit her lip hard, trying to
keep the pledge she had given Ram. He had fiercely demanded, "Promise me ye will never shed another tear!"
and she had promised him faithfully.

England was so much warmer than Scotland, the court
was actually going to have an outdoor celebration the last
day of October. Tina felt like a caged vixen. She wanted to
run to Henry Tudor and demand that he release Ramsay
Douglas, but things were not so simple. She would be lucky
if the king even gave her an audience. She was counting on
Margaret Tudor's letters to pave her way to his exalted
majesty, the King of England. At the back of her mind
always was the superstitious fear that Ram would be the
third unlucky death in the family.

Tina did not expect to be able to sleep in the strange bed
with pictures of Ram filling her mind, but slumber finally
overtook her, and she drifted off to a place where she
would find security. She opened her eyes to find herself
clasped between the thighs of Ram Douglas, who was
astride Ruffian. He was carrying her off to Castle Douglas,
deep in the borders of Douglasdale. She recalled dimly
that he had taken her virginity coldly in the dark of night,
and now she was determined to seduce him, to fire his
blood to madness, to induce such passion in him as he had
never known before.

His reputation as a lover was legendary, and she would
not be cheated ever again. Tina moved against him art-
lessly. Her lashes lifted, and he received the full impact of
her golden eyes. Ram gazed down at the flaming creature
between his legs and cursed himself for a fool. He had
denied himself this luscious woman because of stiff pride.
Now the pride was rapidly evaporating while the stiffness
remained.

At that moment her lovely full breasts brushed across his
swollen phallus, and he almost spilled himself like an untried lad. He slowed his horse, and his borderers thundered past and disappeared over the crest of the ridge,

down into Douglas Valley. Tina knew that all Ram could think of was the fact that he had not yet glimpsed her body. He wanted those full breasts spilling into his hands. He wanted her lying on top of him so he could see the luscious alabaster globes nestle upon his darkly furred chest.

Tina knew they were at last alone. Her golden eyes teased him as they gazed at his hard mouth. Before she was finished with him, she would own that mouth. It would do her bidding and fulfill her every fantasy. The lips would kiss and worship every inch of her flesh, the tongue would surrender and become a willing captive, begging to be imprisoned in her fragrant alcoves. That hard mouth would soften as it whispered words of love hot enough to melt her very bones.

When Ruffian halted, her every sense was filled to overflowing with the heady sensuality of the dark Scot, but gradually she became aware of her surroundings. Surely it was one of the most beautiful spots on earth. Soaring both above and below them was a three-tiered waterfall. They had stopped beside the middle ledge where the water was fairly shallow. The waterfall above them fell down the rock like a misty wedding veil, while the waterfall below them plunged in a smooth torrent into what looked like a deep, bottomless pool.

Tina reached up her hands until she could grip Ram's powerful shoulders, then she pulled herself up against him until she was in a sitting position. "This is the closest to Paradise you and I will ever get," she murmured.

"Hold on tae me," he said huskily, and obligingly she clung while he dismounted. Her flaming hair brushed his cheek, and he buried his face in it, inhaling her fragrance until he was dizzy with need.

Tina smiled her secret smile. Black Ram Douglas seemed to have no idea she was the consummate temptress intent upon enslaving him. He thought the skillful luring was all his idea as his experienced hands denuded her of her clothes and he pulled her down to his nakedness among the dark green grass ablaze with wildflowers.

His caresses were fierce, his kisses savage. His tongue plunged into her soft mouth, ravishing her until she yielded and opened to his plunder. Her thighs too opened beneath his onslaught, and she wantonly arched her mons so that he could sheath his shaft all the more deeply. When Ram Douglas made love, its force was that of a storm at sea. He was frighteningly intense, centering his whole attention upon forcing her body to respond to his. And it did. Her body caught his wildness, reveling in the rough power, matching his passion, excitement, and total possession.

Tina could not hold back any longer. He brought her to shuddering climax, yet he was not yet ready to spend. For one terrifying moment fear swept over her because he would not withdraw. Her pulsations quivered against his marble shaft, making it swell and engorge until she was stretched to the limit, then miraculously her love cream anointed his entire length, and the silken friction of his plunges aroused her to new plateaus of sensation.

Ram took her beyond pleasure. Tina knew she would shatter to bits if she moved one hairsbreadth or breathed too deeply, and then suddenly she somehow knew that if she did give up her last shred of control to this man, it would bring her the ultimate in fulfillment. She plunged up as he plunged down, a blissful scream was torn from her throat, and they both experienced sensations the gods might envy.

The dream stopped, then began again at the very edge of the waterfall. Ram stood behind her with his strong hands cupping her shoulders. His lips kissed the top of her head, her throat, then the nape of her neck. "Dive with me," he urged. Tina shrank back against the naked length of him. Had he said *dive with me* or *die with me*?

"I know ye have the courage for anything, ye just proved it in the grass."

Slowly she felt his arousal grow against her bare back.

This man admired courage more than any other quality, and she knew if she abandoned herself to him and dove down the waterfall with him, she would own him, body and soul, forevermore.

Slowly she raised her arms wide and allowed him to clasp her wrists. She moved back against his magnificent torso until her feet were between his. Together they raised up on their toes and, as one, arched outward in a graceful dive. An exultant feeling of omnipotence engulfed her as they plummeted toward the water. When they hit the pool's surface, Tina awoke with a violent start. She lay still, not wanting Ram to evaporate with the dream. He evoked such powerfully strong emotions, even while she slept. Surely the bond between them could not be severed. Somehow she would find a way to save him.

Ada awoke by six and in her best gown ventured forth to take the measure of Greenwich and the men and women who trod the hallowed halls. Still in a reverie from her dream, Tina looked through the open casement into the gardens. The grass was still a brilliant green, and the scent of the late-blooming roses wafted on the balmy breeze. The flowerbeds were a riot of chrysanthemums, hollyhocks, asters, and Michaelmas daisies. The trees of the park had only just begun to turn color, and a sprinkling of crimson and gold could be seen among the green leaves.

Only servants were about at this early hour, and as Tina leaned out the window to get a better view of Greenwich, she could see the tops of the striped pavilions in the great park. With firm resolution she pushed away thoughts of Ram and vowed to concentrate upon the task at hand.

She carefully chose a gown of Tudor green embroidered with silken roses and wore her magnificent hair loose, held back by only a green ribbon embroidered with seed pearls. Ada was breathless as she closed the door behind her. "You'll never guess—all the Howards are here! Their servants are everywhere and throwing their weight about as if they were England's premier family. It seems Lord Howard's son Thomas is the king's admiral. He's a great hero at the moment. The whoreson pirate captured some Scottish ships near the downs and hanged their captains from their own yardarms."

Tina's hand went to her throat. My god, what if Dacre had already hanged Ram Douglas? Nay, surely she would know deep in her heart if Ramsay were dead. It brought home to her with a jolt that Ram's life hung by a thread. She must do something, anything, to aid him.

Ada said, "The king and court usually attend morning mass, so obviously you must too."

As Tina stepped into the autumn sunshine, she felt its warmth upon her face. For the first time she felt a ray of hope, as if it were a sign from heaven. Here was her golden opportunity to take Fate into her own hands. The morning seemed bright with promise.

She arrived at the chapel early and chose a seat near the front of the church where she could see and be seen. When the chapel began to fill up, she was struck by the resplendent fashion of the courtiers. The men dressed like peacocks, far outshining the ladies in their magnificent attire. Tina thought the shirts beneath their doublets were fancier than the delicate undergarments Ada fashioned for her. High points of lace rose above the neckline of their doublets, and frills and ruffles were at every wrist. The silk brocaded and embroidered doublets and trunks were sprinkled generously with gemstones that Tina had never seen. She was familiar with jet and beryls, but stones like opals, moonstones, orange citrines, jacinths, and chrysolites, she had never even heard of.

When the king arrived, Tina realized it was he who set the fashion and his nobles slavishly copied him. Tina studied him intensely, willing him to glance her way as the music rose and soared about the vaulted chapel. He had a very similar build to her brother Donal and her father, yet he was bigger, like a giant. Bluff King Hal, as he loved to be called, had a great barrel chest and a broad, ruddy face.

He wore a flat velvet cap encrusted with gemstones and
ostrich feather tips over thinning reddish hair.

He had a sandy-colored, close-cropped beard that was
repeated on every male face in the chapel. His hands were
as hamlike as those of Bothwick, but he wore rings on
every finger and even his thumbs. Around his neck he wore
two chains, one solid gold, the other embedded with emeralds. Smaller shoulders would have been bowed down by
their weight.

Tina bethought how her own King James wore an iron
belt concealed about his hips as a penance. Therein lay the
difference between the two monarchs. One had an inner
strength of character; the other was all show and surface
splendor.

When Tina bowed her head to pray, she had no idea that
the lustful eyes of the king were riveted upon her. There
were not many beautiful young women at Henry's court,
and Valentina Kennedy stood out like a delicate crystal
goblet among thick glass jars. The lusty, youthful king grew
hard beneath his codpiece. The tired wife of his deceased
brother, Catherine of Aragon, to whom they had wed him,
did not nearly satisfy his sexual appetite, which increased
daily. Henry made a mental note to ask his chancellor to
find out who she was.

When the service was over, the king left before anyone
else, and the gentlemen attendants who crowded after him
were so numerous, Tina was prevented from catching up
with him outside. She returned to her rooms and found
Ada awaiting her with the chamberlain.

"Madam, if you have messages for His Majesty, I will
present them to the chancellor."

"I had hoped for an audience with the king. His sister
entrusted me with a message of a personal nature."

The chamberlain looked offended. Didn't the stupid little bitch know men lived or died by the king's favor? "In
England we have a thing called protocol, madam. I suggest

you acquaint yourself with it." He glared at her and held out an imperious hand for the letter.

Tina's temper flared hotly. "In Scotland we have a thing called courtesy. I suggest you acquaint yourself with it."

He inclined his head and left her to cool her heels. She would need him before he needed her!

Ada said, "I learned that Lord Howard has just been named head of the king's armies. Of course here at court, the Howards use their titles of Countess and Earl of Surrey. Tina, he could be of vital importance if he could be persuaded to help you."

"God's passion, how can I trust him to help? His son Thomas is admiral and taking every Scots vessel he can lay his hands upon." Tina picked up the sealed letter from Margaret Tudor. "Do you think I was wrong not to hand this over to the chamberlain?"

"No. You mark my words, the chancellor will be our next visitor."

Tina's eyes fell on the wax seal of the letter, and she saw that it had been affixed by a most careless hand. She knew she could flick it open with her thumbnail and reseal it again by holding it over a candle flame. Before her courage deserted her, she broke the small red seal and scanned the letter's contents.

My Dearest Hal:

Fond felicitations from your devoted sister Margaret. The bearer of this letter, Lady Valentina Kennedy, would ask a favor of your most exalted and generous person. She is hand-fasted to Lord Ramsay Douglas, whom Lord Dacre has arrested because he suspects him of being the infamous Lord Vengeance. I know Douglas is not the man you seek, for even as I write this the *Revenge* is raiding along the opposite coast. Douglas is the most powerful clan in Scotland, as you well know, and I am pleased to tell you that I am on intimate terms with the heir to the earldom. I implore you to release your prisoner, for at some future date you may very well find yourself related to the man in question. As you have no doubt noticed, Lady Kennedy is a renowned beauty and will show her gratitude for your divine mercy in any way you command.

Chapter 32

Tina's mouth fell open. The only possible way the English king could find himself related to Douglas was if Margaret married Angus's son—which meant the King of Scotland would have to die!

Were there secret plots afoot in which she was now embroiled? She clutched the letter, knowing she should not pass on such treasonable information, but when she weighed it against the possibility of saving Ram's life, her duty to king and country paled in significance. She quickly read the letter to Ada, then melted the wax and resealed it.

"I saw the king at mass. He's a giant of a man, with a ruddy face and beard. I didn't like the look of him, but his clothes were absolutely magnificent," Tina said.

"I've learned all there is to know about Hal Tudor from the servants. From everything I've heard, he has a pathological need to dominate everyone and everything," Ada reported.

Tina thought of another. "Black Ram Douglas is the most dominant man I ever met."

"Nay, Ram is dominant because he's a natural leader. Henry Tudor dominates every meal, every conversation, every person in the room with him. He dominates his ministers and the clergy. Up until lately, he has been sexually repressed, trapped in a loveless marriage to a *religieuse,* older than himself. It is only this past year that he has dared to defy the Church and commit adultery. Now that his appetite has been whetted, he is constantly on the prowl. He loves to be thought of as bluff, but in reality he is a bully to women and servants. His temper tantrums are legendary, and everyone at court tries to appease him."

"The divine right of kings!" Tina said dryly.

"The consensus is unanimous—he thinks of himself as God," Ada concluded.

Tina tucked the queen's letter into her bodice. "Come, let's go out into the park. If I see either Lord Howard or King Henry, I shall appeal to him. All Hallows isn't until tomorrow, but the celebrations are already under way."

They walked through the gardens, where the quince trees were laden down with fruit and the yew walks were cunningly designed for dalliance. They passed by the tennis courts, the bowling green, and the archery butts that would be overflowing with contestants by afternoon.

Ada said, "None dare win even a game with Henry, he is so childishly spoiled. Apparently the punishments he metes out are viciously cruel."

Tina's knees turned to water at the thought of having to deal with such a monster. The words with which his sister Margaret had concluded her letter rose up alarmingly in Tina's mind. *"Lady Kennedy will show her gratitude for your divine mercy in any way you command."* She pushed the words away and clung to the hope that Henry would be merciful without exacting payment from her.

Out in the great park among the striped pavilions, Tina suddenly exclaimed, "Gypsies! Oh, Ada—the Gypsies are here to entertain the court. They have a vast secret network. I wonder if I can learn if Heath will be here?" They walked past the caravans and the tethered horses looking for a familiar face. This was a far larger band than had ever gathered in Galloway Valley, and Tina realized most of them would be English Gypsies. A swarthy fellow leered at her. Instead of ignoring his insolence and tossing her head as she would have once done, she stopped and spoke to him. "Do you know a Gypsy called Heath? Heath Kennedy from Scotland?"

The man showed white teeth. "We recognize no borders —we are Romanies, not English or Scots."

"Yes, yes, I know," Tina said impatiently. "Do you know Heath?"

He laughed. "Gypsies do not like to be questioned. Perhaps I know him, perhaps I do not."

Tina stamped her foot. She knew he would be maddeningly noncommittal. Gypsies were a closed society, not dissimilar to a clan. Secrecy and loyalty were a necessary part of their survival. "Well, if you happen to run into him, tell him Flaming Tina is desperate to see him."

The young Gypsy leered at her. "If your need is that great, lady, I could serve you in his stead. We need only go into the trees."

"Ohh!" she gasped, daintily picking up her skirts and moving away from him with all speed. "What is the matter with men?" Tina demanded.

Ada shrugged. "Their pricks are the center of their universe, whether they be Gypsy or king."

They passed a Gypsy girl putting her trained dogs through their paces, and Tina thought she looked familiar. She hesitated. In their brilliant red skirts and white peasant blouses, one resembled another. Suddenly she felt eyes boring into her back and whirled about to see a sly, familiar face with slanting eyes and pouting lips glaring at her.

Tina did not recall the girl's name, but her heart lifted in spite of the look of raw hatred being cast her way. She had seen the dark beauty whenever she had visited Heath. Tina walked over to the steps of her caravan. "My name is—"

"I know your name," Zara snarled. "You are the Kennedy bitch." The girl deliberately spat on the ground, and Tina's cheeks flamed. She swallowed her pride. "Is Heath here?" she asked hopefully.

Zara shrugged. "He was but he is gone."

"When will he be back?" asked Tina.

The Gypsy girl looked as if she would like to plunge her knife into the redhead. Tina reached into her pocket and held out a gold coin. Zara eyed it and wet her lips. "He comes, he goes," she said, reaching greedy fingers for the money.

Tina closed her fingers over the coin. "Why do you hate me?" she demanded.

The silence stretched between them as they glared at each other. Finally Zara shrugged. "I was the Ram's woman before you."

Valentina felt a stab of jealousy pierce her heart. It was obvious the sultry Gypsy girl felt a deep passion for the devil-eyed Douglas. Tina decided to take advantage of the girl's emotions. "Ram has been taken prisoner. I believe he's been brought to London. I need Heath to find out where he's imprisoned." Tina gave Zara the gold coin. "Will you help me?" she asked evenly.

Zara went pale, but she threw out another taunt. "Why should I care?"

Valentina abandoned her pride altogether. "You care. I know because I was his woman, and I care. I would do anything to help him, and so would you."

"The women who share his bed will always awaken with a smile," Zara taunted.

Tina shook her head. "There will be no more women. They are going to hang him."

Zara's eyes narrowed dangerously. "He was the first man to give me gold . . . He was the only man I allowed to remove my earrings."

Tina saw she wore only one, then slowly Zara pulled up her skirt to display the saucy black curls between her legs.

Tina's eyes widened as she saw the golden hoop that pierced the Gypsy's mons. *The lecherous whoremaster, let them hang him!* Tina's heart constricted so tightly, she thought it would bleed. Then an inner voice asked, What does it matter how many women have gone before? When one loved deeply, it was all or nothing. She knew she would do anything to save him, and she hoped in her heart that Zara felt the same way.

As Tina turned to leave, Zara asked boldly, "Will you help me meet the king?"

Tina thought wildly, I need someone to help *me* meet the king! She had enough sense, however, to fold her tongue behind her teeth. She nodded her promise to Zara and hoped it was convincing enough.

Ada urged, "They were setting food out under an awning on the lawn. Let's get something to eat."

"I'm sorry, I'm not hungry," Tina replied.

"You must eat something—you don't want to fall sick again."

Tina shook her head. "Food would choke me. You must eat something, though. Come on, I could use a drink, perhaps."

The food tables were laden with the harvest's bounty. Ada helped herself to a meat pasty and a fruit pie, while Tina took a cup of spiced cider. Laughter and men's deep voices filled the air as a crowd of courtiers surged toward the food. When the crowd parted to allow the king access to the table, Tina saw that one of the men he spoke with was Lord Howard. She caught only a glimpse, for there were at least thirty men milling about the king. Before she could push into the throng, other men and women too were drawn to the presence of His Majesty like steel filings to a magnet. Tina and Ada were jostled aside without ceremony until it seemed that every person at Greenwich had business with Henry Tudor.

"If we get separated, you follow Howard and tell him I must see him, and I'll follow the king." Almost before the words were out of her mouth, the crowd surged toward the park and she could no longer see Ada.

Tina followed the crowd, which grew larger and noisier with every yard it progressed. The king's destination was the bowling green. A few fortunate courtiers were selected to give him a match, and the rest fell back about the perimeter of the green to cheer him on and watch him win.

Tina drew the eyes and the hands of the men about her. There was a decided dearth of beauties at court. She felt a hand on her bottom and turned angrily to face the man who touched her so intimately.

"By heaven, the front side is even more attractive than the back side," drawled a fair-haired young man with a long face.

She gave him a ringing slap. "How dare you touch me in public?" she demanded. A sudden hush fell upon the crowd, and Tina realized they had an audience.

"Would you prefer to be private, sweetheart?" he asked with a leer, not in the least deterred by the slap, and the crowd roared with coarse laughter. King Henry looked over to see what amused his courtiers. When he saw the young woman with the flaming hair who had caught his attention at mass that morning, he said to his partner, Lord Howard, "Find out who the little wench is with your son Edmund. I would have intercourse with her," he punned.

Howard laughed at the witty sally, but by the time he glanced across the bowling green, the young woman in question had moved on. Tina moved back to the edge of the spectators. She would have to wait until the king finished his bowls, then she would again take up the chase. Her eyes strayed to the women of the court. She could hardly tell one from another, for they copied each other's fashions slavishly. None of them looked very young, and all of them were full-figured or matronly. Perhaps it was the clothes they wore that made them look like ships in full sail. The gowns were heavy and full, with large leg-o-mutton sleeves and frilled underskirts. They all seemed to be wearing matching headdresses that were embroidered and bejeweled in exquisite patterns but could never match the beauty of a woman's crowning glory.

She stood upon a bench to look over the heads of the

crowd and saw that the king had finished his game. He took a woman's arm in a familiar manner and walked from the bowling green with her. The court trailed after, and Tina picked up her skirts and followed the courtiers. As it reached the gardens, the crowd thinned. Some went indoors, others to the awning where the food was laid out.

At last Tina's efforts were rewarded by a glimpse of the king and the woman he escorted disappearing behind a yew hedge. She hurried after. Lord Howard, Earl of Surrey, caught up with his third son, Edmund. "Back at the bowling green the king saw you speak to a young woman. He seemed most anxious to meet her."

"Prettiest piece I've seen at court in a twelvemonth," said Edmund. "Unfortunately, I know not the lady's name, and I wouldn't share it with Henry if I did."

"Don't be a fool, Edmund—what's a woman between friends?"

"You've dined with him often enough. You know how he consumes everything in sight with that voracious appetite of his. 'Tis becoming the same with women. Elizabeth Blount allowed him a taste—now he devours her daily."

"Good lord, if my eyes aren't deceiving me, I think I've just seen Lady Valentina Kennedy. What the devil can she be doing here at Henry's court, unless the queen sent her?" he shrewdly guessed.

"Where?" Edmund asked.

"She's easy enough to spot, she has the most glorious hair, the color of flame."

"That's the one I spoke with. There she goes, following the king into the maze."

"Oh, my God! Henry wants to meet her, but not I assure you under the circumstances I am visualizing."

The courtiers trailing after Henry had discreetly gone their own way when they saw the king take Elizabeth Blount into the maze. Tina was so intent upon catching up with the king that she did not realize she had entered the labyrinth of a maze until she was inside. Boxwood hedged her in on all sides, and she became slightly disoriented because she had never before been inside a network of shrubs designed to confuse one's direction. She turned a full circle on the path, found an opening, and went through it.

She found herself in a square space that held a sundial. Her fingers trailed over the words inscribed upon its bronze surface: *I measure only the sunny hours.* A small sob caught in her throat. How many sunny hours had she wasted when she could have been enjoying Ram's love? Now perhaps all they both had left were dark hours. She passed through another opening, heard voices, and moved forward toward them. Suddenly, almost in front of her she heard an impatient voice demand, "Up with your skirts, Bessie. Why are we suddenly coy?"

"Please, sire, can we not go some otherwhere than here? In my bedchamber you could remove your clothes and be comfortable." The woman's voice begged, yet her tone sounded hopeless.

"Nonsense, Bessie! I can't undress and dress every time I have need of a woman. What the devil do you think they designed the codpiece for?"

Tina put her hand over her mouth and shrank down against the bushes, trying to conceal her presence. Henry Tudor was about to satisfy his lust not four feet in front of her through the boxwood hedge. She could see two pairs of shoes facing each other. One pair were a woman's slippers embroidered with flowers. The other pair were enormous, square-toed and bejeweled. Suddenly the slippers were turned in the other direction. "Lean over the bench, Bessie, and hike your damned skirts! Don't think to play the cocktease with me!"

There followed such a rustling of garments, followed by grunts and gasps and strange mewling cries of a female in distress, that Valentina was thoroughly shocked and disgusted at the manner in which the amorous king handled a woman. He mounted her from behind exactly as a bull would a cow, standing in the field!

The woman gave a muffled shriek and began to cry. "No need to cry, Bessie, love. I know I'm big, and sometimes I hurt, but that's a small price to pay for the great honor I do you."

"Your jewels have scratched and cut my bottom cheeks, sire."

Henry laughed. "Ah, so they have. . . . I've branded you right well, Bessie. What's a little pain, compared to such huge pleasure? Stop your sniveling and help me fasten this damned codpiece."

As the feet began to move, Tina pushed her way through the middle of the hedge where there was no opening, to avoid being discovered. She heard Henry say, "Make yourself available after the hunt," but the lady's reply was too faint for Tina to hear. After waiting a full quarter of an hour, Tina found her way out of the maze and vowed never to enter another as long as she lived. Her high hopes of the morning were evaporating. She returned to her chambers hoping to find Ada there, but instead she found a page waiting with a message from the chancellor. It asked that she summon him the moment she returned. Tina sent the little page off to locate him and sat down on the edge of the bed to wait. Suddenly she gasped in fright as a dark figure swung open her casement window and stepped inside. "Heath! Omigod, Heath—you near frightened me half to death!"

"Sweetheart, what the devil are you doing in England?" he demanded, not pleased at all by her presence.

She flung herself into his arms. "Oh God, everything is in such a mess! Davie betrayed Black Ram Douglas to Lord Dacre. They were waiting for him aboard the *Revenge.* The English king put a price on his head."

"The vicious little whoreson! He always did make me puke! If they bring Ram to London, they'll probably lodge him in the White Tower." He did not add that the scaffolds were just behind, on Tower Hill.

"The king himself sent a protest, and the Earl of Angus gave me letters from Queen Margaret to her brother saying they have the wrong man, but I haven't been able to get near the king yet."

"Lord Howard, the Earl of Surrey, is probably the most influential man at court at the moment. Does he know you, Tina?"

"Yes, he once tried to seduce me." She lifted her shoulder in a helpless shrug.

"Old lecher! He can certainly find out where Ram is. Speak with him. Seduce him into letting you visit your husband. I'm sure he has enough authority to arrange it for you. If he asks more than you are willing to give, tell him your brother is here with you to protect your virtue."

She looked so wobegone, he reached out a hand to ruffle her hair. "Cheer up, Firebrand—most of the things we worry about in life never come to pass."

When a knock came upon the chamber door, Heath swung his legs over the casement and disappeared before she opened the door. It was the king's lord chancellor. She dropped him a pretty curtsy, and he raised her immediately. "Forgive me, dearest Lady Kennedy. I had no notion you were here as an ambassador from His Majesty's beloved sister in Scotland. The chamberlain has treated you most shabbily. The king hunts this afternoon, so it will be our opportunity to move you to chambers more fitting to a lady with your high connections."

"These rooms are quite adequate, my lord chancellor," she demurred. Heath would have to find her again if she was moved.

"I insist, my lady. If I left you here, it would bring down the king's wrath upon my head."

Tina shrugged an elegant shoulder and consented sweetly.

"I shall present you to King Henry tonight in the banqueting hall."

"Ah, thank you, my lord! It is a pleasant change to meet a gentleman."

The new rooms were exceptionally lovely. The larger chamber was a bed-sitting room paneled in golden oak. The bed-hangings and carpet were Tudor green, and there was a carved fireplace with a small fire burning to keep out the damp of the river. Before the fire was a small table with a pair of cushioned chairs, while the adjoining chamber was designed to be a dressing room with a gilt screen and slipper bath and a trundle bed for a maid.

Since she was finally going to be presented to the king, Tina decided to wear the elegant black and silver creation Ram had purchased for her in Glasgow. It was the latest fashion, with its enormous bishop sleeves and low-cut square neckline. Ada fastened a small silver lace ruff about Tina's neck and assured her that her vivid hair was far too beautiful to hide beneath a coif.

Tina realized she may only get one opportunity to speak with the king, and when so much depended upon his goodwill, the first impression she made upon him would be vital. This was the fifth day since Ram had been taken. He must have arrived here in London by now. Perhaps the king had already been informed that Lord Vengeance was his prisoner and had given orders to hang him.

Tina closed her eyes and offered up a silent prayer, then sent Ram a silent message to keep up his courage. Her stomach knotted painfully whenever she thought of him, and since this afternoon's close encounter she hadn't been able to catch her breath. "Ada, I need air. Walk with me to the stables, and I'll speak with the men who gave us escort. At tomorrow's revels I want them to stick close, for even the gardens and park are not safe for unescorted women here at Greenwich."

They had almost reached the stable doors when there

came such a baying of hunting dogs and pounding of hoof-beats that it sounded like the hounds of Hell had been let loose. All of a sudden the courtyard before the stables overflowed with the returning royal hunt and its carnage. A master of hounds shouted orders to the kennelmen and fewterers who brandished whips among the unruly dogs. The hunt master sounded his horn over and over, half-deafening any who were unfortunate enough to be on hand. The men of the court and a sprinkling of women were laughing and congratulating the king for taking down the most game.

The king's beaters had a score of deer trussed, not all of which were dead. The king's arrows had left some of the stags and does wounded in their haunches, and now to great cheers of encouragement, Henry bent to dispatch them with his knife. He was covered with blood, totally oblivious to his magnificent clothes. He was so immersed in his task, the blood dripped from his elbows, forming great dark pools on the flagstones of the courtyard.

Valentina stepped inside the dimness of the stables and swayed. Ada saw that her face had gone chalk white. She took Tina's arm to steady her. "Take a deep breath."

Tina shook her head, "I can't breathe—I feel as if I'm suffocating." Henry Tudor was the coarsest man she had ever seen. Everything he did, he managed to turn into an obscenity. Even the Highland chiefs like Angus and Argyll, though rough and uncouth, were not this repulsive. The King of England did everything to excess. He was over-sized, overindulgent, loathsome, and offensive. All those about him fawned upon him to such a degree it made Tina want to spew.

As she slipped from the stables, Lord Howard caught a glimpse of her from the tail of his eye and sent his groom to learn where she was lodged at Greenwich. She was an alluring creature, no longer virgin since her hand-fasting, and the thought of her beneath him sent the blood beating in his throat.

Chapter 33

Tina returned to her chamber and stood at the open casement with unseeing eyes. She shuddered at the thought of going to the banqueting hall to dine, but it would be her only opportunity to be presented to the king and give him the letter. She would have done almost anything to avoid meeting Henry Tudor, but circumstances did not afford her such a luxury.

She stood pensively recalling how she had once hated Ram Douglas. If only he could somehow be there with her now to watch over her, she would have felt completely and totally safe. She sighed and told herself to stop her silly, wishful daydreaming. She had a job to do, and she vowed to do it to the very best of her ability.

A dark shadowed figure appeared at the casement, but before she could be alarmed she heard Heath's low, reassuring voice: "I saw them take Ram off the ship. He's in the Bloody Tower which is part of the inner curtain wall. That's the place they've reserved for Scots prisoners."

"Was he chained and manacled?" she demanded.

"Tina, he was alive! For Christ's sake, stop torturing yourself! Concentrate on getting Howard's permission to see him. I'll take care of everything else. We need an official paper."

"You have a plan!" she cried with renewed hope.

"Aye, but you are better off in ignorance. Just get the paper." His shadow merged with the darkness of the gardens beyond her window, and though she had a hundred unasked questions, she felt better able to face the task ahead of her.

She brushed her hair until it crackled, picked up her

silver-handled black lace fan, and walked to the banqueting hall with feline grace. Ada took her place at a servants' table, while Tina waited politely for one of the stewards to seat her. He had instructions to find her a place close by the chamberlain so that he could hand her over to the chancellor for presentation to His Majesty after the meal.

Music floated down from the minstrels' gallery, while pages and squires rushed about the hall doing their masters' bidding. Finally, Henry Tudor and his so-called gentlemen arrived, and the servitors started carrying in their laden-down trays.

Tina crumbled some bread absently as she sipped a little watered wine. Her nostrils pinched together to keep the smell of the roast venison at bay, and she tried to forget the does' eyes, which had been liquid with fear. Of course these were not the same animals, but it would be a long time before Tina would be able to eat anything that had been hunted down.

Ada had told her that the queen, Catherine of Aragon, and her ladies had taken up residence at Richmond, farther along the river, so that she could politely turn a blind eye to the king's pleasures.

Tina paid more attention to the rich garments the courtiers wore than to the people inside them. As a result she did not see the narrowed eyes of Lady Howard, the Countess of Surrey, upon her, nor was she aware of that woman's son, Edmund, observing her from another part of the hall. She was studying a crimson doublet with a white lace shirt pulled through its slashes when her eyes slowly rose to the closely trimmed beard above a frilled collar, and she looked into the familiar eyes of Lord Howard.

Apparently he had been watching her. Tina was so relieved to have made eye contact with him that she sent him a brilliant smile across the room and received a warm nod from him in acknowledgment. For the first time that day, Tina was able to take a deep breath.

Edmund Howard saw the look his father sent the vivid

beauty and cursed beneath his breath. He knew better than to compete with his father for a woman's favors. Mercifully, Tina had no notion that Lord Howard had just saved her.

Finally the board was cleared except for the wine cups and sweetmeats. Henry Tudor took pride in eating and drinking his gentlemen beneath the table each night. The chamberlain bowed before Valentina, then handed her over to the chancellor. He hurried forward with her toward the raised dais before the wrestlers came out to claim Henry's attention. The king was diverted from his victuals as his eyes took in the exquisite face and figure of the young woman who had eluded him since mass this morning.

Tina swept down to the floor as if she were paying homage to a deity. Henry's close-set eyes lit with greed as they licked over her half-exposed breasts beneath the delicious silver ruff.

"Lady Valentina Kennedy has brought a message to Your Majesty from Queen Margaret of Scotland."

Henry held out his beringed hand so that the lady might kiss it, but Tina slipped the letter from between her breasts and placed it upon the King's massive palm. Henry was far more interested in the female his sister had sent him than her missive. He tossed it negligently upon the table and invited the lady to sit with him. With a wave of his hamlike hand, he removed the earl who occupied the seat beside him as if he were the meanest lackey.

Henry splashed malmsey into his large, gem-encrusted goblet and placed it in Tina's hands. She repressed a shiver at the thought of sipping from the same rim where the gross mouth of Henry Tudor had quaffed and covered her hesitation with a shy smile.

"Don't be overwhelmed, sweeting," said the fatuous Henry, patting her knee in a pretense of fatherly affection. "We would share more than our cup with you."

Two strapping wrestlers bowed before the king, wearing

nothing but skintight hose. The king's champion wore
Tudor green, while the challenger's hose were a disconcert-
ing yellow. They were both large, heavy men, and Tina
thought all that exposed flesh most distasteful. Henry bent
toward her intimately. "I wager a kiss that my champion
pins your challenger."

"Sire, he is not my challenger. I know naught of wrestling."

"That is not very sportive of you, my lady. I will teach
you all you need to know of wrestling." He threw back his
head and laughed at his own wit, then smoothed down the
golden curls of his beard. Henry, like an overgrown boy,
wanted to shine before this attractive woman. "My champion is the best. None can match him—save myself, of
course." His eyes lit with zeal. "Would you like to see me
take him?"

Tina could think of nothing she would like less. Her lips
opened as she gasped for breath, and Henry thought she
was overcome with awe of him.

"Come sweeting, wager on me, and win a prize of your
own choosing."

Tina immediately thought of the letter she wanted him
to read and murmured, "No lady ever had a more exalted
champion, sire."

Henry threw his doublet and velvet cap to one of his
gentlemen and climbed from the dais to a chorus of encouraging cheers. Tina was most relieved that he would
wrestle in his shirtsleeves. She had no desire to see the
gross Tudor stripped to the buff.

Tina thought the spectacle before her grotesque. Two
oversized bodies, with arms and legs entwined, heaved and
huffed until both men were red in the face and sweating
profusely. She raised her fan to cover her expression of
distaste. The king's champion was good at charades. He
made a show of being a match for the king until the last
split-second, when he went down like ninepins. The court-

iers cheered and applauded and banged their goblets on the table in approval.

Henry raised his arms in acknowledgment, lapping up the adulation. He was England's undefeated champion whether the sport was wrestling, tennis, jousting, or hunting. He was about to add seduction to the list. His gentlemen helped him back into his ostentatiously ornamented doublet, and he leaned toward Valentina with his sausage-like fingers stretched before him. "Choose a bauble, sweeting—don't be shy!"

"I ask no jewel, Your Majesty," Tina said softly. "All I ask is that you read the letter I have brought."

Henry broke the seal and scanned the contents. Suddenly his lips pursed peevishly. "I've had no word that this self-styled Lord Vengeance has been taken."

"He has not been taken, Your Majesty. Lord Douglas is not the murdering pirate!"

Henry's eyes became covetous as he looked at her mouth, then her lovely breasts. The thought of Douglas fucking her titillated his imagination, as a schoolboy enjoys a dirty picture. His mouth went prudish as he asked, "You are hand-fasted to this Douglas?"

"I am, sire," she said softly.

"A licentious Scottish custom—against the law here in England. 'Tis fornication pure and simple. You live together and share his bed without benefit of clergy." He licked his lips. "Do you deny you are his mistress?"

Tina fanned herself furiously. "It is a time-honored tradition. He is my husband in every way." As she said the words, Tina knew she spoke the truth. Ram Douglas was her husband, and she knew she could never be unfaithful to him.

Henry captured her hand and held it fast when she tried to withdraw it. He whispered huskily, "Wife and whore in one—a tempting combination! Are you rewarding in bed?"

Tina's cheeks were hot, yet it was not shame she felt but anger. Henry enjoyed teasing her. He began to tickle and stroke the palm of her hand with his finger in a suggestive manner, then lifted her hand to his mouth and tickled and licked it with his tongue. Tina's gorge rose, and for a moment she feared she would vomit on his royal person. She swallowed rapidly and prayed she would not disgrace herself.

The Countess of Surrey was worried. She had watched the chancellor present Valentina Kennedy to the king and seen her hand him a letter. It could be from either the King or Queen of Scotland, and it could be filled with lies about the Howards. She lost no time informing her husband of her suspicions and urged him to join the king on the dais. The moment Henry saw the Earl of Surrey approach, he beckoned him with an all-powerful finger. Howard knew a moment of misgiving as his monarch's beady eyes fastened upon him.

"Why was I not informed of the capture of the elusive Lord Vengeance?" Henry asked silkily.

"Your Majesty, I had word from my son Thomas only today that the *Revenge* had been spotted off Flamborough Head. He has an informant who has divulged that a raid on Kingston is imminent, and the admiral has laid plans to trap Lord Vengeance and his ship the *Revenge* in the Humber River."

Henry tapped his fingers thoughtfully. "Your information seems to tally with Margaret's. Apparently Dacre arrested Lord Douglas and had him shipped to London. How could he have bungled so badly?" asked Henry.

Since Lord Dacre was Howard's rival, he took the opportunity offered to blacken his reputation. He shrugged. "Your Majesty offered a great reward for the capture, I believe?"

Henry's fingers tapped faster. "I should have been informed the moment such a prominent Scot arrived at the tower. Though he is obviously not the elusive Lord Vengeance, he could nevertheless prove to be of great value at the bargaining table."

A cold hand clamped around Tina's heart.

"I believe you are acquainted with the delightful Lady Kennedy?" Henry asked, watching the earl's face intently.

"Indeed, sire," said Lord Howard, executing a smart military bow before the lady. "She is one of Queen Margaret's favorites," he improvised. "Her beauty is legendary."

Henry knew lust when he saw it, and it amused him that Surrey coveted the girl at his side. "We want Lady Kennedy's visit to be a most pleasurable one. We charge you, *and your lady wife,*" Henry emphasized, "to do all in your power to serve the lady."

Howard knew he was being warned off the quarry, so the moment Henry dismissed him, he made a show of attending his wife. "She brought messages from the queen. We have nothing to worry about. He asks that we keep an eye on her."

"Henry seems to be doing that without our aid," she said dryly. "He looks like a dog with a bone."

"That's a tasteless remark," snapped Howard, and immediately his wife trimmed her sails as the wind blew. Her husband wanted Flaming Tina for himself and expected her to allay the king's suspicions.

Lady Howard joined Elizabeth Blount and sowed a small seed of disquiet. "Elizabeth, His Majesty neglects you shamefully, but you mustn't be angry with him. Lady Kennedy has quite a reputation for being a honeypot."

"Really?" murmured Bessie. She had been half-hoping Henry's insatiable needs would be met elsewhere tonight, but she was damned if she was going to allow him to humiliate her by openly courting the Kennedy bitch. She took hold of the Countess of Surrey's arm, and they strolled toward the king. Bessie sank down before him, displaying her opulent décolletage.

"Your Majesty dazzled everyone with that superb display of physical strength. Sire, you are unmatched in all of England."

Tina thought the flattery laid on so thickly would be considered insincere, but Henry lapped it up.

"You are often in a position to see me perform, Bessie, and as you can testify, I am tireless."

A tableau from the maze sprang full-blown into Tina's mind. She turned to the king and said breathlessly, "Please excuse me, Your Majesty. I am feeling quite faint. I am sure Lady Howard will be kind enough to see me to my chamber."

Henry looked into her eyes with deliberation and said, "Until later." Then he relinquished her to the Countess of Surrey, called for more wine, and placed a familiar hand on Bessie Blount's buttocks.

Tina sank into a chair before her chamber fire and kicked off her shoes. She felt drained. The tension in Henry Tudor's presence had been unbearable. When his piggy eyes slid all over her, she had felt unclean, but when he actually touched her, she had felt violated. Still, it was a small price to pay for Ram's sake.

Ada undid the laces of her gown. "You look like death warmed up. Have you eaten anything at all today?"

Tina shook her head.

"Why don't you have a piece of fruit?" Ada urged.

Tina selected a pear and took a few bites. "I should be grateful. I suppose my evening was an unqualified success. I was finally presented to the king, who read the letter in exchange for my allowing him to paw me."

Ada could hear the disquiet in her voice.

"Ada, I'm so afraid Henry wants me—and what Henry wants, Henry gets. He strutted before me like a bull in heat. He put on a display of wrestling and sweated like a pig."

"Which is it, bull or pig?" Ada smiled, hoping to lighten her mood.

"I think he can be convinced that Ramsey isn't Lord Vengeance, but he isn't about to let a powerful Douglas out of his clutches."

"Oh, darling, you've done wonders. At least you've removed the threat of the noose from about Ram's neck."

"Perhaps." Tina sighed. "The trouble is, if I call the tune, I have to be prepared to pay the piper."

Ada shrugged philosophically. "It's a man's world, love. All favors must be paid for, but in my experience you never miss a slice off a cut loaf." Ada gave her a warning. "Ram would kill you if he found out, so never let him know."

"He would hate me forever," said Tina sadly. "I would hate myself forever."

"If you're clever, he'll never know," Ada insisted.

But I'll know, thought Tina.

"Let me hang up your gown," said Ada, helping her remove the black and silver dress. Then she pushed a stool beneath Tina's feet so she could rest before the fire.

As Tina gazed into the flames, she fell into a reverie. She could see Ram with the children of Ochiltree. His tenderness had quite undone her. More than anything, she longed to give him a child of his own to love. Gradually her eyes closed, and her head fell to the chair arm as sleep claimed her. Ada left her before the fire, clad only in her black shift, and sought her trundle bed in the dressing room.

Tina opened her eyes and blinked. Someone was knocking on the chamber door. With her hand upon the latch, she asked, "Who is there?"

" 'Tis I, my dear, Lord Howard. We had no chance to speak privately with the eyes of the king and court upon us."

Tina needed a favor from this man, and Providence had sent him. There was no way she was going to refuse him admittance because she was clad only in her shift. She wondered what hour it was and how long she had been asleep. She lifted the latch and looked about for a bedgown, but Ada must have retired without laying one out for her.

"Please excuse my state of undress, Lord Howard. I must beg a favor from you."

He raised her hand to his lips in a gallant gesture. "My dear, I will do anything that is within my power. You know full well how fond I am of you."

A small warning bell went off in Tina's head, so she put distance between them before she asked her favor. "Fear for Lord Douglas brought me all the way from Scotland. I am sick with worry for him. Please write me a pass so that I may visit him in the tower. The king assured me you would help me, dearest Lord Howard."

"It gives me the deepest pleasure to give you what you ask, Lady Valentina. In return, I know you will be more than generous with me."

Tina caught her breath. Dear God, here was another expecting sexual favors! Was this always the currency between men and women? Howard closed the distance between them and pulled her into his arms. His mouth covered hers insistently, and he pressed her close so that she would know how hard her softly curved body made him.

Tina pulled her mouth from his. "My lord, the pass!" When he had written the paper she wanted, she planned to tell him her brother was asleep in the next room.

Keeping hold of her hand, he moved to the desk and picked up a quill. He smiled at her. "You are no longer the green little virgin I knew in Edinburgh." He folded the paper and tucked it playfully between her breasts. "Come, give me all your sweetness now." One arm went about her back, the other under her knees as he swept her up into his arms and carried her to the bed.

He was so much stronger than she, fear washed over her. She sobbed, "Lord Howard, how dare you force me against my will! My brother will kill you for this, sir!"

A panel of golden oak slid open to reveal the massive figure of Henry Tudor in an ermine bedrobe. Howard's mouth fell open. He knew immediately he had made a stupid tactical blunder. Flaming Tina had been in a state of undress because she was expecting the king! She occupied these rooms beneath Henry's only because there was a secret, inner staircase connecting the two apartments.

Henry's mouth pursed tightly. "Is this the way you use a lady to whom I have promised aid and protection?" he thundered in outrage.

Tina was alarmed at the compromising situation in which she found herself. Henry Tudor was so unpredictable, he could order them both to the tower on a whim.

"I am shocked at your licentious behavior, Surrey. No gentleman of my court forces himself upon a lady. Can you not see the child is distraught?" he demanded. "I take great pains to set the moral tone of my court, and then something like this happens to destroy it!"

Tina could hardly believe her ears. Henry Tudor was the biggest hypocrite she'd ever heard, yet he actually seemed to believe his own prim words at this moment. "Leave us, and report to me in the morning. I begin to question my decision to put you in charge of the military."

Surrey bowed stiffly. "I shall leave at once, Your Majesty. I assure you, my interest in Lady Kennedy is a fatherly one."

By now Ada was awake and listening at the other door. She heard Lord Howard depart and knew Tina was now alone with the king. There was nothing she could do. It would be more than her life was worth to intervene between a king and his pleasure. Tina Kennedy was all woman. She would know how to handle Henry Tudor.

Valentina saw the king through a blur of tears. Her lips trembled uncontrollably and Henry sat down and gathered her into his lap. "There, there, sweeting—you are safe now," he said, patting her in a bluff, paternal manner. He dandled her upon his great knee, as if she were a child who had fallen and skinned her elbow. "Come, poppet, dry your eyes." He fumbled for a handkerchief, and at last produced it like a rabbit from a hat. "There!" He dabbed gently at her face.

"Orris root," said Tina, blinking at him owlishly, between hiccups.

"That's right, sweeting. What a clever girl you are. Mmm, you smell of freesia, a most delicate perfume."

Tina was amazed. Apparently Henry was in a mood to play "daddy and little girl." He gave her two quick buzzes on the lips. "There, my kisses have made it all better," he said.

She was terrified for what might come next, so she looked at him with wide, innocent eyes. "Thank you, sire," she whispered. "My brother is asleep in the next room. If he had awakened and found Lord Howard here when I was undressed, he would have run his sword through the man."

The king put his finger to his lips, then to hers. "Hush, sweeting. We don't want to awaken him. I'll just tuck you safely into bed and warn you to keep your chamber door locked in future."

He lifted her and carried her to the bed, but before he put her down upon it, he ran his hand across her breasts in a caress. He put his mouth upon hers and forced it open to admit his tongue. He whispered against her mouth, "Tomorrow evening you will sit with me while we enjoy the Gypsy entertainers. Then you will open your pretty thighs for me, while I give you a loving you will never forget."

Henry enjoyed the anticipation almost as much as the act. The moment when a lady first saw his great size always delighted him, and even though a lady had had previous sexual encounters, it was like being deflowered a second time. He always managed to draw blood when he stretched a lady's sheath with his great sword of state.

Chapter 34

When the king had gone, Tina turned her face into her pillow and cried herself to sleep. The strange nightmares began almost immediately. She stood in a tiny wisp of a shift trying to conceal her breasts with her flaming cloak of hair. Before her stretched an endless line of men. Her father passed her to Patrick Hamilton; he pushed her into James Stewart's arms, who in turn passed her on to Angus. At the very end of the line, she saw Black Ram Douglas waiting for her.

The only way she could get to Ram was through the other men. Angus passed her to a dark Douglas servant; the servant handed her to the steward; the steward to the chamberlain; the chamberlain pushed her toward the chancellor. Now only two men stood between her and her goal —Lord Howard and Henry Tudor.

As she passed from the chancellor's hands to Lord Howard, she glanced down the line to Hotspur Douglas, and suddenly she realized he was waiting to kill her. If she went to Douglas from the king's arms, he would destroy her. She cried out in her sleep and opened her eyes, but she was still dreaming. Again there was a line of men. This time each held out a cup from which she must drink. She trusted none of them. With fear almost choking her, she drank from her brother David's cup, then from Gavin and Cameron Douglas's cups. Next came the cousins Ian, Drummond, and Jamie, followed by Colin who was even more grotesquely crippled than in real life. Then she knew she must drink from Mad Malcolm's cup because it was the only way to reach Ram. Finally she reached her goal and lifted Ramsay's cup to her lips. She drank it calmly, obediently, knowing he had given her poison. She drew her knees up to her belly in her sleep and cried out in agony. She opened her eyes, but she was still dreaming. Heath was there, but somehow he had red hair like her other brothers, and she began to laugh hysterically.

Heath shook her. "Stop, Tina—it's Heath."

She looked at him in amazement. "Oh, God—I thought you were part of my nightmare! What are you doing with red hair?"

"It's a wig. None would believe I'm a Kennedy without red hair. Did you get the pass?"

"Yes, yes, I got it. Where the devil is it?" For a minute or two she couldn't remember, then she shoved a frantic hand down her shift and drew out the precious paper. Suddenly she started to shiver. "Oh, Heath, I hate this place. It's a nightmare sleeping or awake. I'll never, never get to him."

"Here's Ada with some hot tea. I want you to dress warmly. We're going on the river."

"The river?" she questioned, warming her hands on the cup.

"It looks like this," Heath said, drawing an imaginary line across the bedcovers. "Here's the river with the wharf running parallel. We take a barge to this spot on the wharf. We cross Traitor's Bridge, then Traitor's Gate leads into St. Thomas's Tower, which takes you across the moat and immediately on the other side is the Bloody Tower, which is part of the inner curtain wall."

"Must we go through Traitor's Gate to get to him?" she asked with a shudder. "I didn't betray him, even though he believes I did."

"Tina, pull yourself together. Think of it as another adventure we are about to embark upon." He shoved a linen napkin at her. "Eat!"

She wrinkled her nose and asked cautiously, "What is it?"

"Christ, you'd think it was a bloody hedgehog I was offering you. It's oat cakes, plain and simple oat cakes."

She ate them obediently and finished the hot tea.

"Do you feel better?" asked Ada.

"No," Tina said in a forlorn voice.

"Don't tell me all your guts have deserted you," goaded Heath. "Smile, pinch your cheeks to put some color in them. If Ram sees you like this, he'll think he's received a death sentence."

Tina threw back the covers and sprang from the bed. "Ada, give me something lovely to wear." What a gutless creature she was! All she had to do was hold her nose and give Henry Tudor access to her body. If she couldn't charm that gross mountain of flesh into freeing Ram, she wasn't much of a woman.

Ada brought the peach-colored gown with the pleated bodice and stomacher, and Heath opened the wardrobe and took out the luxurious sable cloak. "Do it with panache," he murmured, and she threw her arms about him in a rush of love. She was far more attuned to this half-brother than to her full brothers.

Tina was never more thankful in her life for Heath's support than she was this overcast morning as they stepped from the barge onto the Tower Wharf. A reckless mood had seized her as they sailed down the Thames, but as the White Tower of London loomed before her, her knees turned to butter, and her heart turned over in her breast. She didn't know which daunted her more: the forbidding fortress, or the thought of facing the accusing eyes of Black Ram Douglas.

She was somehow surprised that the paper signed by Surrey got them through Traitor's Gate. She was even more amazed when it gained them entrance to the Bloody Tower. The guard took them past three other cells before coming to a stop before the barred door of the fourth. The tower guard in his military uniform gave them specific instructions before he unlocked the door. "I will lock you in with the prisoner. Call out when you wish to leave."

The Kennedys nodded in agreement, and the turnkey did his job.

When Ramsay saw Valentina he wasn't sure if he wanted to kiss her or kill her. A great wave of love went out to her for risking her life to save his, but at the same time he wanted to take hold of her and shake some sense into her. She was so reckless, so heedless of her own danger, it terrified him. Just the sight of her confirmed his powerful response to her. His heart was racing wildly, and his blood was singing just being in the same enclosed space together. If this woman believed in him, there was nothing he couldn't do.

Tina's heart was in her mouth as she carefully looked him over from head to toe to see if he had been permanently injured. He relief that he was all right made her feel faint and lightheaded. She loved him with all her heart and would do anything on earth to gain his freedom. She must make him understand that she had not betrayed him and never imagined in this world Davie would do so, but before she could find the words to pledge her loyalty to him, Heath placed the red wig over Ram's hair and swung his cloak about Ram's shoulders. Heath spoke quickly.

"The English have been recruiting like mad. They have garrisons at Coventry, Gloucester, Leicester, Nottingham, Manchester, York, and Newcastle, as well as the two you know of, at Carlisle and Berwick. The ports are bristling with ships, and the press gangs are out in full force to equip them with crews. The army is already between twenty and thirty thousand strong, but here's the good news. They are going to war with France before they tackle Scotland."

"Good man!" said Ram with genuine pleasure. "But I can't let you take my place."

"It was my brother who betrayed you," said Heath, "I am honor-bound to do this thing." He grinned at Ram. "You in turn must take my place. You must entertain the king and court tonight at Greenwich. Are you up to riding the ponies and throwing the knives?"

Tina looked at them aghast. They were taking matters into their own hands and exchanging places. "Ram, no! I can persuade the king to let you go."

He took hold of her shoulders possessively, his pewter eyes burned into hers. "I'd see ye dead before I'd let ye ask Henry Tudor for favors."

She could feel the heat from his hands branding her as his woman. "God damn you both, how am I to bear it if you do this thing?" she agonized.

His grip tightened fiercely to reassure her and transfer some of his strength to her. "Hush, vixen." He touched his lips to her brow tenderly.

Heath said low, "Your job isn't over yet, Tina. You must go straight to the king, throw a tantrum, and tell him his prisoner is not Ram Douglas." He grinned at Ram as they gripped each other's arm in a silent pledge. "Zara awaits you."

Tina's eyes flashed their outrage, but Ram threw his arm about her to anchor her to his side and growled, "Call the guard."

If Tina had been afraid on the way in, she was terrified on the way out, but the warden never looked beyond the red hair.

They stood facing each other as the oarsman took them back to Greenwich. They did not dare touch except with their eyes. It wrung his heart to see how fragile she looked, especially with the violet smudges beneath her eyes.

Tina bit her lips to prevent a cry of anguish from escaping when the wind blew aside his collar to expose the raw scar the ship's rope had left upon his neck. There were a thousand things she wanted to tell him, but they all went unsaid. Her throat was closed tight with emotion, and she knew if she tried to utter just one word, she would be undone.

She tried to read what was in his heart, but his face wore

a dark, impenetrable mask. One thing was certain—she might be vulnerable, but Ram Douglas was not. He was stronger than steel, harder than granite. Tina fiercely fought back her tears, vowing not to weep before him. Would he think her courageous or heartless? Did it matter what he thought? She realized it mattered more than life or death. If only they could flee together, but they could not. She was held as fast as Heath in his stone cell.

As Ramsay watched the small figure of his woman climb the Greenwich waterstairs, his eyes softened and his gut knotted with apprehension for her. He had left her safe with all the might of Douglas to protect her, yet she had placed herself in jeopardy to save him. Now her favorite brother was in the Tower of London. Ram's face was bleak; he knew she'd pay any price to save the Gypsy.

Instinctively, Tina knew the only thing that would save her was anger. By the time she swept down the corridors of Greenwich Palace, her temper was blazing. She walked a direct path to Henry Tudor's apartments and stopped only when she reached the royal antechamber. A grenadier guard was posted outside the king's privy chamber, and the chancellor stood between her and the guard.

"Lady Kennedy, I am afraid His Majesty is occupied this morning."

She raised her eyebrows and swept him with an icy glance. "He is with Lord Howard, I presume."

"Yes, my lady. The Earl of Surrey."

"My business concerns him too." She brushed past the chancellor and stepped up to the guard.

"Stop her!" cried the chancellor.

The guard slanted his halberd across the entrance to the privy chamber and the chancellor raised his voice in horror. "You cannot see the king!"

Tina's golden eyes blazed their challenge. "Can I not?" she asked, then threw back her head and let out a blood-curdling scream. Within two seconds the door was flung open, and Henry Tudor filled its frame.

She brandished the paper Howard had signed for her. "The man in the tower is not Ram Douglas! What have you done with my husband?" She ran up to the king and pummeled her fists on his broad chest.

The guard dropped his halberd, grabbed her arms, and twisted them behind her back. Valentina immediately fainted, albeit gracefully.

"Unhand the lady!" ordered the king as he bent to pick her up from the floor. He carried her limp body into his privy chamber and held her on his knee. Henry tapped her cheek gently until she opened her eyes. He watched helplessly as her golden eyes turned a smoky amber and filled with tears. "You've killed him—I know you've killed him!" she wept.

"Dearest lady, we have killed no one. What is this about, Surrey?" the king demanded.

"I—I gave Lady Kennedy a pass to visit Douglas in the tower," he explained. "I saw no harm in it."

"No harm in it?" cried Tina. Her sable cloak fell away from her to reveal the pleated bodice of the peach-colored gown, showing off her delectable breasts to perfection. "Gracious Majesty, help me!" she implored.

"Calm and compose yourself, sweeting." He spoke as if to a very small and wayward child. "Henry promises to look into the matter thoroughly. I want you to run along now and have a little rest. I shall be most annoyed if anything spoils today's celebrations." He looked pointedly at Surrey, but his words were also meant as a warning to Tina.

"I'm sorry, Your Majesty," she murmured contritely. "I promise to be good. I know you will look after me."

He patted her and dropped a kiss on the top of her head before she climbed down from his lap. The moment she had gone, Henry turned accusing eyes upon Surrey. "You were at the Scottish court long enough. Can you identify this Ram Douglas?"

"I most assuredly can, Your Majesty."

"Then send for the damned plaguey fellow, and let's put an end to this farce," directed the livid king.

Two hours later Lord Howard was back waiting to be admitted to the king's privy chamber. He paced about outside the room while inside Bluff King Hal put Bessie Blount through her paces. He was peevish with her. Why the devil was her hair so drab? Lud, she was big as a cow! She couldn't even keep him hard, and he'd only spent twice! Bessie left sniffing back tears, which weren't unusual these days.

Henry came to the door. He wanted to be outside at the archery butts and blamed Surrey for this wretched business, which kept him from his pleasures. "Well?" he thundered.

"Your Majesty, Lady Kennedy was telling the truth. The man below is most definitely not Ramsay Douglas."

"Then who the devil is he?" demanded an impatient Henry.

"Er—he wouldn't say, sire. He said his identity was for your ears alone, Your Majesty."

"Can nothing in this whole damned realm be handled without my personal attention? Oh, go on—fetch him up. Just be sure he's well shackled before you bring him into my presence."

Henry fidgeted nervously with his beard as he awaited Surrey's return. What damned plots were being hatched north of the border? Why the hell was Margaret so eager to save the man's skin? Or had she been forced to write the letter? Henry glared fiercely at the man the guards brought in. His wrists were manacled behind him and chains stretched down to irons around his ankles. "Who the devil are you?" Henry demanded.

The tall, dark young man stepped closer to the king and murmured low. Henry snickered and looked at the handsome young devil with new eyes. Then he threw back his head, and the laughter rumbled up from his barrel-chest. Spine of God, no wonder Margaret was so eager to get the fellow back! "How the devil did you manage to get yourself arrested?" Henry demanded.

Heath replied, "A man in my delicate position has many jealous enemies."

"Just so," chuckled Henry. "Surrey, get these damned irons off the man. We are celebrating All Hallows today. You shall be a guest and join the festivities. Tonight we have the Gypsies to entertain us."

Heath rubbed his wrists. "My humble thanks, Your Majesty, but I dare not dally longer. A lady of our mutual acquaintance, who must remain nameless, is in need of my services. Perhaps at some future date I may be of invaluable service to Your Majesty. My pledge on it," he vowed, his head bent in servitude.

When Heath left, Henry gave a couple of orders. "Follow him, and while you're at it I want Lady Kennedy's servants watched closely—and that brother of hers I've never seen."

Later, as Henry and his courtiers made their way to the archery butts, he thought, sly puss Margaret—but what the devil am I to tell the little redhead?

At the moment the little redhead was packing her clothes frantically. "I'll wear the white gown tonight and my emeralds, but pack up everything else."

"You'll need a cloak. Autumn has finally arrived in England," Ada said.

"Yes, I'll wear the green velvet."

"Good choice. Henry will think you are wearing his Tudor colors."

"He can think what the devil he likes, but I'll be damned if he finds me in this chamber tonight when he steps out of the secret panel. Get the luggage to the stables, and have the men rent rooms at an inn. Give them gold to pay."

Their voices hushed immediately as they heard a rapping on the door. Ada opened it a crack to find a page with a message. "His Majesty the King commands Lady Kennedy attend him at the archery butts," piped the boy.

"Thank you kindly," Tina said, giving him a silver sixpence. "You may take me to him."

The page was happy to oblige. Usually all he got when he delivered a message was a sweetmeat, sometimes only a cuff on the ear. As she followed him through the palace garden, past the bowling green and into the great park to where the archery butts had been set up, Tina was acknowledged by everyone at court. She received bows and nods from the men and curtsies from the women. She blushed furiously. They thought she was the king's latest whore, and she experienced real shame.

When they arrived at their destination, a contest was in full spate, complete with fast and furious wagering. Tina. stood by like the rest of the onlookers, just another puppet on a string who applauded when the king hit a bull's-eye and laughed when he attempted a witticism. She stood patiently for an hour while Henry shot his arrows, drinking a mug of ale between every shot. He remained undefeated, and after he'd received enough applause, praise, and outrageous compliments, he decided to notice her presence.

"Ah sweeting, come walk with me while I try to put your mind at ease."

Tina curtsied low and saw his hot gaze linger on her breasts. After a full minute he raised her and retained her hand in his. "It was a case of mistaken identity all along. How fortunate it was you came to me! No doubt you have seen the gentleman in question about my sister's court?"

"Er—yes, Your Majesty. I believe he is a particular friend of Queen Margaret's," she improvised, picking up on his clue.

"Thanks to you, my lady, the gentleman is already on his way home to Scotland, which brings me to your Lord Douglas."

Tina was faint with relief. "Yes, sire?" she murmured breathlessly.

"I haven't the vaguest notion where the fellow could be,

but I'll bet he never left Scotland. I'll wager he isn't within four hundred miles of Greenwich."

I'll wager he's within four hundred yards, thought Tina, giddy with relief. She went up on tiptoe and kissed Henry joyfully.

He bent toward her intimately. "I shall find out for you where Douglas is, even if it takes all winter. Meanwhile, I shall keep you at my side, where I know you will be safe. Let's stroll through the maze, sweeting. There is a bench at the center where we may be private from prying eyes."

Tina stopped dead in her tracks. "Your Majesty," she stammered, "I have an unholy fear of l-labyrinths and c-closed up spaces due to being l-locked in a wardrobe as a child." She snatched her hand from his. "Just the thought of going in there with you has given me a flux of the bowels! Excuse me, sire." Tina literally ran from the gardens and didn't stop until she found Ada in the banqueting hall.

Tina realized she was hungry for the first time in weeks. As she helped herself to a trencher of beef and a pot of ale, she regaled Ada with the tale. "I didn't lie," she said between mouthfuls, "The king really does frighten the shit out of me!"

Suddenly Tina looked up into the eyes of a man who had been watching her. He averted his eyes so quickly, she knew he was following someone's orders. "Don't look now, Ada, but we have a watchdog. He's between us and the door. Dear God, if the servants haven't taken my things to the stables yet, they'll never be able to sneak them out."

Ada finished her ale and stood up. "We could leave separately. He can't follow both of us at once."

"No, Ada. Don't leave me alone. We'll go to my chamber. The king will be in the park for hours." She hoped the man hadn't followed her to the tower this morning to see her arrive with one man and leave with another. Nay, she would be under arrest by now if anyone knew she had committed such an act.

Tina prayed that Ram had not been followed. Then she

thought of Heath. They were not supposed to know each other, yet any moment he could be climbing in at her casement window while being followed by one of Tudor's watchdogs. Her blood slowed in her veins. Spine of God, the king indeed intended to anchor her to his side. He must have sensed she was ready to bolt. Henry Tudor was insatiable—he would devour her.

Much to their relief the luggage was gone when they went to their rooms. "I'm going to bathe and change now rather than later," Tina said decisively. "Don't call for hot water. I'll just use what's in our water jugs."

Ada emptied the jugs from both rooms into the slipper bath, and Tina sat down in two inches of tepid water. She was out again within five minutes, and Ada helped her into the lovely white gown Ram had bought her. As she fastened the emerald and diamond necklace with trembling fingers, she wished that Ramsay could see her in the beautiful things he had selected for her. Then an unendurable thought came to her: *He would see her!* She would be watching with the king while Ram masqueraded as a Gypsy!

Chapter 35

Before Tina had time to voice her worries to Ada, a knock came upon the door. The king had sent the Countess of Surrey to fetch her to the lawn where they were about to play blind man's bluff. Tina thought it a game for children until she watched the courtiers at Greenwich play their version. The game was purely and simply an excuse for the gentlemen to fondle the ladies and touch the intimate parts of their bodies as they feigned ignorance of the identity of whom they had captured.

Whichever man was blindfolded was aided and abetted by the other men, who pushed, pulled, and shoved the ladies into hands waiting to feel them. Tina's quick wits kept her out of the roaming, grasping hands of the men, but when it was the king's turn to be blindfolded, she did not stand a chance. Thomas Seymour and Charles Brandon delivered her up to Henry, who managed to caress every part of her body as he guessed each woman's name of the court save hers. She wished with all her heart she had not chosen the lovely white gown, for before he was finished with her, the King's fingerprints falsely branded her as his property.

Tonight's feast was to take place outdoors since it was the last time until next spring the climate would permit such an undertaking. Oxen, venison, lambs, and kids were turning on their spits above outdoor pits of blazing coals. Barrels of October ale, apple cider, and wine from Spain were rolled from the cellars to the courtyard, then stacked about the trestle tables that had been set up at the edge of the great park.

The bacchanalia was Henry's idea to celebrate the bountiful harvest and was a great excuse for revelry and riotous drinking. The tables were decorated with huge cornucopias overflowing with fruit, and the dining area was encircled by golden sheaves of wheat cut from the fields that very morn.

To give the festival the atmosphere of a country fair, vendors had been allowed to set up their stands in the striped pavilions to hawk roast chestnuts, hot black peas, tripe and trotters, jellied eels, cockles, mussels and winkles, treacle toffee and spotted dick, a sticky jam pudding.

The Gypsies had set up their fortune-telling booths, and by late afternoon were already doing a brisk business. A Punch and Judy show entertained the gathering crowds and Gypsy musicians strolled about, filling the air with their strange, stirring strains.

The citizens of London had gathered about Greenwich to watch the court indulge itself and marvel at the excess spread before their eyes. The river was filled with little boats and punts, and its banks were crowded with picnickers until the sun went down.

The ladies and gentlemen of the court were arrayed in their finest this evening. The men put the women in the shade with their costly clothes and jewels, and the evening was just cool enough for them to show off the latest fashion—a sleeveless, embroidered coat worn over the doublet and falling to the knee. It was a full garment that swung from the shoulders and added girth to every male figure.

Henry strolled through the park sampling all offerings of food and drink. Lady Valentina was his chosen companion for this celebration, and she forced herself to laugh and respond to his every witticism. Ada trailed after, carrying her lady's green velvet cloak, and one of the king's gentlemen performed a similar service for Henry.

Tina knew she was still being watched. She felt the tension rising until she wanted to scream. Even when he dined al fresco, the king insisted his table be raised higher than the others, and as a servant pulled out the ornately carved chair for her, Tina knew she was the center of attention, sitting high on the platform surrounded by dozens of lit torches to illuminate His Royal Highness.

As they were served one course after another, acrobats and rope dancers performed for their entertainment and the King's gentlemen were instructed to throw coins. Next came a dancing bear. It kept one wild eye on the whip of its trainer and looked to Tina as if it were only performing until an opportunity for escape presented itself. She imagined she knew exactly how it felt and was sorry it was so tightly muzzled. She would have enjoyed seeing it maul someone.

Next came two Gypsy girls with troupes of performing

dogs. Their tricks vastly amused the audience of courtiers, but this time instead of throwing coins, the gentlemen threw morsels of meat and scraps from the table. It caused pandemonium. The Gypsy girls lost control of their animals. Tricks were forgotten as the dogs snatched food from each other, snarling and biting and lashing their angry tails. The crowd was thoroughly amused as one or two serious dog fights broke out, and Henry and his gentlemen placed heavy wagers with each other on the outcome.

When enough food and drink had been consumed to feed half of England, the tables were pushed aside so the king could have an unimpeded view of the entertainment. The court roared its appreciation at the caperings of a fire-eater who chased the king's dwarf about trying to set fire to his derrière. Whenever it did manage to catch on fire, the dwarf's arse was so close to the ground, he simply rubbed his bum in the dirt to extinguish the flame.

Jugglers tossed about lit torches with dizzying speed. Live coals were spread on the ground, and a Gypsy man walked across unscathed, but got no volunteers from his audience to duplicate his act.

"These Gypsies are sly fellows," Henry told Tina. "Every last one is a charlatan. There is a trick to every performance—the fellow doesn't really put his feet into hot coals."

Tina hung on every word, assuring him that he was the cleverest man on earth.

"Here comes a bareback rider. Now this takes skill," informed Henry as a dozen white ponies cantered into the circle of tables.

Tina froze. The swarthy man who balanced on the back of the lead animal wore tight black hose with a scarlet kerchief tied about his neck. She couldn't believe it. It was Ram Douglas! How in the name of heaven had he learned to do such reckless things? His lithe body seemed to glide effortlessly to the ground, then up onto a different animal's back every time. He leaped from pony to pony as they cantered beneath his agile feet, and Tina's heart was in her throat lest he slip where he would surely be trampled beneath the painted hooves. Her attention was riveted upon him, and she saw that his dark eyes smoldered with anger as he saw her with the king.

Henry placed a possessive hand upon her knee when he saw her looking at the handsome Gypsy and said in a voice that carried, "I think the damned fellow envies me."

Tina, afraid of both men at this moment, murmured, "All men envy the king, Your Majesty."

"Come, sit on my lap. Let's really give the insolent fellow something to covet."

"Nay, Your Majesty," Tina cried, shrinking back in alarm. "Every eye is upon us."

The king chuckled. "You are a shy little thing with a passion for privacy." He bent close to whisper, "I should like to kidnap you and carry you off on my barge downriver to one of my other palaces, where we could be entirely alone."

Tina glanced fearfully at the swarthy bareback rider as he jumped through flaming hoops. The look he returned was murderous. Henry's attention, much to Tina's relief, was transferred to the Gypsy dancers, who had just entered the circle. Every man present felt a stir of desire as the scantily clad Gypsy girls swirled rhythmically, going faster and faster, stamping their feet to show off slim brown legs as their red skirts flared from their tempting bodies. They had a wildness in their blood, and any male who watched the flashing white teeth and long black hair felt the wildness enter his own blood.

Henry's hand was no longer content to paw her knees. It slipped higher and higher while at the same time he urged the small hand he held captive toward his own bulging sex. The Gypsy girls went around the perimeter of the tables, teasing the men with the beat of their tambourines, barely avoiding the outstretched hands groping to touch a thigh or a breast.

The music rose in a crescendo, then came to a dramatic halt as a bright red and black target wheel was placed down in front of the king. A hush fell over the crowd as Zara stepped forward like a human sacrifice. The king licked his lips as he watched the beautiful Gypsy girl have her wrists and ankles tied to the wheel in a spread-eagle position.

The crowd gasped as a swarthy Gypsy man stepped forward with a matched set of shiny silver knives. A cry escaped Tina's lips. The man was Ram Douglas, and she knew exactly how dangerous and reckless he could be. If he thought he could prevent war for Scotland and James Stewart by assassinating Henry Tudor, he was valiant enough to attempt it.

Henry's eyes narrowed. "What is amiss? Do you know the man?"

"Nay, Your Highness," she said, drawing her hand firmly from his loins. "I have cut my finger on one of your jewels."

"Surely it was no more than a prick, sweeting," he jested bawdily. The king leaned forward, keenly watching as the beautiful Gypsy girl began to spin on the wheel and her swarthy, brooding partner with the dangerous eyes took deadly aim.

Valentina had never been so tense in her life. Her emotions spun faster than Zara's as she watched Ram throw the silver knives. She was breathlessly afraid that Zara would be killed or maimed. Yet overriding this fear was the dread that Ram would fling a knife into the King of England. The thing that really terrified her, however, was what Ram Douglas would do to her when he got his hands on her. He had watched Henry Tudor paw and caress her body, almost making public love to her.

If only this were a nightmare from which she would awaken! She had not yet confronted the mental horror of submitting to the king when he tired of these revels and the Gypsy music fired his blood to the point where he would demand she leave with him. Tina closed her eyes, not daring to watch the spectacle before her that was exciting the crowd.

When the next-to-last knife was thrown and entered the target between the Gypsy girl's wide-open legs, just touching her mons, the audience went wild. The knife handle looked exactly like a large phallus, and Zara writhed upon the wheel as if it had been plunged deep inside her. Henry gripped the arms of the carved chair with intense excitement. His erection had hardened to such a degree, he felt almost ready to spill.

The onlookers gave a collective sigh of sadness as the Gypsy girl pretended to die, and her head fell forward just in time for the last knife to enter the target where only seconds before her head had rested.

Henry's eyes were glossy with desire, his mouth slack. As the crowd rose to its feet and cheered the performance, Tina leaned over to Henry and whispered Zara's secret into his ear. He looked at her with disbelief.

"Would you like to meet the girl, Your Majesty?" asked Tina, holding her breath.

He nodded avidly and began to stroke himself. Tina stood up and went to the edge of the platform. She avoided the murderous eyes of Black Ram Douglas and beckoned to the Gypsy girl who strutted forward immediately.

"Your Majesty, may I present Zara?"

Henry took the girl's hand, and Tina quietly faded back into the shadows.

Where is Ada? Dear God, let me escape! She slipped quickly past the pavilions and got all the way to the gardens of the palace before she realized she was being followed. Where could she go? The king had had her watched all day, so that it had been impossible to get away from him. The last place she had wanted to be tonight was in her bedchamber at Greenwich, for when the oak panel opened she would be trapped for the night with Henry Tudor. And yet now that his watchdog was on her trail, she reasoned that perhaps if he followed her to her door, he would think she intended to rendezvous with the king and leave off following her for the night.

Like a vixen being run to earth, Tina fled through the garden and into the corridors of Greenwich, hoping Ada would somehow find her. She could still hear the stealthy footsteps approaching as she opened her chamber door and stepped into the darkness. She would wait for perhaps a quarter of an hour and then she would slip away from Greenwich, away from London, away from Henry Tudor forever.

Suddenly she was grabbed from behind. She was gagged and trussed, then something like a blanket was dropped over her head, and she was picked up and carried off. She could not kick, she could not scream. Everything was so black, she could not see, and even sounds came to her muffled and indistinct.

Tina was so afraid, she could not control her trembling, but she knew she must breathe slowly and not panic, or the terrifying sensation of suffocation would overwhelm her. She presumed she would be carried up the secret staircase to the king's apartments, but she soon realized she was being carried much farther than that. When she was finally set down, she knew she was in a boat upon the river. There was no mistaking the roll of a deck or the muffled sounds of the water.

Some of Tina's fear was replaced by anger. The king's words came back to her with a rush. By kidnapping her and carrying her off to another palace, he was fulfilling some sort of sexual fantasy. He was so childish, she wanted to scream. Henry Tudor had to have his own way about everything, and there were scores of sycophants and toadies about him who would cater to his every sick whim.

Her temper was building dangerously. When she was delivered at the king's feet, she would explode and allow her temper full rein. She didn't give a damn that he was

King of England—he wasn't her king, and he had no juris-
diction over her whatsoever. To Tina he was just a man, a
gross, greedy, spoiled, and dominating male who grabbed
whatever he fancied, no matter the cost to others.

It came to her that she had been upon the river for an
inordinately long time. Finally her assailant picked her up
again as if she were a sack of grain and carried her off the
vessel. He carried her a long, long way, and then she felt
herself being handed over to another. This one slung her
over his shoulder and strode on. With her head hanging
down it was difficult to breathe, and she became quite disoriented. When she was finally laid down upon her side,
Tina's head was spinning so badly, she imagined she could
still feel the rocking motion of the boat.

Tina lay there for what seemed like hours. No one came
to release her, and she wondered wildly if she had been
carried off and secretly imprisoned. Perhaps the king had
set watchdogs on Ram and Heath as well as herself and
their plot had been discovered. Perhaps she had been
taken down the river to the Tower of London and carried
over Traitor's Bridge, through Traitor's Gate, and into the
bowels of the brooding fortalice.

Nay, she must stop her imagination from running amok.
This little caper was designed to weaken her resistance and
bring her to her knees. She would try to rest while she
could and gather her strength for the moment she would
come face to face with the lecherous, rampant Henry.

Tina must have been drowsing. Suddenly she became
aware of a man's firm grip as she felt her ankles being
untied, then her wrists behind her back were, freed and she
snatched off the blanket that had almost smothered her
and clawed the gag from her mouth. "You filthy whoreson!" she screamed, momentarily blinded by the rush of
light and her own fury. Her face registered total shock as
she stared into the pewter eyes of Black Ram Douglas. Her
own fury was as nothing compared to the fury she saw in

those accusing eyes. In that moment it would have been far easier to face Henry Tudor.

"I never want tae see that dress again," he said between his teeth, reaching out a powerful hand to tear it from neck to hem.

Tina flew at him with nails and teeth bared. "His paw prints are on the gown because I wouldn't let him put them on my body!"

Ram grabbed her and slammed her against his hard length, but her hands still tore at his hair and the black shirt he wore.

"What about you?" she cried angrily. "Zara's hands have been all over your damned body!"

Suddenly Ram's arms pressed her close, so that her face was against his heart, and he was raining kisses upon her lovely, disheveled hair. Despite her faithlessness she was still in his blood. "We are both so insane with jealousy, we can think of nothing else. I have to get us safely out of English waters—the *Revenge* won't sail herself."

Her eyes widened. "You got your ship back?"

He took his arms from her. "What is mine, I keep," he said quietly. "Ada is in the next cabin," he informed her before departing. Ram Douglas had to get away from her so that he could think clearly. If he hadn't kissed her, he might have killed her. Seeing her play king's whore had almost sent him over the edge of his control. No one would ever know how close he had come to hurling the silver knives into the hearts of Henry Tudor and the female with whom he had been handclasped.

Even greater than his fury had been his towering pride. It seemed like he had been waging a losing battle with his pride ever since he'd laid eyes on Lady Valentina Kennedy. As he stood on the quarterdeck issuing exact orders to his skeleton crew, a part of his mind relived the night he had stormed Castle Doon. He'd found her in the arms of his clan rival, Patrick Hamilton, and thereafter had set about to humble her pride, which rivaled even his own.

She'd had a reputation as a honeypot, and he remembered his feelings exactly when he suspected her of lying with James Stewart and God knew how many of his nobles. Why had he allowed the hand-fasting to be forced upon him?

He knew the answer, of course: She attracted him like no other woman ever had. She was a magnificent flame-haired vixen who wrought havoc with his senses. He remembered acutely the feeling of mauled pride he felt at the ceremony when she fainted and he'd suspected Hamilton had fathered a brat upon her.

When he discovered she was still a virgin, he had completely lost his heart and tumbled head over heels in love with her. But blood on the sheets wasn't proof positive of virginity. Nor was technical virginity a sign of innocence. She could have been sexually active for years and still cleverly maintained her hymen.

As Ram stood behind the ship's wheel with only the wind and the sea for company, the ugly black mists of suspicion fell away from him. He wasn't naive enough to think Henry Tudor would do a kindness for a beautiful female without demanding sexual favors, and he knew Tina was not that naive, either. But it was possible that she had tried to play a game of cat and mouse, promising much and giving little. He knew he would give her the benefit of the doubt. His stiff pride almost choked him, but his heart ruled when Valentina was involved, not his head.

When Tina opened the adjoining door and saw Ada safe and sound with all their baggage stacked against the wall, she burst into tears. The tension of the last few days had been too much for her nerves. The floodgates opened, and Ada was wise enough to know her tears would wash away her tension and soothe her jagged nerves.

Ada helped her out of the torn white gown and poured water so she could bathe her hands and face. "How did you get here?" Tina said. "Were you too trussed like a Christmas goose and carried off?"

"Nay," Ada said, taking a nightrail from one of the bags and shaking out its folds. "One of the Gypsies took me to a caravan where Heath was waiting. He told me he knew he would be followed from the moment the king dismissed him. He soon gave his watchdog the slip, but later in the day he realized we too were being watched, so he had a Gypsy keep a very close eye on you with instructions to abduct you if you fell into danger. 'Twas Heath who discovered where the *Revenge* was anchored. He left a message for Ram and brought me and the two Douglas servants to the ship."

"I've been tied up in that cabin for hours," Tina said, massaging her wrists.

"I had no idea you were there. I was worried sick for you. When Ram finally arrived a short time ago and you were not with him, I almost had an apoplexy."

"Thank God we are all safe!"

"We are still in jeopardy. Ram only has Heath and the two Douglas servants for crew," Ada warned.

Valentina slipped her warm sable cloak over her nightrail and went up on deck. Ram stood at the ship's wheel with his black hair whipping in the wind. He looked at her with an intensity that almost unnerved her. She faced him squarely, hiding her trepidation, and said, "I want to be with you."

After what seemed like an eternity of waiting, he nodded his permission, and she moved to his side shyly. There were things they wanted to say to each other but could not put into words. How could he possibly convey to her how crushed and heartbroken he'd been when he thought she had betrayed him for the sake of revenge? How could he put into words the bone-softening anxiety he'd felt for her when she came to the tower? His fear had been mixed with the exhilarating joy of knowing she cared so deeply about his safety that she had risked all to rescue him. How could he explain that the mere thought of her giving herself to Henry Tudor had nearly driven him berserk?

Valentina drew the furs he'd given her close about her body. How could she possibly convey to him how devastated she'd been when her own brother had betrayed him? How could she put into words that it had been all her fault for wanting revenge? How could she tell him that she couldn't endure living while he thought she had deliberately betrayed him? How could she make him understand that she would make any sacrifice to assure his safety and count it as nothing?

She watched him and knew his restless, savage spirit was as wild and free as the sea. She saw his pride, his loneliness, his courage. She saw his soul. She wanted to become part of him without reservation.

He saw her vulnerability, her generosity, her warmth. He wanted all of it and more, he wanted her love. He opened his arm to her; without a word, she stepped close and he enfolded her against his side. Her eyes filled with tears as they again caught sight of the raw scar on his neck, but she blinked them back quickly before they fell. He would consider pity an insult.

They clung to each other for over an hour. His arm had found its way beneath her fur, where he gently cupped her breast. Her arm was about his waist, her fingers tucked up inside his warm leather jack. At last he murmured against her hair, "If ye want tae make me happy, go and rest until dawn. When daylight comes there will be danger from the English fleet, and no one else aboard can take the wheel. I'll need ye then—we all will."

Tina raised her eyes to the rigging and saw the lithe figure of Heath, who was both lookout and line untangler. He gave the couple beneath him a salute. He thought them so well matched, it was uncanny.

Tina slept until a bloodred dawn broke across the pewter seas, then she and Ada spent the entire day cooking food and boiling water for hot drinks. The men came below one at a time to warm up and dry their soaked clothing at the galley stove, but Black Ram Douglas stayed behind the wheel of what once had been the *Valentina* for twenty-two hours, until it was safely in Leith.

Chapter 36

Winter had already arrived in Scotland. Fortunately it did not take them long to cover the four miles from Leith to Edinburgh Castle where Ram and Heath closeted themselves with James Stewart to make a full report of all they had learned in England. It had been a stroke of genius to use Heath Kennedy to gather information because the Gypsy people were allowed to travel freely from town to town, and men and women confided in them and told Gypsies things they wouldn't even divulge to their neighbors.

James Stewart called all his advisers and border chiefs to Edinburgh. He had the winter months to make decisions about Scotland and whether to declare war on England. The harsh Scottish winter would curtail the raids deep into the country, limiting the skirmishes to a few border forays. Each laird was free to say his piece and offer his advice, but in the end it would be the king who made the final decision.

The Scottish Bishops, led by Elphinstone and Beaton, advised against war. They strongly advocated keeping the peace, thinking that England's might in all-out war would easily subdue Scotland. Some of the clan chiefs urged James to declare war immediately; others agreed to fight England, but cautioned that they wait until spring. The majority of voices urged that James play a waiting game. If

England made war on France, it would take the pressure off Scotland. Let the vainglorious Henry Tudor spend the fortune his father had amassed on war with France, trying to conquer Guienne. Let him expend his manpower, weapons, and ships fighting with the French—then his country would be unable to mount a full-scale war against Scotland.

James Stewart was incensed. He reminded his chiefs that Scotland had signed an alliance with France promising Scotland would march into England if she made war on France. In the end, of course, King James had his way. He decided to use the winter months to recruit an army greater than Scotland had ever had before. He decided to call a justice Ayre in the Highlands of the North and attend himself, urging a call to arms from fourteen earldoms: Argyll, Atoll, Bothwell, Caithness, Cassillis, Crawford, Douglas, Erroll, Glencairn, Huntly, Lennox, Montrose, Morton, and Rothes. He told them, "I rule Scotland, not Henry Tudor, and I shall write it in letters of fire and blood across his borders if I have to!"

Bothwell fiercely supported him. "I'll burn Carlisle!" he offered boldly.

Douglas urged the king to be practical. It made sense to use the winter months to recruit and make Scotland a power with which to be reckoned, but a massive show of strength along their borders would be an effective deterrent. Douglas was totally against honoring the alliance with France.

Ram closeted himself with Angus. Heath had told Ram exactly what the queen had written in her letter to her brother Henry, and Ram decided to confront Archibald Douglas with the information rather than divulge it to King James.

Angus waved a dismissive hand. "I dinna ken what yer on about, laddie."

"Angus, ye crafty old swine, ye know exactly what I'm on about. Margaret hinted the Tudors might soon be related to Douglas. A nod's as good as a wink tae a blind horse, man! When ye read between the lines it means there will be a war between England and Scotland, and if James Stewart is killed as a result, Margaret will wed yer son and be Regent of Scotland."

Angus eyed his favorite nephew and thought for the thousandth time what a pity he wouldn't inherit the earldom. He would make ten times the regent young Archie would make. Angus sighed. "Ramsay, ye know the Scots would rather fight than eat. We are every last one of us cursed with pride of blood. If ye face it squarely, ye know war with England is inevitable. James Stewart will be on the front battle lines. He's a soldier to his bones. He'll be in the front vanguard. I cannot aid his survival, no more than I can guarantee victory for Scotland. My first duty and allegiance is not tae Scotland, nor tae the House o' Stewart. My first duty is tae Clan Douglas. War has a way of plucking the flowers and leaving the nettles tae flourish. Henry Tudor's sister already sits on the throne of Scotland. If Tudor wins the war, I want Douglas power at the helm of the ship of state."

Ramsay almost choked on his anger but thought long and hard on Angus's words. He was not advocating any sort of betrayal. The whole clan would support the king and fight in the vanguard alongside James. The Bleeding Heart of Douglas would be represented by larger numbers than any other clan, but if Scotland went down in defeat, clan Douglas would be there to pick up the pieces as it had for centuries.

Valentina had seen next to nothing of Ram since the king called the council of war. She mixed very little with the women of the court. Occasionally she rode out with Janet Kennedy, and when she could not avoid an invitation from Queen Margaret and her ladies, she took supper with them. But just the sight of Henry Tudor's sister sickened her. The family resemblance was too marked for Tina to be

comfortable in her presence. She preferred the company of
Ada. They sewed new garments for Ramsay, embroidered
shifts and nightrails for Tina, and both of them worked on
a new wardrobe for Ada. Tina took as much pleasure in
the clothes as Ada, and when Angus took her hawking a
couple of times and insisted Ada come along, Tina teased
her woman about the great conquest she had made.

November was half over before Ramsay and Valentina
found themselves with time enough to share an evening
together. They dined alone in their small chamber at Edinburgh Castle. There was no fireplace for them to sit before,
and the chill, inhospitable chamber made them long for
Douglas. It might be dubbed Castle Dangerous, but it was
warm and inviting, even luxurious compared with this pile
of cold gray stone. The bed loomed large before them as
Ram pushed away his plate and emptied the wine bottle
into her goblet. "If this bottle could produce a genie who
would grant me only one wish, it wouldn't be for eternal
life, nor the riches of Croesus." He came behind her, put
his hands upon her shoulders, and dipped his head to
touch his lips to her ear.

Her hand lifted to caress his cheek, and she murmured
seductively, "I know exactly what you would wish for—I
desire the very same thing."

They were in a playful mood, intent upon teasing each
other. His hands slipped over her shoulders, down to her
lovely breasts, as he whispered hoarsely, "Just the thought
of what I want makes my mouth go dry with longing."

"Mine too," she said, threading her fingers through his
midnight black hair. "I want it so badly, I can taste it," she
whispered outrageously.

Ram swung her into his arms. "I am a slave tae my sinful
longings. I'll tell ye what I want if ye'll do the same."

They looked solemnly into each other's eyes and spoke
in unison. "Mr. Burque's *chocolat* truffles!" they said, unable to keep their laughter dammed up any longer. He

swung her about the room until finally they fell laughing to the bed. Their faces became intense.

"I'm starved for ye, sweetheart," he told her, undressing her with infinitely tender hands. When the last of their garments had been banished to the floor, she came up from the bed onto her knees. Ram did the same. They clung and pressed together until they touched from thigh to breastbone, their mouths fused together as if no power on earth could ever separate them again. Their thick eyelashes brushed together, and he held her as if she were part of his own flesh. It was more than an hour later that the fierce clinging and kissing slowed long enough for them to lie down together.

Ram knew the entire winter would consist of one separation after another while he scoured the country for recruits, but tonight belonged to them, and they would savor each other to the full, unhurried as it should be between lovers who had been made for each other.

They had no need for a fire; this bleak winter night, they made their own heat. He had hungered to be buried deep inside her for so long, his shaft probed between her lips of its own accord, and a violent shudder went through him when he found her swollen with need. When the entire hard length of him was within her scalding sheath, he held it still until they could feel each other pulsing, then slowly he raised his head and kissed her temples, brow, eyelids, and the corners of her mouth until his tongue could not be denied. It too plunged within the scalding intimate haven and pulsed and throbbed as violently above as he did below. They savored each other for another hour this way, postponing the inevitable cataclysm that would separate them. When the convulsive climax came, however, it was deeply and completely satisfying to both of them as he filled her with his life.

She lay enfolded in his powerful arms for the rest of the night.

"I'll take ye home tae Douglas if ye can bear the sight of

the place again. I have tae go west and north, and I swear
I'll come tae ye for the night whenever I find myself within
fifty miles."

"Home to me is wherever you are. If you can't come to
me, I'll come to you. I'd follow you to the ends of the
earth." Both knew their love was such that the angels
might envy.

Ram set an easy pace on the ride from Edinburgh, so
consequently the journey of forty miles took up most of the
day. It wasn't long enough for Ram and Tina, however.
They enjoyed every minute of the cold ride through the
majestic southern uplands. The colors of the season were
vastly different than at any other time of year. The sere
branches of winter reached hauntingly against the loden-
colored hills and pewter sky.

They glimpsed red deer through the bare trees and
watched hawks and other raptors circling the skies in
search of prey. When they stopped to water their horses on
the banks of the Clyde, they walked off alone from their
attendants so they could embrace and enjoy a few stolen
kisses where the air was as heady as sweet wine. Though
they had ridden stirrup to stirrup all the way, it was no
longer close enough to satisfy them. When they resumed
their journey, Ram took her up before him in the saddle.

The warm fragrance of her skin and hair mixed with the
scent of horse and leather acted as a potent aphrodisiac, so
that by the time they reached the castle at Douglas, Ram
was incapable of doing anything save carry her to his bed.

Damaris and Alexander stood at the top of the staircase
hand in hand. It had been so long that Valentina and Ram
had spent the night under the same roof with them, they
had despaired of their ever returning.

After sixteen long years Alexander had managed to
make Damaris listen to his story of what had happened on
that fateful night that culminated in tragedy. Damaris believed him with all her heart and soul. She had never really

stopped loving him—she had only been so deeply hurt at the thought that he could poison her, that she had built a carapace about herself that none could penetrate. Now they were as close in death as they had ever been in life.

Alexander had shown her the evil shadow that still lurked at Castle Dangerous, and they had committed themselves to preserving the lives of Ramsay and Valentina, to give their very tenuous love a chance to grow and flourish. They both felt that their deaths would not be in vain if Ram and Tina loved, married, and produced the children that they had been cruelly denied. Together, their power for good would overcome the power of evil that festered at the core of Castle Dangerous.

The spirits were not the only ones overjoyed to see the safe return of Black Ram Douglas. His own moss-troopers as well as Angus's men-at-arms had known of his arrest and had gathered at Douglas hoping he would be able to escape his enemies and return, though none of them had actually believed he could accomplish such a feat.

Ram's wolfhound, the Boozer, rolled in a paroxysm of happiness in the center of the great bed, forcing Ram to cool his ardor until he and his lady had patted and stroked and allowed him to wash their faces with his great rough tongue. So while the lovers lay abed whispering and touching and mating, plans were laid for a great feast. Mr. Burque planned the food, while Colin arranged for the pipers and issued an invitation to every household in the town of Douglas.

It was as if Christmas had come early this year. The spirit lovers were euphoric that Ram and Tina were so wrapped up in each other. No longer were they like two scorpions, circling, waiting for the opportunity to sting. Alex and Damaris had a surprise of their own and plotted and planned a way for Valentina to find Mad Malcolm's lap desk, which contained the history of Clan Douglas with all its ugly secrets. It was the key to revealing the truth about their own tragedy and preventing another.

Ram and Tina arose very late the next morning. When they came downstairs, they saw how everything had been hung with holly, ivy, and mistletoe. In front of everyone Ram put the mistletoe to good use, and Tina blushed at the hoots and whistles of the moss-troopers. He cocked a black brow and warned, "Don't even think of trying this with my woman."

It was one of the happiest days of their lives. When they visited the stables, they saw that the lovely Barbary mare, Indigo, was visibly swollen with a colt. They indulged in a mock argument over who would own it and what its name would be. They even argued over the gestation period for a horse. Tina thought it was over a year, but Ram informed her it was eleven months.

In the afternoon it began to snow, and the company was so merry, they rushed outside like children to frolic and scoop it up by the handful to taste and toss at each other. Tina worried that if Ram and his men rode out at dawn as they planned, they would freeze or be caught in a terrible snowstorm. But Ram only hugged her to him and laughed. "How can I ever be cold again with ye tae warm my heart?"

The meal was perfect. Mr. Burque had even allowed the other cooks to prepare the traditional haggis. What went into it was a fiercely kept secret, and Mr. Burque held his fastidious nose as they carried the obscenity to Ramsay for his approval.

The villagers were all crowded into the hall, jostling one another for a glimpse of their lord and his lady and the magnificent haggis. All went well until Mr. Burque became alarmed that Tina was actually going to consume some of it. He shook his head desperately and went as far as to snatch the pronged fork from her fingers. He rolled his eyes and warned, " 'Tis all ears and arseholes!" Those who heard him fell down howling, and Tina laughed so hard the tears ran down her cheeks.

Ram said, "Man, yer a rare treasure. Not only do ye

cook better than any chef in Scotland, ye provide the entertainment while we dine."

"And he's so easy on the eyes," added Tina with a wink.

Before the reels got too wild and while there was still a semblance of order, Colin presented Ramsay with the promised portrait of Valentina. It took his breath away. It was so lifelike, he could almost smell the heather and burn his fingers on her flaming mass of hair.

Tina knew a terrible moment of misgiving. Where had Colin concealed the naked portrait he had painted? When Ram was safely away, she decided to confront Colin about the whole thing. The other painting must be destroyed before Ram accidentally laid eyes on it.

By dark, the serious fun was under way, but any man who didn't have a hard head for drink knew better than to imbibe too heavily. Black Ram Douglas would depart at sunup, and any man in his service unfit to ride would not be tolerated.

Ram lured Tina from the hall early. They went up onto the parapets to view the surrounding countryside, now covered in its pristine blanket of snow. The music and laughter from the hall were muted up here in the frosty night air, and Tina caught her breath at the beauty of the moon above the upland mountains.

She enjoyed every moment of Ram's seduction as he lured her back to their chamber and pulled the heavy fur cover of the bed in front of the blazing fire. "We only have till dawn," he murmured, drawing her down to him. She knew she was falling more deeply in love every day. She enjoyed being courted and wooed and longed for him to ask her to marry him. Ram smiled a secret smile and knew he was wearing down her resistance. He enjoyed the wooing as much as she did.

He whispered, "Each time I come home, I'm going tae ask if ye love me and if ye'll wed me, until the answer comes back a resounding yes!"

She brushed his face with her lips. "Court me just a little

while longer. I enjoy it excessively." She pushed him back against the furs and trailed her hot mouth down his muscled chest and across his taut belly. Ram groaned with deep pleasure as the curtain of her glorious hair bathed his loins and hid the intimate things her lips did to him.

Damaris was slightly frustrated. She had been present when Mad Malcolm had asked Jenna to give the laptop desk to Lady Kennedy. Damaris was aware of the secret compartment that held the Douglas history, though Jenna was in ignorance. Because of Malcolm's death and because Tina had been so very ill, Jenna had put the desk away for safekeeping and obviously forgotten about it.

Damaris stood behind the Douglas maid and whispered into her ear. She urged her over and over to give the little desk to Tina. It took an hour of persistence, but eventually Jenna recalled the small antique desk she had set aside in her wardrobe for Lady Kennedy. She knew that Lord Douglas had retired for the night and that Valentina would not be about until the next day. She pondered on what she should do and finally decided to take the desk to Lady Kennedy's woman, Ada, who promised to give it to Tina first thing in the morning.

Damaris's sigh of relief was so great, it made the candles flicker beside Ada's bed. Ada shivered and drew the heavy curtains tight across her window to keep out the drafts. Damaris wanted Tina to read the pages while Ramsay was still at the castle to protect her. The danger must be effectively removed before Tina was left alone and vulnerable. Damaris looked for Alex to remind him to keep a vigil regarding Ram's leavetaking at dawn. She shook her head with tolerant amusement when she found him watching Mr. Burque make love to a plump and ripe Douglas wife, whose husband lay snoring beneath the very table upon which they sported.

"For shame," Damaris chided. "I thought you were above such spying."

"I'm no' spying, I'm receiving an education," Alex said in awed tones of admiration at Mr. Burque's inventiveness.

Ram Douglas was up long before the cold, gray light of dawn filtered into their chamber. He had no intention of waking Tina. He wanted no tears at his leavetaking—he wanted only to carry the intimate memories of the night with him to warm his blood on the freezing trek into the Highlands. He regretted that he had seen neither of his brothers but wrote a letter to each advising them to paint out the name of *Revenge* on their vessels as a precaution against being taken by England's new admiral, Thomas Howard.

His men had already broken their fast and were lining up in the courtyard, eager for the gallop that would see them in Stirling before the hour of noon. Letters in hand, he looked for Colin. He wasn't in the dining hall, so Ram ran upstairs to Colin's chamber. The door was not locked, though Colin was nowhere to be seen, so Ram propped the letters on his mantelpiece. As he turned, a painting on an easel riveted his attention. Tina lay nude amongst the wildflowers beside a loch where he had once made love to her. It was apparent he was not the only one who had done so. The feral look upon her face made her look like a vixen in heat. The howl that burst from Ram's throat was that of a wounded animal.

The spirit of Alexander flew into the chamber, and he cursed at himself for allowing Ramsay to see the erotic portrait. " 'Tis a lie, a filthy lie!" he cried, but Ram burst past him like the angel of death.

Damaris was frantically trying to send Ada into Tina's chamber with the hidden papers before Ram departed. Suddenly she heard the heavy door to the master bed chamber crash back upon its hinges. She flew to Tina's side in a panic, just in time to see her roused from sleep.

Black Ram Douglas towered over her garbed in leather and chain mail. His knuckles clenched his knife hilt so tightly, they were bloodless. "Strumpet!" he thundered, almost blinded by fury. He unsheathed his knife and slashed savagely at the woman in his bed.

Chapter 37

Damaris moved so quickly, the draft caused the bedcurtain to blow protectively across Tina's naked figure. Ram snatched his knife from the tangled curtain and cursed the Kennedy bitch. He slammed his knife back into its sheath. "Ye deserve each other!" he flung before he quit the room.

Damaris saw Alexander. "What happened?" she cried.

"He saw the nude portrait," Alex explained.

"Don't let him leave! Don't let him leave her here with Colin!"

Alexander flew after Ramsay, while Damaris stayed with Tina.

Ada came into the room carrying the laptop desk. "What on earth has happened?" she asked, taking a sobbing Tina into her arms.

"The painting! He must have seen the nude painting. He nearly went mad!"

Ada locked the door. She was aware of the Douglas temper. He was not called Hotspur merely because of his riding skills.

Alex materialized through the locked door. "He's gone. I couldn't stop him."

"Dear God, Alex, sometimes a tragic event is stamped so indelibly upon a place, it is doomed to happen over and over again. She's already been poisoned, as I was. Colin painted both of us, and now Ram has seen it as you did. Murder will be done again if we don't do something!" Damaris cried.

"I'll go after him and bring him back!" swore Alex.

"I don't think you can leave this place," Damaris whispered hopelessly.

"Yes, I can, if I bond with a living being. I can go where he goes."

"Be careful, Alex," Damaris cried.

"Sweetheart, nothing can happen tae me that hasn't happened already."

Tina wiped away her tears and reached for her bedgown. "Oh Ada, everything is such a tangled mess." Tina threw back her long hair impatiently. "Only last night he told me he loved me and asked me to marry him. Now thanks to that twisted, sick Colin Douglas, everything is spoiled! I could kill him!"

"Calm down, love. The damage has been done, but once Ram is gone, we have all the time in the world to confront Colin and get possession of the painting. Lock this door after me. I'm going to go to the kitchens and get you some breakfast, and I think I'll ask Mr. Burque to help us. We should have the protection of a man when we challenge Colin."

"That's a splendid idea, Ada. Oh, that's the desk I gave poor old Malcolm."

"Yes, Jenna brought it to me last night. She said Malcolm made her promise she would give it back to you."

Ada went to the kitchen, and Tina carefully locked the door behind her, then she went back to the antique desk. She opened the drawer and touched the carving that opened the secret compartment. There lay Malcolm's history. How poignant it was to touch the pages he had written! He had been so obsessive about the history, it had filled the endless hours of his days and made them bearable for him. Somehow Tina felt absolutely compelled to read what he had committed to paper.

Tina's brows drew together in puzzlement. She thought his history would deal with Douglas ancestors, perhaps starting with the first earl, but if he had written of the early times, those pages were not in the desk. In fact, there weren't many pages at all, certainly fewer than a dozen, and Tina's attention became riveted as she realized it told the story of what had happened sixteen years ago, the night Damaris had been poisoned.

The spirit of Damaris stood at Tina's shoulder so they could read the pages together. The writing was lucid, organized, and far clearer than Malcolm had ever been when Tina had spoken with him. As she read the pages she realized that Malcolm had not been bedridden sixteen years ago when the tragedy occurred.

It was so unusual for the newlyweds to exchange angry words that I made myself scarce so they could argue in private. Before the afternoon was over however, their raised voices could not be ignored, and the reason for Lord Alexander's fury was revealed. Colin had been painting a portrait of Lady Damaris, and when it was finished we all admired his great skill, but apparently Alex discovered that Colin had also sketched her naked. In a fit of jealousy, Alex accused her of faithlessness. Colin was nowhere about to answer the accusations, so Damaris had to face Lord Douglas's temper, which was infamous.

I recall that the afternoon closed in quickly, and dark came early. Lady Damaris took wine and was immediately poisoned. Alexander forgot his jealousy immediately. She was in so much agony he was distraught. Even in those days I was called Mad Malcolm because I was somewhat reclusive and often got drunk, and marched to a different drummer than other men. Alex accused me of poisoning the wine and refused to let me help him with Lady Damaris.

She died so quickly, there was nothing I could have

done in any case, but she died with the accusation of
"Poisoner!" upon her lips, totally convinced that her
husband had murdered her.

Alexander was like a madman. He waited for Colin's
return with a black heart, thinking he had seduced his
beautiful wife who now lay dead. When Colin learned
Damaris was dead, he went berserk. The two men drew
their swords and flung terrible accusations at each other.
Colin told Alex the poison had been meant for him, not
Damaris. Colin thought he was heir to the title of Lord
Douglas. Alex flung at his younger brother the secret he
had kept for years: Colin was a bastard and the title of
Lord Douglas would pass to his cousin Ramsay in the
event of Alexander's death. Alex and Colin were so intent upon killing each other, there was nothing I could
do to prevent bloodshed. I took a jug of whisky and
locked myself in my tower room. I had consumed most
of it when I saw them out on the parapets.

Alexander was the superior swordsman, who slashed
Colin so fiercely, I believed him doomed. I saw Colin
wounded several times and knew he would be cut to
ribbons. I must have passed out. The next day Lord Alexander's body was discovered in the courtyard, and his
wife lay poisoned in her bedchamber.

The Earl of Angus descended upon Castle Dangerous,
as well as the Kennedys, thirsting for revenge. Somebody
said Colin was off fighting in the king's Highland cam-
paign, and I feared I would be the prime suspect for
murder. I locked myself away and drank. The naked
painting of Lady Damaris was discovered, and it was
concluded that Alexander had poisoned her in a jealous
rage, then committed suicide by diving from the parapets.

Coward that I was, I was so relieved that I was not
charged with the double murder, I kept my mouth shut.
When Colin returned home a week later, crippled with
his war wounds, I was the only one who knew that Alex-

ander's sword had maimed him for life. He kept me well
supplied with whisky, and for more than a year I stayed
drunk day and night. Later, whenever I tried to bring up
the night of the tragedy, people nodded knowingly and
called me Mad Malcolm.

I reasoned that things could have been worse. At least
Colin did not inherit the title. Ramsay became Lord
Douglas, and the role fit him like a glove. The chief of
the clan, Archibald Douglas, Earl of Angus, was well
pleased with Ramsay, who was born with the qualities
necessary for leadership. So in the end, the evil one did
not benefit from his crime. Colin carried his twisted
body every day of his life as a reminder and was doubly
punished because no woman would ever look at him.

I would probably have kept my lips sealed forever if it
had not been for the arrival of another beautiful Lady
Kennedy. I knew Colin lusted for her, and I knew he was
evil enough to poison Ram so he could have Ram's
woman. I decided to break my long silence by committing it to paper. Since my legs went, I fear for my own
life, but now I also fear for Ram and for the beautiful
Kennedy lass who has been so kind to me.

Malcolm Douglas

"Dear God, it was Colin who killed Malcolm by poisoning the wine. I drank some by mistake." Why, oh why
hadn't she discovered these pages before Ram left? Tina
unlocked her chamber door and went down to the kitchens
to tell Ada and Mr. Burque what she had just learned.
Damaris did not want her to leave her room but was helpless to prevent her. All she could do was stay beside her.

Valentina found Ada and Mr. Burque leaving the kitchens. She quickly told them both what Malcolm had revealed. "Colin is a dangerous man—we cannot confront
him unarmed," she added.

Mr. Burque agreed with her. He took down a sword
from the stone wall of the hall. He was not a trained

swordsman, but he was well muscled and agile, and he had all the courage necessary to protect Valentina. He sent Ada to the knights' quarters for any men-at-arms Ram Douglas had left behind. Without hesitation, he moved toward the castle stairs. At that moment they saw Colin Douglas poised at the top of the staircase. The looks on their faces immediately alerted him to danger.

"I didn't mean tae poison Damaris. I loved her!" Colin cried.

Tina looked up at him, her face ashen. "You murdered Alexander, you murdered Malcolm to silence him, and by putting poison in the wine you murdered my baby!" She was so incensed at all the pain and suffering he had caused to both the Kennedy and Douglas clans that she rushed up the stairs ready to attack him with her bare hands, unmindful of any danger to herself.

He drew his knife with his left hand and grabbed her. His lips were drawn back from his teeth, his face as contorted as his body. "If I couldn't have ye, I wasn't going tae let that arrogant swine Hotspur have ye! He already snatched my title from me!"

Black Ram Douglas rode at the head of his moss-troopers on their way to Stirling. The pace he set was punishing, but his men-at-arms knew better than to protest when their leader was in one of his murderous moods.

Some of the blinding, bloodred mist had cleared from his brain in the bitter cold air, but as his temper cooled, an icy hand gripped his heart. The ghostly specter of Alexander Douglas rode pillion with him.

"Turn back, turn back, man! Valentina is in danger!" urged Alex.

Ram's face was grim and closed. He could not rid his mind of the erotic portrait.

"Colin poisoned Damaris and Malcolm and lusts for Tina. She is in terrible danger from him," insisted Alex.

As Ramsay's mind searched desperately for a reason, a

small niggling doubt intruded. How could his beautiful vixen give herself to Colin? Ram knew him well—knew he was ugly on the inside as well as the outside. He'd suspected him of keeping Mad Malcolm well oiled with whisky all these years, and when Malcolm was found dead, Ram had been suspicious. He had been too concerned with Tina's recovery at the time to investigate, but he had known better than to leave her unprotected at Castle Dangerous.

Alexander was alarmed at the distance widening between them and Douglas.

"Turn back, Ram! If ye love her, go home!"

The Douglas men-at-arms stared at their leader in amazement as he suddenly drew rein and pulled to a halt. The great black destrier Ruffian pivoted on its hindlegs and pawed the air as he turned the animal. He waved his arm and called out their destination. "Douglas!"

If they thought the pace was punishing on the ride out, the ride back was brutal. Though they tried valiantly, none could match his speed and determination. None could keep pace, and one by one they fell behind.

"By the power of God," Ram cursed softly, "I know she loves me and would not do such a thing."

Mr. Burque stared up the staircase with dread in his heart. Tina was always so headstrong, yet so courageous, she was ever unmindful of danger. Colin had his arm about her throat and looked insane enough to plunge his knife into her heart.

Mr. Burque stood indecisively, holding his breath, wondering if he dared rush up the stairs in an attempt to disarm or wound the desperate swine. Suddenly the Boozer spotted Damaris's cat. Folly spat at the dog and flew up the stairs. The Boozer rushed after it with frenzied anticipation. The animal charged into Colin, unmindful of anything but the pleasurable pursuit of the feline.

Colin immediately lost his balance and, because of his crippled leg, could not regain it.

Tina fell to her hands and knees on the steps. Colin pitched down the staircase and impaled himself upon the sword Mr. Burque brandished. The horrific tableau was witnessed by Ada and two burly Douglas men-at-arms who had been left behind to guard the castle.

Mr. Burque was white to the gills and visibly shaking. The men thumped him on the back, praising his skill and his courage in saving the lady and dispatching the evil that was Colin Douglas. He had been like a hidden viper in a nest, and Mr. Burque had single-handedly rid Black Ram Douglas of a formidable enemy. The Douglas guards had a new, healthy opinion of the handsome French chef.

The men told Ada to take their lady away before they took care of the gory business of removing the sword from the disemboweled body. Tina walked on unsteady legs to the hall, where Ada sat her down before the blazing fire. She sat gazing into the flames as if she were in a trance. In reality she was reliving the events that had led up to the tragedy of Damaris and Alexander Douglas. The present dissolved into the past, and she lost track of time.

Her thoughts came tumbling back to the present as a powerful dark figure strode into the hall. The swarthy Scot who came toward her was a formidable sight in leathers, chain mail, and iron helm. Tina arose from the settle, a hand at her throat as she saw the fierce pewter eyes. She took a step toward him, her hand going out in supplication. "Ram."

Tina's limp body slipped unconscious to the floor. He swept her up into his arms and lifted her against his heart. When Tina opened her eyes, she was in the wide bed with an anxious Ram Douglas sitting beside her. He had captured both her hands between his, and when he saw her open her golden eyes, he raised those hands to his lips and kissed them reverently. He had removed the helmet, and his black hair was wildly disheveled from running a distraught hand through it. He poured her some whisky, tasted it first, then said, "Drink this." He brushed back the flaming tendrils from her brow. "Can ye forgive me once again for my suspicions?" he asked humbly.

"Why did you come back?" she asked, hoping for a certain answer.

"I sensed ye were in jeopardy. When my jealousy stopped blinding me, I knew ye could never be unfaithful wi' a miserable excuse for a man like Colin."

"Did they tell you everything that happened?" she asked.

"Aye. May I read for myself what Malcolm wrote?"

Tina handed him the pages so that he could read the fantastic account of what had taken place sixteen years ago. When Ram finished, he kissed her brow. "Thank God history wasn't allowed to repeat itself. God's passion, no wonder their spirits still walk this castle."

"Perhaps now that the truth has come out, they will be able to rest peacefully."

"I'm going tae destroy the paintings and sketches he did of Damaris, as well as the ones he did of you. I can only guess at his unclean practices behind the closed door of his chamber."

"He's the third Douglas to die," Tina whispered. "After Malcolm and the baby, I feared it would be you when you were taken prisoner."

He enfolded her tightly in his arms. "And I feared it would be ye, especially when ye took the poison from my own hand." His voice broke. He paused, then forced out the words, "How can ye ever trust me again, my little vixen?"

Tina looked into his stormy gray eyes and the corners of her lips lifted in irony. "Ram, it is you who must learn to trust." She slipped from the bed and stood before him.

"What are ye doing?" he demanded.

"I'm not lying in bed all day. Let me help you off with your mail."

"I forget I'm wearing the damned ugly stuff." He stood and lifted it off himself.

"I'm sorry to keep you from the king's business—nay, I'm not sorry at all! I'm so glad that you are here to comfort and protect me today. I always feel safe when you are by me."

Ram reached out a hand to touch her fiery curls. "Tae hell wi' the king's business. Douglas business comes first—always has, always will. But ye are so right. I've never learned tae trust anyone. Not the queen nor even the king. I wouldn't trust Angus as far as I could throw him. Only look how David and Colin betrayed us, and they share our blood. I've gone through life trusting only myself. I tell ye I love ye, and yet my actions prove I don't trust ye." He shook his head at the riddle.

Tina went to stand at his side and leaned her head into his shoulder. "Ram, I think we love each other, but we haven't learned to like each other yet. We became lovers without first becoming friends. The basis for any friendship has to be trust."

They curled up in the big chair together and talked for hours. They had never known this kind of closeness before, not even in their most intimate moments. One by one the barriers came down between them as they shared their fears and emotions, as well as their hopes, feelings, and ideas. They had started to do this once before, but circumstances had intervened and driven them apart. This time Valentina was determined that nothing would ever interfere with their personal lives again. She vowed never to oppose him again. She would stand with him against family, against king and country, against the Devil himself. From this moment on, they would be one mind, one heart, one soul. She would be Black Ram Douglas's woman and damned proud of it.

Ram stayed two more days so he could be certain she didn't suffer any ill effects from the shock she had received. The only time they left their chamber was to take an occasional walk by moonlight in the crisp snow. He would wrap her in one of her soft furs, and handclasped they would wander out, sometimes as far as the frozen river. They stopped once at the place beneath a copper beech where Damaris and Alexander were buried.

"I used tae think she was restless because her grave was next to Alexander's, but now I think it right that they are together. If ye agree, I'll get the bishop tae consecrate the ground—or do ye think we should move him tae Castle Douglas tae lie with his ancestors?"

"I think they should stay together through eternity," whispered Tina, brushing away a tear.

They hurried back to their chamber, where a roaring fire and sinfully sensuous dishes prepared by Mr. Burque awaited them. When Ram finally departed it was the hardest thing he'd ever done in his life. As he kissed her goodbye he whispered, "Will ye marry me?"

She clung to him whispering, "Mmm, perhaps. Ask me when you return, you devil—not when you're departing."

Chapter 38

Ramsay Douglas gave his all when he recruited for the king. He traveled farther and faster than any of James Stewart's lieutenants, obtaining signed bonds pledging men-at-arms from every branch of Clans Douglas, Kennedy, Campbell, Drummond, Erskine, and Graham. He kept his pledge to Valentina to return for the night whenever he was within fifty miles of Douglas, but still they saw each other only once in every six weeks. The long, forced absences made their brief reunions so much sweeter, and they longed for a time when they would be allowed to live a life together, unclouded by the demands of impending war with England.

Slowly but surely, over the winter months and into the spring, James Stewart gathered his forces for war. It was a large undertaking to amass an army greater than Scotland had ever had before. Manpower was not all that was needed. Horses to carry the cavalry, oxen to pull supply wagons, and the mounted, heavy iron cannon were needed by the hundred. Thousands of weapons would be needed to wage war—not only the usual swords, knives, and lances, but spears for the spearmen, arrows for the hagbuts and harquebuses, baggage wagons, oxcarts, and weapon sleds.

Ram's job was one of communication. Basically, he traveled back and forth tallying numbers. Argyll was already Governor General of the Army, and Arran, Lord High Admiral of the Navy. The king decided to keep Bothwell's hot-headed Hepburns as a reserve unit. The rest of the borderers would be united under the command of Lord Home, with the exception of Clan Douglas. Since there were so many branches of Douglas, not all of them borderers, they would be commanded by Lord Ramsay since the Earl of Angus was now past his fighting prime. The Earl of Huntly was to command the Gordon Highlanders, while the king and his good friend the Earl of Crawford would command the Scottish center made up of their clans, Stewart and Lindsay. The Earl of Lennox was put in charge of all Highlanders other than Campbells and Gordons.

Since Stirling was the strongest fortress in Scotland, the king used it to call together all his chiefs who had mustered their clans to swear the oath of fealty. A total of fifteen earls, five bishops, and a score of lords and chiefs gathered to give James Stewart the oath. Each noble placed his hands between the king's and swore into his service their lives, their goods, and the lives and goods of their clan and liegemen.

Beautiful spring weather returned to Scotland, and with it came a reprieve. Henry Tudor sailed his army across the Channel preparatory to making war on France. In Scotland, a joyous relief pervaded every county. City and country dwellers alike wanted to push thoughts of war from the forefront of their minds and celebrate the lovely short summer.

A few shrewd and astute nobles knew war with England had only been postponed. King James Stewart, the Earl of Angus, and Ramsay Douglas in particular knew of Henry Tudor's naked ambition. He would use any method—conquest, assassination, intrigue, or bribery—to gain control of Scotland. The English nobility, like their king, were power-hungry, waiting like jackals to swallow the kingdom.

Ram left Edinburgh Castle with his usual complement of forty moss-troopers. They made it to Douglas in just over two hours. The guard on the walls had alerted Tina of the Black Ram's return, and she ran up to their chamber and out upon the parapet walk, waving a silken Douglas banner so that he would see her from a great distance. By the time he reached the bailey, she was running down the outside pentice staircase.

Ram vaulted from Ruffian's back and caught her in his arms, anxious for the clinging to begin. He kissed her over and over. "My honeypot, how I've missed ye."

She was vividly radiant. The setting sun turned her flaming curls to molten red-gold. In his arms her golden eyes turned to smoky amber, and he knew himself the luckiest man alive. Tina was weak with the nearness of him. She did not see the sweat and dust of the hard ride—all she saw was the dark Scot, towering above her with his magnificent weatherbeaten face. His body was as hard as rough-hewn granite.

"I love you, Ram," she said breathlessly.

He swung her about, then set her feet to the ground and bent her backward, kissing her as she'd never been kissed before. "Ye'll marry me, vixen—I'm yer destiny!"

Tina's eyes sparkled with love and pride. She woul⟨ never tame him. It was so typical that he told her she'd we⟨ him, rather than ask, but she was so far gone in love, sh⟨ could deny him no longer.

Ram held her in one strong arm, and before his dark hardened men-at-arms he called to Jock, "Fetch the prie⟨ from St. Bride's church—and hurry." The deafening Doug las war cry echoed off the castle walls, and the Boozer loping over the drawbridge from his daily hunt in th⟨ woods, launched himself at the embracing couple wh⟨ meant more to him than any other humans on earth.

Ram and his men stabled their mounts. They all pre ferred to care for their own animals rather than leave then to the grooms. Tina stayed at Ram's side while he unsad dled Ruffian and gave him a rubdown. Before they left th⟨ stable, they went along to look at Indigo.

Tina gasped when she saw her beautiful mare was lyin⟨ in her straw. Ram spoke to the head stableman to learn i⟨ aught was amiss with the prized mare, but he reported n⟨ problems before today. Ram went on his knees in the stra⟨ and ran his hands over Indigo's sleek, satin belly. "I thin⟨ she's near her time. It feels like she'll foal soon."

When Tina stroked her neck and spoke soft words t⟨ her, the mare responded and managed to get on her fee⟨ A frown marred Ram's brow. She was such a finely bre⟨ Barbary, she might easily have trouble birthing a colt sire⟨ by Ruffian. He kept his fears to himself, but told the groon to watch her closely and call him if she showed signs o⟨ going into labor.

They emerged from the stables into the courtyard whe⟨ Jock returned with the Douglas priest.

"Marry us where we stand before the vixen changes he⟨ mind," directed Hotspur. His energy was barely containe⟨ and she saw the muscle flex in his jaw and wondered if he'⟨ be able to stand still long enough for the priest to say th⟨ words over them.

Every man and woman in the castle came out into th⟨

bailey to witness the joining of Lord Douglas and his woman. Valentina pretended outrage. "Aren't you even going to bathe first, you barbarian?"

He leered down at her, feeling the surge of his own pulse. "We'll do that together. It will be your first duty as Lady Douglas." He clamped her to his side as the priest raised his voice.

"We are gathered together in the sight o' God and in the face o' this congregation to join together this mon an' this woman in holy matrimony, which holy estate Christ adorned and beautified wi' his presence, an' therefore is no' by any tae be enterprised, nor taken in hand, unadvisedly, lightly or wantonly; but reverently, discreetly, advisedly, soberly, and in the fear o' God. I require an' charge ye both, as ye will answer at the dreadful day o' judgment, when the secrets of all hearts shall be disclosed, that if either o' ye know any impediment why ye may no' be lawfully joined together in matrimony, ye do now confess it. Wilt thou have this woman tae thy wedded wife? Wilt thou love her, comfort her, honor, and keep her, in sickness an' in health; and forsaking all other, keep thee only untae her, so long as ye both shall live?"

"I will," Ram Douglas pledged solemnly.

"Wilt thou have this mon tae thy wedded husband? Wilt thou obey him and serve him, love, honor, and keep him, in sickness and in health; and forsaking all other, keep thee only untae him, so long as ye both shall live?"

"I will," Tina Kennedy said clearly.

"Who giveth this woman tae be married tae this mon?"

A long silence followed the question and none stepped forward. Finally Mr. Burque decided to take the honors upon himself, to the accompaniment of a great cheer.

"I, Ramsay Neal Douglas, take thee Valentina tae my wedded wife, tae have and tae hold from this day forward, for better for worse, for richer for poorer, in sickness and in health, tae love and tae cherish till death us do part, and hereto I plight thee my troth."

Tina's eyes widened as he produced a wedding ring from the recesses of his leather jack. "With this ring I thee wed, with my body I thee honor, and with all my worldly goods I thee endow."

Tina repeated the vows. The priest declared them wed. "It is my pleasure to gi' ye the new Lady Douglas," he said.

The rough borderers had been waiting for this moment. They picked up both bride and groom and carried them laughing into the castle hall with cries of "A bedding! A bedding!"

Ram managed to extract himself from his moss-troopers. He stood on the dais and held up his arms. "No way! I'm the one who'll do the bedding. Break out the casks, and enjoy yerselves!" The men protested when the couple tried to leave, but Ram told them firmly, "I have tae fulfill my vow. Did I no' promise tae honor her wi' my body?"

When Valentina heard his outrageous promise, she picked up her skirts and ran. He gave her no quarter, pursuing her ruthlessly until she lay imprisoned beneath his powerful body in the center of their huge bed.

Damaris and Alexander had watched Ramsay's homecoming reception with delight. They both agreed that these two vital people had been made for each other. They were almost dizzy at the speed with which the marriage ceremony had been performed, but they also had a feeling that this was right, this was meant to be. The clans of Kennedy and Douglas were at last joined in a blood-bond that would produce magnificent sons and daughters.

Damaris's hand lay in Alexander's. "This is a perfect ending to the story of Tina and Ram, yet it isn't the end, it's just the beginning."

Alex squeezed her hand. "It's the end of our story, my love. We should be moving on."

"Oh, Alex, we cannot leave them alone. War is threatening, and what about when Tina tries to carry another child?"

"Sweetheart, we can't live their lives for them. I too want tae stay until I know the outcome o' thc war, but our time here is over. This is their time, no' ours."

"Alex, I'm afraid," Damaris said.

"I'll be wi' ye, lass. We'll go together."

His eyes glittered with wicked amusement. "Ye trust me, dinna ye?"

Damaris flushed. She hadn't trusted him for sixteen years, then she had learned that her love had not been misplaced after all. Trust was what love was all about. She reached up on tiptoe to brush her lips against his. "I trust you, husband. I cannot trust you with my life, but I can trust you with my soul."

"Come up tae the parapets wi' me," Alex urged.

Damaris searched his face. Neither of them had ever ventured out upon the parapet walk since that fateful night so long ago.

"There's nothing tae fear, beloved. Trust me."

Silently the wraiths ascended to the castle ramparts. "It doesn't seem very inviting, this other world," Damaris said with trepidation. "Will it be Heaven or Hell?"

"Perhaps neither, but it is the final test of our faith and our love for each other," Alex assured her.

"You are so valiant, so brave. What must I do?" He could hear the faint tremor in her voice.

"Simply step off the edge into the void of infinity, or remain behind without me forever."

"Oh no!" she cried, and ran from him back into Castle Dangerous.

Alexander's heart contracted. He had fully believed she loved him enough to join him in the long journey. Why had he not been able to convince her? He knew without a shadow of a doubt that the sixteen-year delay could not be prolonged. Alex was filled with a sadness greater than he had ever experienced. How many more years would Damaris be condemned before she realized she had no choice but to move forward? It was the final truth each one

of us must acknowledge—we must go forward. It was so
unbelievably cold up on the ramparts all alone, but Alex
knew he must go without her.

Suddenly he saw her floating toward him with her beloved cat in her arms. She laughed up into his dark face. "I
couldn't go without Folly!"

Alexander's heart soared. He took her hand and hoped
they would be together throughout eternity.

Ram was naked, Tina wore a silken nightgown. They
knelt upon the wide bed, molded together from lips to
hips. "Tell me again that ye love me," he demanded. "It
took ye far too long tae admit it."

"I love and adore you, you devil-eyed Douglas!" Tina
hugged to herself the knowledge that she was again carrying his child. She would keep the secret awhile longer. She
was dizzy with relief that he had insisted upon marrying
her before she'd told him of the child. This way she was
secure in the knowledge that he loved her and wanted her
for his own and not just for the heir she would give him.

A low knock came upon the chamber door, and with an
oath he flung it wide, indifferent to his naked state. A
stableboy stood with Ada, his face beet red. He opened his
mouth, but no words came out.

Ada said, "Indigo has gone into labor."

"I'll be right down," Ram said to the stableboy.

"You mean *we* will be right down," Tina asserted, slip-
ping a fur cloak over her nightdress.

Ram threw on chausses, but didn't bother with a shirt.
They hurried out to the huge stables, the Boozer close
upon their heels. The mare was extremely restless and
voiced her apprehension with a plaintive whicker. Ram
again ran his hands over the animal.

"Barbarys are very highly strung and nervous. The colt
hasn't shifted down much yet. I think we're in for a long
night, wife."

Tina soothed the mare by talking to her quietly. Their

presence seemed to have an immediate effect as the horse quieted. Ram made them a bed in the next stall with fragrant hay, and they lay close together with her fur over them to wait out the vigil. The Boozer lay at their feet with his nose upon his great silver paws.

"I never expected tae spend my wedding night playing midwife," he said, enfolding one strong arm about her.

"You are doing this for me because you know how much I care for her. I think that is very gallant and also very romantic." Her fingers threaded through the thick curls on his chest, loving the feel of him and the smell of him. In the fragrant hay he was intoxicating! Ram's lips brushed her temple. "The truth is I'm no' gallant at all tae wed ye just before I go tae war. I'm selfish!"

"But surely the threat of war is diminished now England is fighting France?"

He was silent for a few minutes, then murmured, "I know better. Jamie Stewart will fight."

"I hear a note of regret in your voice," she said softly.

"I think it's ill advised. I've always believed in force. I believe in swift and terrible retaliation for any assault by an enemy, but I believe this time we should remain in Scotland and concentrate upon making our borders invincible. James has done right tae muster the clans and gather this great army, but I believe the show of power is all that's necessary."

"You think he'll take the army into England?" she asked with disbelief.

He didn't answer her question. Instead he said, "I could kick myself for wasting so much time wi' you. There are so many places I want tae take ye, so many things I want tae show ye."

She snuggled close. "Tell me, tell me about every one of them."

"I'd like tae take ye north wi' me when I go for the wild horses. It's primeval in the forests of the Highlands, as if time began there. It has an otherworldly quality about it—

silent, majestic, shrouded in mist. The animals are so wild and free, it breaks your heart tae separate them.

"We could spend a year traveling about Douglas strongholds. I want ye tae see Tantallon. It's something special. It's all pink sandstone spires on a cliff overlooking the sea. Even more spectacular than Tantallon is Dunbar Castle. The fortress is erected atop stacks of naked rock, rising in columns from the sea, all linked together by bridgelike covered corridors of masonry. 'Tis the most curious thing ye've ever seen."

"It sounds intimidating," she ventured.

"Only tae an enemy," he assured her. "I'd love tae take ye tae the Isle of May out in the Firth of Forth. 'Tis fearsome in winter, but on a summer's day the North Sea slaps against the sheer, serrated cliffs, and ye feel like a god at the top of the world. 'Tis uninhabited by man, and thousands of puffins and kittiwakes swirl about yer head, totally unafraid. In the spring there's hundreds of gray seal pups born there. The rock pools in the crevices can be an inch deep or twelve feet. The king often uses it as a retreat. You'd like it. It's almost a mystical, spiritual experience."

They came up from their bed of fragrant hay together as Indigo screamed. Tina went to her head. "Easy, easy, m beautiful girl," she soothed. Ram felt the position of the foal. "It has moved right down. She's presenting a leg."

Tina could see his brows creased with worry. "Is tha bad?"

"Just one hind leg isn't good," he said low, taking i firmly into his hands and pressing it back inside the mare. Indigo's eyes rolled wildly, then she began to pant and sheen of sweat covered her purple coat.

Tina took a warm Douglas plaid to cover her, while Ram filled a leather bucket so she could have a drink. Ram eased the mare's pain by massaging her belly with long firm strokes. He kept it up for most of an hour, then finally Indigo went down in the straw, unable to stand on he quivering legs any longer.

"Ram, do something," Tina begged. "If it's too big to come, put her out of her misery."

"Nay, Vixen, we won't give up that quick." He laid a length of rope across his knees, then gently eased a hand inside the swollen mare. After what seemed like hours, Ram finally gave a satisfied grunt and Tina saw his hand emerge holding two tiny hooves. With infinite patience he tried over and over to loop the rope about the small back legs and tighten it without doing irreparable damage. Tina marveled how such large, callused hands could perform the delicate maneuvers required to gain a firm hold on the elusive, slippery colt.

She talked to the mare ceaselessly, stroking her velvet nose, and craning her neck to watch Ram perform a miracle. He was a naturally strong man, but it took every ounce of that strength to bring forth Indigo's foal. He struggled for another full hour, then finally with a great whoosh the offspring came into the world, encased inside a great membrane. Ram acted quickly to free the foal's nose and mouth so it could breathe, and Indigo was up on her legs, nuzzling her baby before Ram could remove the rope. He cleaned the little creature with handfuls of straw, and they watched with fascinated delight as it tried to stand up on its long, wobbly legs. "It's a male!" Ram shouted triumphantly.

"Oh, he's beautiful!" cried Tina. "What will we call him?"

"How about Hazard?" Ram asked with a laugh.

Tina sat back in the hay to watch the dam and her foal, while Ram washed in the horse trough and dried himself with a Douglas tartan. Valentina's face was radiant as she lifted it to look up at Ram. "That was a spiritual experience."

"Rubbish—it was bloody hard work!" he exclaimed. A wicked light came into his dark face as he eyed her appreciatively in the hay. "I'll give ye a spiritual experience!" He dived into the hay, sending a million dust motes into the

air. Before she had been thoroughly kissed, a stranger ap
peared to stand looking down at them as they cavorted.

"Lord Douglas?" he asked almost hesitantly.

"Aye," came the impatient reply.

"I've a message from the king, my lord."

Ram sighed and slowly got to his feet. His embarrassed
bride tried to sink into the shadows. Ram held out his hand
for the message and admonished with a stern face, "Don'
let on tae Lady Douglas I was rolling in the hay wi' a
comely wench."

"Nay, Lord Douglas," the messenger assured him.

"I suppose it's morning. Go tae the hall and break ye
fast. I'll join ye after I've bathed and dressed."

Tina giggled all the way to their chamber, but when Ram
read the message recalling him immediately to Edinburgh
she sobered quickly. She sent Ada scurrying for the ser
vants to fetch bathwater and laid out Ram's new velve
doublet and hose.

He stripped off his chausses and stepped into the water
"Sweetheart, I'm so sorry. We've been cheated out of ou
wedding night." He held out his hand to her, and sh
placed hers in his.

"Must you go today?" she asked wistfully.

"Come in wi' me," he coaxed. She slipped off the sil
nightrail and stepped into the water. As he reached up t
draw her down to him, a breathless moan broke low in he
throat, and she became caught in the web of passion h
wove. Ram sat in the water with his knees bent, and Tin
lay between his legs, her lovely round breasts crushe
against the solid wall of his chest. She shivered delicately a
the mastery of his touch. His sexual energy cried out fo
release as his mouth moved over her wet, satin skin, arous
ing her until nothing mattered in the whole world save hi
magnificent body beneath hers. She couldn't get enough o
him. She pressed her face into his flesh until his heartbea
was beneath her ear. Her tongue came out to delicatel
trace and tease his diamond-hard masculine nipples. Sh

wanted to be irrevocably a part of him, lie with him forever, endlessly yielding while he endlessly took. She thought her heart would burst with love for him.

Her ripe body between his thighs almost scalded his loins. He set his hands to her tiny waist and lifted her. "Wrap yer legs around me, slowly," he instructed. Carefully she straddled his lap, impaling herself upon his rampant, pulsing shaft. At first his movements were deliciously slow and fluid, initiating the primitive play of male and female. Then he began to teach her his power, stroking deep, honoring her with his magnificent body. She received him fully, joyously, yielding herself body and soul. Their mouths so close were in a perfect position to kiss and lick and suck. Their needs were so great they almost savaged each other.

Then he slowed his thrusts to a powerful, undulating rhythm, and her golden eyes flew open to stare into his pewter depths as they rode the rising crest of passion, then hurtled down into a molten sea of flame. They clung together, not wanting to separate, for each knew the separation would be endless. Ram had not disclosed the contents of the king's message other than call him back to Edinburgh. There was no need. She knew.

"Take me with you," she begged.

"Ye know I cannot," he said as he dressed with care. "If ye'll stay up here, I'll come back tae kiss ye good-bye. Don't dress—I want ye naked."

She nodded, unable to speak for the lump in her throat. She knew he hated tears and forced herself to blink them back. She knew it would take the men some time. Each had a war chest with armor and weapons, each had a warhorse with protective armor. Baggage wagons with supplies and fodder, packhorses and oxen teams with their harness and sleds must all be readied before the cavalcade from Douglas could ride out.

A fear gripped her that he wouldn't come back upstairs as he had promised. Perhaps he had decided this way was easier, but finally she heard his firm step at the chamber door, and she flew into his arms. She caught sight of his badge, the Bleeding Heart of Douglas, and was almost undone. She felt a foreshadowing, as if she were giving him up to Death. In that moment, it all seemed so clear, so inevitable. She choked back a sob as he put her from him.

"Good-bye, Lady Douglas. Be brave, my little vixen."

Tina flung her sable fur over her nakedness and ran after him. She could not keep up with his long strides. He did not turn back to look at her. She ran from the castle out into the bailey where all seemed organized confusion. He did not turn to her until he had one hand on the pommel of Ruffian's saddle, then he snatched her into his arms. She opened her fur to offer herself naked and a low, savage cry was torn from his throat as he crushed her against his chain mail.

The Boozer stood with ears erect beside Ruffian. This time he was determined to accompany Ram. As Lord Douglas vaulted into the saddle and turned to wave, Tina had to fall upon his wolfhound and clasp him about the neck to prevent him from following his master.

Chapter 39

Muster the army!

James Stewart sent out the order to every clan in Scotland. They were told to gather at the Burgh muir of Edinburgh, a moor above the city that was the traditional mustering place for Scotland's armies.

Every nook and cranny of Edinburgh Castle was packed with the king's earls, bishops, and lords, each chief deter mined to voice his opinion and not be overruled by a rival clan. Rumor was rife over what had prompted James to finally decide upon all-out war with England.

The bishops reported that the pope had threatened to excommunicate James Stewart if he broke his solemn treaties with England. The king was incensed and sent back an immediate protest that England had already broken the treaties and that Henry Tudor was slaying, capturing, and imprisoning his subjects. James was enraged when the protest went unanswered. Bishop Elphinstone urged caution and prudence, but James and his earls could not swallow the insult.

Another envoy arrived in Edinburgh bringing an appeal for help from Louis XII of France. Henry Tudor had taken an army to Flanders in an attempt to conquer and regain Guienne, which had once belonged to England. The Auld Alliance between Scotland and France promised that either country would stage an invasion if the other were menaced.

As the clans began to gather above Edinburgh, James Stewart's confidence soared. A thousand banners and standards fluttered bravely in the summer breeze. The sunlight blazed down upon the steel of a score of thousands of fighting men. James knew it was the largest and most glorious army a king of Scotland had ever led, or was likely to ever lead again.

England and Scotland's navies had been virtually at war all summer. England's admiral, Thomas Howard, had a fleet of a thousand sailors, and it was taking a full-scale effort for Scotland's admiral, the Earl of Arran, to keep them out to sea. Sea battles raged from St. Abb's Head to the mouth of the Firth of Tay. Arran's navy was now a sizable one. He commanded not only the king's warships—the *Margaret,* the *Lion,* and the *Great Michael*—but also the converted merchant ships from every ruling clan.

Ram Douglas envied his brother Gavin and his cousins, Ian and Drummond, who captained Douglas vessels and were keeping the English fleet out beyond the Isle of May, well out of the estuary of the Forth, where Scotland's capital was situated.

Ramsay had been chosen to lead the Douglas men-at-arms, since Angus was considered too old for battle, and in truth Ram would have been supremely insulted had it not been so. Both Angus and Ram knew their clan would obey orders from none other.

The ranks swelled every day as more and more clansmen obeyed their chief's call to arms. The Earl of Huntly brought his Gordons, Argyll his Campbells, Lennox his Stewarts, and Bothwell his Hepburns.

James Stewart inspected his growing army each day and consulted with his earls, lords, bishops, and advisers each evening in the great hall of Edinburgh Castle. Tonight Ram could sense something in the very air. Tempers had been building to flashpoint, and it would take an iron hand and an iron will to keep the chiefs in check much longer. When James Stewart stood and held up his hands for silence, an odd hush fell upon that whole assembly. "I have had an appeal from the Queen of France. Henry Tudor has churlishly dismissed an ultimatum to leave Thérouanne in Flanders. England and France are at war! The French queen has named me her champion and has invited me to step one pace into England, to strike one blow for her."

A deafening cheer rose up and rolled about the hall like a great wave. Ram Douglas felt the hair stand up on the nape of his neck. He was alarmed because Heath Kennedy had ridden in with news of an English Army twenty thousand strong, gathered at Newcastle.

The Earls of Atholl, Morton, and Crawford stood and urged the king to march into England immediately. This was followed by another uproarious outburst, confirming the chiefs were ready to depart on the morrow if James would but give the order. He asked Argyll for a tally of guns, cannon, weapon sleds, ox carts, and baggage wagons. Argyll consulted with Glencairn and Montrose and reported an excess of fifty thousand pieces in the baggage train. Next, he asked how long it would take an army of this size to march to England. Lord Home, who was familiar with the border country between Edinburgh and England, estimated it would take five days.

James was accustomed to taking the advice of Angus in matters of paramount importance. He urged him now to stand and give his blessing. Archibald Douglas's harsh voice rose. "Lord Ramsay Douglas commands our clan in this war. He wishes tae voice wise words o' caution. I ask ye tae listen tae him."

As Ram got to his feet, none cheered him. Throats were cleared, feet shuffled, and the eyes that looked up at him were almost hostile. Clearly this gathering was in no mood for caution. Ram's deep voice carried around the hall. "I've had reports today an army equal tae the size of ours is gathered at Newcastle." Voices drowned him out. They would not believe such a thing possible when they had been told Henry Tudor and his army were fighting in France. Ram's voice rose again. "This army is led by a man who was at our court until last year—Lord Howard, Earl of Surrey." The babble of voices again made it impossible for him to be heard. James Stewart stood beside Ram Douglas and held up his hands until the crowd quieted. "My spies tell me this is true. Let Douglas speak," admonished the king. "I would hear his advice."

Ram's eyes were black tonight, his face grim. "It will take us five days to reach the border. I think we should align our army on this side of the Tweed. We should keep Scotland's army in Scotland. We should challenge England tae take one step intae Scotland. When they see our force matches theirs, I dinna think they will take that step!"

Shouting and cursing drowned him out. Some agreed, but more disagreed, until fighting broke out in the great hall. Loud shouts of "coward" could not be borne by Ram Douglas. His voice thundered out, "I challenge any and all tae personal combat! I'm no' afraid tae mount a raid intae

England! I'll lead my Douglases and put Carlisle and New-castle tae the torch. But I still say Scotland's main army should remain on Scottish soil!"

Angus studied James Stewart's face, and he knew this was not what he wanted to hear. The king was impetuous, eager to show off his reckless courage. Angus held his tongue. The king wanted to go to war with England. So be it.

James Stewart held up the turquoise ring that the Queen of France had sent·to him. He grinned. "Louis has sent us twenty thousand French pikes. Let's put them tae good use!"

That night as James Stewart lay abed watching the fireshine play over Janet Kennedy's hair as she disrobed for him, he had a premonition that he might never love her again. "Jan, sweeting, this is our last night together."

An icy hand clutched her heart, but as she walked to the bed, she gave him her most brilliant smile. The last thing a man wanted from a woman was tears. She saw that he had removed his iron belt of remorse to please her and wished fervently he would not wear it when he rode into battle. She knew he would not be merely a spectator, and it would hamper him. She did not mention it, however, for she knew what his answer would be.

Janet had gilded the tips of her breasts, and as James toyed with them, their color reminded him of something he must say. "Jan, you'll find gold in the bottom drawer of my desk. Take it all in the morning. It will serve you better than pretty jewels."

She kissed him to stop his words, but he lifted his mouth from hers until he had said what he must. "Keep our son safe, Janet. Explain to him that he is the son of a king and the brother of a king, but that·he must never try to become a king."

"My love, I will bring him up to serve James V after you are gone, but we will have years together yet."

He gathered a handful of her flaming hair and brought it to his lips. "Thank Angus for lending ye to me for a little while," he said outrageously, and she threw back her head to laugh up at him. She saw the turquoise ring upon his little finger from the Queen of France and knew he could never resist an appeal from a woman. Then they loved each other as if it were for the last time.

The very next day James Stewart and his chiefs joined their men camped on the vast Burgh-muir, and on the last day of August the Scots army was on the march. It was a magnificent show of strength. Its orderly ranks clad in their brave plaids stretched out well over two miles.

The weather was glorious, and on the fifth day of the march, as predicted, they crossed the River Tweed into England. The standard bearers led the way, carrying Scotland's flag, the Red Tressured Lion on Gold. James Stewart rode at the head of his cavalry magnificently clad in red, black, and gold, telling the whole world that here indeed was the King of Scots. Each clan had its own pipers.

James had scouts out to keep him informed of the progress of the English Army and to choose the most advantageous high ground in the Cheviot Hills, where the Scots could make their stand. The spot they chose was high above the Till Valley, where three hills formed a formidable, natural fortress southwest of Norham.

Moneylaws Hill was at the center, Branxton Hill to the left, and Flodden Hill and Edge were on the right. James Stewart had outmaneuvered the Earl of Surrey to set his army upon these hills, and on that early September morning Scotland's position was unassailable.

Ram commanded over four hundred Douglas. Fewer than a hundred were mounted. Only his and Angus's mosstroopers were trained to the sword. The rest gathered from the far-flung Douglas territories were spearmen, as were the majority of soldiers. All Scots carried knives and dirks, and some were proficient with hagbuts, and others were

trained to man the artillery and cannon that could deci-
mate an enemy when used effectively.

Ram knew he need not wet-nurse his moss-troopers before the battle. Jock, his first lieutenant, was so well
trained, he could handle the men without Ram's direction.
So he concentrated his attention on the Douglas spearmen. He ordered them to don their iron helmets and never
remove them. He forbade them to use the seven-foot
French pikes with which they were unfamiliar and ordered
them to stick with their short spears and knives.

When the Earl of Surrey sent his herald under protection of a red cross to James, he challenged him to fight two
days hence on open ground below the hills. Ram Douglas
was happy with the king's reply. The Scots would fight
where they stood, not on ground an English earl had chosen.

Douglas and Bothwell came up with an idea of fortifica-
tion, and since it was their suggestion, they were the ones
chosen to implement it. They fortified the east escarpment
of Flodden Edge with sharpened timber stakes thrusting
outward at an angle that would rip the belly from a cavalry
horse if it tried to jump the trench.

The next day English battle lines were drawn on the
eastern bank of the River Till. Surrey saw that all the
marshy ground was covered by the Scots artillery, and
when they would not come down to fight, he wisely abandoned his position. He retired his army to the north and
reformed below Branxton Hill.

Douglas and Bothwell urged the king to fall upon the
English as they retreated across the River Till. They knew
they could defeat an army in retreat as it crossed a river
with only one bridge, but James refused to give the order
to leave the high ground.

When dawn arrived the following day, it brought rain.
Under cover of the thick smoke when the Scots burnt their
camp refuse, James moved his army from the crest of Flodden to the ridge of Branxton Hill, four hundred yards

above the English. Bothwell and Douglas again urged the
king to order a charge while the windy rainstorm blew the
smoke down the slope, hiding the Scots from the English.
The coarse wet grass, streams, and bog where Surrey's men
were forming their battle lines resulted in hours of confusion, but the king delayed giving an order until the day was
almost spent and the sun began to set. By this time, the
English had their artillery and cannons in place.

James Stewart finally gave Scotland's master gunner an
order to fire his artillery. The Scots guns could not be de-
pressed enough downhill to do damage, but Surrey's can-
noneers worked their pieces with deadly skill, killing Scotland's master gunner and a good number of the waiting
spearmen.

James Stewart should have withdrawn his divisions out
of range to the far side of the ridge and waited for the
breathless English to reach the top, but he could no longer
control his anger and impatience. With foolhardy and reckless courage, he led his magnificent army down through the
rain and the smoke. James led one central column, and the
Earl of Crawford led the other. The center advanced
steadily with lowered spears, but it soon became a wild
slide of barefoot men on a slope of wet grass.

Ram Douglas and his men made up the left flank with
Lord Home and the Earl of Huntly's Gordons. As James
moved his column down the center, the borderers were
away against the nearest English. Surrey's third son, Edmund Howard, was leading a division of Cheshire men.
Ram Douglas broke them, and they were slashed to pieces
by the swords of the border moss-troopers.

Amid the clash of steel, battle cries, and screaming
horses, Ram Douglas astride Ruffian came face to face
with Davie Kennedy, who was fighting under the banner of
Archibald, Earl of Cassillis. The youngest Kennedy had
disappeared from Doon after he had betrayed Ram Douglas. He had hidden out from Angus's men and from his
father's, fearing he would swing for what he had done.

When war was declared, he had come slinking home, begging for a chance to vindicate himself by fighting with his clan for his king and for Scotland. Davie Kennedy knew that a man could cover himself with glory in battle, and he imagined he could be such a man.

His father and his brothers cast him out and refused to speak to him ever again, but the chief of the clan said they would need every Kennedy.

A look of stark terror came over Davie's face as the dark pewter eyes of Douglas blazed into his. Clearly he expected the man he had betrayed to dispatch him to Hell with his dripping broadsword.

Ram Douglas felt sick to his soul over the lack of decisive leadership. Discipline was the thing that won battles, in his opinion, and neither James Stewart nor the men he was leading to their destruction showed the slightest scrap of discipline. Ram snatched up Davie Kennedy's bridle in a bloody hand. The betrayal was not foremost in his mind. All he saw to his great horror was the extreme youth of the boy. Surely he could not be any more than fourteen. He brandished his sword. "Flee! Flee this damned place, Davie lad!"

The boy turned his half-maddened horse and obeyed both Douglas and his own instincts. Ram Douglas's borderers, along with Bothwell's had vanquished the Cheshire men and now raced toward the English camp.

Lord Dacre, in charge of fifteen hundred horsemen spurred forward to join battle with the borderers. Davie Kennedy in full retreat easily recognized Lord Dacre whom he had known all his life. Fate must surely have been smiling on him this day. His enemy Douglas bade him flee and the only man who stood in his path was a friend. As David cried out with relief, a sudden look of surprise altered all the features of his young face. Dacre wielded his swordarm with deadly accuracy. Before he thundered past Davie Kennedy, he had sliced him open from throat to heart.

Dacre's cavalry and the Scots borderers were well matched in a fiercely fought battle using swords, spears, and lances. The Earls of Lennox and the gnarled Argyll were engrossed watching the fighting below their ridge, when the clansmen were suddenly surprised by disciplined English bowmen bringing up the rearguard, led by Sir Edward Stanley. The rain of English arrows decimated the Stewarts and the Campbells, leaving Lennox and Argyll among their bloody dead.

The center of the field was becoming a slaughterhouse. The English footsoldiers were armed with a bill—a short shaft of oak topped with an ax blade and a curving hook. The Scots who carried the seven-foot-long French pikes were unbalanced as they advanced downhill. The Scots who stuck with their own familiar spears were no better off, for the English soldier simply lopped off the head of the Scots spears and killed their defenseless owners.

When Sir Edward Stanley's bowmen finished off the Highlanders, they came down the ridge behind the Scots. Surrey and Stanley now had the core of James Stewart's glorious army surrounded. They gave them no quarter. One by one each commander died with his men. The Earls of Crawford, Erroll, and Montrose lay dead in the field.

James rode deep into the English Division with one target in mind. He knew that in a sword fight with Surrey, he would emerge the victor. He would have succeeded, but by the time he came face to face with the hated Lord Howard, the king's body was riddled with arrows, and his head had been severed by an English bill.

Ramsay Douglas, as part of the left flank of the Scots army, fought on valiantly. They were holding their own, but they suspected the other divisions were not faring as well. Mercifully they had no idea that James Stewart, King of Scots, lay dead on Flodden Field, along with twelve earls, two bishops, fifteen lords, and nearly ten thousand brave followers.

It was almost dark. Ram saw only the man in front of

him. It was Jock, his first lieutenant, and he was in trouble. Ram swung his broadsword with an arm that was numb with fatigue. He dispatched two of the English to hellfire, wounded another, and let out a satisfied Douglas war cry as he saw Jock's horse stumble away. He swung Ruffian about on his hindquarters, and his eyes widened in shocked surprise. Where had all these Englishmen sprung from? Suddenly he was alone in a sea of English. It seemed to Ram that he and his destrier received their wounds at the same moment. As he took the steel, Ruffian went down beneath him. Ram struggled to arise, but it was impossible. A lance had pierced him through the belly and pinned him to the earth. He could neither feel nor move his legs, and yet he was aware of a great heaviness, as if Ruffian were lying on him. Ram Douglas was inured to pain, and he kept his mind tightly closed upon it, but there was a warm, comforting feeling seeping over him that he almost welcomed. So this was death, then. He sighed once, then everything went black. His warm blood and Ruffian's mingled as it seeped into the earth beneath their bodies.

Chapter 40

Lady Valentina Douglas found that she could settle to nothing. She felt like a prisoner in her own castle. If only she had been born a man! They had the easier role in life, riding off to glorious battle. Ram Douglas would cover himself with honors on the field of valor; then, when he rode home to her, he would be insufferable.

Tina caught back a sob and fled out upon the parapet

walk. She pressed the back of her hand to her mouth to prevent the sob from escaping, for she knew if she uttered one, a hundred, a thousand, or perhaps a million would follow it. When he rode home to her, *when he rode home to her . . .*

A whole month had dragged past since that day at the beginning of August when he had wed her and ridden off to war. There was nothing glorious about war, she finally admitted. It was hideous, it was obscene, it was madness. She dashed the tears from her eyes and searched the hills endlessly as she had done morning, noon, and evening since Ram had departed.

Tina had never been one to admit fear. When its specter had raised its ugly head, she had denied it vehemently, laughed in its face, and miraculously the fear had always receded. Up until now. This time she had allowed fear to gain a stranglehold upon her, and she knew that any minute she would lose control.

Her hands began to tremble as they cupped her abdomen. It was their special miracle that she had conceived another child so quickly. Would Fate cheat her once again? She hadn't told him of the baby, and now Ram might die without ever learning of the child. She cursed herself for not telling him. The knowledge would somehow have protected him, given him reason to live at all costs and return home to her—to them.

Something inside her exploded, and she knew if she stayed cooped up one more day, she would go insane. "Ada, Ada!" She picked up her skirts and ran to find her. "I'm going to court. News will reach Edinburgh long before it comes to Douglas."

"Do you think that wise?" Ada asked doubtfully, knowing a dutiful wife's place was at home until her lord returned to her.

"Wise?" questioned Tina. "When the hell did I ever do a thing because it was wise? Pack our things immediately— we'll leave at sunup. I will not wait longer!" Suddenly

Tina's knees turned to water, and she sagged down onto a stool. "Ada, the truth is I cannot wait longer. Disaster is in the very air I breathe. I cannot shake off this feeling of impending doom."

"I doubt if any of the men will desert their posts and disobey Ram's orders to escort you to Edinburgh."

"Mr. Burque! We will take Mr. Burque. You pack, I'll ask him now."

When Mr. Burque saw her and heard the hysterical note in her voice, he understood completely that she could no longer remain passively waiting. He realized she might not be taking the right action, but for Tina in this state, any action at all was better than none.

"Rider approaching!" came the cry from the gate. Tina forgot what she was saying to Mr. Burque. Her feet flew over the flagstones, through the studded castle door, and out into the courtyard. She raced across the drawbridge, then went rigid where she stood as Heath thundered up to the portcullis, dismounted, and swept a protective arm about her.

"All is lost. Our army went down in defeat, Tina. The king is dead. Every earl who fought with him is dead. There are mountains of dead lying on Flodden Field!"

"No!" Tina snarled.

"Yes, love. The Scots went down in defeat, I'm sorry to say. It was total annihilation." He smoothed back her wild red tresses with a gentle hand.

"No! Don't touch me!" she screamed.

He swung her into strong arms and carried her toward the castle. "Angus is less than an hour behind me. I met up with him at dawn. He's devastated."

Heath carried Tina into the hall. "Whisky," he ordered the first servant he saw. He propped her on the wooden settle and held the raw liquor to her lips just as Ada arrived on the scene. Tina knocked the whisky to the floor, her golden eyes blazing with anger. She tried to struggle to her feet, but Heath held her down with one strong arm. He repeated what he knew to Ada: "I came straight from the battlefield. The Gypsies made camp at Kelso, not ten miles from Flodden. Archibald Kennedy, Earl of Cassillis, is dead. I don't know about our father, Tina."

"No! Let me go!" she cried.

"Tina, where are you going?" Heath asked wearily.

"Hush lass, hush," he soothed. "There hasn't been time to identify all yet, but the list is already long. The king is confirmed, and Crawford. So is Argyll, Lennox, Montrose, and even Bothwell." His voice cracked. "Early reports say a hundred Kennedys—two hundred Douglas."

"No!" Tina eluded him and stood defiantly, hands dug into her hips, tossing her disheveled hair back over her shoulders. "The king may very well be dead, and Lennox and Montrose and Cassillis and Crawford, and even Bothwell and Argyll, but Black Ram Douglas is not dead, so do not repeat your foul lies to me!"

Ada was white and shaking. She exchanged meaningful glances with Heath. Both of them knew Tina was about to give them more trouble than she'd ever dished out in her life. "Are you packed and ready? We will leave today rather than tomorrow."

Ada again looked at Heath. "We were leaving for Edinburgh tomorrow. Perhaps it would be best if she joined the court."

Tina looked at Ada as if she had lost her reason. "I'm not going to court now, you fool, I'm going to England, to Flodden."

"Stop it, Tina!" Heath said severely. "You cannot go there. The carnage is unbelievable. 'Tis like a massive slaughterhouse of bodies and body parts."

"You don't understand," Tina said fiercely. "Ram and I were married before he left at the beginning of August. I'm Lady Douglas. I must find my husband."

Heath was heartsore for his beloved young sister. "Tina, I will go and search for his body. If I am lucky enough to find him, I'll bring him home to you."

"Thank you, Heath, but that won't be necessary. I am going myself."

Heath was alarmed. He knew what Tina was like when she got something fixed in her head. He knew he would have to physically restrain her and was contemplating getting her drunk when Angus and his small Douglas escort clattered into the bailey.

Heath said to Ada, "I hope you have an adequate supply of whisky on hand. It's the first thing Angus will call for."

Ada sent a servant to fetch a barrel, and as Archibald Douglas entered the hall, the first word out of his mouth was "Whisky!" Angus flung off his gauntlets and sank wearily into a chair.

Tina came to him and laid her hand upon his shoulder. It seemed to her he had aged a dozen years since the last time she had spoken with him. "I'm so sorry, Angus, that the king is dead."

He lifted his eyes to hers, thinking her the bravest lass alive to be comforting him when she needed comfort herself. "I feel the loss o' Ramsay far more keenly than I do the loss o' the king," he admitted.

"Ram isn't dead, Angus. We were wed before he left. I'm going to find him and bring him home."

Angus searched her face, then his eyes sought Heath's. Heath gave a helpless shrug.

"There is no need fer that, Valentina. My men will find him. We are on our way now tae gather our dead, as is every other clan in Scotland. The hearts o' Douglas heroes are always buried beneath the altar in the chapel."

Tina pressed her hands over her ears. "Stop it! You all look at me as if I am deranged, but I know he is alive! Ram and I are not just man and wife—we are bonded, we are one! Don't you think I would know if he were dead?" she cried. "Go and gather your dead, Angus! My brother tells me there are over a hundred Kennedys and two hundred Douglases. I will never allow England to keep him. I found him there once before against all odds, and I shall find him again. You seek the dead, and I shall seek the living. Excuse me—I must see if Mr. Burque is ready."

Heath and Ada and Angus looked bleakly after Tina's determined figure. "It is a sort o' temporary madness that keeps us sane, if ye understand me," explained Angus.

"I understand," said Heath quietly. "She will never let go until she sees for herself how impossible it is to find one man among ten thousand corpses. I'll go with her. She will need me when she sees and smells Flodden."

Ada said quietly, "I too will go."

Angus sighed. "So be it. We'll go together."

As Tina helped Mr. Burque gather the things they might need, he was the only one in the castle who didn't think her temporarily deranged. He marveled at how much she had matured since she had left Castle Doon just over a year ago. She gave one hundred percent of herself in any undertaking—that was her secret. That was the reason any man who had ever met her lost his heart to her. Tina lived life with a passion, experiencing all its joys and all its sorrows, yet she never let it defeat her, no matter the blows it dealt out to her. Just as now, instead of being prostrate with grief, she was being practical, efficient, and tenacious as a terrier.

"We may need linen for bandages," she reminded him. "What else will we need besides poppy and rue for pain?"

"I think yarrow would be advisable," Mr. Burque said quietly.

"Yarrow?" Her lovely brows drew together.

"It's a yellow powder to sprinkle on wounds to clot the blood."

"Oh, yes," she agreed, crossing herself. "I'll get needles and thread, just in case."

Within the hour they were in the saddle. The weather was glorious, showing off to perfection the unequaled beauty of the border country through which they rode. The sun shone so brilliantly, it seemed a sacrilege when the

flower of Scotland's nobility lay dead and defeated on the
field of valor. Surely the gods themselves should be weeping in their heavens at the almost total annihilation of such
a proud realm!

Tina's back was straight as a ramrod. Ram's wolfhound
loped along at her side. None had argued when she insisted the Boozer accompany them.

Angus had thought to set an easy pace, but the decision
was taken from his hands. Valentina rode at breakneck
speed that carried her far ahead of everyone save Heath. It
was up to the others to keep pace or fall behind. She paid
them not the slightest attention. Her mind was focused
upon one thing, one goal.

When dark descended she would have ridden on, oblivious to whether it was day or night. Finally Heath dragged
on her reins with his superior strength and dragged her
mount to a halt. He could see she was ready to fly at him.
He knew she was reckless enough to carry on alone if they
refused to accompany her, so Heath said the only thing he
thought might stop her. His voice was harsh and dispas-
sionate as he laid the blunt facts before her.

"Tina, if you ride farther tonight, you will kill the horse.
I know you don't give a fiddler's damn for poor old Angus,
but I don't believe you want animal abuse on your conscience."

Tina was immediately contrite. Angus's men set up cam-
paign tents, and she, along with the men, wrapped herself
in a Douglas plaid and tried to curb her insatiable impatience until the hour before dawn. Her fists clutched the
dark blue and green plaid in desperation as the hours
dragged slowly by. She was alone at last to think, without
the others hemming her in with their anxious eyes upon
her. What had they expected from her? Tears? Fainting?
Hysterics? These were petty, womanish things, not nearly
adequate to assuage the rage she felt within her! She
wanted to lift her hand and destroy the universe and everybody in it.

An irreverent inner voice mocked, *You need not destroy Scotland, she has destroyed herself!*

She bit her lips in impotent frustration. She would sell her soul for a handful of thunderbolts. Just one fistful of deadly thunderbolts would do nicely. One for Henry Tudor, and another for that ugly bitch, Margaret Tudor. The Howards needed destroying, and that swine Dacre who had arrested Ram. She wanted to call down fire and brimstone upon each of them and watch them burn in the everlasting fires of Hell.

By first light, she accepted the fact that she could do nothing except mount her horse, straighten her back, hold her head high and resume her mask.

As they rode closer to the English border, they passed many mounted groups both coming and going. All had the same destination, all the same heartbreaking task: to gather their dead, their mortally wounded, their maimed.

Carrion crows circled in the sky above the battlefield, and if this did not tell them they were close, the stench did. As they sat upon Flodden Edge, the hot wind wafted up a smell like nothing they had ever experienced. Gunpowder, excrement, blood, horse sweat, rotting flesh, and the evil, sweet smell of death formed a miasma that insinuated itself into the nostrils, mouths, and throats of any who were foolish enough to approach the carnage.

"Abattoir," murmured Mr. Burque hopelessly.

Angus thought that once Tina had glimpsed the horror of a battlefield with its mountain of dead men and horses, she would give up the unthinkable task of searching for Ram. Heath and Mr. Burque, however, knew her better than that.

As she squared her shoulders and urged her mount down to the field, they resigned themselves to aid her in her fruitless search. She went slowly now, carefully, painstakingly picking her way through the bodies riddled with arrows. Some were headless, many more were missing arms and legs. Some of these were still alive, and Tina closed her ears and her heart to their pitiful moans. Ada tried to emulate the courage of Lady Douglas, but when she saw a gang of looters stripping bodies of knives and badges, she was violently sick. Tina immediately attended to her and tore a strip from her fine shift to wipe Ada's face. When there was no more Tina could do for her, she moved on.

She decided not to remount but stepped delicately between the dead, leading her horse behind her. Finally, even the horse revolted at the mounds of quivering horseflesh, crying in their death throes. It shook its head wildly, blew through its nostrils, and took off toward a dozen or more destriers who had survived the battle and were patiently awaiting their masters at the edge of a stream whose waters still ran red.

Tina knelt beside a fallen man with black hair, but when she managed to turn him over, she recoiled in alarm at the extent of his dismembering. From that moment on Heath insisted on going before her to examine the features of every man with black hair.

In her heart Tina now realized the task she had set herself was an impossible one. After searching for four straight hours, all the corpses started to look alike. After five hours she began to get cramps in her feet, and when she reached down to massage them, she saw that from the knee down she was soaked with filth and blood. Suddenly she began to fear for the child she carried. Under no circumstances must she harm the precious burden. Ram would never be dead while his child lived. The light was beginning to fade from the late afternoon sky when she decided to give up the search. She stumbled and Heath lifted her in his arms and knew she had no more strength. As he carried her through what had been the English camp, he heard the Boozer barking and yelping in a frenzy. He called the wolfhound to heel—then it penetrated his tired brain that perhaps the dog had found something. Tina too, had heard the commotion the Boozer was creating. She struggled in Heath's arms, and together they stumbled over dead English to get to him.

Ram's body was half beneath that of Ruffian's. The horse had had its belly ripped open and in death it looked ugly, almost obscene. Ram, in contrast lay at peace, his swarthy face pale and bloodless. A lance had gone through his middle and pinned him to the earth.

Heath gave a great shout and waved to the others. He had already removed the lance by the time Mr. Burque reached them.

"The yarrow," Tina whispered, and though Mr. Burque knew it was pointless to sprinkle yarrow upon a corpse, he did exactly what Tina expected of him. When he had finished lacing the wound with the yellow powder, he bound him tightly. It was not until Angus's men arrived that they could free the body from the weight of the fallen horse. They carried him to the edge of the field.

Tina laid a soft hand on Heath's sleeve. Her face was at peace. "If you can fetch a Gypsy caravan, I'll take him home." The lump in Heath's throat choked him so that he could not speak. He caught a wandering horse and thundered off in the direction of Kelso.

The two Douglas men-at-arms laid down their burden and went to speak with Angus. They would soon need to set up the tents again but were loath to do so at this foul and accursed place.

Mr. Burque knelt down to Tina as she crouched beside the body of her husband. The light was now almost gone, and he thought for a moment his eyes were playing a trick on him. He thought he saw Ram's still body take a shallow breath.

"*Mon dieu,* is it possible that he lives?"

"Of course, Mr. Burque. Did you doubt it for a moment?" she asked serenely.

When Heath returned with the caravan, he would not believe them when they told him that Ram was still alive. When they gently lifted him inside the painted wagon and he saw for himself that Ram's rib cage lifted slightly in an uneven rhythm, he wondered if Valentina had somehow resurrected him from the dead. As he watched them together, the poignancy was tangible. How bittersweet that Ram had lasted long enough to die in his wife's arms!

Angus was totally undone, and Ada gave all her attention to the sobbing old earl who showed his vulnerability for the first time in his life. They traveled in slow stages, one day at a time, and it took them five days to reach the Castle at Douglas.

Ramsay had remained unconscious on the journey. Angus, Heath, Ada, and Mr. Burque knew this was a bad sign. Tina only thought how merciful it was that he could not feel the jarring of the caravan as it crawled along through the rough cut tracks of the borders. She knew she was taking him home to die.

Chapter 41

> Black is the color of my true love's hair,
> His eyes are wondrous fair,
> Warm are his lips and strong his hands,
> I love the ground whereon he stands.

Valentina was most grateful that they carried Ram upstairs and laid him gently in his own bed, but she washed his body with her own hands, and they left her alone with her husband. She had no idea what would happen to her, or to Castle Douglas, or even to Scotland now that they had been defeated by England, but she did know what would happen to Ram when he died.

She would assert her authority. She was Lady Douglas. She would not allow them to cut out his heart and place it in a casket, as Douglas tradition demanded. His heart belonged to her, and she would see that he was buried intact. She knew there was nothing more she could do for him. Very gently she lay down beside him and took his hand.

Ironically it was not the wound Ram sustained in the battle that had brought him to death's door. At least not directly, for the lance that pierced clean through his flesh, pinning him to the earth, had destroyed no vital organ. It had chipped bone, torn muscle, and severed blood vessels. He was close to death because too much of his lifeblood had leaked away. He had lain for three days unable to move while his blood had dripped slowly from his body into Flodden Field. Miraculously, now that the flow of blood had been stanched, his body gradually began to gain strength.

Tina must have slept, even though she had been determined to keep vigil. It was still pitch dark when she opened her eyes in panic. Dear God, Ram must have slipped away into death while she slept. He had closed his fingers about hers, and they had stiffened in death to a grip she could not break.

A sob escaped from her throat, and as her eyes became accustomed to the dark, she fancied that he lay watching her. She caught her breath, not even daring to hope. Her throat closed as she struggled to speak. "Ram?" she managed to whisper at last. She did not see his lips move, but she knew he was alive and that he would recover because he answered her. Vixen! He had whispered the word *vixen,* and it was the loveliest sound she had ever heard.

As she pried his fingers from hers, her tears fell upon his face and mingled with his. She eased from the bed and ran to tell the world that Black Ram Douglas was still master of his own castle.

In an amazingly short time, Ram was on his feet. As

Tina entered their bedchamber, she cried out in alarm
when she saw him struggling into his clothes.

"Dear God, what are you about? 'Tis not three weeks
since you lay on the battlefield near death."

"The English couldn't kill me, but by Christ, ye and Ada
and Mr. Burque might accomplish what the enemy could
not, if I lie here one more day!"

"Whatever do you mean?" demanded Tina, thoroughly
offended after all the tender ministrations she had lavished
upon him.

"If ye change my dressing one more time, I'll strangle ye
with the bandage, and if Mr. Burque fetches me one more
bowl of broth, I'll crack his bloody French skull wi' it!"

"We've done our utmost to nurse you back to health.
The servants have tiptoed about so they wouldn't disturb
you. I've kept visitors away so they wouldn't upset you with
their horror stories of the war. I've sat with you for hours
playing chess so you wouldn't be bored. I swear, men make
the very worst invalids!"

"Invalid?" His pewter eyes narrowed dangerously. "I'm
no' an invalid, and I'm no' a bairn. I'm a man, Tina. And
while we're on that subject, I don't need a nurse, I need a
bloody woman! Sometimes I could swear ye don't want me
at my full strength again because ye like giving the orders.
Well, as of today, Lady Douglas, ye will start fulfilling the
vows ye made when ye married me. Ye pledged tae love,
honor, and obey me. So now ye can start doing as yer told.
Don't shrug that saucy shoulder at me, Vixen!" he warned
as he fastened his belt and pulled on his boots. "I heard
Angus ride in, so I'm going down tae talk man tae man. Ye
will occupy yerself moving yer things back tae this chamber."

"I didn't want to disturb you," she protested quietly.

"Well, ye *do* disturb me, every time I hear yer voice, or
smell yer fragrance, or see yer breasts when ye bend over
me tae feed me that bloody broth!"

The corners of Tina's mouth lifted for the first time since

her wedding. If his sex drive was asserting itself, he must indeed be almost recovered.

By the time Ram arrived in the hall, Angus and his men were on their third whisky. Angus came toward him and walked about him in a circle. "Yer lookin' a hell of a lot better than the last time I saw ye, laddie."

Ram stifled the urge to take Angus in his arms. Archibald had aged all of a sudden, and Ram could see his years were numbered. Any affection on his part, however, would be considered pity, so Ram decided the kindest thing he could do for Angus was insult him.

"I wish I could say the same fer ye, but ye look like hell, man. Are things that bad, Angus? Is doomsday upon us?"

Angus drained his whisky and poured himself another. The thought of downplaying the situation because of Ram's health never occurred to the toughened earl, and Ram knew he'd get the bald truth from him.

"I won't deny we suffered a massive defeat at Flodden. The clans lost thousands. James was a fool, but he's dead and we won't speak ill of him. Even the English were impressed by his reckless valor, according to the chronicle I got my hands on. It said, "O what a noble and triumphant courage was this for a king to fight in a battle as a mean soldier."

"So what happens now that Argyll, Lennox, Bothwell, and all the other earls are dead?" asked Ram.

"Believe it or not, we go on much as we did before. There is a new Earl of Argyll to lead the Campbells, a new Lennox to lead the Stewarts. Fortunately every earl had a son tae take his place. Ye underestimated Margaret Tudor, but I did not. She won't allow her brother Henry tae swallow her kingdom, whether he won the battle or no'. She'll see that her son rules Scotland, not her brother. We've a new king, James V, and until he's old enough tac rulc, there'll be a regency council consisting of Margaret, Douglas, Arran, and Huntly."

"So the loss of a husband meant less than nothing tae her," Ram said with contempt.

"Weesucks, laddie, I never thought ye naive. She's about tae wed my son Archie. Ye did know he lost his wife a few weeks back? The Hepburn lass never enjoyed good health."

Ram's pewter eyes studied Angus from beneath shrewd, lowered lids. How much he had orchestrated he'd never know—never wanted to know. He was even cynical enough to bet Angus was comforting a grieving Janet Kennedy.

"Will ye come tae the capital, Ramsay? Scotland is in need o' strong leaders just now."

Ram weighed Angus's words carefully. He was offering him carte blanche. He raised his eyes as Valentina came into the hall, and in a heartbeat his decision was taken.

"Thanks, Angus, but I'm a new bridegroom and have neglected my wife long enough. Within the month I'll be back patrolling the borders so that James V remains secure on his throne. What I want is not in Edinburgh—it is at Douglas."

Before the week was out Gavin and Cameron were home. Their cousins had been lost in a sea battle, but they knew they were more fortunate than other families to have three brothers survive.

Tina's father rode over from Castle Doon to see how they fared. When he told them David had died at Flodden, but Donal and Duncan were expected to recover from their wounds, Tina felt truly blessed.

When at last all their visitors departed for home, Ram pulled Tina into his arms. "The weather is lovely today, but we won't have many warm days left. Let's go fishing."

How could she resist? One of the happiest days they'd had together had been spent fishing.

Tina lay in Ram's arms on the riverbank. They had devoured the delicious food Mr. Burque had packed for them, and now Ram was intent upon dessert. He unfastened the laces of her gown. "Come for a swim," he coaxed.

Tina was shy. She knew that if he lured her from her clothes, he would discover her secret. She traced her finger along the hard line of his jaw. "I once dreamed we swam together at a three-tiered waterfall. It was the most beautiful sight I'd ever seen. We stood on the ledge and dived together into the river below."

"There is such a place in the borders, where Kirkcudbright joins Douglasdale. I dived it often when I was a lad. Do ye think ye'd have courage tae dive it wi' me in real life?"

"Of course," she said without hesitation, knowing full well she would do no such thing.

"Liar!" he teased. "Ye don't even have the courage tae take off yer clothes and swim wi' me."

She pulled from his arms and stood looking down at him. "Do I not?" she said, tossing back her flaming hair and stepping from her gown. His eyes became intense as he watched her remove her delicate pink undergarments, then they widened as realization dawned upon him.

"Flaming Tina Douglas, you shameless honeypot, tae cavort naked in yer condition!" he crowed joyfully.

She laughed down at him. "What about your condition?"

He pulled her down to him, their swim now forgotten. He cradled her beneath him while they whispered between long, slow kisses. "We'll call him Archibald," he teased.

"You devil! There'll be no Archibalds. I want beautiful names for my children like Neal or Robin if it's a boy, Kathe or Rebecca if it's a girl."

"Nay," he said tracing her lips with the tip of his tongue. "If it's a lass, I'll call her Vixen!"

Author's Note:

I chose the name Kennedy for my heroine's clan because Janet Kennedy was a real mistress of King James IV and was often referred to as Flaming Janet. For contrast, my hero had to be a Black Douglas, the most feared name in Scotland.

The immediate family members of my two clans are fictitious, but all the earls and heads of the clans are real historical figures, and all fell at Flodden with the king.

Every castle is authentic, as are the tartans, devices, and mottos. The hearts of the lairds of Clan Douglas are buried beneath the altar of St. Bride's Church in Douglas.